He may be new to readers, but E J Goldberg-Phillips has decades of writing and life experiences. World travel, politics and environmental activism have connected him with the good and the great including prime ministers, actors, musicians and writers.

Born in Australia, Eddie uses his fertile imagination and wealth of memories to conjure up sinister, at times disturbing, images of the seedier side of life—and death. For him, society divides itself and the fight for wealth competes with that for mere survival.

His debut book, *Achilles Heel—Your Stalker Solution,* is still available on Kindle and Amazon paperback.

E J Goldberg-Phillips

NO ONE WILL HEAR YOU SCREAM

GHOST-WRITING HAS SOME DANGERS.
SO DOES FINDING OUT THE TRUTH.

AUSTIN MACAULEY PUBLISHERS™

LONDON * CAMBRIDGE * NEW YORK * SHARJAH

A CIP catalogue record for this title is available from the British Library.

ISBN 9781528983860 (Paperback)
ISBN 9781528983877 (ePub e-book)

www.austinmacauley.com

First Published 2021
Austin Macauley Publishers Ltd®
1 Canada Square, Canary Wharf
London, E14 5AA
+44 (0)20 7038 8212
+44 (0)20 3515 0352

To Michelle Gray, without whose analysis and thought-provoking ideas this book would never have been as it is.

To Marieke Pingen, who kept me right and brought her analytical, scientist brain to spot inconsistencies.

To authors—Michael J Malone and Caro Ramsay—who unknowingly made such useful suggestions to help me improve the final product.

To my family: Edwina, my wife; sons, David and Joe and my mum, Nancy, for their support and encouragement. A million thanks.

Introduction

No one will hear you scream is the second in a series of novels following my debut, *Achilles Heel-Your Stalker Solution* (available on Amazon, Kindle and in paperback), and follows the unfolding career of Lizzie Spector. Lizzie was an unexpected heroine in the first novel, a young researcher on "Squawk FM", the local radio station. She manages to unravel an extraordinary involved criminal plot, assisted by a plethora of others, and as a result makes her name and is subsequently headhunted to a major TV company, Channel 8. The story develops as does her character, love life, ambition and truth seeking/exposing. I quite like this girl who I see as a young version of Stacey Dooley, or Hermione Grainger, though the comparison is only my own. Lizzie is the centre of this story but, as ever, she isn't alone. The world she inhabits is full of huge egos, prima donnas, criminal types and charlatans. Lizzie Spector is anything but an excellent role model—headstrong, fiery, self-opinionated, a maverick when it suits her. Maybe I like her because I see similar qualities in myself at that age, ones that lead me to socialism, something I still find myself in complete sympathy with. The first book dealt with a stalker and how a secret organisation was able to ostensibly take him out. This book has an entirely different theme and ends with a twist I confidently doubt any of the readers would work out in advance. There is also a "whodunnit" thread weaved into a large part of the book. You'll need to read on to find out who actually did it! Enjoy.

Chapter 1

Andromeda and the Blackhole

Andromeda Galaxy Smyth, you're in a fucking blackhole. And she was! Who? How? Where? Why? Ann Smyth was in a situation not necessarily of her making or choice. It was more to do with being there in the line of duty. Her duty was finding out the truth. The truth could sometimes be secreted in the most unimaginable and excruciatingly difficult places—such as down a well. She would need to go wherever the truth lay. The truth lay at the bottom of this well. And the smell. That stomach-wrenching, awful smell. Indescribable but they all knew what was responsible for it. The aroma wafted up the twenty-foot funnel. The long-abandoned well, probably still with some water despite the dry period and due to the very wet time that had preceded it. Absolutely no one needed to be told what was at the bottom of it. Quite obvious. Not just a smell, but a hum. They knew what was making that as well.

Ann Smyth was one of the first from the Kent Police Forensics Team to arrive. America had made Crime Scene Investigation appear sexy, almost glamorous. The reality was anything but. It was something that was needed to be done. Having got her BA in biology, she had then spent time as a serving constable; Ann was now a reasonably new member of the Kent Police Forensics Unit. Her team leader, Jack Jordan, had done the job for nearly twenty years, her only a tenth of that time. Other members of the team were all a bit senior to Ann but the six of them were a team.

So what had happened to bring out their team, a dozen uniforms, including a Chief Inspector? It seemed that a report had been passed to them by an anonymous member of the public—no one ever seemed to want to own up to alerting the police to anything suspicious—of the smell that emanated from that long-abandoned well near Cobham in Kent. The caller said that he had to pull his lurchers away as they were both howling something awful. He described the pong as worse than a badger's arse. He must have had some rubbish sense of smell. No living badger's anus could have emitted that! A patrol car took a detour and confirmed the smell. A sergeant came up and confirmed the smell. At this point, it was obvious that something didn't just smell in the State of Denmark! A van arrived and the uniforms decided to get the blue and white "incident" tape and wooden stakes out and do a perimeter of the well. They had noticed some other tyre tracks, some small, possibly dog, footprints and several shoe and boot prints. Clearly, something had happened there. It wasn't up to them to speculate, just secure the area.

Next to arrive was a solitary forensics guy, Jack Jordan. The police knew Jack as he was always on the crime scene. It was to be determined if indeed it was a crime scene.

'Jack, think this one's a real bad 'un,' said Chief Inspector Gary Stevenson. The two had worked together on numerous cases in the past so the CI knew what he was talking about. They both bent under the tape and approached the well. Even at four feet, both of them were conscious of the putrescence. 'I'd wear a mask, Jack, before you look down.'

It had just gone dusk on an early August night and it was light but fading. Jack took out a large torch and, ignoring the warning, turned the torch on and peered over the edge of the well, which had a rusty wrought iron grating screwed down that had clearly been opened recently. The top of the well still had a modicum of daylight for about four feet, then complete darkness. Jack was hit in the face by a thousand flies. He'd been too slow to close his mouth and got a mouthful of them, some up his nose, even one in an ear. He staggered back and spat out what he could and blew his nose. Nothing came out.

'Fucking told you. Never listen, do you?' CI Stevenson felt an "I told you so" moment but resisted the temptation. 'Did you see anything then?'

'Something's down there and it ain't moving.' They both agreed that it was time to call in Kent Forensics—euphemistically nicknamed "The Heavy Team".

Ann got the call and shouted to the others. 'Case. Here's the address,' and they jumped in the van, her in her car. Henry, Lewis, Ralph and Richie plus her. More of a truck than a van, which was just as well because of the equipment and they would possibly require it all. They arrived at eight that night and Ann went up to see Jack. It wasn't that she was second-in-charge or anything, just less jaded than the others who had been doing the job longer. *Bright-eyed and bushy-tailed* was how Ralph had described her. Had she known; she'd have agreed with him. The team started to set up their equipment: forensics tent next to the well, arc lights and a lot of other equipment that would be required. The top of the well was covered. By ten, it was all done. They all called it a night and let the uniforms sort out guarding the scene until the next morning.

Next morning, Ann was the first of the team to arrive in her car and about ten minutes later came the others, including Jack, in the van. It was a fairly wide well, a good seven or eight feet in diameter at the top but narrowed to five or six feet halfway down. Probably a medieval construction, Jack thought it might be useful to get the old plans for the area to check out what was down there. They duly arrived from the parish council; it had been abandoned since before the First World War.

They took the cover off. It was now after 10 am and light. Another flurry of insects escaped. Jack, Ralph and Ann came over with large industrial flashlights and facemasks to try to see what was at the bottom causing such a stink, as if they didn't know. They shone their lights down for about twenty seconds each then stepped back. Even in that small amount of time, the smell was overpowering. They could make out a fairly large object, or objects, but it wasn't at all clear. They tried again with no more vision of it than the first time.

'Drone?' said Jack, and they all agreed. Richie was the "drone boy"; it wasn't just his job, but he'd one of his own at home. Richie went back to the van where they had four drones of various sizes. He selected the Mini Quadcopter Drone. Small, manoeuvrable, just what was required. It even came with a VR headset so that the operator could be wherever the drone was. Nevertheless, this would be tricky.

The team set up a monitor connected to the drone so that they could watch, and if anything was spotted, Richie would be alerted to it and could take a closer look. It was radio-controlled and whilst normally that would be fine, in the confines of a well with thick stonewalls, it could present problems if the signal was interrupted at all. Control would require finesse and dexterity. They were all just about ready. The drone—the size of your hand—was actioned, given a test run and all was ready to "rock and roll". The first thing they wanted to do was get some pictures of what was down there before deciding any further action. The drone, its four tiny rotor blades and minute light and camera hovered at the top of the well. Very slowly, Richie had it descend inch by inch down the centre, noticing that the further down it went, the damper the well walls became, with moss and lichen everywhere. In some places, the vegetation was missing as if it had been disturbed by something, possibly by whatever was down there. Ten feet down and still nothing, still searching. Richie was becoming aware of slight control difficulties. He said to Jack, 'Anyone out there on a radio?'

Jack spotted a uniform using his phone. 'Hang up now. You're disturbing our signal,' at which the officer did exactly that.

'Thanks, getting something now,' and with that, he gasped, and the drone went offline. The picture became static. The drone had joined the contents of the well. Bummer. Ralph was so pissed off at losing his toy.

During coffee, the team viewed what the drone had recorded before disappearing. It had recorded several seconds of clear vision before either hitting something, the wall or who knows what, or possibly just losing the signal. It was always going to be tricky; Richie was good, but everyone had their limitations. They all discussed what they thought they were looking at.

'Is that a head?'

'Possibly. Right shape.'

'I think it's more than just one head.'

They ran it back and re-examined the footage frame by frame. Clearly, they did seem to be looking at remains. 'Stop!' Ann had noticed something. 'Where's the arm?'

'Arm?'

Ann pointed to the screen. 'There! That's a body but it's lost an arm.'

Lovely! Meanwhile, Jack was back at the van on the phone to the office. It was clear to him that there was reason for suspicion of felony but they needed to now treat the well as a major crime scene. He wanted to get the perimeter extended as well as get another piece of equipment to be able to examine what was at the bottom of the well. It was lunchtime and given that they could do little until it arrived, they stopped for lunch. For at least one of them, holding on to that lunch in the afternoon could be a challenge.

'Send down another drone maybe? What about a light and camera on a pole?' suggested Jack, clutching at straws. They all knew what the answer was.

'Sorry but there's no other way. Someone will need to go down, record, take photos and tissue samples,' said Ann. Immediately, the entire team looked at her and she just knew what they were thinking.

'Me? Fuck!'

Jack then pointed out that, given the narrowness and restrictiveness of the lower part of the well, the size of the team members as well as their weight might be a problem, and with her dexterity, she was the ideal person. Ann had never been asked or "volunteered" for such a task before. It wasn't that she wasn't up to it, she fitted the bill in terms of size, nimbleness and ability; it was just…well, she suffered from claustrophobia, something she fought to control but nevertheless, it might be an issue. Ann thought maybe she should have mentioned this when she had applied for the job but it was far too late for that now. Jack took her aside and explained what they needed to do.

Normally, they might have just used a Bosun's seat to gently lower her down but there was a slight danger that her feet could disturb the body, so possibly they could lower her down headfirst. The half-serious, half-devilish idea was shelved. The problem would have been her disorientation and being able to do what would be necessary. This needed to be considered.

Ann hadn't been claustrophobic at all until an incident when she had been ten. As punishment, her father had locked her under the stairs and there had been no light. After an hour of battering the door and pleading that she would be a good little girl, she was eventually let out, but it left a profound scar on her regarding dark enclosed places. Like almost drowning, Ann shied away from situations that might require her to repeat such an experience. She now saw that small, dark space as the Grand Canyon compared to what she would soon be facing. It may have been nineteen years, but she still got flashbacks and a shiver would shoot up her spine. Ann hid this fear. The team met to discuss what the next step would be. Jack said it was straightforward but intricate, requiring patience and dexterity. Could Ann handle it? She nodded her belief that she could. This was a mixture of bravado and duty. The intention would be to fit up a pulley and rope over the well entrance, fit a lightweight plastic seat to the rope, secure Ann and lower her down to where the body was. She could then fully photograph and document the scene, take tissue samples, etc. Great precautions would be required to protect her and to ensure that the least possible disturbance was made to the scene. She donned a blue boiler suit with fluorescent attachments for visibility on the rope, a hard hat with a fitted torch, as well as a helmet video camera, a tool belt containing a selection of instruments including tweezers, scalpel, scissors, etc. Her shoes were removed and protective blue plastic bags with elasticated tops were put on to ensure that no contamination of the site took place. Surgical gloves and a facemask with a built-in mic to allow her recording and audio contact as well as an earpiece connected to the surface. She stood before her team. 'How do I look?'

Two of them pissed themselves laughing whilst Jack just said, 'Very pretty,' with a smirk.

'Let's do this,' she said.

It had gone 8 pm when they began to lower Ann down. The camera and sound were playing and working well. It wasn't a smooth-walled well like many but a kind of a "dry stone" construction with stones jutting out here and there, not exactly conducive to what she was about to do. The men started to lower her very slowly and gingerly down the well shaft, monitoring her all the time via her camera. She was now far out of her comfort zone, but the only way was down. It may inadvertently cure her of her fear. She had no fear of what she was about to find down at the bottom—they couldn't harm her. She got down another ten feet, not far to go. Dusk had been falling even as she had stood at the top but where she was now, the only light supplied was from her helmet. She could hear Jack saying, 'You've only another four feet. Try to keep your legs as near the wall as possible,'

She could feel the jagged wall on her heels. It then occurred to her, *Andromeda Galaxy Smyth, you're in a fucking blackhole.*

'What was that, Ann? Repeat,' came the voice in her ear.

I bloody said that out loud. Muppet. 'Nothing, Jack. Another two feet, then stop.'

By now, Andromeda—sorry, Ann—could see something and if it hadn't been part of her job, Stephen King could have described the tableau in one of his horror books. At the far wall opposite her, was a sight. Two feet from her face was a green, possibly blue, definitely grey, face with mouth wide open and eyes infested with insects. There was now a constant buzz. The head on top of that body was physically attached, welded onto another slightly bigger body. The eyeless face of the second body at the wall was incomplete, missing a nose and a chin, the complexion of both was grey-green but not yet totally unrecognisable as human beings. They more accurately resembled Notre Dame gargoyles. They were both casually dressed, and a rope was clearly visible around both of them. The second one had an expression Ann had never seen on any other person, alive or dead. It seemed to be a mixture of anguish, terror, disbelief and blind anger. This cornucopia of emotions on a corpse had no doubt been a result of what had transpired between these two, definitely men, in their last moments.

'Subject A, missing the right arm. I don't think it was that long ago, looking at the socket.' The arm had detached and slid out of the jacket sleeve before plunging out of sight of her camera. In order to look at the empty socket, she needed to pull off the still attached jacket sleeve. Ann took out a knife and carefully removed some skin and flesh and placed it in a specimen container and sealed it.

'There seems to be a surprising amount of tissue remaining on both bodies, raising some doubt over how long they've been down here. They may have been here a considerable length of time. Hard to estimate the age of these cadavers. I'm now going to take a sample from Subject B, the noseless one.'

Ann took a sample from the chin. It was clear from this one that blowflies had been at work. She observed that Subject B had good teeth, not just a normal set.

'We'll need to secure them for raising them out. Can you see if it's possible, Ann?'

Ann had a good look at them. She did a touch test; the bodies were unquestionably in a state of advanced deterioration but—in all probability because of where the bodies were—were now starting to show some immediate signs of putrefaction. It was her very presence, raising the ambient temperature, that had started it. She thought she'd better get out before they deteriorated any more.

'Pull me up now, please,' and within three minutes, she was at the top of the well. Her claustrophobia had been side-lined whilst her professionalism had taken centre-stage. The expression on the face of Subject A was unquestionably one that she would remember for a very long time.

'Let's look at what you've got,' said Jack as Ann started to take off her accoutrements, putting the specimens into a cold box. Despite the chilly conditions in the well, she was sweating profusely and would have liked a shower. However, there was still some work to do. The team was, on occasion, required to travel too far from their homes for them to be able to return every night, and this was one such occasion. Their office had booked them into a nice small local hotel. It was now approaching 11 pm and they would have a quick look at the recording evidence, pack things up ready to go to the crime lab and then head off to the hotel.

Having set off—Ann in her car and the rest in the van with uniforms still in attendance—Ann decided not to go to the bar as she was exhausted, and not just physically. Her experience had not exactly cured her fear of enclosed spaces, but it had certainly reconciled that fear with the requirements of being a forensic technician. She took a quick shower to get rid of any lingering smells and went straight to her room after bar snacks with the others on account of the time, leaving the others propping up the bar. As she bid them all goodnight, they all shouted in unison, 'Night, Andromeda!' with a devilish laugh. *Oh well, boys will be boys*, she thought. Ann called her other half, Raheem. It was a short chat, mostly about their four-year-old daughter. 'Think I might be here a few days. Will try to get back for the weekend.'

The next day, the team met up at breakfast. On the drive back to the site, the men chatted about things, mainly politically incorrect stuff about Ann's garb and the little thing that she had inadvertently let slip. They could have teased her about her name but decided to keep it for another time. Work to do. This was a most unusual case, but other revelations were awaiting them all. At the site, Jack had a meeting tent erected alongside the incident tent. The first job was to have a talk about the conditions at the bottom of the well and consider all available information and statistics to decide what was required. Jack recognised that the bodies would need to be extricated from a very testing environment and the fact that an arm was missing, cause unknown, suggested the degree of internal decay that was present. They needed the lab report on the age of the cadavers, pronto. Ralph went on the blower to the lab, trying to rouse them up. Given the condition of the faces, software to determine identification would be hopeless but there might be DNA that could identify them. Normally, the hands of the corpses would be cut off so that fingerprints could be taken. The precarious conditions, both of the corpses and of the environment, made this process even more difficult, with every possibility that the hands would not be able to be secured. They spent most of the morning reviewing the footage and thinking what to do. If the corpses were in such a poor condition that an arm had already been lost, getting them out using conventional means was unlikely. They would come out in very many bits, making the job of identification and that of the coroner more difficult. They would need a better plan.

'Thanks, Gus.' Ralph came off the phone at 2 pm from the lab and told Jack that they had some initial results from the samples.

'Lab must be quiet. Bloody quick,' said Lewis.

'So, what gives?' asked Jack.

'Well, the DNA results will take a bit longer but, and wait for it, the bodies have been deceased over 18 months ago, probably a good bit longer than that!'

'They're in a remarkable state of preservation for that age. Normally, they'd be virtual skeletons.'

Jack looked at the statistics sheet. 'Must be a combination of the temperature and moisture content, which slowed down putrefaction. Weather as well. That dry spell might have caused some mummification. The problem is how to get them out in one piece, or at least not too many pieces. Any ideas, anyone?'

A lot of blank looks. 'Freeze them.' Even more blank looks. 'No, really. Freeze them and lift them out. No one else has come up with anything else, have they?' said Henry.

'Is it even possible? Won't it damage the cells?'

'Boss, how much more damaged cells can they have! Bloody dead aren't they! Will be coming out in dollops any other way.'

They all resisted a smirk. 'OK. Why not do some research and if it is a runner, we could try it. I'm telling you though, if it all goes pear-shaped—' rasped Jack at Henry.

'I'll get onto it right away. Shouldn't take very long.'

The others looked incredulous. 'Freezing! Contact Iceland, eh!' The others laughed but funnier ways of getting bodies removed had been tried before. 'Remember that time we were going to contact Dyson?'

Jack was seriously considering this novel option but there were considerations such as tissue and internal organ damage, unfreezing difficulties, etc. If it was a way to do it then he would go for it but first, they would need to contact the cryonic experts.

Chapter 2

Ruby and that Bloody Woman

'Ruby Latimer? I'm Lizzie Spector, C8 News. I think I've been reading your books since I was about ten. Brilliant stuff, by the way. I'm not going to be interviewing you but as the researcher for the channel, I just wanted to check a few things regarding your books. You have sold over 12 million books, I believe; is that right?'

'Twelve million and six hundred thousand, so far, Miss…Spector? Still got a long way to go to catch up with Jo Rowling but can't complain.'

'Where do you get your inspiration from? I mean, some of your themes are quite unique, some of them historic, and some, if you don't mind me saying, a little bizarre.'

Ruby frowned. Ruby was somewhat tetchy. Ruby was more than a little pissed off but like any VIP, she didn't outwardly show it. This young upstart of a girl who probably hadn't achieved anything in her entire life had the temerity to suggest that some of her themes were a little bizarre!

'I don't really know where I get my inspiration from, Miss Spector. (Definitely pissed off.) It's just there. It's like it's the corner and I just fall over it. Both my agent and publisher have asked me the same question and I don't really have a good answer for them either. It just seems to happen. I'm no Barbara Cartland; hell, I don't do conveyor belt writing. I hope my stuff has got better quality than that.'

Lizzie wasn't certain who Barbara Cartland was—way before her time—but had seemingly touched a raw nerve. It was what this young researcher inadvertently did, occasionally deliberately, and did it consistently and annoyingly well. Lizzie had only been with C8 News for a brief time, about 18 months, having been headhunted. In that time, her work had been fairly routine, and this was just another continuation of it, as far as she could see. Setting up an interview with the author who had developed airs and graces from a considerable number of years of success and was being lauded by all and sundry for her so-called "brave" writing. As a good researcher, Lizzie knew the titles of all the Ruby Latimer books, had done some background checks on what most of them were about but hadn't been able to either find the time or inclination to actually read any of them. That comment about reading her books from the age of ten was just for effect.

'I hear a film company bought the option on *Tamara's Treasure*. You must be really pleased about that.'

'Ah well, let's just wait and see if anything comes out of it. I've had false dawns before so maybe this one will prove to be the one.'

For any author, the Holy Grail was getting that elusive book-to-film trick. Few people who wrote novels actually got them published. Of those that did, only about one in every 25 made any money out of them at all. It was the same in many professions and sports where a handful made an exorbitant amount of money whilst the vast majority took home a mere pittance. Writing was a dog-eat-dog profession with only the best surviving and thriving. Ruby Latimer was one such survivor.

'You have any more questions for me, Lizzie? Just that your man's wanting to interview me very soon and I need to do a little preparation myself.'

Ruby was nothing if not direct. Lizzie smiled and just said, 'Thanks.' Only having met once, both were equally wary of each other, sensing a certain defensiveness and not necessarily appreciating just why. Could it have been that Lizzie Spector, despite her tender age, had sussed intuitively that Ruby Latimer was a complete fucking cow? Could it have been that Ruby Latimer was positively that fucking cow, knew it and had sussed intuitively that Lizzie Spector wasn't just unlike her but had more brains in her little finger than this famous author had in her entire body?

Sometime later in a TV studio, Ruby Latimer wasn't exactly relaxed. The comment about some of her writing being bizarre had really rankled her. A feather-ruffled author about to be interviewed by some literary cretin about something he had little or no interest in or any deep knowledge of, save that which his researcher had given him, wasn't exactly reassuring. The sound engineer wired her up as she was seated, facing an already wired-up interviewer. Across from her sat Nick Rogers, arts correspondent of C8 News. The channel had gotten wind that a film deal was going to be struck whereby one of Ruby

Latimer's books would be the subject. After both had shaken hands and sipped water, it began.

'Ruby Latimer, a book prize winner, welcome to C8 arts. Your last book, *Foragers Fair*, about a Dorsetshire family after World War II went down particularly well in the West Country. Can you tell us a bit about the background?'

'Thank you for inviting me, Nick. I have some relatives in Devon and when I went to see them, I found this fascinating story told to me by my cousin about a family who lost three boys during the Second World War. I did quite a bit of research and discovered a really tragic story and a community that was bound together by common aims and interests and a love of the land. This book was my first sojourn into the rustic way of life. I really loved writing it. It was a complete departure from what I had previously written.'

'It was well written, I will give you that, Ruby; indeed, all your books are very readable. The only problem was that not as many people apparently read *Foragers Fair,* as some of your previous books. What would you put this down to? Do you think that your old tried and tested formula needs to be given new impetus, or did you feel that your readers were becoming blasé about what you were giving them?'

'Nick, I don't write for my readers, I write for myself. Readers deserve the best I can give them, and the book we're talking about here was, for my part, the best I could give them. If I don't like what I'm writing, how can I possibly expect the public to like it as well? Not every book is going to be a literary landmark. Even Dickens wrote the occasional dud. I'm certain not every book I've ever written is perfect, but I do think I have improved with time.'

The interview went on for 15 minutes and as it did, interviewer Nick Rogers felt the hackles rising inside his guest. Whilst not exactly Grace Jones versus Russell Harty, it was clearly not the most amenable of interviews to have taken place under the auspices of C8. As the interview was drawing to a conclusion, Nick turned to the subject of Ruby Latimer's next book.

'I hear you've got another book in the offing. Can you tell us what it's about? I'm sure the viewers would really love to get a sense of what the next Ruby Latimer book is going to be about.'

'My next book is well underway. It's going to be quite a departure from my previous books in as much as it is going to be set in the present day, be very dark, have at least one murder and, well, I don't want to give away too much at this stage. When it's finished, the world will be able to read it. Nick, I must say I'm really disappointed that you haven't asked me about the book that's going to be made into a film. I would have thought that this is something your viewers would really like to hear about.' Over her shoulder, out of the corner of her eye, Ruby could make out hand activity.

'I see your producer is telling us to wind up so maybe I could come back another time and tell you more about it.'

'Ruby Latimer, thank you very much and yes, we may well come back to discuss your film.'

The interview was over and rather than wait to be disconnected from the sound system, a furious interviewee ripped the microphone from her blue woollen cardigan, threw it at Nick and stormed off shouting, 'Fucking arsehole, couldn't even score with an open goal.'

A somewhat red-faced interviewer stood chatting to his producer, shrugging his shoulders and wondering what the hell was up with that woman. "That woman" was still seething about her pre-interview chat with the young researcher. Ruby Latimer had actually started to panic. The panic was about the fact that she was 90,000 words into a book and had tried everything to finish it. It remained unfinished. She had the cursed writer's block.

Ruby Latimer had had writer's block before. It was many years since it had been quite as bad but she knew this time, it was different. When she had been much younger, it was normally just due to tiredness. She would work at fever pitch for weeks on end, totally exhausting herself mentally and physically. She would be like some demented thing, pacing up and down, drinking gallons of coffee alone in her flat, never venturing out until the task had been completed. In those days, the task would always be completed. They were the good old days. Where had they gone? She understood that as you got older, you became less resilient, but this was not just like resilience deprivation, this was altogether more worrying. She just couldn't understand where she was going to take this next book. Where she would really have liked to take it was to the wood burner in the basement with a can of petrol poured over it. The problem was—as it was for everything these days—the book was on her laptop.

Also, in those days, she had been less touchy, more secure, tactile, quite a charmer really. However, she'd realised that charm was a very wasteful commodity, and, in any case, most people saw through it. This woman was, if she told the truth to herself, vacuously one-dimensional, with only an interest in what the outside world thought of her and almost nothing else. For almost a couple of decades now, she had kept the outside world at bay, but her defences were not always up to scratch these days and this young researcher for C8 News had clearly gotten under her guard. Instead of shrugging it off and just getting on with things, she was more inclined these days to, in a Trump-like fashion, file it away with every intention of returning to it in the not-too-distant future and get revenge—whatever that would entail. Only one thing that Ruby Latimer lacked was good judgement and knowing just quite who she was taking on. Know thy enemy.

Chapter 3

Ruby and her Writer's Block

'Finishing off this book is driving me bloody mad. Aaarghhh! Just can't do it. Tried everything to come up with a new angle. I just seem to be completely out of inspiration. Maybe I just need a holiday. Time for a drink.'

Ruby Latimer, writer extraordinaire. Found fame writing a trilogy about the not so "holier than thou" Mormons in the 19th century and how they were involved in various intrigues—all fiction, of course. Yeah, right. From the moment Ruby found herself a literary agent—a feat in itself for anyone those days—Ruby felt that she was truly on her way to becoming an author. The fact that she had written one moderately interesting novel, which, to be quite frank, was considered by potential agents to have been fairly dull and remained unpublished despite her best efforts and that of her then-not-so-great agent, was neither here nor there. She knew, she just knew, that there was at least one riveting, exciting and saleable tome in her head. If only she could come up with it.

The problem at hand was when she had started writing, she had been but a strip of a lass, full of literary enthusiasm, a first in English literature, lots of boyfriends and quite a few contacts. She started to write, and write, and rip it up and start again. That elusive first idea to take to her agent was just around the corner. What she hadn't realised was how sharp that corner would be and how long it would take her to manoeuvre it, not to mention all those hurdles, water jumps and the odd Beechers Brook! She had needed some help. Help had been provided.

She was now no longer a strip of a lass. She was no longer waiting to have her first novel published. She had a score of them behind her. At first, having started, she had begun to find it quite easy. Her real breakthrough novel, her fourth, *Mormon Mayhem*, had gotten mostly rave reviews, invites to various book fairs, TV interviews and chat shows as well as a few local radio interviews and most importantly, had sold a quarter of a million copies, and all this before Kindle! A good start for a young girl barely into her twenties. She got a two-book deal as a result. Publishers were very picky about their novelists and for her, it would be no different. The fact that she was a real looker, of course, was somewhat of an advantage. Having a photo of the author on the dust cover of the book, particularly if she was very pretty, was likely to increase the sales of the book to men in particular. A few ideas down the road, she decided that "if it's not broken, don't fix it", and with that went on to write *Tabernacle Terror*, which, given her burgeoning reputation, sold as well as her first breakthrough book, leading to more publicity and, it had to be said, more than a little contention with the Church of Jesus Christ of Latter Day Saints. That was nothing that she or her publishers and agents couldn't handle.

For her third book in this particular series, Ruby had decided to close down her fascination with Mormon society by concluding the trilogy with *Salt Lake Scandal*. Many writers sought inspiration from the real world unless they were science fiction, science fantasy or some sort of Gothic horror writers. Ruby was one of the former and could be described as a "factasy" author, blending historical facts and scenes from the past into a narrative that kept the audience on the edge of their seats. By the end of *Salt Lake Scandal*, her sixth book to be published, she was in overdrive. She was now an established novelist. *Salt Lake Scandal* became Ruby Latimer's first 1 million seller. From a financially struggling young woman, she was now becoming very comfortably off indeed, able to demand a decent share of royalties. She was now also capable of writing three novels every two years and her publisher pretty much expected her to do this. By her 30th birthday, her novel tally was well into double figures.

Ruby Latimer was now motoring. Her agent told her that he had been approached by a film company who were interested in one of her earlier novels. He told her that he told them to talk to her publisher about it and that they would do so. Neither her agent nor herself heard about it again, something of a disappointment, but as long as the books continue to sell, and they did, all was well. Her only problem was continued inspiration and finding those precious, occasionally elusive, ideas for every new novel. With every passing year and every new novel written, the expectation was that the next one would be better than the last. The pressure was on, it was always on. Writing, launching your book, PR and marketing, book signings, readings, TV and radio, literary reviews, etc. in her 20s had been really fun, in her 30s, it had still been fun but getting harder. Now she was fast approaching 40. Now she wasn't having so much fun. The gloss had worn off along with the novelty. Occasionally, she would ask herself, *Is this really what I still want to do?* She was now a victim of her own success.

Like most writers, Ruby became utterly engrossed, obsessed, in what she was doing. When she wrote, she put her heart and soul into it; when she wrote she was on the page in the book, second-guessing what each of her characters might be about to do. For her, writing wasn't just an idle pastime, it was her very *raison d'être*. In her short life, she had known nothing but being a writer, something she utterly loved. But things were changing in the industry. E-books and self-publishing had transformed her industry much more than the Net Book Agreement ever had. It brought opportunities but also unappreciated pressures. She began to wake up in the middle of the night in a cold sweat, she would get the occasional panic attack, on the odd occasion, she would forget important things. In short, she was approaching a mid-life crisis and she was approaching it on her own. Time to change.

After that bloody TV interview that, as far as she was concerned, had been utterly unsatisfactory and not helped by a young upstart fucking researcher—cheeky young bitch—Ruby Latimer returned to her two-bedroomed semi-detached flat in Hounslow. Why would she need anything bigger? After all, she lived on her own; yes, she did have a certain entourage of hangers-on or, as she liked to refer to them, "friends". She supposed that many people in her circumstances would have a bunch of fawning disciples and of course, she did have. All were related to her profession. Apart from the occasional "fans" who were wetting themselves about her latest book and just wanted to meet her, shake her hand, thank her for all the pleasure she had brought to their pathetic existence and would no doubt never see again, she had maybe four or five groupies who she would disparagingly describe as "regulars".

Her "regulars" were ostensibly part of the novel industry. Of course, there was her publisher and her literary agent. Then there were the PR people, a few journalists, the odd photographer, but as one could gather from this list, there was just no one currently special in her life. Well, there was. There was Ruby Latimer. She had fallen hook, line and sinker for her own publicity, which told her that she was the best thing since sliced bread, and she could do virtually anything and never fail. The problem about being surrounded by sycophants was that nobody told you the truth. Sycophants, by their very nature, told you exactly what they thought you wanted to hear. The idea that you could actually listen to criticism of yourself or anything that you did seemed to be a total anathema. Those fawning hyenas followed you about, praised you, ingratiated themselves with you and offered…what? So that they could come back the next time and do exactly the same thing.

Walter was one such of these people. Walter came to Ruby's house every few weeks. He actually went at the behest of her literary agent, Arthur Newell. Arthur must've had about 40 or 50 authors on his books, two or three of them who actually were a bit more successful and a bit more prosperous than Ruby. These other authors were 10 to 15 years older than she was, had at least a couple of films in which they had been screenwriters or technical advisers, whilst another had diversified into children's books as well as adult literature. Walter, in his 20s, got a real kick out of meeting what he considered to be the great and the good. He had the hots for Ruby big-time, but this would be yet another case of unrequited love. Truth be told, Walter was a little bit of a sad wee git. He thought Ruby liked him, when in fact she was being polite at best; most likely, she couldn't give a shit. As far as she was concerned, when he turned up, Walter was there purely to carry out business, collect a disk or USB far too important to be left to the post, dealt with it, smiled and left. He was her courier.

Greville was quite another matter. He was one of the senior management at Laurel Publishers who, for the best part of 20 years, had been Ruby's meal ticket. He was relatively new to her but she could see from the very outset that he knew what he was all about. Greville was just one of those guys who oozed confidence. No comprehensive school or secondary modern for this guy, he clearly had a background in business. Whenever he turned up, a couple of times a year, it was normally because Ruby was behind schedule, was required by the publishers for some matter or other or possibly because she had some content difficulties with the book. On every occasion when he visited her, he'd added something to her writing, reassured her in her own abilities or, dare it be said, inspired her to do better or revise what she had already written. He was not her friend, what was that? At best, Greville could be described as a confidant, but nevertheless a very useful person. In the army, he would have been a regimental sergeant major!

Marion was a Ruby Latimer editor. Saying "a Ruby Latimer editor" was no slip of the pen. Marion had been editing books for longer than she cared to remember. In editing Ruby's latest book, Marion had commented to her that this was the seventh book that she had edited for her. It took quite a lot of skill to be an editor and Marion was certainly one of the best. It was clear, however, to her that her author was struggling more than she had done in the past. It had been suggested to Ruby that it might be an idea to take a break. Sometimes authors reached a point where they hit a brick wall and Ruby was clearly at that point. For Marion, there were some tell-tale signs around the flat. A half-empty bottle of gin was quite a good indication that all was not well, given that Ruby was ostensibly a coffee drinker. Ruby had smoked in her youth but hadn't done so for decades. However, she was now vaping. Booze and nicotine were clearly having no effect on our author's inspirational requirements. It wasn't Marion's place to advise her employer of sorts. However, as it became clear that the amount of editing she was required to do was becoming sparser and of a poorer quality, Marion felt duty-bound to have words with her boss.

'Ruby, I mean, Miss Latimer, is everything OK?'

'Absolutely fine, Marion. Why do you ask?'

'It was just…well, normally, your manuscript is pretty well complete by now.'

'Just what are you suggesting? Am I not writing fast enough for you then? Don't you like what I'm writing?'

'Oh no, sorry, Miss Latimer, not being critical, just concerned for you. You're normally so quick when you write but…well, it just seems a bit sluggish compared to normal. Hope everything is OK with you.'

'I think we'd better call a day, don't you, Marion? I'll let you know when I've got more to edit.'

Marion got up, put her notes away in her briefcase and, slightly red-faced, smiled and said goodbye to Ruby. It would be quite a while before she saw her again. It transpired after the "discussion" that Ruby asked her publishers if they could supply another editor, presumably one who wouldn't ask her awkward questions. Marion was clearly getting a bit too close to the truth. Shame, really, because all the woman was doing was showing sisterly concern for someone who might have needed to confide her problems in another human being. Ruby Latimer was totally self-contained but the older she got, the less self-assured she began to feel about her own talents and abilities. A crisis was looming, and it wouldn't be long before this author hit the proverbial buffers.

Chapter 4

Lizzie and the Art of Diplomacy

Beep. 'Morning, Miss Latimer, it's Gretchen here. Wondered when we could come to see you next about the Fan Club Annual General Meeting? We were hoping that this time, you might actually be able to be there so what we thought was if we could give you some dates to check in your diary, you could let me know. If you could phone me back or text me with some possible dates, we would really, really appreciate it. Many thanks. Byeeee.' *Beep.*

Gretchen Turner had just left yet another answerphone message on Ruby Latimer's phone. Ruby Latimer never ever picked up when she heard who it was, unless it was press or media…or her agent. Sometimes messages would wait, unplayed, for almost a fortnight. Most people bored her rigid and her "fan club" (she had a fan club, bloody pretentious or what?) consisted of Gretchen and her sister, Lucinda, and possibly another 200 or so people—the exact number she didn't know and cared even less, but hey, they bought her books, talked about her, some—apparently for reasons unknown to her—seemed to actually idolise her, something that was met with a mixture of personal disinterest and disdain. She had met Gretchen on a couple of occasions, not by appointment or design but through sheer accident. Once was at a book fair that she was attending— serendipity maybe—and another at a social gathering; the Turner twins had been there because they had been given tickets. Lucinda commented, 'Serendipity,' Ruby on the other hand just thought *Pair of sad losers, these two*, smiled that watery smile that she had perfected over years and luckily, at the last minute, had remembered who they both were. Needless to say, these two bored her with their fawning attitude and about how wonderful the fan club was doing, how great her last book had been (mediocre really) and about the film? Pure sycophancy in stereo, although the Lucinda tweeter was more of a muted echo compared to the Gretchen.

Miss Gretchen and Miss Lucinda Turner were two upper middle-class types with a rich daddy, stay-at-home mommy, older brother who was a successful city man. Both were still living at home in beautiful Bishop's Stortford. Lucinda had done an internship—unpaid, of course—in a lawyer's chambers with the hope of becoming employed in Law. That wait was still continuing but given her connections, or more properly, those of her father, she would surely get the job she wanted. Gretchen on the other hand had done Sweet Fanny Adams, not really knowing what she wanted to do so the fan club had been set up, in which Lucinda occasionally helped with and was both a pastime and a possible way into the publishing industry, or so she thought. She had read "Mormon Trilogy" long after they had been published; indeed, she had struggled to get the first one as it had been out of print but had managed to get one on a second-hand book website. For some reason unknown to herself, it seemed to strike a chord deep within in her. It had filled her vacuous life.

Two years before, Gretchen had written to both Ruby and Laurel Publishers enthusiastically suggesting that a fan club could be set up and that if they didn't mind, she would undertake to do it herself. The publishers had written back to her, politely suggesting that as long as the author didn't object to the suggestion, they would be quite happy to endorse the fan club on the understanding that it wouldn't cost them anything. Gretchen had waited four weeks for a reply from Ruby, which predictably hadn't materialised. So, on the basis that the author hadn't objected (most people would bet that she hadn't even read Gretchen's letter), she had gone ahead and set it up anyway. First had been a Ruby Latimer Fan Club website, Facebook page, Instagram, etc., and from that she had established a core of interested people who signed up to be members of the fan club. Maybe this was something Gretchen Turner could be quite good at? Better than sitting at home, dildoing.

The Ruby Latimer Fan Club had grown under Gretchen as secretary and Lucinda as honorary chair—an almost meaningless title. A number of other people had expressed interest in getting involved but as with these organisations set up by needy individuals, Gretchen and, to a far lesser extent Lucinda had wanted to do it all by themselves. The thought of somebody else being as enthusiastic as them coming in with new ideas had been viewed particularly by Gretchen as some sort of threat, a takeover bid by Johnny and Jenny-Come-Latelys. Needless to say, such offers of assistance had been ignored or rejected. The title of the organisation might have been Ruby Latimer Fan Club, but it was really the wholly owned property of retchen Turner. None of these people would be getting their grubby hands on what she was going to be doing.

Gretchen had a great friend called George. The reason neither was a virgin any longer was all down to this local stud. George was very different to the two sisters. He lived in Bishop's Stortford, but on a council estate with his mum, his dad having to work away frequently. George was 25, worked in the main supermarket in the town as a store boy. He was swarthy…you know the type. On one of her regular visits to the town centre, Gretchen had spotted George on a comfort break outside the supermarket. She had passed by him, he had been having a smoke, she had smiled at him, he had returned it, offered her a fag, which she had politely declined, and that had been basically it. The next week, she had managed, quite by coincidence of course, to pass the same place at the same time and of course, he had been there and this time, they had exchanged a few words. He had asked if she wanted to have a coffee sometime. They had arranged to have one the next day, his day off.

George fancied himself as a bit of a ladies' man. Indeed, George WAS a ladies' man! There were two predominant kinds of people in Bishop's Stortford, his type and her type. There was no point being a ladies' man if the ladies thought you were a bit of a dick. George Pope was no dick, in days gone by, George would have been regarded as, well, a gigolo. Young enough to be attractive to women, yet old enough to know what to do with them. The secret of George's success was patience. He would work on them for a few weeks, tell them all the things he thought they wanted to hear, flatter them, pour his heart out to them of how unfortunate he had been and had triumphed against all odds, and when he saw that look in their eyes, he knew he would be pleasuring them and himself soon. Gretchen wouldn't be the first and Lucinda not the last.

So, back to Gretchen. They had that coffee—Americano for him, flat white for her—found out all about her, poor little rich girl, such a shame, daddy didn't understand her or appreciate her…you know the kind. So, after an hour of listening to this drivel, George started to tell her about himself. Yes, of course, George was working at the supermarket as she well knew, but he was there earning money to go to university to study religion, a subject close to his heart (oh Pinocchio!) so that he could do good in the world. He liked reading and had a real taste for all the Greek classics—Mezze, Dolmades, Keftedes to name but three. Yep, George was really full of shit. Full of shit he may have been but Gretchen, four years younger than him, was already under his Svengali spell. She agreed to go out with him for a meal. That virginity of hers was now in grave danger. At least, she hoped it was.

Lizzie, our dear young Lizzie, the girl who had never achieved anything in her life unless you counted exposing a stalker of royal lineage, revealing the existence of a super injunction and the exposing of a high-ranking paedophile ring…well, compared to writing several novels, this really wasn't much of an achievement. Lizzie Spector was one of those irrepressible forces of nature who, through any means possible, would accept nothing but success. She sat in the canteen at C8 as Nick Rogers, fresh from an interviewing debacle, strolled through the swing doors clearly not a happy camper. He fixed his gaze on Lizzie, who he really quite liked but not on this occasion. This time, Nick felt somewhat aggrieved.

'Lizzie, just what did you fucking say to that mad bitch of an author? She stormed out the studio like something demented, accusing me of not asking her the right questions, but I think it was more likely about something you must have said to her. What exactly did you say to her?'

'Can't really remember, Nick. Far as I can recall, I was very polite to her, complimented her on her books and possible film and might have said that some of her ideas were bizarre.'

'Bizarre! You said to one of our top authors that you thought some of her ideas were bizarre and then left it to me to get on with it. Thanks a bunch, Lizzie; in case you didn't know, the interview was a "disarster, dahling". Doubt if we will ever be able to tempt her back into the studio again. Do you think that in future, you could be a little more circumspect on your use of words? After all, these people are our bread and butter. Lecture over. She was a mad fucking bitch anyway.'

'I'm really sorry, Nick. My big mouth gets me into trouble now and again. Other things on my mind, as you possibly know.'

Lizzie was sitting at one of the canteen tables dressed very smartly as ever— nice cardigan, blue skirt, flat shoes. When Nick came in, she had obviously been deep in thought, fidgeting with the sparkler on her third finger, left hand. It hadn't been there before so maybe it wasn't all that surprising that she was a little preoccupied. Her knight in shining armour had finally landed his prize. She was happy, or so she thought. Almost 24 years of age, still the whirling dervish that Squawk FM had developed and let loose on an unsuspecting public, captured scoops like there was no tomorrow and left them for bigger, better things. As she grew older, her horizons altered but the fire in her belly remained. This was Lizzie Spector, scourge of the establishment.

Just when Lizzie had finished and about to take her coffee cup into the staff kitchen, she heard a voice and smiled. 'Heard you'd been a naughty girl again. Make a note, Miss Spector. We must try and not upset the celebrities, the suitably touchy.' A broad beaming smile crossed Lizzie's face. Craig Endoran, C8 News producer, had just popped in for a quick coffee himself. He could see by her rigid posture and hunched up shoulders that she was a little uptight. Since she had arrived at C8, he'd had to deal with her that way a few times. She was a brilliant researcher and opportunities for advancement were waiting for her just around the corner. All she needed to work on was one thing that she didn't possess—patience.

'Yeah, I know, bloody did it again, didn't I? Me and my bloody big gob.'

'Big, beautiful sexy gob you mean. Stop blaming yourself. Of course, sometimes it can be your fault…'

Craig thought that maybe he shouldn't have said this, but she seemed to take the criticism in her stride,

'We're all capable of the occasional faux pas. Fuck, if I had a pound for every bloody time I'd done it myself, I'd be a millionaire. Just put it down to experience; take a breath before you talk to these types who are generally up their own arses, something we all need to remember. Was just wondering how you will get on with that MP bribe case. A tough one, I know, but still… Must dash. See you later. Have a good day…and bloody well cheer up!'

And with a coffee cup in one hand, cheese-on-brown-bread sandwich in the other, the whirlwind producer whirled off to see his intrepid band of scribes and reporters about the evening programme. A lot of water had passed under the bridge since Lizzie Spector had joined C8. Her last job at Squawk FM had led to the arresting of a paedophile ring. Lord Forbes of Ashby had inadvertently turned out to be the owner of C8 and had had a connection with some of those arrested. Embarrassing? Yes. Unfortunate? Most definitely. Detrimental to her career? For a short time until it all blew over. Time having passed, Lord Forbes had thought of discontinuing his ownership in the media and had divested himself of C8. Things were looking up for our Lizzie and she was newly engaged. Lucky guy, whoever it was.

Chapter 5

Fun with Gretchen and Lucinda

Not sure that all authors were like Ruby Latimer. For some, success brought other benefits apart from money, fame and privilege. These elusive "other benefits" could be contentment and satisfaction. Seemed that in Ruby Latimer's case, her interest in such other benefits was absent. She'd always wanted to be an author, and at a fairly early age, she achieved her ambition. For some people, it was not their end goal but the journey that was all-important; for others, when one goal was achieved, they turned their attention immediately to the next one. Contentment permanently eluded them. It could really be a curse and in Ruby's case, oh, how cursed she was. It had turned a hopeful, optimistic young author into a paranoid zealot. In many such cases, by the time someone reached her age, she would have had multiple lovers, possibly a stable relationship, maybe even children. Ruby Latimer was childless, lover-less, partner-less, and she was loving it. She was, for all intents and purposes, the most un-needy, self-contained person imaginable. While some might say more to be pitied than scorned, she viewed other people in families, relationships and such with a certain disdain. She was above all that. After all, she was a successful author.

Some people could be described as people persons. Liking other people, outgoing, sociable, gregarious. A minority on the other hand were like Ruby. When she was in public, meeting "her public", she would put on a face, smile at all and sundry, act happy, outgoing—you probably know the type. Fact was, it was all an act, just for show. Inwardly, when she met them, she analysed them, judged them, scored them and dismissed them depending on their "career use value". She often thought to herself *if these arses only knew what I really thought of them*, but her guard was never down. All those years and her reputation as an amenable, accessible, cooperative writer had remained intact, difficult though it may have been at times. Ruby Latimer was a real PR pro. She sometimes wondered herself how she kept up this façade, the charade of nice. It was solely to do with being able to continue to write, sell books, be in the public limelight and basically, that was all. Sex was a complete anathema to her. It was not that she was unattractive—God, how she was attractive—it was just that quite frankly, she had no interest in men, women or in having sex with anyone at any time. Her libido was non-existent. She had had an orgasm-free life to date. Suppose it might change, and that was a really big "suppose", it would have meant sharing herself with another person. Ruby Latimer didn't do "share". After all, she was a successful author, a self-made literary artist.

In stark contrast, sex was anything but a complete anathema to Gretchen Turner. Chance would have been a fine thing. OK, at school, she fooled around, had pyjama parties, minor bits of curious intimacy with other girls and was intrigued about what that thing above her vagina did. One night, Lucinda took the time to show her and…well, think you know the rest. One of Lucinda's classmates had shown her on her phone. It seemed to be the way most teenage girls got their sex education. Gretchen was certainly interested in having sex with someone as long as they were a Ruby Latimer fan. After the dirty deed was done, they would need to talk about something. George, on the other hand, hadn't got a clue about Ruby Latimer. For all he knew, she could have been an Olympic swimmer, the latest pop sensation or a reality TV star. Don't get me wrong, George could read. The *Daily Mail*, the *Sun*, and on a bad day, he might even read the *Star*, which he considered a quality paper. George had the gift of the gab but he wouldn't exactly have made the Oxford University Debating Team. Still, no one was perfect. He thought he might Google this Ruby Latimer tart. After all, if he could wax lyrical about her, he might get his end away with Miss Gretchen bloody Turner.

It had been a couple of weeks since they had met. They had gone for a coffee and a piece of cake. He had offered to pay but she would hear nothing of it.

'George, um…me and Luci are having a party on Saturday night. House is ours. Thought you might want to come.'

George, party, lots of lovely girls, free booze, food, probably drugs. Difficult decision.

'What time?'

'Nine o'clock.'

'OK, I'll see if I can make it.'

George was already considering what different flavours and textures of condoms he would need to buy. Unknown to him, Gretchen was ahead of the game. Her condom supply was already in her room. As they departed, he thought it appropriate to give her a kiss—not just a normal goodbye peck on the cheek, but a proper full-on-the-lips smooch. He resisted using the tongue, but she didn't. He was actually starting to care for her a little bit. *Careful, George*, he said to himself, *don't want to fall for this one, do we?* Fact was that gigolo George was starting to like her. He smiled and put details of the party in his phone.

'We're having a party on Saturday night, sis, hope you can make it.'

Lucinda was taken aback. 'Party? Didn't know about this. So, who's invited?'

'George.'

'And…?'

'Not gotten around to the rest yet.'

'No Gretchen, what you were hoping was that nobody else would turn up and you could get your grubby hands into him all for yourself. Well, it's not going to happen. If we're having a party, a proper bloody party, I'll invite some of my pals. Get over it.'

Gretchen's bottom lip began to quiver. She had decided that Saturday would be VD Day—Virginity Deflowering Day. Her spoilsport sister was intent on ruining it all. From then on, Saturday would be a battle of wills and Gretchen was determined to be the victor. Why couldn't Lucinda just go out or do one? She loved her sister, but she could be a right pain at the wrong time, and this was definitely the wrong time. The battle was on and Gretchen was in marine mode. "Operation Penis" was going ahead.

Lucinda never gave it another thought after that. She had more important things to think about. Her internship at the lawyers was going to be over in a matter of months and she really hoped it was going to lead to a job either in those Chambers or in another Inns of Court. As far as the legal profession was concerned, Lucinda Turner had very narrow horizons. One good thing was that she was liked by most of the lawyers, and one in particular—a QC called Spector—always had a kind word to say to her. Maybe he was just an old letch, but more likely just a nice guy. There had been a girl called Elizabeth Spector in her old school in the same year but a different class, and Lucinda had been a prefect. She wondered if there was any relationship. Maybe he was nice to her because he'd mentioned to his daughter about this girl who had gone to her school and she might have put in a good word for her. Nevertheless, she wasn't forward enough to ask him. He was, after all, a Queen's Counsel. Maybe she should have summoned up the courage to find out. She was still just a mere strip of a girl and while she was quite confident, her confidence did have gaps.

Gretchen had never seriously intended to invite anyone apart from George to the party that Saturday. Lucinda, on the other hand, just to spite her errant sister had a list of 20 she was going to invite, which became seven and by the time she had phoned them, most had already made other arrangements. Four of them said they would definitely be there so that was better than nothing. She told Gretchen she would pass them her mobile number just in case she got delayed. Gretchen decided that she would have to cater for them herself, so she got in provisions—booze, crisps, a tray of sandwiches—and that was it. Not exactly a feast but then again, it was Gretchen we were talking about here. You wouldn't believe sisters could be so different—one scatty, one not. Lucinda decided to go out for a meal that Saturday night, leaving Gretchen to her own devices. What happened next would not have been unpredictable. 9 o'clock came and so did George, spot on. And there was Gretchen, done up, looking quite gorgeous to be honest, which wasn't that hard because…well, she just was. Her hair, clearly quaffed by a quality hairdresser, blood-red lipstick, yellow dress, red three-inch heels. Stunning. Half an hour passed by and still nobody else had arrived. 9:45 and Gretchen's mobile got a text. *Sorry G, car fucked. Waiting for RAC. Might get there later. Have a good evening.* Gretchen read it and didn't know whether to be disappointed or relieved. Much easier to get your end away when there wasn't any competition.

Anyway, there was Gretchen, George, booze, food, music, an empty house (parents were on holiday) and a year's supply of condoms. Nice. So, for the best part of two hours, Gretchen and George were left to their own devices. She was starting to get more than a little tipsy, whilst George could hold his drink a lot better than her. Not being backward at coming forward and certainly not a rapist, George flirted and flirted and flirted; Gretchen reciprocated. Virgins were so last year. Off came her heels. They slow-danced. They talked. They kissed and cuddled. And laughed. Things were moving forward. Time to show him her room.

It was after midnight. The remarkable thing was that it had taken George almost three hours to bed this woman. He was amazed at his own self-restraint. He couldn't think why. Normally, by this time, he'd have shagged the woman once, done her again for good measure and kissed her goodnight, never to see her again. Normally. However, this time, he hadn't. He really liked this girl, he really did. Yes, she seemed to have hang-ups, particularly over some bloody author, she appeared a bit fragile but...well, she was not only drop-dead gorgeous, but was genuinely fun to be with. They just clicked.

Half past midnight. The front door opened and in came Lucinda in a foul mood. She'd gone for a meal with a man seven or eight years older than her, one of the many dating sites on the Internet. He had been a total prick. He knew it and she knew it but still had to sit there and listen to him chundering on about his bloody sports cars, all three of them. As if she cared. She normally got taxis to wherever it was she was going. So, after a dreary evening with this guy who was so forgettable she'd forgotten him already, in she came, desperate for a drink—not that she hadn't had one or two, possibly more, to deaden the pain of listening to a boring arsehole. The first thing she did was kick off her high heels as her feet were killing her. She hadn't worn stockings so bare-footed and glass in hand, she swayed somewhat, hoping to seek out the one person who just might understand how shite her night had been—her sister, Gretchen. So up the stairs she went to Gretchen's door.

'What a fucker of an...'

Lucinda was stuck for words. The glass of red wine now lay at her feet on the rug, now red and sticky. She would normally read a note on Gretchen's door—go away or some similar pleasantry—before entering but she was so irritable and frustrated and just bluntly annoyed at her evening, she wanted to vent her spleen on someone and that someone had to be Gretchen. However, Gretchen was, shall we say, somewhat occupied. So was George. Red stains on the carpet were reciprocated by equally red stains on Gretchen's bed sheets. Trouble consummating their union had meant doggy fashion on the bed, hence the blood. Gretchen Turner was now an ex-virgin.

Losing your virginity could apparently be quite painful. However, for Gretchen, it hadn't been painful, mostly thanks to the alcohol and a gentle lover. Lucinda was still in a state of shock, coupled with uncharacteristic envy of what her sister had just achieved. She had hoped she would have been the first to be no longer a virgin. Not now! Too late! The eyes of the sisters met. It was a most uncanny of exchanges. Gretchen was now clearly a woman whilst Lucinda, in her own eyes, wasn't. A bottle of champagne on the dresser still had some left so—and this was a first; Lucinda went over and downed the contents in one. All three of them were soon well pissed. The difference was that George had more capacity to hold his drink.

It was one of those evenings for doing the uncharacteristic. Gretchen and George were naked. Lucinda thought to herself, *I'll have some of that*, threw caution to the wind, said to them, 'Room for one more in there?' and in 30 seconds had stripped down to her bra and panties and jumped on the bed next to George. Had Gretchen been sober enough, sober at all, she might have objected, put up a fight or something. However, by this time, Gretchen was so out of it—not to mention a bit bruised and bloody—that she hardly knew her sister was there. George, being a red-blooded man, just couldn't resist. Lucinda didn't try to resist. In 10 minutes, a fresh stain was added to one red stain on the carpet of wine and one in the bed of menstrual blood. What a great party it had been!

The next morning was an entirely different story. The disaster area, formerly known as Gretchen Turner's bedroom, resembled something from a Salvador Dali painting. Indeed, so did Gretchen. Lucinda. Oh my dear God! The inhabitants of the bedroom slowly woke up and then it hit them. The two young women sat up in bed, both naked, both examining their red raw fannies, both in a little discomfort with a handsome young man between them—in Gretchen's bed, not between their legs! —possessing a smile wider than the Grand Canyon itself. From that moment on, the realisation of what had happened hit the two women, embarrassment quickly set in and Gretchen ran to the bathroom and locked herself in. Lucinda, on the other hand, decided that after her first journey into sexual relationship, she would try it again—and she did! George was a prolific stud and how! Lucinda decided she quite liked sex. After her second shag, she picked up her clothes and ran to her room. George thought he'd better scarper before Gretchen came back and wanted seconds as well. He was right knackered and no joking!

Gretchen returned to the room, totally oblivious that her sister had been there and had been fucked twice no less by her man friend. She was feeling rather delicate in more ways than one but was starting to improve. She thought she should better change the bedsheets that were clearly the worse for wear. She looked at them, stained as they were with God knows what—drink, semen, blood and…more blood? She just about remembered George and her having a spot of rumpy-pumpy but didn't remember doing it twice! Oh well, maybe they did. In any case, she had gotten it out of the way, the albatross around her neck, that weight off her mind, and all those other clichés. She hadn't really enjoyed it, it had it been really quite painful? Couldn't remember, but George had been a gentle enough fellow in the circumstances. It would take a couple of days for her to heal down there and then she could try again with George, and hopefully this time, she would maybe enjoy it.

Naked Lucinda was back in her room, clutching her clothes—she vaguely remembered taking off her shoes in the living room downstairs when she had gotten back from the rubbish date—shut the door behind her, leant against the door, crossed her legs and groaned with pain, not because of George but due to the doorknob in the small of her back! She quickly went into her en-suite bathroom, ran the shower and got in quickly. She felt like a complete slut. Fancy bedding your sister's boyfriend and she had still been in bed with them both! Having examined her body, she was without blemish but there was blood running down her legs and she knew just why. She leant against the tiled shower wall and slowly sank down and sat under the showerhead, which continued to cleanse her. For the first time in her life, she felt dirty, not the kind of dirty that miners used to deal with, but a moral type dirty. All that sex education in third and fourth year. Such a waste of time. She felt like crying, but she didn't really know why. Had she lost something or gained something? Her moral handcuffs had been removed, and she began to cheer up. She was at that time a lawyer in the making, pretty and she knew it, and now she had experienced sex. Could it get much better than this? *Oh please, let it get better than this*, she thought.

And as for George! He would be able to get free pints off the lads in his local for years to come, recounting the story to them of when he pumped two virgins in one night in the same bed. Oh yes, our George and his Jack the Lad tale would be doing the rounds for quite a while whilst the two objects of his lust would never so much as hear about it. He expected he would see Gretchen from time to time as she passed by his supermarket. He really liked her and would definitely see her again; the difficulty was Lucinda. George thought Gretchen knew that he had screwed Lucinda in Gretchen's own bed; what he didn't know was that Gretchen had no recollection of what had happened and Lucinda had no intention of rectifying that memory lapse. Whitehall Farce or what? So, Lucinda and George knew that George had screwed Lucinda, but Gretchen didn't know. Oh dear, what a tangled web we weave!

Chapter 6

Arthur Meets an Aspiring Author

Arthur Newell, owner and sole agent ("Arthur Newell: literary agent"), this long-suffering dogsbody, gopher, human punching bag and all-round put-upon guy was the agent of the extremely high-maintenance Ruby Latimer. He was quite simply a terrific agent. He needed to be with prima donnas like Ruby on his books. He had others, of course, quite a few, but none were as hard work as this one and she was getting harder! 20 years previously, when she had just been starting out, she had been advised by a former BBC journalist, 'First thing you need to do, Ruby, is get yourself an agent. You won't go anywhere without one and it needs to be a good one. Bad agents are ten-a-penny and are as likely at getting a publishing contract as Bill Clinton is at keeping his dick in his pants.'

So, with that advice, Ruby Latimer began the search for the Holy Grail: a good agent, one that believed in her and could get her a publishing contract. She learned how valuable such a person was to her author aspirations. Her first book written, she enthusiastically spent money making it into manuscripts, posting it out to dozens of publishing companies, both big and small, and waited, and waited...48 manuscripts dispatched, three replies, three rejections and all asked her not to bother them again as they only dealt with agents and did not view unsolicited mail charitably. This was lesson number one in the school of hard knocks.

Her first novel remained unpublished and she remained agentless. Back to the drawing board. Novel two. *Even better*, she thought. This time, having learnt the lessons of her first venture, a friend had pointed her in the direction of a literary agent. Francis Forbes had just set up and was young and enthusiastic. One of Ruby's friends had recommended him to her. Big mistake. Ruby's friend was, at that time, having a torrid affair with the young man and obviously or possibly via pillow talk had mentioned to him about her friend, the young female author. Francis, who had just started to grow his business and was always looking for new writers, agreed to interview Ruby with a view to taking her under his wing. Whilst he was several years her senior and had worked in agent offices, he still lacked experience and, more vitally, contacts. She signed with him on the understanding that he would definitely get her a publishing contract. He read her first novel and understood why publishers had rejected it. He also agreed, however, that her second novel was a great improvement. He started the rounds of the publishers and thought he'd cracked it with one, only to be disappointed. He continued to try but with little luck. They met up again, he conceded defeat, she had been a bit tearful—she had been so young and capable of emotion—and left distraught. She wondered despairingly if she would ever realise her dream. "If at first, you don't succeed…"

Then it happened. One of her friends who knew she liked writing phoned her up to tell her that there was a novel competition in a national newspaper and she might be interested in entering it. *Nothing to lose*, Ruby had thought. She looked at the terms: you had to be an unpublished author without an agent. Check. Winner would get their book printed by a major publishing firm. She had gone off the notion of getting her second novel published, maybe she could return to it in the future, but she was already halfway through her next novel with the working title of "Daggers Drawn", a historical piece set at the start of the 19th century in Dublin. She liked researching interesting and obscure history and giving it her own twist. She duly submitted the first 3,000 words along with a 600-word synopsis and thought to herself, *I need something that will make them read it*, and with that, she got a friend, a good photographer, and arranged a photo shoot to go along with her submission. With the start of the novel, synopsis and picture for the front cover all duly submitted, she fully expected that would be the last she would hear of it. It wasn't!

Ruby got a phone call quite unexpectedly telling her that she had been shortlisted for the prize. This would mean a trip to London and attendance at the announcement followed by a press conference. The award ceremony was being held at the home of the sponsoring national newspaper in Wapping. For a twenty-something, this was the opportunity of a lifetime staring her in the face. If she won this competition, she would be made for life, or at least for another novel. She would take her friend who had told her about the competition, power-dress and even write a few words of thanks. As usual with this confident upstart, Ruby expected to win. Hope sprung eternal. So, her friend and herself boarded the train from St Albans, arrived in London, took a taxi to Wapping, all paid for by the newspaper. On arrival, she showed the letters to the security guards at the gate and was ushered in. There was a small anteroom with a number of mostly men and a couple of women drinking wine, nibbling on finger food, chatting and laughing. Despite her bravado, Ruby wasn't calm, anything but! The butterflies in her stomach felt like the size of owls. She small talked with a couple of people, trying to find out who the rest of these worthies were. Seemingly, they were a mixture of journalists, politicians, friends of the newspaper owner and presumably other hopefuls or, as Ruby saw them, competitors and losers.

After about forty minutes of milling about, they were all shown into a plush conference room with a big screen at the front, three chairs and rows of seats for everybody else. Being seated, the event started. The chair, the editor-in-chief of the sponsoring newspaper, introduced the other two on the platform—the head of the publishing house that would print and publish the winning entry and the "trophy wife" of the owner, who was in America. *How very equal opportunities for them* thought Ruby. After the usual platitudes about how marvellous all the potential winners had been, the chair asked his two colleagues to announce the winner. Ruby was ready, prepared, halfway out of her seat. 'And the winner of the Falcon Award 1998 is...' Everyone held their breath. 'Da, Lavidica Purcell for her brave and imaginative novel in outline, "False Promises".'

Ruby sank back into her seat, applauding, but was inwardly heartbroken. Her big chance had been snatched away from her by someone with a posh name. The winner was ushered into a room for a brief press conference and the rest into the large executive dining room for luncheon.

The crestfallen Ruby sat quietly and just picked at her main course. A woman sitting across from her asked if she was OK.

'Fine. I would have loved to have won though.'

'What's your name?' enquired the woman.

'Ruby Latimer.'

'You came second. A very interesting read, I thought,' as if to make her feel better. It didn't. 'Keep trying.'

'Been trying for over 18 months now. Seem to be getting nowhere fast.' Ruby tried to fight back her frustration and only just succeeded.

'Until now, dear girl.'

Intrigued by this comment, Ruby asked, 'What do you mean?'

'You don't recognise me but that's OK. Helen Stone. I was on the judging panel. I read your composition and synopsis. You have real potential, but you just need someone to sponsor you. As an author, I can't get you a deal with a publisher but what I can do is get you an agent, my agent, best in the business.'

'You are serious, I hope,' a quizzical Ruby asked her. The woman just smiled, nodded and handed Ruby her card. Ruby was not a great one for reading other people's books but had just googled the woman's name under the table. She was indeed a famous author. This was outstanding news.

Ruby had forgotten that coming first in competitions didn't always mean success, just like coming second wasn't always a failure. It just showed that the old adage, "keep trying and you will succeed", was very true. This was after all the age of "Cool Britannia" and a twenty-year-old at that time could achieve many things. All that was needed was talent and that lucky break. Things were definitely looking up.

Ruby and her friend travelled home to St Albans in a much better mood than they should have been, given the disappointment of the day. The next day Ruby was to phone Helen Stone, get the number and email address of her agent and take it from there. Helen's agent, a man called Arthur Newell, was indeed a very good agent. She phoned him to find out that Helen Stone had already contacted him, was expecting her call and invited her to come in and see him. He was in London so again, a trip on the train. She brought with her the manuscripts of the first two novels along with the half-written third one, which had failed to win the prize. They chatted for over an hour, she left, he promised to look at her work and get back to her.

Two days elapsed. She got a phone call from the man who was to be her new best friend.

'I can see that you have developed since the first book you wrote. Thought it was quite superficial but has some potential. Second one was much better. This unfinished one—now you're talking!'

Ruby was gobsmacked. Read two and a half books in under two days! Some going. Really!

'So, what now?' she enquired.

'Finish the book, get the rest of it to me pronto, I'll find your publisher!'

If only he could have seen her face. It was a combination of ecstasy and relief. The guy was different from the last total shyster agent—a slightly unfair characterisation but "if the boot fits…"—who had failed her. If this Arthur

Newell character was as good as his word, she would be as good as hers. She got him the rest of the book in six weeks. It was rough, but it was ready. He could now take it to hock it around and get it published. It took longer than he thought but nevertheless, he persuaded a decent publisher to take her on board with a two-book deal. Things had definitely started to look up. It was still not going to be a cakewalk, but she had never expected it to be. She was now going to be a published author. It had been a hard slog but she was knocking on the door of being something she had always wanted to be. Her next book would be even better. If only she could think of a decent subject. She now searched for inspiration.

Chapter 7
Rumours in the Coffee Set

Marion French had been an editor of books, journals and magazines for about 10 years. In that time, she'd built up an encyclopaedic understanding of what she was doing, what worked and what didn't. She worked on the basis of payment by results. The parts of the publishing industry where Marion inhabited had no one-size-fits-all approach to what she did. A bit like the music industry, an editor was like a session musician, dependent on the stars who wanted to record their latest song. When offered a job, they could either take a one-off fee at completion or, in the rare event, a percentage of the book profits. It was normal practice to take a fee. Marion worked on the basis of a bird in the hand. She edited on behalf of the publisher, delivered the final text and, when it was published, received her fee. It worked very well and paid her rent. She was considered a safe pair of hands and her publisher trusted her implicitly.

An old adage, "if you can't do it, criticise it", or in her case, edit it, could apply to the likes of editors such as herself. Marion started very modestly as a teenager, doing it in her spare time while studying for exams. Back then, she wasn't making much money but what she did make came in very handy. She was then still living at home with her parents but as soon as she was qualified, she moved out. She shared accommodation with three of her friends. The attractions of the big city were irresistible to a young female. They always would be. She was very well qualified in English Literature and had a propensity for correcting other people's mistakes—something that was quite annoying to her friends who saw it as almost an obsessive-compulsive disorder but tolerated it as it was their pal, Marion. In those early days, she read things in a very literal fashion, hot on grammar and punctuation but soon learned that a writer would have their own style, phraseology and attitudes. Her part-time employer called her into the office for a chat. She left with advice and a full-time permanent job offer.

Fast forward to now. Years had gone by, Marion had been in several relationships, married once, divorced once, pregnant once, given birth to a boy who had tragically died after only six weeks and now she lived alone. Since her divorce, she had had a few men friends but none that serious. Marion was a serious type, maybe she exuded an intensity or something and just maybe that was why she had difficulties keeping men interested in her. The expression, "it's not you, it's me", came readily to mind. She wasn't particularly unhappy about the situation, being quite self-contained, but variety was the spice of life. Pretty, but probably carrying a stone she could do without, Marion had no reason not to indulge, and she did. And then there was the love of her life—her work, which had developed and was now in tune with her six or seven authors, quite a feat when you think of the variation between them. They could be at various stages of development in their latest tome and whilst it was not her job to criticise what they had done—many of them were overachievers—she would make her own notes about their style, direction of travel, inconsistencies in the writing, etc. You would think that being surrounded by all these literary "geniuses"; Marion would fancy a bash at writing herself. No way. Having observed the creative process and the ravages it took on those creators, she thought her job easy by comparison. After all, if they have one failed book, it could be curtains for that writer, while she would still be employed and making money.

Marion had a few friends, three of whom were also editors. They met up for coffee from time to time to compare notes. Editing was more of an art than an exact science. The result was people in the industry were constantly gleaning tips from others about how to do it. Marion, whilst being very good at what she did, was circumspect enough to realise that she could always do better. There had been occasions when she'd edited someone's book and had been less than totally satisfied with the result. OK, there had been the ultimate satisfaction of knowing that the silk purse in the local national bookshop chain was the sow's ear that she had helped make readable and saleable and possibly had even gotten a small bonus from the publisher for doing so.

Tuesday morning, Charing Cross, London, in a well-known coffee shop, four women sat with Americanos and croissants at the ready. It was the bi-monthly book editors get together. The four of them had edited over a hundred books between them. They had met at a book launch organised by their own publisher and had discovered that they were all in the same line of work. That had been three years ago. Ever since that day, they had met regularly for a chat/gossip, and this was that day. And boy, did they have a lot of gossip to catch up on! Not just about editing, you see. Husbands, boyfriends, children growing up, things in the news, etc. Then they would talk about their latest editing challenges. A problem shared was a problem halved and of course, you always had problems with prima donna authors including one Ruby Latimer.

There was Abigail Roberts, considerably older than the others, lived in Eynsham, just beside Oxford; then there was Mary Callan, early 40s from Windsor; and finally, there was Rebecca (Becky) Letts from Orpington, just a bit younger than Marion. Their "literary chewing the cud" days were always looked forward to. The last thing they always discussed was the current project, whatever that happened to be. Each and every one of them had experiences of Ruby Latimer that had always ended in conflict. It wasn't that she wasn't a very good author; she was a very good author indeed and a very successful one. It was just that…well, her ego tended to get in the way of her ability, and they all had come to the same conclusion that her inability to take constructive criticism made her very high maintenance. At the end of the day, all of them would work with her regardless of her prickly nature; after all, they wouldn't be asked to sleep with her, just edit her books—and get paid for it! She was known to throw tantrums and report various editors to her agent for insubordination! The agent then saw to it that another editor took over until Ruby had calmed down or completely forgotten what she had been angry about in the first place, which didn't take long!

'Thinks she's struggling with this latest one,' Marion said to the girls. 'It's really not like her. She's so fluent normally. Getting old, that's what it is.' The others just laughed at this relatively young woman making that kind of comment.

'It happens to them all eventually,' said Abigail. 'They just run out of steam. It can be a kind of meltdown, like the inspiration's gone and they can't find a way to get it back. Oh, they try this, try that, some of them try crack cocaine, some of them…well, try other things, if you know what I mean!'

Marion thought she knew what she meant; the other two showed no indication that they did.

'In time, it normally comes back to them. Most of them just need a change of scenery for a bit. Maybe Miss Latimer needs to go away for a holiday, do something different, get laid, nuff said.'

By this time, the others had cottoned onto the gist of the conversation. Abigail had always been firmly of the view that to be a sustainable author, you also needed to be a sustainable human being. For her, that meant only one thing—kids. She had two grown-up children, a boy and a girl, plus a fifteen-year-old daughter. Her oldest daughter was in the later stages of pregnancy, having got married the year before. Life experiences were, as far as Abigail was concerned, an essential part of being a good writer; otherwise, you were just basing your ideas with your own imagination, not having done any of it yourself. Never regret the things you've done, only those you haven't.

'Heard you'd been away on holiday, Mary. Nice, was it?'

'Brilliant it was. Norwegian fjords. Just a week mind. Pre-Christmas break. Bitter it was. Still, George and me (her husband) kept warm, got to know each other again.'

Marion and Becky looked both bemused and confused. Get to know each other?

'Great sex was it then!' chirped Abigail. A broad, ruddy smile and a couple of almost invisible nods of her head confirmed to the others that Mary had indeed had a good time—and so, presumably, had George! So, it seemed that everyone was in the pink and doing quite nicely.

'What about you, Becky? How's your love life doing?'

'Love life! Do me a favour. Chance would be a fine thing. Last bloke I had was a right swine. Didn't realise he was a compulsive gambler. He ended up selling my bloody washing machine. Never saw him again and he's still got the key to my flat. Needed to change the locks so that the bugger couldn't get back in. Good riddance. I really do pick 'em, don't I? Maybe the next one'll be Mr Right!' Becky sipped her coffee.

She was the least experienced editor and listened intently to the others to garner tips.

It was an accepted convention of the girls that they could talk, in strictest confidence, about content of books, things you liked or disliked in them, but never name whose book they were currently editing. Nothing to do with protecting the authors, it was just that they dealt with so many different authors, it wouldn't matter anyway which one they were editing for. Ruby Latimer was only different because all four of them had worked with her at some time in the past. Their publisher was oblivious to their "coffee mornings". What his view would have been of them was uncertain; he might have considered them quite useful or he might have been apprehensive about what they talked about. After all, if they were talking about the contents of unpublished books in a public place, someone else might overhear them and pinch some of their ideas—highly unlikely though this would have been. The girls' meeting drew to a close and soon they would go their different ways until the next time. They always got ideas about editing that they applied to their latest task. If it had been lunch, it would be a working one. The next time they met, none of them knew it would be somewhat more dramatic. It would be a matter of life and death.

And then there was Greville Walsh. *Mormon Mayhem*, *Tabernacle Terror* and *Salt Lake Scandal* had all made Mr Walsh a very wealthy man. Not that he hadn't been wealthy before he signed Ruby Latimer, he was just a little bit wealthier now—and so was she. Back in the days of Larry Parnes, the famous impresario of the 50s who had discovered multiple talents in the music industry, time had moved on. Authors, agents and their publishers were the ones making money. Greville Walsh was the kind of publisher who had no concern whatsoever for the morality of what he did—personal sensitivities or indeed legal conventions. What he did best was sell books and boy, did he sell them! Like anyone in any industry that measured success by the quantity of items sold and the amount of profit made, publishing was an unsafe industry. Before the technological revolution, the Net Book Agreement, computer games and so many other wonders of the modern world, books had reigned supreme. Nowadays, with so many competing interests, unless you were JK Rowling, there was fat chance of you making it. Some would, and it was people like Greville who would decide just who they were. Greville Walsh a.k.a. literary kingmaker.

'What's that old bugger Newell wanting now?' he asked his secretary who was on the phone.

'Another brilliant find, he says,' replied Alice, Greville's PS. 'Says she came second in a major national novel writing contest. Says she's the best thing since sliced bread. Wants you to meet her. What will I tell him?'

'Tell him to get lost. I've got enough dross to contend with.'

'He says he'll buy you lunch!'

'Well now, there's a first. This author guy must be good then.'

'Apparently, it's a she. I did tell you that.'

'So, you did. Oh, all right then. Tell him to bring her along, my choice of restaurant, Thursday. No promises, just a chat. Hope she's got nice legs. No Alice don't tell him that! I was just thinking out loud! You just can't get the staff these days. Yes Alice, I did mean you.'

Greville was an unreconstructed male chauvinist pig. He did like to banter though, and Alice took it in good spirits, like she had a choice! Today he might not quite rank alongside the likes of Harvey Weinstein, but his mindset wasn't dissimilar. That had been in the late 90s, of course. Today, Greville was older, not necessarily wiser but mellower. For all his sexual innuendo, he was just a flirt, a middle-aged one. In his publishing house, most of the authors were women, not because he had any designs on them, but because they were all excellent writers. He was not perfect in regard to his judgement; one or two good'uns had slipped through his fingers, including some guy Follet, but most of his stable made money for the company, for themselves and, most importantly, for him. He was unlikely to make "The Sunday Times Rich List" but he didn't care because he was rich enough. The invention of Kindle had added a few zeros to his bank balance and that of his authors. It just got better and better.

Back to those heady days of 20 years ago. Mal Maison restaurant, lunchtime. Greville arrived to be greeted by Arthur who introduced a gorgeous young author called Ruby. First impressions mattered in every profession and industry and Ruby had power-dressed again for the occasion. She just knew that this was her main chance. Arthur had told her to say little or nothing, to leave it all to him, that was his job. Arthur then proceeded to give Greville the hard sell, the emotional blackmail stuff, poor young girl just wanting a chance. Greville sat impassively listening to this trite nonsense, stuff he'd heard from many agents many times before. He let Arthur continue and then just said, 'Let's eat. I'm starving.' In other words, *shut the fuck up, Arthur, quit while you're ahead.* Arthur took the hint. The three ordered and continued to chat and drink.

'What do you think of this man, Ruby?'

'If he can get me a publishing contract, I'll screw him in the toilets today. Sorry Arthur, only kidding, wine talking.'

'I think I like you, Ruby Latimer. You are a feisty young thing, aren't you? Come in and see me on your own on Monday, I'll get Alice to draw up a contract. We always start off with two-book contracts. You happy with that? Well, of course you are!'

After two hours, Greville got up and left. Arthur and Ruby sat and finished off their coffees. Arthur was as pleased with the outcome as Ruby was shocked and amazed, not least with her "screwing Arthur in the toilets" comment. She had no idea where it had come from or indeed why she had blurted it out. It could have gone badly but it hadn't. She was on her way to fulfilling her dream.

'Should I take my manuscript in to show him on Monday?'

'Yes, by all means, but don't give him a finished version and don't sign anything; bring it to me so that our lawyers can take a look at it to make sure he's not trying to screw you over. He drives a Bentley. Who do you think pays for it? Once I get the contract checked out, make any suggestions or amendments if required, then you can sign it. Then you will be an author. Well done, Ruby. He's right. Feisty.'

Chapter 8

Removal of Two Stiffs

The forensic unit had waited a day for anyone from CryoScience UK to appear. Jack had bit the proverbial bullet and contacted their office to ask if someone could come out to look at the situation and advise. CryoScience UK was a private firm that dealt with cryogenics—freezing dead people to possibly resuscitate at some point in the dim and distant future, or possibly never. It was for the hopeful rich whilst the rest of us just accepted that life and death happened. A Professor Jones duly arrived, complete with white coat and case. Jack took him aside and explained the situation to him.

'I'll need to take a look.'

Jack showed him the photos and video. 'How long have they been down there?'

'Not absolutely confirmed but our lab has estimated that the cadavers are between 18 and 24 months deceased.'

The professor was now deep in thought.

'And they are still with substantial tissue? Remarkable!'

Both understood that the action of putrefaction would be expected to start when rigor mortis had worn off. In such circumstances, the amount of intact cadaver mass of both victims must have meant that they could have still been living when they had entered the well bottom. Both shuddered at this likelihood.

'You haven't tried to remove them then?'

'No, they're both too fragile plus the well walls aren't smooth, so we would likely damage them or worse, lose bits of them on the way out. We're loath to do that. Do you think you could help here?'

The professor had one hand on one elbow, the other stroking his grey-bearded chin.

'OK, this is what I think we should do…' and then outlined an approach.

Jack thought about it and said, 'Yes, it could work. We need as little tissue damage as we can manage, and the thawing period?'

The professor took out his phone, did some rough calculations based on the likely weights of the bodies and showed Jack.

'Fine. OK, let's give it a try.'

With that, they shook hands.

'I'll be back tomorrow with our equipment. We will need to take them back to our centre to control the thawing process. I expect you'll need to have someone present to protect against any unintended cross contamination.'

The professor certainly seemed to know forensics, as indeed he should.

'Jack. A hitch. Will need to construct a receptacle to enclose and contain the bodies before we can freeze and uplift. Will take a couple of days. I suggest sealing the well to prevent it heating up,' Professor Jones suggested this to Jack Jordan on the phone. The forensics unit, all six of them, were at a major crime scene kicking their heels until the CryoScience UK lot had all that they needed. Jack knew a lot about many things, but this was virgin territory. He studied some information on the Internet so that he had relevant questions, but he was still uneasy about the outcome. Had he known that the CryoScience people felt the same, he would have been even less confident. Anyway, the dye had been cast. On Friday, a lorry came with…guess what was written on the side. Not Iceland! Out came four men, all in virtual spaceman garb, Professor Jones being one.

'We'll take it from here.'

Having spent over a day taking plaster casts of tyre tracks, footprints, possible blood and tissue samples from around the circumference of the well, at last something seemed to be happening. Jack had his fingers crossed behind his back, so apparently did the professor. Jack and the professor went for a walk whilst his team unloaded the contents of the lorry.

'I take it you know what's involved, Jack?'

'You're going to tell me, aren't you?'

'It's like this. To remove bodies and have them able to be medically examined will take a fair degree of skill, care and, at the end, dry ice. We need to chill the bodies down. Normally, it would be minus 130 degrees but probably minus 80 will suffice for your purposes. The term is "Cryoprotectant Vitrification", which is to protect cell damage during freezing and stop ice crystals forming. If it's good enough for frozen embryos, it's good enough for them,' pointing to the well.

52

'So how will you get them up?'

'First things first. I'll need Tom to go down to assess the situation. He'll not disturb anything but if they are attached to the wall, it will need to be rectified.'

Tom, all geared up, was lowered down the well and in fifteen minutes, returned to the top.

'Fucking stinks down there. Need a pipe and gemmy to get them unstuck from that wall.'

A pipe and hose were duly supplied and a large crowbar. Down went Tom and ever so slowly hosed liquid nitrogen onto the wall, which made the lead body even more secure against the wall.

'Give it ten minutes, then I'll start.'

Ten minutes elapsed and Tom began to prise the first corpse away from the well wall ever so carefully. The freezing had made it easier. In a few minutes, the two were free. They were still supported by the wall, just not attached to it anymore.

Tom came to the surface, his part of the job completed.

'Jack, now the real process can begin. Get out the chamber.'

The lorry's back door opened, revealing a large, cylindrical rigid grey plastic chamber that would fit into the well cavity. It was open ended. Now Jack could see the plan.

'This is stage one. We will lower and place the tube over the bodies, begin to freeze them. Ten degrees only in stages up to minus 80 degrees, by which time they should be solid, then we fill the spaces with ice, drop the temperature to ensure the bodies are tight and secure, then lift the tube to the top.'

'Hope it works,' said Jack, more in hope than expectation. It would take three to four hours, but it was worth a try. With everything in place, the tube and Tom again descended to the bottom of the well. Once there, he helped carefully manoeuvre the chamber over the bodies, ensuring that the one previously attached to the wall was free. Then, inch by inch, the plastic chamber was lowered until it was in place.

'Can we get the ice first?'

A flexible plastic tube about eighteen inches in diameter, twenty foot in length, was lowered into the well until Tom had hold of the handles. He directed it to the top of the chamber. 'Slowly,' he shouted. A rush of noise shuddered down the tube, which he directed in all directions into the chamber, filling every bit that wasn't corpses. Task done, he then said, 'LN pipe,' and what looked like a garden hose was fed down to him. He was fully kitted out to prevent any danger to himself and it was just as well. LN could bring on frostbite. The corpses, however, were packed in ice so it was not likely to affect them. He started to spray the contents into the chamber, which saw mist appear from below and above it. That was the first phase. Tom then returned to the surface. A nice cup of tea, then lunch.

'Happy with it so far, Jack?' asked the professor.

'So far so good. What happens when we get them up?'

'We need to take them back to our centre. It will take the same amount of time, maybe slightly longer, for them to return to room temperature. We can keep them cool if the PM (post-mortem) people want, until Monday.' Jack nodded.

'However, still to get them out. Need to do it very slowly. Lunch, I think. Jack, you buying? Only joking.'

This was the professor's attempt to lighten a sombre atmosphere. Lunch was back at their hotel. The team minus Richie—didn't do vegan at the hotel so he'd brought his own to eat—had a nice lunch and the ten started to chill a bit, just like those in the well. Ann, the only woman in the room, got chatting to one of the Cryo guys. She was interested in how he had gotten the job, what he did when he wasn't getting bodies out of wells, etc. They all did some bonding. Then it was back to the grind.

'Now, remember that the well has walls that are anything but smooth. Gently does it.'

'Still got three hours of freezing to do before then,' said Henry. They returned and the freezing continued until almost five in the afternoon. Then it was done. Tom came back up.

'Right now, easy does it. Inch at a time.'

Literally, it was brought up that slowly. Tom went down to chaperone it to the top and it took twenty-five minutes of ensuring that the chamber didn't catch a protruding brick in the well wall and that the contents of the chamber were secure. The chamber arrived at the top. A trolley was awaiting it and it was placed on it as the lorry was backed over to the well. Its doors opened and a refrigeration unit opened to take the chamber and its contents.

'As I said, Jack, we'll have this ready for the PM people Monday morning. Take it that's who we will send our invoice to.'

Chief Inspector Stevenson, who had been hovering, nodded in the direction of Jack, smiled and said, 'Kent Police. Thanks for your help.'

A good day's work all around.

'Richie, still one thing to get. Did you think we would just write off your drone? Forensics isn't made of money, is it?'

Richie had hoped the boss had forgotten. He hadn't. That was why he was the boss. They shone a torch to see if they could locate it, but it was nowhere to be seen. They went back to tidy up around the well and secure the rusty metal grill. Ann took a peek over and recoiled.

'That stench. Way too strong if everything is now out, in my opinion. Residual odour shouldn't smell like that.'

'It is. Strange,' said Richie. 'I thought the cause of the smell had been removed. I know we might need to fetch out that arm but that surely can't be the cause of the smell?'

Given the circumstances, it wasn't unusual for aromas of that sort to linger long after everything had been removed. They still had a missing arm to locate.

'The smell stopped when they froze the bodies. I'm with you. Something else must be down there.'

'Fuck, we can check it out now or wait. Long day, folks. Whatever else is down there, it can wait. It's not going anywhere.'

The forensic unit was made up of dedicated professionals. They also had families who they would dearly have liked to spend the weekend with. They had booked out of the hotel and had intended to all go to their respective homes. Jack went up to CI Stevenson and the others could see them talking. He came back.

'Off home, team. Uniforms will secure the area until Monday. A job well done.'

Monday, they returned, and by the end of that day had discovered much more than just a rotten smell. It was a mass murder site.

Chapter 9

Lizzie and her Rude Awakening

It was a Sunday morning in Greenwich. A man lay next to Lizzie Spector in her bed. He was on his back and his hairy chest was visible. He was motionless and asleep. Lizzie Spector also lay on her back next to him, the thin silk sheet that covered him halfway up his chest covered her nakedness. Her right hand twiddled with the diamond ring on the third finger of her other hand. She gazed at the ceiling, lost in childhood reminiscence. She occasionally smiled, glancing at this body next to her. She had been deep in thought for an hour and still was. She was in love with this man, she thought. She heaved a deep sigh and glanced at him furtively. Would he still be the one lying next to her in 50 years? Another deep sigh and another deep thought.

She thought back. Ten years ago, when she had started to discover her sensual body. As a new teenager with friends from school, she had been invited to a sleepover—pyjama party—one weekend. The girls were slightly older than her, just a few months. At that age, a few months could be the difference between theoretical carnal knowledge and total innocence. Young Lizzie was then most definitely the latter. Saturday night, Jamie, Lily and Andrea were in Jamie's house and in her room at 10 o'clock at night in pyjamas, James Blunt on TV. The four laughed, carried on, wrestled and tickled each other.

In those days, you could download stuff onto a DVD and watch it, old hat now. Jamie put on a DVD and the three began to watch it. Two young women were getting very friendly with each other. Lizzie remembered being a bit uncomfortable and blushing. Two of the others weren't in the slightest bit fazed by it. It was apparently a great laugh. Lizzie noticed something else though. Andrea was sitting propped up against a wall in her sleeping bag, watching the DVD. Her hands were both inside the bag. There seemed to be some movement and she had a strange, almost pained expression on her face and her forehead

56

was wrinkled. Lizzie asked if she was OK and Andrea replied, 'Will be soon,' and giggled. The other two girls looked at each other and laughed. Lizzie had no idea what the joke was.

'Don't you know what she's doing? Juicing,' Jamie told Lizzie. Lizzie was clearly confused.

'You know, masturbating.'

Lizzie had heard of this but had no idea what it was. The three other girls laughed, and Lizzie went red in the face, not knowing if she was the butt of the joke.

'You do know what masturbating is, don't you?'

'Course I do!' lied Lizzie.

'Well, what is it? You say you know what it is. Tell us.'

Lizzie remembered that she had blushed again. The other two just shrugged their shoulders and looked at each other. 'Think we should show her?' chirped Lily.

The other two smiled and said, 'Sure thing.'

'Want to see what juicing is, do we? Juicing is having sex on your own. Want us to show you how it's done?'

Lily stood up and pulled down her pyjama pants and stood, legs apart in front of Lizzie's face. 'This is juicing,' as Lily moved her index finger briskly back and forth across what appeared to be a small raised piece of hard skin.

'That's my clit.'

Lizzie, eyes red, tears dripping down her face in sheer embarrassment of what she had just seen and at the idea that she hadn't known about it. It wasn't just for peeing then! "Les Girls" had just taken some of Lizzie's innocence. It would never come back.

Midnight approached; the mood had changed to one of quiet tiredness. It was Jamie's room, so the bed was hers and the other three had inflatables and sleeping bags. After a round of goodnight, they turned in for the night. Not Lizzie. Lily had shown her something fascinating but what did it actually do? She had seen the technique. She also saw the sweaty, scintillating outcome. She absolutely must. She just knew she had to. Her right hand descended and found that spot Lily had rubbed so vigorously. She fiddled and fiddled, juiced and juiced. Nothing. Ten minutes; nothing. Another five; still nothing. The others heard her. 'What's up?' asked Jamie.

'I don't really know,' sobbed Lizzie.

The other three were now sitting up around her. Lily asked her, 'You been doing what I showed you?'

Lizzie just sobbed more and nodded. 'Nothing happened. Doing just the same way as you did.'

Lily, who by now had sat next to Lizzie, put her arm around her shoulder and said, 'The first time can be hard. It was for me. Once you get the knack, you can come every time.'

Lily gave Lizzie a "hands on" lesson. In under ten minutes, Lizzie remembered that she had had her first glorious experience. She also remembered that she had shuddered and cried with pleasure and relief. The other two had broken into muffled applause. Lizzie hugged Lily out of sheer gratitude. Her childhood had partly ended that night and life as an aware adolescent began. This was not a lesbian experience, just being shown what that part of her anatomy existed for. After that, they all slept and Lizzie slept the soundest of the four. So many questions had awakened in the mind of Lizzie Spector, few of which the other three could possibly answer. She asked them; they, of course, gave her answers either made up, incorrect or just plain mischievous. At her tender age, she would have had difficulty deciding which of them were right. Lizzie Spector's age of innocence had indeed ended, and her age of curiosity had begun. What about boys?

Lizzie's mind returned to where she was, still in bed next to her fiancé, who was still asleep. She grasped his right hand with her left, but her hand quickly vanished under the covers to somewhere else. She recalled that those girls had been fun, the boys even more fun. She thought back to her first boyfriend and heterosexual experience. Both of them had been just sixteen, the difference being that she had known what to do. His name had been Jerry. They had gone up to his room after school one day and fooled about. It had gotten a bit hot and serious but even though he had been ready for it, she hadn't. They had done the next best thing. He had dropped his trousers; she had dropped her skirt and knickers. His mouth had not been on her mouth and nor hers on his. After two minutes, it had been all over for him. His ecstasy had stopped hers. His mouth had been full of gratitude whilst hers had been just full. She remembered running into the bathroom, gagging and spitting. She had learned that day that men, boys, once satisfied, lost interest in their partner having satisfaction. So, it was cheerio Jerry.

The man in Lizzie's bed stirred but continued to sleep. She thought back again to that special person, the one she had been saving herself for, The One. It was funny how life would take over when you least expected it to. Just having turned eighteen, school, disco, lots of drink, lots of boys on the prowl for sex. She thought back to that one boy who had taken her virginity that night. Funny thing was that she couldn't visualise him. It was the least romantic sex, back of his dad's car for a minute or more, blood and…and him cursing at the bloody mess—literally! —that she had made of his dad's backseat, as if he hadn't made a contribution! Yes, it had been truly wonderful, something she would treasure! Lizzie sighed. If only she had known how much better all those experiences… She was prone to make mistakes. It was called being a human being. Did she regret it? A bit but well, not really. At least she hadn't gotten pregnant. Happened to some girls all the time. Happened to a couple in her class at school. It hadn't been rape, just youthful stupidity. Lust. Her right hand had been busy between her legs and she was now quite wet. Time to wake up her champion. Her left hand had also been busy. He woke up, smiled and was ready.

'Engagement party, Friday. You will be there?'

'What do you think?'

He answered with a haughty smirk on his face. 'Difficult to have one without me, I would have thought. What's for breakfast?'

'Apart from me, you mean!' she said with a smirk. Fifteen minutes later, he got up, walked naked into her kitchen and five minutes later was back with two coffees.

'Good chance for our parents to meet as well. Soon this will be us all the time.' She just smiled and nodded.

'Looking forward to it, I take it, darling?' Again, she just nodded and smiled.

'We've got a lot of arranging to do after,' said Lizzie, stating the bleeding obvious.

'Our mums will no doubt take over as they always do. I need to nobble yours. Mine has rather more unorthodox ideas than yours might. Need to ensure it isn't something weird like a naked ceremony; just kidding. Anyway, need to put the "Lizzie" stamp on it.'

They drank their coffee and both got up to go into the living room, turned on the TV and watched the Andrew Marr Show. He rubbed her leg and she rubbed his arm. Not exactly love's young dream these two but nevertheless, they were well-suited. 'I'll need to go back to the office later,' to which she replied,

'And I've got some work to catch up with as well.'

They both had busy lives and tried to share them as much possible, but it wasn't always easy. In under half an hour, he was dressed and, on his way, out the door.

'See you tomorrow?'

'Not if I see you first!' smirking in his direction. They kissed again, he left, and she shouted after him, 'Bye, Craig.' Her mind had momentarily asked herself the question, *Am I really happy or just prepared to settle for second best?* She put this firmly to the back of her oh so busy journalist mind.

Chapter 10

Walter and the Agent's Office

Young Walter Sims, a bright and dedicated young man in his 20s, started working in the publishing industry straight from school. At school, he had been, at best, average. One thing he liked to do was read, something he had done at school at every opportunity, something that led him to be seen as an outsider. It was true that he wasn't very sporty, wore glasses, which he had now changed to contact lens, would have been picked on by the school bullies except for one thing, the left hook that he possessed. He had only ever used it once. He had had a couple of books under his right arm and been on his way from class to the library at the start of the lunch break. One of the lesser-known toe rags had decided to relieve him of his books. As Walter had his right arm occupied, he had just brought his left fist under the bully's chin, end of bully and story. Funnily enough, after that, he had been left alone. Bullies, cowards, same thing.

He left school early without sitting exams because a relative knew someone who could get him a job. The job was with a man called Arthur who was a literary agent. It wasn't great, starting off as the office dogsbody—poor pay, strange hours—but for Walter, that wasn't the point. He didn't mind being the "gopher" as long as he was learning the tricks of the trade and meeting interesting people. He knew that it would be a long learning curve, but he was a patient lad. On his first day, he met all the women who worked for Arthur and they of course, all being in their 30s and having young children, had wanted to mother him. He had let them.

After a couple of weeks of making tea, taking letters to the post office—Arthur Newell, Literary Agent, still operated as if they were in a different century and to some of the women could have been the 19th! —young Walter got his first real piece of responsible work: collecting a manuscript from one of the authors. This was quite a common practice. Laurel Publishers would be the recipients of the finished product; however, Arthur always insisted on having a sneaky little look at any finished work. After all, if it was shit, it could reflect on him and his company, not that he would have any say in the matter. Only after he had read it on the only decent computer in the office would he let it go to Greville. He let every single one he read go to Greville. Arthur thought Greville didn't know he did this but of course, Greville knew everything. It was the nature of printing and publishing. Extra quality control, he figured.

Walter would collect completed chapters from various authors each week, leave them overnight with Arthur and deliver them the next day to Laurel Publishers, having been thoroughly scrutinised by Arthur. The editors, working on an ad hoc, payment by results basis, would work on the chapters, visiting the author only to clarify or ascertain certain nuances within the completed text. Rather than screw up the process, this actually was more efficient because by doing the editing in small manageable chunks, the editors concentrated better and made fewer mistakes. Authors were more likely to see Walter than the editors who were only likely to call a couple of times during the book writing process.

Walter harboured a secret ambition, that of being a writer himself. He wasn't confident of achieving this. Walter wasn't confident about much. However, what he did was occasionally meet various authors, the odd literati if they happened to be visiting one of the authors when he was accidentally there. He started off as a teenager, quite shy but in time came out of his shell. He would listen to what they said and if he heard anything relevant, he made a note of it back at the office. He needed ideas for a book himself but couldn't really think of anything. It would no doubt come to him in the fullness of time. No doubt many people in this industry were very protective of their ideas, which was not surprising given the paranoia surrounding intellectual property. It was almost like posters seen during World War II stating, "careless talk costs lives", except it was changed to "careless talk costs ideas…and money!" What scraps of information, ideas, he got from his eavesdropping were pretty useless. Nevertheless, he clung to the hope that surely if he just carried on, listened and took notes, eventually, that elusive idea would hit him. He just kept going. He wondered how he could get into becoming an editor. He asked one of the editors and she told him. For most of them, it was because they had English teaching backgrounds. He, of course, had nothing of the sort. There might be a back way into the profession through Arthur. If he showed enough initiative, reliability and was given the chance to prove he could do it, then just maybe Mr Newell would allow him a shot. He approached Arthur, who said maybe in a year. That had been four years before.

At 23, Walter was still a virgin. He ploughed all of his energies into his job; any spare time he had; he wrote. Writing rather than girls was his passion. It wasn't that he didn't have male urges, he had normal, shall we just call them "male sexual responses", that anyone of his age and sex would expect to have. He would either ignore them or deal with them as most sex-deprived adults did. Anyway, as stated earlier, he did have the hots for one particular author who really had no interest in sex at all. Like him, she was interested in her career and that was all. Life could be funny, with all kinds of twists and turns, so you never knew exactly what was around the next corner. A famous author and a message boy. Go play with yourself! He did.

Walter Sims, despite the lower pay and apparent lack of appreciation— particularly when he would love to be editing other people's work and was being frustrated in this aspiration—decided to carry on. Being in a bit of a rut but still in employment was better than nothing. He saw for himself what his old school mates weren't doing. They had left school and were, in most cases, signing on for various training schemes with little prospect of a job at the end of them. The bullies in particular, he laughed to himself internally, had proved to be the biggest losers. It was now his turn to feel superior. Walter was an eternal optimist and believed that becoming an editor at the publishing house would be a turning point in his life. Maybe one of his beloved authors who he had served loyally for almost five years would be able to help. All he needed was the courage to ask them for their support. Maybe he should ask Miss Latimer?

He had occasion to visit her to collect a USB, which contained a minuscule amount of text as she was having continued problems with this book. He arrived at the appointed time to collect the USB. It was never just to hand but rather somewhere in her study. Ten minutes later, she appeared, looking sort of harassed, with the USB.

'Miss Latimer, may I ask you something?'

'Very busy. Won't it wait till next time?'

At this point, Walter decided to ask. 'I was wanting to become an editor and was hoping you might recommend me. I've been coming here on and off now for five years. I hope you see I'm reliable and trustworthy. I would like to move on to editing but would need the recommendation of—'

'Walter, is it? Walter, dear boy, I don't have the time for this right now. We can discuss it again next time you call. I must go.'

He was never sure just where she always seemed to be going to, but it was always urgent when he came to call.

Young Walter left with the USB, somewhat crestfallen. She hadn't said no but she hadn't said yes either. Maybe she just needed to think about it. What Ruby Latimer really thought about was that the idea of her using her reputation to help somebody else was just ludicrous. Doing so would be a first. This young guy would visit her every few weeks, collect stuff, exchange a few words and leave. She had no idea that he was more than a collection and delivery boy. This, despite the fact that on several occasions, he had mentioned to her that he read and wrote. You needed to be interested in other people to remember such things. This wasn't about herself so why should she remember or show any interest. That would go totally against Ruby Latimer's self-centred grain. At times, she made a certain Mr Clarkson look three-dimensional.

Five weeks passed. Walter was due to visit Miss Latimer again, full of hope and anticipation. When he arrived, he collected yet another USB with precious little text on it. Walter knew that this author was writing very little and mostly rubbish. He had heard the odd remark about her not being as quick as normal. It usually took her under six months to complete the draft up to the final editing stages. She had taken nearly a year and it was still quite some way from completion. There was the usual rummaging, trying to find that blessed USB, which she found and gave to him.

'Well, Miss Latimer, did you think about what I asked you last time I was here.'

'What was that again?'

'Me being an editor. You said you would give me a recommendation.' In fact, she had said nothing of the sort, she had said nothing at all, but Walter was learning to chance his arm on the basis that she wouldn't remember in any case. Ruby looked both confused and embarrassed. Had she really said this?

'If you want to write it out yourself and bring it to me next time you're here, I'll sign it.'

Result! His sheer cheek had brought him nearer to the prize. He returned in a week with the recommendation for her to sign. She wasn't in. Where was she?

Chapter 11

Ruby: Up, Up and Away?

Frustratingly, Ruby Latimer was no further forward with the book. If anything, she was further backwards than she was forwards. She poured herself a drink, a large G&T, and she had a fag. Having given up smoking in her teenage years, this showed the state of her mind—despair, desperation and resignation all lumped into one. She looked again at what she had written, shook her head, hunched up her shoulders, took another drag and a sip and reread the last completed chapter of her book. Something was definitely amiss—but what?

"…Nancy and Barry Truman, at first glance a loving couple if there ever was one. Married for 10 years and off to enjoy their wedding anniversary in Rome. It was to be a lovely trip, first-class flight, champagne, flight attendants fawning over them. Barry, a thirty-something very successful executive in a transnational corporation specialising in mining lithium. A self-confident, determined, focussed individual if ever there was one, Barry knew his mind and how to get on in the business world. It was all about networking. He already had a penthouse apartment in Central London where they occasionally lived. Nancy, apart from fuck him did, well, fuck all. Nancy hardly ever did even that those days. The wedding anniversary was an attempt to rekindle lost libido—hers, not his—Barry had married Nancy for sex, she had married Barry for luxury.

"They were still childless because…well, that would have meant sharing and neither of them were sharers in any real sense. Maybe one day or maybe not. "If it's not broke, don't fix it." Was she his trophy wife? Absolutely. Nancy was twenty-nine, quite tall for a woman and slim. However, she did more than dabble with the old Botox, not that it showed much. At her age, it was more a case of safeguarding her looks to safeguard her meal ticket. They had met at a debs thing where she had spilled (accidentally, really!) her drink on him. The rest was sex,

less sex and even lesser sex. Love wasn't always connected to sex but it sure went some way to oiling the tracks. Still, they both appeared to be reasonably content."

Ruby read it and was quite happy with where the story was going. Barry, though she would never admit it, apart from genitalia could have been her. She continued…

"Take-off from Heathrow delayed an hour, so off to the VIP lounge. Free champers and luxury nibbles. Take-off and a three-hour flight ahead. As I said, champagne, nibbles, lots of fawning."

Ruby saw the repetition, but it worked so she just left it in.

"Two hours into the flight and flying over the Alps, Nancy was gazing out the window when it slowly appeared. Just then, a weather balloon below, apparently on the left side. Something strange though, it appeared to have something dangling from it long and straight. She looked again—and gasped.
'Oh my god, Barry! Barry, look! LOOK!' she yelled and nudged him. She thought she recognised the "long thing". Barry had his smartphone, leant over her and started to video the object/s. Then they were gone from view.
'What was it, honey?' he asked her.
'A body. It was a body.'
'Couldn't be. Could it?' He quickly viewed the video.
'Not sure what it was but…just not sure.'
'Page the stewardess.' A young female member of the cabin staff answered their call.
'My wife thinks she saw a weather balloon with a body attached to it. I don't know. Here's what I got. See for yourself.' The all-singing, all-dancing state-of-the-art smartphone had a very good picture of the item lasting eight or nine seconds. The attendant looked at it and asked how long ago it was taken.
'Was taken about three or four minutes ago.' She asked if she could show it to one of the flight deck officers. No problem. This was just the start.
"On landing, the flight attendant brought the phone back and asked if the couple could hold back a few minutes. Barry had, without telling anyone, sent the video to his brother in London; why, Nancy wasn't sure. He always shared

videos with him. It seemed the Carabinieri wanted to get more details. Carabinieri Inspector Liberio took them into a small interview room and talked to them in broken English about the circumstances and Barry went through it once more. He asked the inspector what he thought. His reply was both candid, probably inappropriate and shocking.

'We are aware our Comoro sometimes use these balloons to disappear victims but until now it was only a suspicion.' Until now.

"After a pleasant weekend of mostly sightseeing and dining out, it was back to London. When they arrived, a phalanx of photographers was there for some celebrity feeding frenzy or other, no doubt. No, it was for them! Apparently, their video was on YouTube and had gone viral! Interest in them was at a premium and as soon as they had collected their bags and were on their way to the taxi, a man approached them about doing a TV interview. Out of weakness and a large degree of vanity, they accepted. Major mistake!

The TV interviewer was just not going to let this one go.

'What do you really think it was you saw?'

Nancy started to answer, 'It sure looked to me like a body, Michael—' but her husband interjected, 'Hard to be sure. Maybe the experts can identify what it was. After all, it was over in a few seconds, wasn't it, dear?'

Nancy chimed in, quite irate, 'I saw a body. I know I did. That's what I saw.'

After the interview, Michael, the interviewer, said that one of his friends on a national newspaper was an investigative journalist and would maybe want to pay them for an interview. Would they mind? Absolutely, they would mind! They had had quite enough of reporters, thank you very much. They took the card anyway. In the TV company paid-for taxi, on the way home, the issue came up again. Nancy wasn't interested in the idea of more boring talk about "it", but Barry thought it might be interesting, so he gave the guy a call. A day later, Enfield Pottinger, who was a member of the Institute of Investigative Journalists, called back and was invited to the Truman flat that night. He had seen the YouTube video and there had been a voice-over (Barry's brother?), speculating on what it was and there was a blurry close-up of it. Even blurrier, there was the unmistakable sight of a body-like shape dangling from a weather balloon, arms apparently dangling down, lifeless. After taking details of how the video was taken—for the umpteenth time—Enfield told Barry he was well into writing a story about how the Comoro had been using weather balloons in Sicily and Southern Italy for at least a couple of years to spirit away bodies of opponents, snitches or people who just caused them inconvenience. It was almost the perfect murder as bodies could end up virtually anywhere in the world but most likely in an ocean and they didn't even need to dig a hole! Barry nodded.

'Carabinieri told us that in Rome.'

'Did they? Wow! Thanks. Corroboration at last.'

Nancy was listening rather than being involved but started to get a little worried though she said nothing until this reporter had left. She had concerns.

'Who's this Comoro guy?' Barry had obviously not married her for her intelligence.

'Mafia, darling.'

'I'm getting a bit concerned, Barry.'

'What about?'

'Well, if it's organised crime doing this and they find out where we live, we could end up on the end of one of their balloons.'

'Unlikely, dear, but you may have a point. Better safe than sorry.'

Barry thought about where this was going and decided to take the kind of action that the rich alone had available to themselves. That was to just up sticks. Next night, he came home and announced to his beloved, 'Pack a bag; we're moving out into a hotel. I've put the house on the market.'

Nancy sat down to take it in.

'You are taking this seriously, aren't you! Thought we'd have moved into the London flat.' (the Mayfair penthouse)

'Better safe than sorry,' he replied.

'Off you go. Just enough for tonight. Estate agent thinks this will sell within a week. Not surprised. He's also looking at houses outside the M25. Seems there's quite a choice in villages and suchlike.'

So off to the hotel they went, then back the next day to collect more stuff, her expensive jewellery, clothes, etc. Removers would pack up the rest and put it in storage until a new house was bought. It was a torrid time, but Barry seemed as ever to be in control. Everything seemed to be going ahead like clockwork. They would just disappear for a while. That was their erstwhile hope."

Ruby stopped again and had another mouthful of booze. It had only just gone noon. She sighed, wondering just what was not right about this. Were weather balloons not a good way for the Mafia to rid themselves of their enemies? Was there no possibility of them being intercepted? Wouldn't people notice them on the ground? She did some research. Nope. These balloons could stay up for at least a month or more at heights where only Jumbos could go. Radar might spot them but they were weather balloons! No, the idea was sound. An ending was still absent though. She carried on…

"*Two weeks later, moved out of the hotel, house and flat sold—penthouse flats in Central London just go! —off they moved into a four-bedroom villa in a secluded part off the green belt in the Crawley area, three miles from the local village. A local station was handy for Barry's work, not that he was likely to use it much, if at all. It was beautiful and felt safe with a high fence and security cameras. Safe as houses.*

"*Five weeks went by and nothing much happened. Then Nancy—who by all accounts was…well, shall we say not the brightest button in the box—was reading the paper when she spotted an article about their very item by, of all people, Enfield Pottinger. But the article was not by him but ABOUT him. Enfield Pottinger was missing. His car had been found abandoned, seemingly having been side-swiped by another vehicle and there were signs of a struggle and no papers, laptop, mobile phone or suchlike had been discovered in the car. At this point, Nancy found herself hyperventilating. She called Barry to tell him.*

'*I'm fucking scared, Barry. Think they might have done him in.*' *He assured her that they were perfectly safe for now.*

"*It was September. Barry's birthday in a week. Doorbell rang. It was a delivery truck.*

'*Delivery for a Mr Truman,*' *the driver said, showing his ID.* '*Four boxes. Mr Truman's instructions were to leave them in your garage.*'

"*Nancy pointed it out to the driver, and he and his associate promptly put them in the garage and left. That night, Nancy said to Barry,* '*You got a delivery today; I told the men to put the boxes in the garage. What was it then?*'

'*Birthday present from me to me. Stargazing. You know I like all that stuff.*'

"*So that was that. Stargazing. Funny how he'd never revealed that side of his nature. Married people had secrets or maybe it was just indifference by the other partner. Or maybe she just didn't listen to him. Bed. Nancy had a headache so took a couple of painkillers and retired early. No sex tonight, dear. Nothing new there. Truman sex had become something of a rarity. Even on the trip to Rome, it had been predictable. She was out sound asleep in five minutes. Barry was still up. He was up to something. A 4x4 arrived, its lights off. He let it in through the gates. Three men dressed in black appeared. Apparently, he'd been expecting them. They and he had an ulterior motive.*

"*She felt something shaking her. Bleary-eyed, she slowly became conscious of someone more than Barry being there. She saw someone in black and began to scream but felt a pain in her arm and went promptly limp. She was now back in the chemical land of Nod. Two men in black were in the garage. They opened two of the boxes and took out the contents and laid them on the grass in that enclosed, secluded back garden. Now it became apparent what had been in the boxes and what was about to happen. Nancy opened her eyes. Her legs. They were completely numb. Part of the plan. She was now outside on a dark mild night in her nightdress. She was confused but this confusion was just about to turn into abject horror. Barry was kneeling over her.*

'Darling, this is goodbye. Got you a one-way ticket to the moon.'

'What are you fucking talking about?' she said in a slurred, muted tone.

'Not only am I bored and frustrated with you and your sterility and frigidity but I'm looking for a younger model—model Tina Forde from HQ to be exact. You just don't do it for me anymore so it's goodbye to you. And thanks for the idea.'

'What the fuck are you talking about?' A large, dark, long, oval form was slowly taking shape behind her.

'Our little video, dearest. I got to thinking and made a few calls, bought the equipment, so easy to do, you can't imagine, you never could, well, could you? So, you can go stargazing, permanently!'

The helium canister had almost totally inflated the weather balloon behind her.

'You will just float away, disappear, and if anyone is suspected, it will be the mob. Have a nice trip, dear.'

"*Her mind was racing but she couldn't move her legs. She screamed but who was going to hear her in such an isolated place in the middle of nowhere at half past midnight? No one would hear her scream. The men in black were now showing a sense of urgency. Balloon tethered, awaiting its payload, they wanted to finish their task. Barry knew that these boys were good at this. You'd almost think that they had done it before. Maybe they had! Yet, he'd sought them out through the Dark Net and was paying them handsomely in Bitcoin for their work and discretion.*

"Nancy was now carried over to the balloon, her hands bound with duct tape and attached to the tether. Seconds later, she was up, up and away. Seemed the record for a weather balloon being aloft was 46 days. Barry was thinking maybe they should have knocked her out before cutting her loose, but that gold-digger deserved what was coming to her. Seeing herself rise higher and higher, getting colder, air getting thinner. And then the terror of it all. Her screams got further and further away, then nothing. Nancy was gone, sailing into the clouds, gone out of sight. Barry felt no remorse, just relief, and now he could get on with his life and get himself a younger model. No marriage this time.

"Then he spotted something unexplained. Two similar boxes in the garage. What were they? Oh well. At the same time, he overheard two of the men in black talking about 'her having company up there with that fucker reporter'. The third one was…where? Then a sharp pain on his head. Nothing. Black. Opening his eyes, he saw nothing but black, stars and a few birds. He was rising on the end of a balloon himself. It all made perfect sense. These guys weren't some random hoods but the real deal who were doing a contract on him and her to get rid of balloon enemies and suchlike. Weather balloons were never found. And of course! The men had his house to strip it of valuables. Handy having a Chelsea tractor then. A real plan. As he rose, cold, and struggling for air, he regretted a lot of things. He regretted not being a better husband. He regretted not having children. But most of all, he regretted that bloody state-of-the-art smartphone. He sensed muffled and increasingly louder talking coming from his pocket. His brother was on speed dial to him. Man in black must have done it. Bastard. He regretted nothing more. Cold. Black. No stars. No birds. No air. Then, nothing.

"Having thoroughly cleaned out the house, taken the boxes away with them, made it look like a burglary and closed the gates as they left, the driver laughed and said to the others, 'At least he'd have got a decent signal up there. Three down, one to go. Brother, where art thou? We know where you are and we're on our way. Then back to Roma. Fredo, Angelo…you two fancy a drink first?'"

Ruby had grave reservations about this plot twist with these men. You could drive a coach and horses through this patently obvious semi-ending. She had a fag and another gin. She went to press "delete" on her laptop but hesitated. Now what? She just couldn't think up a way to finish the book. She'd already spent the advance from the publishers, Arthur was owed his cut, they were pressing her for final copy, and she was still 30,000 words short. She was fucked. Well and truly. She'd never considered getting help as that would be a sign of weakness. She wasn't prepared to show this to the outside world. She was tired, she was unhealthy, she was snappy. She needed a break. Maybe she should talk to Arthur and get his advice. She did.

'Take a break abroad, love. No point flogging a dead horse. Come back refreshed, finish the bugger off.'

Sound advice. She really fancied Switzerland. She went to Google.

Chapter 12

Life Begins at Forty

A quiet wet Sunday afternoon in Oxfordshire. Abigail was pottering around and tidying up, having read the Sunday papers and discussed them with her better half. She had some editing work to do but not much. Despite the rain, it was a very beautiful summer. And then her phone rang.

'Hello, Abi, it's Mary here.'

Abigail breathed a huge sigh of relief. Her friend was back in touch at last.

'Mary, oh hi, didn't expect to hear from you. What's up?'

'I needed to talk to someone. Well, for what it's worth, I'm…well, I'm up the duff. Just found out today. Abi, this wasn't meant to happen to me! I mean, I'm 41, my fallopian tubes are buggered, never expected this. Thought it was just George and me. Was totally resigned to it.'

This was indeed a bolt out of the blue.

'Mary dear, of course, it was you and George; who bloody well else could have been! Did you two not think of taking precautions? Clearly not.'

'Precautions! Abi, what for? I can't have babies. Sure, when we were much younger, we wanted them, tried like mad, but nothing doing. Went to doctor. Got examined and was told about my tubes. From then on, it was pointless taking any kind of contraception. It was that bloody cruise. All that sea air, all that drink—'

'And all that's how you father, Mary!'

Abigail was hugging herself with maternal pleasure. She thought about her first pregnancy and how she had told her man about it, how ecstatic he had been.

'Nicely put. Don't know how George will take it at our time of life. Thinking of an abortion. Smart move maybe, Abi?'

'Mary!' said a horrified Abigail. 'You're asking me, someone about to become a nana, about an abortion. I think you might need someone more neutral about the subject. All I can see here is that it may have been a bolt from the blue, more likely a pre-menopausal last throw of the dice, but it looks as if you have gotten what you wanted all those years ago. I think you know where this is going.'

A scared and confused Mary had been hoping against hope that Abigail would have given her blessing to proceed with an abortion. It clearly wasn't going to happen. Subconsciously, she had selected Abigail precisely because she had known that she was the most likely not to encourage her down that road. Mary was just terrified of the thought of parenthood. She was seeking reassurance that everything would be all right.

'How will I tell George?'

Abigail couldn't believe this. Mary still hadn't told her husband!

'Oh, Mary. Joyfully, just with joy. Don't you get it! Your long marriage apprenticeship has ended. Welcome to my world. You'll be fine.'

Seven weeks down the line. Usual coffeehouse, Charing Cross. Three women sat with their coffees and croissants.

'So, Abigail, anything exciting happening?'

'Usual stuff, Becky. Looking for a smaller house. Starting to get a bit beyond us. How's things with you, Marion? Not got a lover yet?'

'Me! Men? Nothing but bloody trouble. Only good for one thing, taking out the rubbish.'

'It doesn't need to be a man, if you know what I mean, not these days.'

'Becky, it bloody well does. I'm no lezzy, but I don't need a man either. So, what about you?'

'Got one. Nice fella, does it for me, if you know what I mean.' The other two smiled. They knew exactly what she meant.

'Where's Mary? Have you heard from her? Abigail? Marion?'

Both looked unknowing though Abigail blushed a little. 'Well, as a matter of fact, I—oh, here she is,' as Mary strode into the coffeehouse, half an hour after the others had arrived.

'Nice of you to join us.'

'Sorry folks, doctor's appointment.'

'Nothing serious, I trust,' asked Marion. A smirk crossed Mary's reddening face.

'Wouldn't call it serious. More like impending.' They all looked at her with slightly puzzled expressions. Abigail, however, was smiling. Then the others spotted it, smiled, stood up and had a group hug. Mary was clearly showing.

'Thought you couldn't have kids?'

'That's what I thought as well but Mother Nature and of course, George, had other ideas. He didn't tell me, but he'd been taking Viagra to keep himself in tiptop condition and he certainly was. Sneaky old bugger.'

All had a laugh at this. George may have surprised himself as much as Mary. Some aphrodisiac!

'He was pleased, I take it.'

Mary looked confused. Then blushing, she smiled.

'You mean at the pregnancy, oh yes, delighted, shocked but ecstatic. Says he feels like a proper man now. He always has been a proper man to me.'

'How long have you got to go?' they all wondered.

'Six months. Wanted to wait to be sure. Get the first trimester by. No celebrating too soon. No coffee. Orange juice is all I can handle right now.'

An hour later, they actually stopped talking about the bump and talked about editing. Marion had heard rumours about Ruby Latimer's problems in trying to finish off her latest novel. It became the main topic of conversation, mostly due to a dearth of other things to talk about. Before Mary had arrived, they had discussed politics, fashion, holidays and so on. Marion wasn't keen on doing any more work for Ruby Latimer for a while. She suggested that maybe one of the others might want to volunteer. Becky thought she might.

'Got to keep this new fella in Viagra as well, oops, sorry, Mary, better be careful, don't want to end up preggers too, huh!'

Becky wanted to find out for herself how much trouble Ruby Latimer might be in. She was intrigued. Could be there was a disc or USB of her work waiting to be edited. She decided to follow it up.

'Same time in a couple of months?'

'Wouldn't miss it for the world; anyway, baby will need an outing.' The others just laughed, hugged and went their merry ways. Their next meeting could prove interesting in many ways.

Becky was naively honest. Coming from a working-class background, her folks had moved to Orpington due to work. She had moved out at eighteen and, following a few bad relationships, had managed to get settled in a Council house, someone pulling a few strings for her apparently. That said, it wasn't an uncommon occurrence seemingly. Becky wanted kids sometime but was pretty fussy about who to have them with. Maybe this bloke would be better. At least he worked! She had been through comprehensive education and had done pretty well, but didn't fancy going into teaching; she just wasn't inclined that way and earned mostly from the editing and had a weekend job in a shop that helped out with her fairly happy but modest lifestyle.

It was hard to imagine what the four editors had in common—apart from editing. They were from vastly different and varied backgrounds. Happened sometimes, disparate upbringings leading to similar interests. They all had siblings but they rarely came up in conversation. Becky had a younger sister, Kirsty. Like other siblings, these two were different. Becky, despite appearances, was academic and read a lot. Kirsty was the opposite. Unmotivated, she bobbed up and down on the waves of life, being tossed in one direction then another. The sisters—seven years separated them—met up from time to time, normally in Becky's flat—Kirsty shared a bedsit—and over a bottle or two of wine would catch up. The wine was certainly a tongue loosener.

Kirsty did things that she kept to herself. She indulged in drink-fuelled one-night stands and had had loads of them. She wasn't fussy about who it was with, although she was always *compos mentis* and took precautions. Unlike her big sis, she wasn't into relationships. Unlike her big sis, she was also sexually very practiced and aware of the needs and desires of men and unlike her big sis, she looked drop-dead gorgeous. Not that Becky was unattractive—she showed the facial wear and tear of someone who came from a poverty-stricken background. Kirsty knew she had something special and men knew it too. She was manipulative and whilst she liked good men, she preferred bad'uns more. They were much more experimental, if you see what this meant. She didn't work but seemed to do OK, one could only surmise how. Kirsty was not particularly intelligent but was sly, streetwise and could spot an opportunity when it presented itself. She might not have to wait very long.

Chapter 13

The Publisher, an Agent and the Ticking Clock

It really wouldn't have been fair to call literary agent Arthur Newell and publisher Greville Walsh blood brothers. Whilst both would cheerfully take your last pint of blood, neither would call each other brother. They were, however, inextricably bound together in a cutthroat industry that was indeed their lifeblood as much as it was the bane of their lives. The literary sausage machine called publishing required both, along with a myriad of other people. It wasn't known if they ever met regularly in any formal setting save functions, though clearly, they had spoken on the phone many, many times. The sausage machine operated thus. Arthur, as the literary agent, would decide whether or not to sign an author; the author would then write/complete their book; on completion, it would be edited by Arthur's people and then Arthur himself looked at it before passing it on to Greville's lot. The publishing house would further edit it and at that stage, Arthur and Greville would probably talk on the phone. Given that Arthur might have a number of books per year, these conversations could be every fortnight or so.

Arthur Newell was tight. He didn't redefine the term, but his doyen was Hal Roach, the man who had stiffed Laurel and Hardy for a small fortune whilst they had made him a very large one. He knew that most authors, unpublished when they arrived at his doorstep, had very little bargaining power and quite often a large degree of desperation, having normally done the "agents' merry-go-round". He used to talk to authors who had just turned up at his door but nowadays, he only accepted those recommended to him from reliable sources. The more gravitas the recommender had, the better the deal that the authors were likely to achieve.

'You'll get 40%,' but he never explained what it was 40% of. In fact, it was 40% of what was left after everyone else had taken their cut. For her first published book, Ruby had been getting a massive 25p a book. He was normally already in the driving seat when they arrived. Result—a very poor deal for them, a brilliant one for him. If Jo Rowling had appeared at his door clutching a manuscript of *Harry Potter and the Philosopher's Stone*, the chances were that she would have been incredibly poorer than she was today. Agents, as well as publishers, had the power to make or break a budding author. Ruby was lucky that she'd struck a fairly good deal from day one due to him recognising her worth. After all, killing the goose who laid the golden egg would have been short-sighted. Just as well that she had gotten Arthur in a positive mindset. Be under no illusion, his authors in the main made a tidy living from their work, just not as much as they maybe could have. It was after all what they were legally bound to—the contract.

Arthur had been in the publishing industry for decades. How he got into it was surrounded by a plethora of urban myths. Absolutely no one knew the entire truth. He claimed to be the man who had Alistair Maclean as his first author. It was claimed that Maclean's publishers had paid him princely sum of one-pound sterling advance for *The Guns of Navarone*. The story was more likely to be true than his claim to have been his first agent. Arthur just loved making up such stories. One thing he did know was a good novel when he read one. Ruby Latimer's first novel had been utter shit but had potential, or at least she herself did. By the time she had written the first blockbuster, he knew she was ready. He was ready to make packets out of her, while she also made lots of dosh. Arthur Newell, literary agent, mover and shaker, entrepreneur extraordinaire. Tightwad.

Greville Walsh. Whilst Arthur Newell had an important part in the "sausage production", without him having access to a publishing and printing company, nothing would have happened. Publishing of books was a rare skill. Virgin authors, having completed their masterpiece and thinking they had written *For Whom the Bell Tolls*, when it was probably just another mediocre piece of drivel. Weekly, any publisher could receive several hundred unsolicited manuscripts from eager-to-be published writers, all expecting their blood, tears, toil and sweat to be gleefully jumped upon, printed and ultimately make them a small fortune. The crushing facts were that not only would their hard work not make them a penny, it wouldn't be published or read and would most probably end up in an unopened pile of manuscripts or shredded. Publishers in today's industry just didn't do unsolicited manuscripts yet people still insisted on sending them in. They got stockpiled and unceremoniously pulped or shredded every month to save space. One major publisher had received nearly a thousand unsolicited manuscripts in one week! They only ever accepted them from a bona fide agent, and it would need to be a bloody good one. Arthur was quoted in this area.

Greville dealt with numerous agents, and all of them had wonderful, talented and thrilling authors just champing at the bit, waiting to be published. Arthur was a brilliant exponent of shit-speak on occasion, whilst Greville knew bullshit. Arthur was a champion bullshitter. Greville knew he was as well. He also knew that sometimes Arthur actually came across the occasional gem. Ruby Latimer had been one of them and still was. She had made both of them pots of money whilst not doing too badly herself. Greville had an eye for the possible. He was a pragmatist who operated a literary triage system. If you were brilliant or if you were rubbish, you had no chance with him. As "championship" rather than "premier league" publishers, he believed that the best deserved the very best and so would move on to Random House or some other global phenomenon, regardless of their contract. However, if you were a decent writer with great potential, he would take you on board because he knew you would develop and that hunger for success could drive you on to better writing. He expected that most first novels would not be great but subsequent ones would be better. He knew how the business operated. Ruby Latimer was one who didn't get away. Her gratitude—and her advances—kept her put and kept Laurel Publishers through some lean times.

The literary agent and publisher were not fabulously, obscenely wealthy but were…well, pretty well-heeled. It would be wrong to say that it wasn't about the money. Life for them was all about the money. It was also about ego. Whilst the authors basked in the reflected glory of their latest novel, the publisher knew who had pulled the strings as did the agent. At every book launch—and boy, they had attended many—they were both there, team-handed with their entourage along with various authors. E-books had certainly had a huge effect on the industry as had audio books, but there was still money to be made and making it they certainly were. Greville's publishing company was superb at marketing whatever book happened to be just out. The author was expected to play their part in this campaign and emphatically did. After all, who would benefit? Ruby Latimer had been at a score of these events and knew exactly what to do. She was a public performer, God's gift to any publisher. Arthur wanted to know when the damn book would be finished as Greville was trying to work out a timetable for the launch. She just bullshitted about things but eventually had to concede that she had run into difficulties.

'Take a break, love, blow away the cobwebs. Holiday. Get yourself pampered. Come back refreshed. Finish the job. Leave Greville to me.' Arthur knew what she needed. Ruby went back to her laptop and looked at Switzerland again.

Ruby knew a little about Switzerland, but then again, she knew a little about a lot of things. She knew, for example, that there was a place called Davos. She knew that it was where the World Economic Forum took place every year. She knew that it was a place for rich people. She could afford it. She tried one of these discount holiday websites. Well, the forum was finished, hotels had emptied, there was little skiing due to a consummate lack of snow—climate change—yep, a good time to book. She went on one of her favourite sites, found a good deal of a lovely luxury hotel, which had all the mod cons. She had a concierge service, Abel Group, and got a good deal. Her years of frugal living before making it big had ingrained financial prudence into her. If she left in three days' time, she could be basking in obscene unadulterated luxury at a fraction of the price paid by Donald Trump. This would be a week to relax, unwind, chill out. She couldn't wait to go. God, she so desperately needed this holiday. She would be in perfect bliss and hopefully come back, literally with cobwebs blown away, writer's block destroyed, business resumed as usual. Seemingly, this may ultimately prove to be a forlorn hope but no harm trying.

You might be tempted to think from this explanation of the rich author seemingly counting the pennies for a luxury holiday that she was as tight as her agent. Not the case. Ruby Latimer had a disorder that was the bane of the *nouveau riche*, something a certain Ken Dodd had also suffered from—the fear of losing it all. She had seen it happen to quite a few other successful people. They thought success was permanent and spent like there was no tomorrow, lost whatever they had, ended with nothing. Yes, she needed a holiday, a good one but she was still cautious. She vowed to have a cruise as a treat to herself once the book was completed. In the meantime, she consoled herself with the thought of a soft bed, room service, fabulous food, serious pampering. It was a hard life, but somebody had to do it.

Ruby Latimer arrived at the airport—red designer high heels, stockings, designer suit, chic Gucci sunglasses. A porter took her bags as she went into the VIP lounge. She swanned around the lounge hoping to be recognised, her flight was called, she left heading for her first-class seat. Her air miles had come in handy and had been used to the maximum. A two-hour something flight over and there she was, being picked up by the hotel courtesy car and whisked to her "prison" where she would be incarcerated for a whole hellish week. Sleep, eat, drink, get pampered, repeat. Yep, this was just what she needed. She wasn't aware of it yet but she just might get a bit more than that. Lucky Ruby?

Chapter 14

Craig and the Time of his Life

Lizzie had been working at C8 News as the researcher for 18 months from the day she had started with them, after she had left Squawk FM. She had been lured there on the express understanding that she would be going places. She certainly had gone places; unfortunately, it had been places to do research, not exactly what she had in mind when she had been enticed there by the TV channel. Now, having proved herself yet again, she was getting impatient. She wanted to be a reporter. The man who had promised her this left C8 a month after she arrived and took with him that promise. However, a knight in shining armour had been recruited as a senior news editor, Craig Endoran. Craig had waved goodbye to Lizzie when she had left Squawk FM. Nine months into her tenure as a C8 researcher, she had met Craig again. It was obvious to him that she was disgruntled, dissatisfied and possibly looking around. He knew from his own experience how amazing she was. If he had his way, and he would, Lizzie Spector would be a reporter and a damn good one at that.

Craig had said to her that as soon as an opening for a reporter materialised, Lizzie's name would be in the frame. There had been a national award ceremony in which C8 News was up for an award. Craig was going and he thought it would be a splendid idea to have it engineered for her to be part of their table. She had no difficulty accepting, unaware who had been behind it. It had been a black-tie affair with men dressed formally, women in black evening dresses. Lizzie had always known how to dress to impress. She started off the evening sitting with people she didn't know, apparently someone connected to one of the advertisers and his wife. The meal took place, small talk and compliments, then the award ceremony, interspersed with bottles of champagne. C8 News as expected didn't win. The boring old couple soon left, leaving Lizzie on her own with a glass of champagne and some dark thoughts. Craig, who had been one of those left towards the fag end of the evening, took his glass and wandered over to one of the empty chairs next to Lizzie. Both were merry but not drunk. Lizzie was more morose than actually merry and was trying to get drunk. Craig found out why.

Elizabeth Spector had no illusions regarding her own prodigious abilities. Able, fiercely single-minded, indefatigable, perspicacious. One could say she suffered from what might be described as a surplus of self-esteem. These were the qualities for which C8 News had recruited her. She was, however, getting somewhat disillusioned with her underutilisation and lack of upward mobility. She was thinking of looking for another job. Despite her forgiving nature, Lizzie still remembered from time to time how she'd split from Brian, her ex-boyfriend. He'd betrayed her, had sex with someone else but had always protested that he had done it to get Lizzie information about the super injunction she had got wind of. Brian had told the truth, Lizzie had kicked him out, taken him back but the damage had been done—to Brian. He had slid into alcoholism and they'd parted. This had been such a shock to her. She had been planning a future with him— marriage, children, the lot. Her hopes had been totally dashed.

Craig sat and listened to this initially cringe-worthy account, but the more he heard, the more he began to understand that that young woman was plunging herself deeper into her work in order to forget about this heartbreak. The more she talked, the more she got upset, the more Craig wanted to hear her speak. It had been a very long time since anyone had confided in him to this extent. It was clear that this had been building up inside her for quite a while and she'd had no one to discuss it with. Normally, she would have just kept it to herself but the occasion, the wine, the hurt had just overwhelmed her. An emotional dam had burst, and Lizzie let it all out. Many a man would have taken advantage of such a situation with a vulnerable, tipsy young woman. However, Craig Endoran wasn't just senior to Lizzie, he liked and admired her. There were things he could do for her, and others over which he had no power.

At the end of the night, Craig ensured that she had been placed in a taxi, her address given to the cabbie and safely taken home. He made sure of this by being in the cab with her. It had been tempting for him to accompany her to her home, but he thought the temptation would have been too great. The rest of him was proud at the self-restraint he'd shown with a work colleague. Lizzie had never told him but in fact she had felt a little insulted that he hadn't tried it on. What was wrong with him? Was he gay? Was she ugly? She might have been drunk, had been upset, but she still had sexual needs. However, she had come to the conclusion that Craig was a really nice guy. How nice she would try to find out, all in the fullness of time.

During lunchtime the next day at the C8 canteen, a young woman had sat down on her own, nursing a cup of black coffee and wearing sunglasses. Given that the canteen had no natural light and it was overcast, people drew their own conclusions to the wearing of the shades. A well-dressed man sat down in front of her.

'Rough night then, eh!' he said. She just grunted.

'Craig, I think I have a lot of apologising to do. I was totally out of order unloading all my shit on you at the function. I'm really sorry, I really am.'

'You needed to talk to somebody about it. We men can be very…well, self-centred. Not all, just 95% of us.'

A brief smile flashed across Lizzie's mouth. She thought to herself, *Maybe he's not gay after all. He is really quite nice.*

'I was thinking what you had been saying and might be able to help. One of the reporters has handed in his notice. Want to apply for his job?'

Lizzie took off her sunglasses. She bent over the table and kissed Craig on the cheek. 'Take that as a yes then!' She just smiled. Three weeks later, Lizzie moved from researcher to reporter.

Her promotion, whether overdue or not, had been forged through a drunken conversation at the night of the award ceremony. It had had other consequences. It started to forge a friendship between Lizzie and Craig that would be built on mutual respect, common interests and sexual chemistry. The latter had always been there, but both were in denial. At Squawk FM, he had been the boss, she the researcher. There had been very little interface between them. Now there was likely to be a bit more. Lizzie was still hurting from the love she had lost, her Brian, and Craig also had been through a fairly recent, fairly friendly divorce. Both needed a lust sabbatical. In not too long a time, both of them would shrug their shoulders, admit defeat and get on with it—but not just yet. The reason for this was quite obvious. They loved journalism.

Very soon, the two would meet with other journalist colleagues at work in the local pub and discuss all the juicy titbits that journalists knew about but couldn't put into bulletins or programmes. Quite often, the others would leave the pub first, leaving Craig and Lizzie chatting, flirting, getting on in good style. It became obvious to both of them that there were only two ways for this to go—abandoning nights out or going to bed. They knew which one they would both choose. It was a no-brainer. Brian was a thing of the past, Craig was divorced, there was nothing really stopping them. They didn't make plans to have sex, it would just happen naturally, unplanned, spontaneously.

You see, for Lizzie Spector, sex wasn't the be all and end all; well, not normally, but occasionally a certain time in the month, it could be. Brian, her ex, had been a good lover but not an outstanding one. Oh yes, he could give as good as he got and that would normally be plenty and often. However, it wasn't quantity that counted but quality. It could be a fairly one-sided experience with most of the "benefits" coming his way, no pun intended, and with her being left with a rosy glow and an occasional happy ending. It never happened enough so when it did, it was special and lovely. Brian was very good at what he did but being younger than her—and she had been only in her early 20s at the time—he hadn't much experience at lovemaking. *Maybe that was why he had had sex with that other woman*, Lizzie had mused to herself. She had, on one occasion, tried to show him the art and technique of female satisfaction, but it had been a waste of her time and effort. For him, barely out of his teens, sex was about the woman satisfying her man, end of.

Craig, however, would prove to be different. No longer a boy, something he hadn't been for a decade or more, he had been married young but separated and then divorced from his first and only wife three years previously. They had just grown apart, him being in broadcasting and her as a retail buyer. He and his wife, in the first flush of their marriage and before, had been very active sexual partners. They had become proficient in mutual satisfaction, or so he'd thought. It had been some years since he had practiced such pleasurable techniques. Work had taken over their bedroom activities to the point where they had been lucky to get it on more than once every couple of months. Craig hadn't fancied a woman for nearly five years, and then along had come Lizzie. Lizzie Spector was very different from his ex-wife. It was very hard to quantify or qualify just in what ways, suffice to say she just was. Coming from journalist backgrounds was certainly an advantage. His ex-wife had also been driven like Lizzie but in her own particular sphere of work. Conversations at night had clearly been of a one-sided nature, neither having the slightest interest in their partner's working life. Sex was never enough to sustain a long-term relationship. It hadn't been there either.

It was the last day of a holiday weekend. Both Craig and Lizzie had been on duty and this was before they became an item. The shift had just finished and both were on their way out of the main lobby exit. Craig let Lizzie out first, then quickly followed. Outside, they smiled and chatted briefly about one of the major political items of the day. 'Fancy one for the road?' Craig had suggested.

'Why not?' Both headed for the Red Lion pub in Whitehall. It was a short taxi journey, but it was always awash with various journalists, MPs, lobbyists, etc. A kind of a "busman's holiday" venue, you could say.

'G&T?'

'Oh please.'

'Hard day?'

'Hard week. Trying to unravel a story about this stalker body, you know the ones who expose them. Can't find a lead or anything. Thought they'd have disappeared after that cop, DC Peake, had been abducted by them but not a chance. Still seemingly on the go and still scaring stalkers shitless. Robin Hood syndrome. Fucked if anyone will talk to me about them. Totally zilch.'

Craig sipped on a pint. He was a strange sort of hack; he wasn't an "alki" like most of them. Preferred his excitement from real life rather than real ale. The two talked about work stuff, then there was a pause.

'You not going to ask me out then?' Craig's goose was cooked, and his face looked roasted as well. 'Thought I'd better do the asking or we'd be beating around the bush for another three months. Yes, I'd love to go out with you. Where are you taking me?' Forthright as ever was our Lizzie.

Fast forward one week. Craig and Lizzie were sitting in a plush West End restaurant, looking through the exorbitantly priced menu—what the heck, it was their first date. He'd waited months for this and now this was his reward. Lizzie was no stranger to fine dining. Her father being a QC had occasionally visited her and treated her to an expensive lunch, so she really did know what *cordon bleu* was about. In any case, to hell with equal opportunities, someone else was paying. After two hours in this restaurant and a full bottle of expensive shampoo, as well as a lot of flirtation, schoolgirl giggling—blame the shampoo—the couple left and went to a jazz club. They both kind of knew where this was leading them that night – especially Lizzie – and of course it would. In truth, both would have been equally bloody disappointed if it hadn't. Lizzie was in control and knew what her intention was. If the meal was the starter and the jazz club the main course, the desert would be well worth savouring. They left the jazz club, hailed a taxi and headed for Greenwich. Funnily enough, by an absolute coincidence, Lizzie just happened to live there.

So, there they were, in Lizzie's spider's web. The flat where Brian and her frequently had had lots of fun. Brian had thought that sexual satisfaction was entirely for men. Lizzie knew differently. Most of the time, it was him, and him alone, who had left with a post-coital smile. At times, she had thought that he considered her to be just a human trampoline on which he could practice press-ups. He had never asked her ever *how was it for you?* He had just presumed that she had enjoyed it quite the same as he had. Young men just didn't get it, did they? Anyway, the fly in Lizzie's spider's web that night was one Craig Endoran. She hoped that he would be a more considerate lover than Brian. They arrived at the flat, more than a little merry. She put on some mushy music and they had a smoochy slow dance...and a few more drinks. Very soon neither of them would be *compos mentis* enough to do anything except perhaps sleep or throw up. She showed Brian into her boudoir. Having arrived at the flat fully dressed, they were now semi-dressed. In five minutes, neither was dressed at all.

Morning arrived. Lizzie's bed had now two naked, entwined, smiling occupants. She was rubbing her fingers through his brown hair; he was kissing her hand.

'What happened last night, Lizzie? I can't bloody remember.'

'Nothing fucking happened,' she said incredulously, given the present closeness. Realising what she'd just said, she giggled. 'Had something happened, it would have been a bloody miracle, given your state! You couldn't have raised a smile, let alone anything else.'

'You weren't exactly all that capable either, Lizzie Spector!' Craig retorted acerbically.

'I never planned to shag you then, in any case. I don't take advantage of drunken men, not much point. They never remember it anyway.'

The couple continued to caress as sobriety slowly returned. Lizzie got up and in five minutes, returned with two cups of coffee and a hint of Chanel. She wasn't finished with Craig yet. Hell, she hadn't even started.

Lying in bed, each of them squeezing, rubbing, hugging, talking and laughing. Lizzie then came to a serious point.

'Brian hurt me. I don't just mean emotionally. He liked rough sex and he was rough. He thought I did as well, but I was always raw for a couple of days afterwards. I could have put up with that, but he just didn't really know how to satisfy me sexually. Do you know how to sexually satisfy a woman, Craig?' Craig blushed. It was a forthright, honest question from our modern woman. He thought about it for a minute. It had really taken him by surprise. He recalled lovemaking with his ex-wife and had never been totally sure about how satisfied she'd been. She'd sounded satisfied if that was anything to go by. He went to say something but as he began to, Lizzie shushed him whilst simultaneously taking his hand to that place of pleasure on her body that men really should not just visit with their member. She then demonstrated what he must do and directed his hand to that part of her, and within three minutes of vigorous hand movements, Lizzie was lubricated and ecstatically convulsing next to him. He had never seen his ex-wife display such pleasure at his touch. He sighed, pleased at the response he'd just produced in her. Lizzie, who had been breathing quite heavily, making noises of encouragement, removed his hand and kissed it. Brian had never done that to her. Craig would do. They would do. She made a mental note—*next time, his mouth.*

Chapter 15

Ruby Goes to Switzerland

Three months had flashed by since the editors had last met. In that time, quite frankly, not a great deal had happened. Spring had sprung, Marion had made up with Ruby—kind of; Abigail had become a granny; Rebecca—Becky—had done very little work but was just about surviving. They had met in the usual café in Charing Cross. As before, there was quite a lot of small talk, gossip and not a little laughter.

'So, Marion, the Wicked Witch of the West saw you wearing sackcloth and ashes and took you back. How do you feel?'

'I don't know. It's all a bit strange. I mean, well, the book's finished and I've been editing it but, I don't know how to put this, it just doesn't feel right.'

The other two looked at each other, wondering what she could mean. The group was still one short. Abigail looked at her watch. They had been there for over half an hour. The coffeehouse door opened and in breezed Mary, a bit red-faced, slightly out of breath but with a certain *je ne sais quoi* about her, saw them and beamed an instantaneously radiant smile across at their table. The three smiled back, got up and there was what one could only call a group hug.

'No need to ask how you are, girl. Kind of obvious.'

'…And it's a boy. George is over the moon.'

Nana Abigail and childless Becky were more enthusiastic about Mary's condition than Marion. Whilst she smiled and tried to at least give some pretence that she was equally pleased, in her heart of hearts, Marion was quite sad and still hopeful that someday she too might also experience what Mary was experiencing and hopefully end up with a baby as well. The thought of single motherhood wasn't appealing to her, at least not yet it wasn't. In the meantime, she mustn't spoil Mary's moment. They all returned to their seats as the waitress came over to see what Mary wanted.

'I need to pee first,' and off Mary walked to the ladies. The only one with existing kids, Abigail, flashed a knowing "been there" smile. Five minutes and then Mary returned.

'I would really love a coffee, but it gives me such heartburn right now, so could I have a green tea, please? Oh, and a scone, no, two scones please.'

'What would you like on your scones, Miss?'

Mary smiled, flashed her wedding ring and laughed.

'Butter and Marmite, please.'

The waitress opened her eyes wide, spotted Mary's bump, smiled and said, 'Of course.' Only Becky looked surprised.

Abigail started, 'I remember so well, Mary. Bloody annoying, those strange cravings. Why, I remember when I was—'

'…and peeing with nothing coming out at three in the morning. And…'

The others cleared their throats as if to say, "enough please". The conversation then reverted to Marion who had been talking about Ruby Latimer's latest novel. Marion was also very keen to change the subject. Talk of babies had now become a bit irritating to her. Subject exhausted, the conversation turned back to their professional lives. The new Ruby Latimer book and all its interesting nuances.

'As I was saying, Miss Latimer's book, really odd.'

The others looked at her intently.

'In what way?' Becky probed.

'Well, as you know, I've been editing her books for a few years now and I thought I could almost guess where she was going with them. Could, until this one. Most of it was fine, usual style, predictable innuendo, dramatic in parts but nothing that the reader couldn't handle. Either she has been taking lessons from someone with an entirely different train of thought or…'

The others were waiting. This was good stuff! 'Or what exactly?'

Marion cleared her throat, lowered her head towards the table in a very furtive manner and the others did likewise.

'…or…somebody else wrote the bloody thing!' she whispered in a conspiratorial tone of voice. The other three looked gobsmacked. If this was true, it would be absolute dynamite. Of course, writers had been known quite often to be assisted in their writing; you could even get one on Google! But this was the great Ruby Latimer! For her to do so would be highly improper, particularly if she took the credit for all of it.

Abigail asked, 'Did you ask her about it?'

'Must be bloody joking. I've just got back in her good books. Last thing I'm going to do is muddy those waters. I'm telling you though that it looks as if she's trying to pull a fast one. I've edited it as best I can, trying to stitch it all together to make it appear to be coherent and consistent and hopefully, it will turn out fine. But I'll tell you one thing, never doing this again. Shame, the writing is different but it's a bloody marvellous conclusion, full of invention and understatement.'

The other three had by then latched onto why Marion was unhappy. It was as if she had been asked to be party to an elaborate piece of subterfuge that she really objected to. Not all the women present exhibited those same high literary and ethical standards as Marion, but no one was heard to disagree with her either.

'So, what's the bit at the end like, rubbish then?' Mary enquired. Clearly, her pregnancy brain had affected her hearing as well.

'No, not rubbish at all, conceptually brilliant, different in style. It felt like trying to knit together cotton and silk, both really nice fabrics, just somewhat mismatched. Whoever wrote the ending is quite a talent in the making, it just wasn't Ruby Latimer.'

'What are you going to do about it?' asked Abigail.

'Nothing I can do really. I'm not the whistle-blower type. Apart from that, I like my job and would quite like to continue doing it for a few years more, thank you very much. If it gets out, then I'm the only person who could have done it. Just too big a risk. Keep all this to yourselves, for God's sake.'

The three ladies nodded their agreement to say nothing about it. Apart from Marion and Becky, none of them had been in contact with Ruby Latimer for a couple of years or more. It was unlikely that in her present state Mary was going to be doing much editing, Abigail had a new grandchild to fawn over, Becky's interest in the matter, if indeed she had any at all, certainly wasn't apparent. The next time they met, they would either be only three of them, possibly four, possibly even five! It was all a matter of timing.

And just exactly where had the subject of these four women's discussion returned from two months previously? Switzerland, actually. Ruby's plane had touched down. First-class travel was such a bore but hell, needs must sometimes. All that champagne, salmon sandwiches, *cordon bleu* food. And that only on the plane! All on the publishers' expenses naturally! She hoped to claim them for it (inspiration-provoking expenses). Then there had been the limo ride from the airport, the five-star plus hotel, room 509 complete with balcony, Jacuzzi bath, spa, swimming pool and various punishing treatments. She had paid for the hotel, but the publishers had agreed to pick up the tab for the "extras". Oh yes, that week was going to be the week of renewal, invigoration and inspiration that she had been requiring badly for most of the previous year. That had certainly been the plan. It must work or else she was finished as a writer. If she didn't finish the book soon, certain things would start to happen. In the first place, the publisher would be looking for the return of the advance; her agent would equally be pressurising her for a completion date; the literary press would be writing her obituary. By the summer, her career and reputation would be in tatters. All this because she couldn't find a few thousand words to finish that damned book. Not so much "Monte Carlo or bust" as "Monte Lenovo Hotel or bust", and she hadn't the slightest intention of going bust. It was just too horrible a concept for her to envisage. "Take a week, relax as best you can, clear your mind, enjoy." She had no real concept of the kind of "enjoyment" that awaited her at the Monte Lenovo Hotel.

Chapter 16

Oh Lars, You're So Good with Your Hands!

So, there she was, at the Monte Lenovo five-star plus hotel, Davos, Switzerland, transported by the hotel limo, dressed in black, red high-heeled shoes, designer sunglasses perched on the top of her head like some Hollywood starlet. In fairness, she was richer than many of them but still clung on to her Hounslow flat, like her lifestyle was only temporary. Her bags were portered to her room by the bellboy on one of these posh four-wheeler luggage carriers with the brass handles, and there she was. She thought to herself, *Well, if I'm going to go down, I might as well have fun doing it.* The maid unpacked for her, putting her clothes in the cupboards and drawers. Ruby, in a somewhat hoity and dismissive tone, told the young woman to run her a bath as she poured herself a glass of champagne from the complimentary bottle in her room. She asked about the hotel facilities and was told about the spa, pool, treatments, etc. She really loved the sound of some of the wonderful massages and exfoliant treatments— Thalassotherapy—and mused about which ones to get as she luxuriated in her jacuzzi bath.

It was coming up to five, so she decided to phone reception to book some treatments. She wanted a couple of facials and a daily massage. Bummer. Since the WEF was over and many of those who had come for the "extras" as much as for the forum meant that she could get the facials OK and the spa area and pool were there for her any time; however, the regular masseuse, Heidi, was on a week's holiday, recuperating from the constant massaging of world dignitaries after the World Economic Forum. This was more than a little disappointing and she made her displeasure known to the poor little receptionist. All this money— well, all somebody else's money—and no massage available. The receptionist said she would see what she could do.

After breakfast the next morning, Ruby Latimer was passed a note by one of the waiters. It asked her to come to reception as they had information for her.

'Miss Latimer, the hotel wishes to apologise for our inability to provide you with the masseuse you requested. We have managed to contact one of the local masseurs, one who would be available for you from today and for that week. Would you like us to have him call upon you? His name is Lars, from Sweden, and as he is not under contract to the hotel, you would need to pay him directly. I hope that is a slight inconvenience, but nevertheless a good solution.'

Despite the incorrect English, Ruby got the message. She'd have preferred a masseuse, but she thought to herself, *Any port in the storm*. Probably some hunky big blonde guy with rippling muscles and a shiny, waxed chest. A mischievous smile crossed Ruby's face. She booked Lars for four. Plenty of time for that facial, hot tub, steam room and a few lengths in the pool before lunch, then a bit more of the same after lunch. Sounded like a plan.

After relaxing all day, four o'clock arrived as did Lars the masseur. Ruby polished off the last of her champagne and went into the bathroom to change into a new bikini whilst Lars set up his massage table. She hadn't really looked at him when he had arrived as she had been on her way to get changed. When she came out of the bathroom, there he was—over six feet, white t-shirt and shorts, white sneakers, whiter teeth, Bjorn Borg haircut—pretty much what she had been expecting. Without him telling her, Ruby got onto the table, face down with her face through the blowhole.

'I am just putting warm Bergamot oil on you. I hope you will enjoy it.'

Oh God, did she not half enjoy it! It felt like the most beautiful warm bath ever. He had started on her neck and shoulders. His large muscular arms powered his long delicate fingers that massaged her neck and shoulder blades. Whatever he charged her; it wasn't enough. He then began on the other end of her. Each foot in turn got the full treatment followed by her calves and upper legs. At the start, her legs had felt quite heavy but now they felt light as feathers. He then moved back up to the middle of her body.

'Miss, I want to massage your back. Can you please loosen your bikini strap, or would you prefer me not to… May I?'

She was so relaxed at this stage, champagne and all that, quite frankly, she wasn't much caring what he did. She undid the bra strap. Ruby could feel his warm oily hands on her back, using some pressure and moving up and down, again massaging her neck.

'Miss, you are very tense. Your neck and shoulders have many lumps and bumps. I will massage out the lactate.'

She could feel his fingers pressing down hard and moving about what seemed to be small marbles on her shoulders. He seemed to spend a long time doing this. How wonderful this felt. His hands moved down the small of her back to the base of her spine. He was massaging her but studiously avoiding her buttocks. 'Would it help you if I took off these?' indicating her bikini bottom. Lars said nothing. Without waiting for his reply, Ruby quickly removed them and lay back down. She could feel the warm essential oil on her buttocks, hands firmly grasping and kneading them almost as if they were two piles of playdough. She could also feel the oil dribble down between her legs. What came over her next, she would never know. Just what had she been thinking? Maybe he had accidentally reawakened something in her past that she thought had been forever lost. She had never had much of a libido. Maybe it had been the relaxing erotic occasion. Maybe it was the Moet! What else could it have been! Whatever it was, she had grabbed his arm, drawn him close to her face and whispered. She knew what she wanted and now so would he. She spread her legs. Would Lars oblige?

It seemed like decades since anyone had asked or allowed to really touch her, get her worked up. She never had had anyone special in her life and while she wasn't a virgin, sex had never really been a force in her life. She had gotten virtually everything she had wanted in life and husband and babies had never been part of her agenda. Now, there she was, face down, naked on a massage table covered in warm oil with a six-foot muscular blonde male who had touched virtually every part of her body. Not much left. She smiled, winced a bit before his hands found their target. And there was more!

'Please turn over so I can do your body front.'

This she did. He continued as before, massaging her from head to foot—and everywhere in between. It never occurred to her how exhilarating a massage from a Nordic man could be, countries where open sexual pleasure was not some kind of embarrassing taboo. Clearly, her request had not been the first of its kind that he had ever received. Maybe she was just an English prude. Whatever she was, she had had a bodily function she hadn't experienced almost in living memory. And only the first massage of the week! It was a massage with a happy ending even though she had never in her life had one like that.

Massage over, Ruby Latimer slithered off the table, knees almost knocking from what she had just experienced, and scurried into the bathroom, her bikini top and bottom in her hand at the door. She then immediately thought what a ludicrous action, given that he had seen and touched everything! Two minutes later, she re-emerged wearing one of the hotel dressing gowns, goodness only knew why such false modesty in the face of Swedish sexual modernity. 'Lars, that was wonderful. You have such a wonderful touch. Same time, same place tomorrow?' as she placed money in his hand, which included a little "extra".

'Yes, miss. Will you require the same treatment? If so, then extra items.'

Ruby had no idea what he was referring to. She would be in for a pleasant surprise the following afternoon. A small pink oscillating surprise. It was as if in all her writing and reading, she'd never come across sex toys. Once again, it had been of no interest to her so maybe that explained it. For an hour or more, every day that week, Ruby Latimer sighed, exhaled writhed and groaned at the behest of her masseur and some of it was a result of being massaged! On the second-last day, after the massage, Lars noticed that for the four previous days, his client had seemed to be totally relaxing but on this day was getting uptight once more.

'Is there something worrying you, miss?' Lars asked in a slightly concerned tone.

Ruby sighed. 'Nothing you can help me with,' she said, and in a totally uncharacteristic display of emotional frustration, trustingly she told Lars about her writing dilemma, never dreaming for one minute that he could be of the slightest help.

Ruby's last day. There would be two surprises for her. The first was the most wonderful "happy ending" to her week in every sense of the word! She would certainly remember it. The second was two gifts from her masseur, one that worked with batteries and one that could possibly prove to be the saviour of her literary career. Lars was more than a Swedish masseur working in Switzerland. His boyfriend/partner was not only a talented writer himself, he was also, by the sheerest of coincidences, involved in an organisation capable of solving her writer's block problem. The card, in the little pink zipper bag that contained the pleasure device, contained a phone number. Lars told her to call it when she got home and they would provide her with the help she needed. Given this information, Ruby embraced Lars in a manner she had never done to another human being that hadn't been one or other of her parents. Then she was off. She looked at the card. All it said was "GW" and a phone number. She really hoped that whatever it was, it would deliver for her. She had not been inspired or thought of any new ideas, so this was likely the last chance hotel.

Back at her flat in Hounslow, Ruby Latimer, far from unpacking, was on the phone. A man answered, 'Hello. GW. How can we help? Contact name please.'

Ruby said one name, 'Lars.'

'Thank you.' There was a minute of silence, then the man continued. 'We are a completely confidential bespoke literature completion service. If you have an unfinished manuscript, we guarantee to complete and return it to you in 28 days at a cost of £9,600. Your references are in order, Miss Latimer. If you wish to proceed, please have your manuscript available for collection two days from today, 10:30 am. Our courier will collect it from you as long as your bank transfer is deposited in our account. Please be aware that we operate on the double-blind principle of neither ourselves nor you will ever know the identity of your assigned person. Nor will the assigned person ever know the identity of the author. Please remove all indications of your identity from the USB. It will be done expertly.'

Ruby was at first a little hesitant. £9,600! A lot of money but compared to making nothing more from writing, it was a veritable no-brainer.

'I'll have it ready to be collected. Send me your bank details so I can deposit the money.'

And they did. And she did. And as if by clockwork, at 10:30 am on the appointed day, a motorbike dispatch rider arrived at her door and left with a USB containing the unfinished novel. 28 nerve-wracking days would ensue. Had she been a complete fool? Would she ever see the completed manuscript? Was her career as a novelist finished? These were questions for which answers were awaited.

Chapter 17

Ruby is All Done!

Twenty-six days had expired since the courier had come and collected her USB. Ruby Latimer had returned from Davos a bit more relaxed and bodily, shall we say, sexually exfoliated. Unfortunately for her, that just wasn't enough. She had hoped to have come back fired up, full of inspiration and ideas to finish her book. As the week had ground on, it became crystal clear to her that it just wasn't going to happen. She had just retreated into a sort of passive resignation that for her, the game was up—the game being as a celebrity author. At least she thought so until she made that phone call. Someone else was on her side and someone else in two days' time would be returning her manuscript novel completed and hopefully as brilliant an ending as any one of her "Mormon Trilogy". Yes, those were certainly the days, halcyon days, glory days. Her inability to rediscover in her mind the kind of unique interpretation of life could have been caused by anything. The sad fact was that in just the same way that a songwriter, sportsperson, artist could all of a sudden run short of or out of inspiration, ideas or words, possibly it had just happened to her. It was a shudderingly unpalatable thought. She certainly hoped it wasn't the case.

For over three weeks now, Ruby Latimer had been living in what was for her virtual stasis. Normally, on the completion of a novel, there was a ritual. The finished product was taken to Arthur who, after a few days—time enough for him to have read it—would take her to lunch to discuss it; thereafter, he would phone Greville in a chirpy tone of voice saying stuff like, 'Greville, got a real cracker for use this time', 'she's really outdone herself in this one' or 'I think we might have another blockbuster on our hands', cranking up his anticipation and hopefully adding a few zeros to their sales prospects. That was the way it had gone for well over a decade. This time, everything seemed a bit more muted.

She had always delivered her manuscript on time before, always. Once or twice, she'd been close to the wire but Ruby had always delivered. The non-delivery of her latest novel on time, not by a matter of a few days, not even a few weeks but well over half a year, was quite unprecedented. Laurel Publishers had been pressing her agent for ages and were now making not so idle threats about legal action to regain the advance she had received. Arthur had told her that this might happen. Greville, for his part, certainly didn't want it to happen but the publisher's accountants were nervous of not taking action as this would look bad when the Annual Statement of Account was published and they would need to show that they had at the very least been trying to recover the money. Greville and Arthur talked to Ruby on several occasions and on those several occasions, she had assured them that there wasn't a problem and the book would be delivered even if it was a bit late.

Ruby Latimer continued to suffer from what could only be described as "writing inertia"—being stuck between the end of her previous novel and the beginning of a new one. Her confidence in coming up with a new idea, let alone being able to finish it, had dwindled almost to nothing. The problem was that she had come to the end of her present publishing contract and given the fashion that the present, as yet undelivered book had taken even after the exhortations of many people, she was not confident that the publisher would want to take up their option. The only hope was that when the manuscript came back, it would be such a profound work that it would save her bacon. Was she grasping at straws? Only time would tell. Meanwhile, she continued to do nothing. For many women in a similar situation, they might have found solace in family or friends. Because of her life and lifestyle there was a total absence of either. She was going to have to set that out on her own. A totally self-contained individual, she had been quite happy with her solitary existence until that moment. Now she was on tenterhooks, almost as if counting down the hours and minutes until that knock on the door. She went back to the box where the card was, thinking to herself that maybe she'd better phone them. Picking up the card, she looked at it and flicked it against her other hand. However, her gaze meandered past the card to the box itself. She remembered that Lars had given her another present. She opened the box and took it out. All sense of time and space was momentarily lost.

It was now dark. Ruby had a headache and thought lying down in a darkened room would help. She also thought this small contraption from Lars might also help her relax. She lay on the bed and turned it on. It made a near silent buzzing. An hour later, she came back out to her living room, not exactly satisfied but at least her headache had gone. She thought she would try watching some TV and as she was doing so, her mobile phone pinged a text message to her. "Package delivery to your address, 10:30 am tomorrow." Her stomach began to churn, and her breathing increased. D-day would come 24 hours earlier than expected. She started to feel surprisingly upbeat at what might be getting delivered to her. The bottom line, she supposed, was that it would be utter rubbish and she would have wasted £9,600… She would be finished as a writer. Maybe she was being unduly pessimistic. After all, she trusted Lars; he had no axe to grind, and those hands! She wasn't a very trusting person but still, nothing ventured, nothing gained. She really would have liked a drink, but she needed to keep her senses about herself to be able to read the manuscript the next morning. Another sleepless night beckoned. Tomorrow, the dye would be cast, her future, if she had one, determined. She went to bed without a headache and with Lars' "gift".

The next morning,10.30 on the dot, the front doorbell rang. She opened it to be confronted with a helmeted courier who gave her a package and then he (or she) was gone. Ruby Latimer wasn't one for lolling about in her pyjamas, having been dressed since 8. At her dining room table, she had her laptop open and raring to go; she opened the package. *Unexpected*, she thought. The contents of the package contained one USB along with a manuscript. Leaving the USB to one side, she examined the manuscript. The A4 version on her computer, unfinished as it was, stretched to 185 pages; this manuscript had 225 pages! Whoever it was had at least the decency to go through the motions of expanding on what she had written.

She started reading from page 182 and in a few minutes had reached the point where her writer's block had prevented her from continuing. A deep intake of air followed. Her future life, in the hands of a complete stranger, would in a matter of next hour or two be unfolded before her. Triumph or disaster? *Here goes nothing*, she thought. A half hour went by and she had reached page 188. Her apprehension had turned to expectation. Having no idea who had written this, she was quite dumbfounded at the insight and, being honest, sheer genius of what she was reading. Page 208. Laughter, unbridled joy. Page 214. Tears. Page 221. Ruby Latimer couldn't stand it anymore. Having decided to take a short break for coffee, she just marvelled at the ingenuity, the consummate skill that she had been reading, more an artist than a writer. Better than anything she could have written. Genius, a word that she had been resisting but now used over and over. Having returned to the book, she continued to read until she reached page 224. *Oh my God! I never saw it coming. It was bloody well there all the time the... How the...couldn't I see it?* Ruby Latimer—in awe of what she had just read; relief that could be she had been premature in writing herself off; returning confidence: she may not have finished the book but most of it was hers and whoever it was couldn't have done it without her. She just wished she knew who it had been.

'Arthur, Ruby here. Guess what.' A deep sigh of relief. '...Yep, it's finished. Tell Greville to call off his dogs... Editing? You'll send Marion over on Wednesday. Fine. Be here waiting for her. Now I need a good drink.'

So that seemed to be that, or so she thought. She thought to herself, *Grab yourself a bath*, and started to run it. Thinking back, Ruby Latimer considered that luck had smiled upon her, being in the right place at the right time, having the right man with the right contact with the right writer and so on it went, her mind racing about...well, virtually everything. She went into the bathroom and turned off her nearly full bubble bath. As she prepared to go into the foam, her mind once again turned to that darling man, Lars; she made a mental note to really thank him for his card—and his other thing, which she picked up and took into the bathroom with her. *This is waterproof, I hope.* Another wonderful memento. She plunged under the water and came up giggling hysterically whilst a muffled buzz was submerged somewhere in or around her person. Her now increasingly ecstatic person. For someone who had lived without thanking anyone this was a new quality emanating from the author—gratitude. No doubt it too would quickly subside. Things were looking up again.

Chapter 18

Pennies from Heavenly Hell

A couple of days later, young Walter arrived to collect the USB from Ruby Latimer's house. Walter was still quite a naïve young man in some ways but not in others. Shy regarding women but quite streetwise in the business sense. Normally, if he had something to collect or deliver, he'd spend two or three minutes chatting idly with whomever the author happened to be and, on a rare occasion, fifteen or twenty minutes if offered a cup of tea, something that almost never happened. At Miss Latimer's house, on this occasion, he found her in what one could only describe as an uplifted mood. She was quite unlike the normal moody, morose, impassive self of the past few months. He couldn't work it out, then it hit him and he smiled, a smile she returned, a first.

'Miss Latimer, you seem happy today,' stating the bleeding obvious. 'Have you completed the book then?'

'Would you like a cup of tea, Walter?'

Wow! Another first! *Must be a red-letter day*, he deduced.

'Yes Walter, the book is now complete and all I can say is thank fuck.'

Yet another first here. He had never known this author to swear, not that he'd spoken to her much. They drank tea and chatted. This was the most animated Walter had seen this author but given the relatively short length of time he had known her, and all that time she had been struggling with this particular book, he'd just presumed that that was the way she was. Essentially, Walter was correct in this assumption. They actually talked for almost an hour, once again unprecedented for Ruby Latimer when in the presence of a minion. She talked and he listened, smiled and nodded. What else could he do? It wasn't exactly a meeting of equals.

'God is that the time! I really must go. Many thanks for the tea. I expect the editor might want to pop in to check it over with you before it gets passed on,' showing a degree of experience that Ruby Latimer had not expected. And then Walter was on his way.

'Miss Latimer—'

'Ruby please. Call me Ruby.'

'Miss Latimer…Ruby, you may remember you promised to sign my letter of recommendation to be an editor. I've typed it out. Would you like to read it?' Ruby, still high on the adrenaline of the moment, just clicked her fingers at him. Walter was truly elated.

'Pen. Where do I sign?' And that was it. Walter had what he hoped was his passport to becoming an editor.

Ruby didn't really like anyone. Her self-esteem gene was purely personal and non-transferable. However, this young man had been prepared to listen to her catalogue of trials and tribulations and so had gained some brownie points in her book. Of course, it didn't mean they were friends, just someone who, the next time he called, would possibly show her the respect she deserved. If insincerity had been an Olympic event, Ruby Latimer would have been on the podium with a gold medal.

A couple of days dragged by, then Ruby's mobile phone rang.

'Ruby, my love (another first), Arthur here. What have you been eating for breakfast? I've read all your books…' He winked at Walter who was coincidentally in Arthur's room at that exact time. 'Well, of course I have, I'm your bloody agent, but this one transcends anything else you've done. I sense another prize-winner in the offing, my dear! Marion's been given a hardcopy transcript and should be coming to see you in the next few days just to do the usual clarification. Then the three-ring circus will start again. Keep your diary free; I expect it will fill up quite quickly. The delay will just add to the anticipation.'

Arthur had hardly taken a breath, whilst Ruby had moved the phone away from her ear, such was his enthusiasm. Did she feel a tinge of conscience? After all, it wasn't all her own work and she knew it fine and well. Luckily, she was, apart from the co-author, the only person who did know this. Ruby Latimer was determined to keep it that way at whatever cost.

Four more days elapsed and the author, still on cloud nine of utter relief, was certain that all was going to be well. Her bag buzzed. Several seconds of buzzing—she had considered changing the ringtone to something less mundane, like Beethoven's *Fifth* or Snaps' *I've Got the Power*, but that might not be appropriate quite yet.

'Miss Latimer, Marion's French.'

'Yes, Marion, and what can I do for you?'

'Just to let you know I have the manuscript and it's basically complete. Can I come and see you on Friday to just tidy up a few sequential and consequential issues?'

There seemed to be a certain momentary hesitancy in Ruby's voice. 'Yes, of course,' and they arranged a time. At the appointed time on Friday, Marion arrived. This time, unlike their last meeting, Ruby Latimer was uncommonly civil. The last time they'd met, Marion had shown some concerns, but the author had been either too hung over or too stressed out and had quickly shown Marion the door. This time, however, she was not only all sweetness and light, (insincerity overflow) but even offered her editor something to drink! This was certainly a side of "Her Authorship" that had been sadly lacking on previous occasions. Marion was puzzled. Who was this woman and what had she done with Ruby Latimer? It wasn't as if she hadn't received back a completed novel before, a number in fact. On those other occasions, whilst there had been a few minor questions, she'd certainly not been shown much—if any—level of courtesy, let alone the offer of hospitality that she'd been given. Strange days indeed!

Maybe Ruby Latimer thought Marion French had rumbled her. Maybe this show of feminine understanding was to throw her off the scent when in fact this couldn't have been further from the truth. Marion, far from being suspicious, was quite in awe of the finished product. She had a few questions regarding textual context, some syntax and one slight inconsistency in the plot line needing to be changed, but apart from that, she loved the work. Ruby listened and discussed these points and within a few minutes, they'd been corrected and the USB copy updated.

Having finished her tea, Marion prepared to leave. 'Oh, Miss Latimer, just one final thing…'

Having been relaxed, buoyant and cooperative, Ruby Latimer seemed to visibly and momentarily tense, as if the crushing Detective Colombo killer question that would have stumped her utterly was about to be launched. 'Will you be requiring any further input after today? I'm going away for a week to some friends and for the sake of continuity, I wouldn't want to have to pass this to somebody else.'

Ruby Latimer's raised shoulders lowered as if what she'd been expecting hadn't been chucked at her. 'No, that's fine, Marion, hope you have a good time.' And with that, Marion French left.

Driving home, the radio was tuned to Squawk FM for a little light relief. Some mouthy rock DJ was going on about fake news and he came out with the line, 'You can't bloody well trust anything these days. Why, even that President, you know the guy, has been caught out tweeting bullshit. Even that Jordan bint has written six bloody autobiographies. Slag can't even write her name let alone do her life story. No doubt she got the best ghost-writer money could buy.'

Marion thought about this. She began to wonder if it was possible that this fine upstanding author, this paragon of all that was true and honest and decent work, had pulled a fast one. Marion was determined to read the end of the book a couple of times more to see if her suspicions had any foundation. This just wasn't adding up. Had she been taken for a ride? But before she started to throw about accusations of impropriety, she'd better be bloody well sure of her facts. If she did go off on the deep end, the consequences would be enormous, not just for the author but for her employer, colleagues and herself. She thought back to all those famous sexual deviants who had gotten away with it for years only because of who they were. It could be her word, that of a nobody, against that of an internationally renowned author. She started to have doubts, began to think maybe she should just leave it alone, but too late—she'd already opened Pandora's Box in her mind and it just wouldn't close.

Meanwhile, back in Hounslow, Ruby Latimer was feeling quite pleased with herself. What could have been the Spanish Inquisition had turned out to be a total damp squib. Her editor had left the building apparently, unaware that she'd just been reading the words of two entirely different people. At least that was what she thought. She'd been tense at times during the meeting, but she reckoned that it had probably gone unnoticed. She considered herself a not entirely untalented actress and reckoned she'd played Marion like a strad or should that have been a fiddle. Truth was she considered that everyone she came across had been put there either for her use or amusement, possibly both. Her ability to underestimate the possibility that there were a few other people on the planet with a brain didn't always register with her. As far as she was concerned, a possible danger to her being exposed as a charlatan was now gone. The book would go to her agent and publisher and would very soon be hitting the bookshops everywhere as well as the e-book and audio book phenomenon. She'd once again soon be laughing all the way to the bank, as she had always done. She fancied a celebratory bath and oh, a bit of fun with her little pink contraption. Well, didn't she deserve it? She was starting to realise that maybe she was becoming ever so addicted to self-pleasure. *Better late than never*, she thought. If she was never to write anything else again, she'd better find herself a good hobby…maybe.

Chapter 19

Bob the Builder and his Team

Scroungers United emblazoned the headline regarding this unfortunate family. The article in question in a national tabloid paper went on to assert that they were "*...career criminals, lazy, indolent wastes of space.*" Like most of these papers, they knew that there was an audience for that kind of punk journalism. The gutter press knew how to sell papers! In truth, their description of this family wasn't totally inaccurate but as usual, they tarred the entire family with the same condemnation even though half of them didn't deserve it. Yes, it was true that half of this large family was involved in various small-time illegal scams but in truth, it was all very penny ante stuff. The rest of the family, even though they lived under one roof, had found jobs in one sector or another and didn't deserve to be lumped in with the others. Not exactly a non-story but it did paint a rather distorted picture. There were many worse examples of feral families that they could have picked upon. The members of this family were veritable babes-in-arms compared to the organised outfits that existed and who even the police steered clear of. There was "Orpington's Finest", the Grisham family, for example.

In 1983, the first of the Grisham brood came into existence, produced by mum, Ellen Fraser, and dad, Ted Grisham. Ellen and Fred got married in 1984 and went on to produce more. Ted and Ellen had moved from London's East End with their respective parents, bombed out of their hovels and moved to temporary (prefab) housing followed in the early 60s to a more substantial council-built home. It was a front-and-back-door so was heaven compared to what they had been used to. Life was still pretty hard in those post-war years and Ellen and Fred were born into a life of post-war poverty. For many, the way to move up the social ladder was simple—have kids of your own. In the early 80s, the so-called "property owning democracy" of Mrs Thatcher plus homelessness legislation opened the door a bit and by 1985, Ellen and Ted's folks had bought their respective council properties and were already grandparents to Ray and Bob. The next generation of the Grishams saw procreation as a money-spinner and fucked for prosperity. It seemed that was the height of Ted and Ellen's aspirations. That and buying a council house appropriate to their growing family and its ever-increasing social and economic needs. Their kids were not all like them. Some would prove to be competent criminals, others huge disappointments.

Now, let's see, who exactly have we got? Well, there was Ray, oldest and thickest, though you would have to appreciate that other dumb ones were as yet to be born. Next to come along was Bob, who would get the nickname, "Bold Bob" for reasons that would become apparent. Bob was the brains of the family, the criminal brains. Even in primary school, he was really nothing but trouble; in secondary, he was regularly excluded, threatened with expulsion and was quite clearly one of the school bullies. He showed little academic inclination but developed a slyness that was to become his trademark. By sixteen, Bob was bigger than his father and the parents felt uncomfortable around him, threatened a bit by his presence, not that he would have done anything to them. He hung around with other lads, not bad boys, just bored, and they got up to no good. He began to build a reputation that he would use to his advantage later in life. Approaching eighteen, Bob was itching to leave home and get a place of his own. He got a local flat and it became a den of iniquity, parties, drink, lots of shagging…you name it. He was having fun, but that wasn't enough. Bob Grisham wanted recognition and respect as well so that was where the Grisham Team got started in its reign of terror.

The Grishams were an eclectic bunch. Most of them followed in Bob's wake. The first set of twins, Tony and Marilyn, a couple of years younger than Bob, thought he was cool and tried to act just like him. The only problem was that they weren't quite as sharp as he was. Marilyn would sharpen up. They were nevertheless an integral part of their undertaking. Next came Frank, or Franny, as he would be known. One day a local shopkeeper who decided not to pay up—protection money—made the big mistake of calling him "Fanny". The next day, that shop had been burnt to the ground. Bob had sussed that his fearsome reputation plus that of his family had become a money-spinner rather than a disadvantage. The entire estate, shops, businesses, pubs, bookies and so on, knowing that the police were both shorthanded and short-arsed, could do nothing to stop them. In that part of Orpington, the Grishams ruled the roost. In a sense, they had themselves become the law, the burnt-out shop just sought to underline what would happen if they were crossed by anyone.

Four more of the Grisham Corporation. The second set of twins, Mike and Linda. Both were Grishams but with a twist. Linda, whilst initially part of the "local insurgency", had decided remarkably that it just wasn't her cup of tea. She had opted out and become administrator in Graham South, Funeral Directors. As you would say, no accounting for taste. Mike wasn't keen on a life of crime either. Off he went as an eighteen-year-old to the local butcher's where he became an apprentice, then a fully-fledged butcher. How could the owner refuse? It must have crossed Father Ted's mind that the twins neither resembled him nor did they have the normal family ethics. Only Mother Ellen would know for sure and she certainly wasn't saying anything. Finally, the two absentees. Alf, a loner and a violent, alcoholic thug who was so disruptive that he had been thrown out of the house. Finally, there was Pete, the youngest. Pete wasn't as bad as his slightly older brother, Alf, but had similar problems. He'd been in jail for drunken affray and assault on three occasions. He could never be part of the burgeoning crime syndicate as he was, just like Alf, a total liability. Business, after all, was business.

Bob had started modestly enough, terrorising a few small shopkeepers into giving him a weekly bung. As the weeks went, he expanded his area and the money just kept coming in. He now needed other family members to collect for him. At the start, he often went collecting alone. He was a big boy and he didn't find many around to give him any lip, certainly not if they had any sense. Then he started working on the local shopping area. Within ten days, he'd made the pubs, fast food takeaways, bookies and even a chemist pay him what he described "safety money". He was now raking in well over £1,000 a week. And that was just for starters. The more shops and businesses he visited, the more he depended on other family members to visit them to collect their weekly "contribution". Of course, it wasn't all plain sailing. Like the guy that Franny had encountered, two or three of them had second thoughts and decided to tell one of the collectors to fuck off. Bad mistake. It wasn't just about money. Well, it was mostly about the money but was also about disrespecting the family—and about the money. Local shopkeepers would find that local customers were "encouraged" to shop elsewhere. Virtually forced into bankruptcy, they'd quickly see the error of their ways and start to pay again. Bob Grisham couldn't let anybody off. If he did, where would it end? They would all need to pay and continue to pay. In perpetuity.

And what would the police do about this? It was a very strange environment. Fair enough, a reign of terror existed in the community, but paradoxically, crime had drastically reduced. The Grisham Team "business model" had resulted in the unexpected consequence of none of the other thieves, tossers and other assorted arseholes being brave enough to try to rob any of the places known to be under the protection of the family, and as they didn't exactly know where all these places were, even ones that weren't paying protection money would be left alone—no robberies, no assaults, nothing. In these circumstances, local police were actually getting accolades from higher up about their reducing crime figures; as no one in the community had the balls to let on what was going on, the Grisham Team carried on, emboldened by their success.

Bob was now sitting upon a fairly impressive and steadily growing cash stash. The next bit was going to be more difficult—how to benefit from all the money. Bob had his limitations and imagination was certainly one of them. Luckily for him, young sister, Marilyn, was quite good on the computer and did a bit of digging and discovered some ways to invest their money. Property. Rundown property. Lots of it around. *Homes under the hammer* was their starting point for tips!

Bob and Franny decided to celebrate their good fortune and increasing wealth—like an excuse was ever needed—by a visit to one of the area pubs, the Horseshoe, on Saturday night. It wasn't a bad pub, quite lively, plenty of birds, live band and so on. Nine o'clock that night, a couple of lookers rolled in, slightly the worse for wear and drink, no doubt having done a bit of vodka "pre-loading" at home before coming out and were giggly and talkative. The girls, dolled up, were chatting with each other, voddies loaded, and standing at the bar when Franny was up getting in a round; he bantered a bit with them, asked them to join him and his brother. Two minutes later, over they came.

'Girls, Bob, how you doing? You've met Franny already.'

'Good to meet you, Bob, Franny. Kirsty. And this is my big sis, Becky.'

Chapter 20

Gretchen Loses her *Raison D'Etre*

Time had inevitably moved on and Greville had been as enthusiastic about the book as Arthur. *Heavenly Hell* had been quickly printed and distributed in the normal manner. Advanced orders had exceeded all expectations. For the author, this was a mixed blessing. Ruby Latimer was happy to be back in the black as well as being back in favour. It had been almost a decade since her last notable success, and while she had continued to sell her back catalogue in very respectable numbers, she realised that her books had shown a downward trend in customer orders and sales.

'It's terribly hard to keep coming up with fresh ideas, intriguing storylines and…well, maybe I have struggled, but now I'm back,' she told Arthur.

'Well,' he retorted as he offered her another glass of champagne as they sat for lunch in Mayfair, 'I will grant you this, Ruby love, it's a veritable *tour de force*, the way you slogged through the first half, lulling us all into a sense of false security, only to rattle our senses at the end, and what a final chapter! I don't know where that came from; it was brilliant. Never saw it coming. Your time in Davos was certainly money well spent.'

Outwardly, Ruby Latimer was totally impassive in hearing these comments. However, internally, it was an entirely different matter. Inwardly, she was right royally pissed off. *Sense of bloody false security. Bastard.* Just at that moment, in walked Greville, beaming from ear to ear. He sat with them and another glass was requested. After the usual congratulations, he dived into his pocket and pulled out a letter.

'You might want to hear this,' and he read it out.

"We have pleasure in announcing that the novel 'Heavenly Hell' by author Ruby Latimer, published by Laurel Press, has been shortlisted in the category of

Novel of the Year. The award ceremony will take place on 18 June. We have yet to complete the entire shortlist and would appreciate if you would kindly refrain from making this public until our shortlisting process is complete. We look forward to seeing Laurel Press representatives at the forthcoming award ceremony and invitations will be duly dispatched.

Signed—AFC Scimitar Chair of Judges."

Arthur smirked, saying, 'Not at all surprised, love. As I said before Greville appeared, it really was, is, something else. Visit to your favourite boutique beckons before the big day, yes?'

Of course, it did. Ruby got home and thought, *This time, two months from now, it could be me picking up the biggest prize of my life. Man Booker eat your heart out.* She went to her small drinks cabinet and poured herself a bourbon with a touch of soda. She sat down and kicked off her shoes. She glanced at her feet and thought, *Need a pedicure badly.* She also thought, *Fucking ghost-writer,* and sipped her gin. What she really thought was that she was very fortunate to still be in business, her talent had maybe somewhat diminished, but she was still there for a little bit longer. She also thought that maybe she should call it a day if she won this most prestigious prize, but it then occurred to her—to do what? No kids, no husband, no one. For two decades, this had been her world, a world she had desired, sacrificed everything for, backstabbed anyone who had crossed her, even betrayed old friends, all in the pursuit of art and success. It didn't make her proud nor did it make her ashamed. For her, it was just the world she inhabited, her *raison d'etre*, or so she thought. *It would have been nice*, she thought to herself, *if there had only been a friend*, someone she could have taken out with her to buy that dress and someone to accompany her to the ceremony. Plenty of time for that yet. Ruby, now relaxed, crossed her legs and lifted her glass. "Thanks GW whoever the fuck you are" in an ironic self-toast.

George Pope in the meantime was still living at home in Bishop's Stortford, still working at the local supermarket, but that weekend opportunity was definitely knocking. His mum and her partner had decided to go away for a long weekend, leaving him, poor boy, to cope all on his own. As it happened, that weekend he wasn't working. So a quick text to Ms G Turner, inviting her to come and have carnal knowledge with him. If nothing else, he was straight and to the point. He got a one-word response, "YESSSSSSS" and a dozen smiley-face emojis.

Since her loss of virgin status, Gretchen had fully recovered and was raring to go. Telling her mom and dad that she was away to a fan club weekend, like they would really care, she packed a few things—clothes, underwear, laptop, large supply of Johnnies. She just hoped she had enough clean underwear and Johnnies. And as they say, the rest was to be history.

Sunday morning and a score of fucks later, Gretchen had been strenuously exercised—in a manner of speaking—for several hours. As a result, she hadn't checked her email for a couple of days, or used many condoms. It was normally just junk, adverts, inconsequential. However, there was one very intriguing. It was from someone called Henry. Not for one minute did she, Miss Gullible herself, consider that the sender was really called Henry and when she read the email, it just confirmed this.

"The secretary of Ruby Latimer Fan Club,
Your author is a complete fraud.
"Heavenly Hell" was not written by her.
She has claimed it as her own.
Read it and you will see.
Look at the last 40 pages.
Two different people have written this book.
It should stand out a mile.
Shame on you, Ruby Latimer.
Shame on your fan club as well."

Gretchen, who had for the best part of two days been bathed in—if not exactly—affection, at least the exotic experimental lust of her lover and had at last sown her wild oats, was now plunged back into the reality that her revered author might not be all she appeared. It could, of course, have been untrue. It could, of course, have been the vexatious attempt by another author to blacken Ruby Latimer's name. Her head was filled with confusing thoughts, but she couldn't dismiss the idea out of hand. The first reading of the book by Gretchen had been superficial. She had set up the fan club, she had read all Ruby Latimer books beforehand and when they had first come out when she was but a kid. Since then, she had read each one the very week of publication and had done the same with *Heavenly Hell*. Even at such a quick read, she'd wondered about a few things. Now, after this cryptic email, she decided that she'd better reread the novel.

Sitting in the kitchen of George's parents' house, which whilst small was clean and fit for purpose, as was his bed, with her laptop out and him rubbing her bare back and shoulders.

'Everything OK, lover?'

'Not sure. Maybe there is something funny about this book.' Gretchen was clearly uneasy about the email. George poured her a coffee and tried to distract her by kissing her neck. She adored this, one of her newly discovered erogenous zones, closed her eyes for a few seconds, but was not going to be distracted. They had the rest of the day for that. She read on. Uncharacteristically, George had noticed that after reading the email, her shoulders had tensed up. She was now reading the book on her laptop and her shoulders had dropped. This was not a sign of relaxation, more of despair.

George, and particularly Gretchen, had had a wonderful experimental few days of lust fest, which she had needed more than he had. Her "bit of rough". Just as well his house was empty. Noisy as fuck they were. However, given that the girl had built up in her mind that Ruby Latimer was not just a wonderful authoress but also a role model for her and a paragon of virtue, to read that she wasn't possibly all she made out to be had come as a complete shock. Sorry George, but sex had to take a backseat whilst she thought about this and just how she would deal with it. There were options but first of all, she needed to talk to sis, Lucinda. After all she was Honorary Chair of the Ruby Latimer Fan Club. She would need to be the next port of call.

Gretchen went up to the bedroom—the kitchen had become too cold to be sitting about—and put her stuff in a bag. Gretchen looked around the bedroom, remembering it and her time there, got dressed and trotted back down the stairs.

'You leaving then? Something I said?' enquired a puppy-dog-faced George.

She kissed him and said, 'Something important I need to do. Talk to my sister about this.'

'What will I do without you then?' Gretchen was no longer that naïve. She gave him a playful stare, a dirty laugh, raised a hand in a fashion as if it was holding something and moved it back and forth.

'I'm sure you know what to do, don't you!' and then she was gone.

A lot had happened to Lucinda. Her internship had finished. Her dad and others had asked around but had not had any luck finding a vacancy in that side of the law. Her dad was friendly with Jeremy Spector QC and in a conversation with him had discovered that Channel 8 had just restructured and brought its legal services in-house. They might have something and as his daughter knew one of the bosses—both literally and biblically—and it appeared had gone to school with her as well, she may be willing to put in a good word for her.

Lizzie had known Lucinda in passing at the school they had both attended before both going off to their respective universities but that had been ages ago. She took a copy of her CV that had been passed to her and thought it was quite impressive. She gave it to her fiancé who was so loved up, he was putty in her hands at that time, so he did his best, she got an interview and bingo! The job was hers.

The first Friday after she began, they both went for a lunchtime drink to catch up on the names of old school friends—there were a handful—and discovered mutual likes and hates. They reckoned they could end up good mates. Both were competent and ambitious. Both knew how to play the game. Both were going places. It was just that at that point, those "places" remained largely undefined and unrecognised. One thing they both knew; it would be fun travelling the road to those destinations.

Chapter 21

Lucinda Helps Unearth the Truth

The mind of Gretchen Turner was in overdrive. Having had her first truly sustained sexual encounter, it was rudely interrupted by an email capable of tearing her world of make-believe apart. The woman she had put on a pedestal, Ruby Latimer, was dangerously close to falling off it. She was being accused of deception of the most heinous kind for any author, falsely claiming to have authored the work of someone else. When she had read the advance copy that she had an encrypted e-book version of, on the first read it seemed slightly different from the author's normal style, but she just put it down to literary development. This e-mail could have been mischievous, even vexatious, but if it wasn't, then her doyen would have been found severely wanting.

Gretchen drove home, went straight to her room, locked herself in and proceeded to read the e-book cover-to-cover—in a manner of speaking. Several hours later, she'd finished. She referenced several other Ruby Latimer titles to see if there could be any validity in the wild assertion. The more she researched, the more worried she became that it might in fact be true. There did seem to be at the very least a need for in horseracing parlance, a "Stewards Enquiry". She needed to discuss with another party but who? lightbulb moment—sister, Lucinda. Who else?

Lucinda Turner, honorary chair of LLFC, could be trusted. She might even know someone who might be able to verify Gretchen's suspicions. Whilst she hoped against hope that she was wide of the mark, her need to confirm or dismiss was killing her. That Sunday evening, she had a confidential sisterly chat with Lucinda. A very long sisterly chat. The upshot of it was that Lucinda would investigate if there were any reliable experts who could be called upon to look at the book and give an informed opinion as to whether it was the work of a sole author or not. The next night she came home and gave Gretchen a scrap of paper with a name and phone number on it.

'If you phone this person, she might just put your mind at rest or alternately destroy your illusions. Your call here.'

Gretchen took the bit of paper and, going to her room, phoned it. She explained to this person, seemingly an expert professor in literary authenticity (yes, there was actually one!) who was capable of analysing old manuscripts and not just by handwriting but content, authenticating works and ascribing others to different people. The Bard himself had been subject to such scrutiny. Emeritus Professor Llewelyn was always very busy, but she was fascinated by this case. Gretchen arranged to see her and travelled to Bristol in hope that it would not end in despair.

The professor met her. Far from a crusty old academic type, even though she was in her early 60s, she was dressed casually and had, maybe not that unsurprisingly, a Welsh accent. The professor wanted to know more. Gretchen had a hardback copy—signed—that she gave her and pleaded with her to keep silent about the matter until an appropriate time in the future. Not only did the professor agree to this, she even offered to do the deliberations pro-bono. This seemingly was a match made in heaven!

Gretchen and the professor parted company and the academic promised her that she would be in touch as soon as possible but couldn't be more definite regarding when that would be as she would be researching it herself. The journey back home by train took a while but Gretchen would at least know with some degree of certainty the answer to this conundrum. She decided to get on with other things in the meantime, trying to put, as best as she could, the matter to the back of her mind. It wouldn't be too long in fact before she was to get her emphatic, authoritative answer.

Lizzie was out, not with Craig, but with Lucinda, with whom a burgeoning friendship had begun to develop and flourish. Lucinda might have had an entirely different type of professional specialism but given that Lizzie's dad was a QC, she could converse on many matters legal with a fair degree of understanding—and about men, etc. as well! Lucinda, having recently lost her cherry, hadn't been too hasty about sealing the deal with a number of guys and so they did have something else in common.

On the Friday in question, Lizzie was joined by Ambreen, a C8 News producer. Ambreen Gubta was decidedly older than the two girls and was keen to integrate into their "scene" so going to the pub during Friday lunchtime seemed as good a way as any. Ambreen was a modern Asian, preferring to adopt Western customs, and so C8 was the perfect starting point for her. She came from a traditional Muslim background but had defied her upbringing, preferring to adopt a lifestyle that would allow her individuality rather than subservience. It had taken years of family conflict for her to gain her independence as well as escaping her uncle's clutches—Pakistan, circumcision, forced marriage and who knows what—to follow her dream. After a few years being upstaged by white male competitors, Ambreen finally had been given her chance to shine, show what she could do and prove her worth. Channel 8, an equal opportunities employer, if ever there was one.

Lizzie, newly promoted to news reporter, had started to work on some minor pieces, part of the learning curve, but as she was a fast learner, she was ready for bigger, more public, political challenges. What better way to get this across than in casual conversation in the pub, drink in hand.

'I'm pretty bored, to be frank. I was hoping to get my teeth into some meaty issues, but they just keep asking me to investigate dross. It's not as if I can't handle big stories. For fuck's sake, I blew *Stratfordgate* wide open—that's why I'm here—so you'd think they would trust me with something with a bit more gravitas, not all this petty "cats up trees" stuff. Sorry to get heavy here, folks, just a bit annoyed, that's all.'

'Why don't we get them to move you onto my territory then?' suggested Ambreen. 'We're currently investigating some shady dealings in parts of the London area. You might want to come to the "Secret Society" programme. We're looking at a lot of exposing of the criminal classes. What do you th—?'

'Absolutely. Terrific. Can I?' Lizzie was almost salivating at the thought of some really in-depth exposes.

'Need to get it okayed but would love to have you.' Lizzie could hardly conceal her joy and relief. A real reporter on real stories!

Meanwhile, the Grisham brothers, Bob and Franny, had clicked with the two girls they'd met in the pub that Saturday night and, as expected, got their ends away at Becky's pad. Pad! Council flat really. Franny and her in one room—the one with the bed—whilst Bob and young Kirsty had the couch all to themselves. They all had a screamer of a night. Kirsty was a screamer in more than the metaphorical sense! Anyway, it was the start of something, maybe not love, possibly not even lust but certainly a bit of fun. It might have been called "slap and tickle" in the post-war years but now it was a bit more…well, full on. It wouldn't be a regular occurrence but would happen again for certain. In what you would call pillow talk, Kirsty found out that Bob boastfully thought of himself as the estate's "Mr Big". Kirsty thought to herself, *Mr Bighead for sure*, but the more he talked, the more she listened. Kirsty would be filing away this boaster's crack for future reference. The next morning, the two guys left without a by-your-leave. Typical men, use em', leave em'. It would prove to be a meeting that would lead to unexpected repercussions. Franny and Becky did exchange phone numbers as well as…

Kirsty and Becky were left alone in the flat. Despite being several years her junior, Kirsty was more streetwise than her sister and had just spotted an *opening in the market*. That opening was one Bob Grisham. He had been less guarded than he normally would be, drink and sex being the tongue loosener. He had alluded to things about himself that, whilst unsavoury, were also wealth-providing. She could tell from his suit, his shoes and his gold chain—the only thing he had kept on were his socks, yuck! —no doubt expensive socks, that he wasn't just bullshitting her. Kirsty didn't mind him, the closest to affection that she was capable of expressing. After a coffee and a fag each, they chatted about the night before.

'Have fun then, Becks?'

'Nah, shite in bed he was. No conversation. And yours?'

'OK, not bad, had better.'

And that was the depth of the discussion. Becky was naively trusting of her sister. Kirsty, on the other hand, had no scruples of any kind and would have betrayed their own mother—she indeed had done so but had gotten away with it—so betraying her sister wasn't an issue if the opportunity presented itself. Kirsty was a listener and mental note-taker. Becky was now nearly sober so spilling any sort of beans wasn't going to happen. Not then. Kirsty thought about this. *Maybe soon a drinking session with big sis*, she thought.

Time to get back to work. Lizzie, Ambreen and Lucinda all headed back towards the C8 studios, Lizzie being by far the happiest of the three. Lucinda was by then musing about what her sister, Gretchen, had revealed to her but said nothing about it for two reasons: she had promised to keep silent on it and until the fraud was verified, there really wasn't a story. She did, however, think that if it proved to be true and there was a "Secret Society" tale to be told, who better to tell it than Lizzie Spector?

They got back to the studios and Lizzie detoured up to Craig's office. 'Is he in?' she asked his secretary who nodded. Normally, people waited to be invited into his room, but the secretary knew who Lizzie was, her relationship with Mr Endoran and, apart from that, wasn't brave enough to even try to prevent her. He was alone in the room. She marched over to his desk where he was seated and before he could utter a word, gave him a very passionate, tonsil-vacuuming smooch.

'What's up?'

'I'm moving to "Secret Society". Perfect. Just thought you should know.'

'Yeah, good move,' he said unenthusiastically. She was somewhat taken aback.

'Not delighted for me, then?'

'Course I am. They will appreciate you there.'

She thought about that for a second. 'Appreciate me! So, I'm not appreciated where I am then.'

'It's bloody Tony. Got the producer in his pocket. Won't let you near him. Think you know why.' Even after a couple of years, Tony the "Rottweiler" remembered her from *Stratfordgate*, their encounter in the Strangers Bar at the Commons, and didn't trust her. It now made sense. At "Secret Society", she'd show them all.

The coming together of disparate souls in different locations, different backgrounds and differing objectives would lead to the *Law of Unexpected Consequences* itself having an absolute field day.

Chapter 22

Professor Plum in the Library

Craig Endoran had been married only once. It had been initially a very happy marriage, but both were determined not to be defined by who they were married to rather what they themselves as individuals were. That would have been fine enough, a logical stance, but for one thing—their personal and divergent ambition. Neither considered the other when it came to career choices. Valerie, his ex-wife, had been different from Lizzie in looks. Lizzie was oh so cute, but at five foot and maybe half an inch, she came up to his chin on her tiptoes. Valerie, on the other hand, had been quite tall for a woman and had a not dissimilar temperament to Lizzie.

A senior buyer in a Knightsbridge department store, Val could spend days away, seeking new goods, taking product providers to task for the quality of their merchandise and on it went. She had already been well-established and upwardly mobile, a bit ahead of her husband. Given the diversity of their jobs and the fact that she earned more at that stage than he did, it would lead to conflict, but that wasn't all. Val was two years older than Craig, Lizzie eight years younger than him. Craig and Val were then still in their mid-twenties and financially secure. The problem was aspirations. He had shown signs of broodiness and hoped she too might be that way inclined. On the rare occasion, very rare given their work schedules, that they made love, in the afterglow of coital expression, he had asked her about children.

'I'm not very maternal, besides that I've my career to consider.'

So, there was his answer. What she had really meant was "I've got my career to consider". From that point on, the marriage drifted and they eventually agreed to call it a day, clearly desiring differing things. Craig decided to concentrate on his career, saw a vacancy at the managerial level at Squawk FM, applied and got it. Craig Endoran was a "mover and shaker" of a different horse, but still one. He helped the embryonic radio station take root.

For Craig, however, life and relationships were more than just about sex and babies. Valerie was in retail, him in broadcasting. Neither the twain would meet. Their conversations, whenever they took place, either face to face—a rarity—on their mobiles or nightly on Skype increasingly showed that his interest in her day job was as false as hers was in his. Their common interests were uncommon. He really needed someone in his own line of work as did she. Their split was amicable enough and they got a quickie divorce, allowing both to go their separate ways.

After their divorce, Craig moved from Squawk FM to Channel 8 News production. He liked it there but from time to time felt the need for female company. Given the absence of such, he just immersed himself totally in his work. The Lizzie thing wasn't planned, it just kind of happened as these things do. Another wedding planned a year down the road. He was a bit apprehensive on account of his previous venture into matrimony, but he did love her; Lizzie Spector was, in his eyes, the one, whereas Valerie had flattered to deceive, and his desire to spend his life with this heavenly munchkinette was the overriding consideration.

Lizzie was good for him; Craig was good for her. Still, they had a lot to discuss and he hadn't broached the "B" question with her. Marriage was more than baby-making, it was filling in those gaps in both the partners and that took time and effort. They were both young and had years before it became any kind of biological imperative for either of them. They could always freeze embryos, putting it off for a decade or more. Neither would be defined by each other, only who they were. They were journalists.

Three weeks had elapsed and still Lucinda was no further forward knowing if Ruby Latimer was an out-and-out fake or if it was just a drastic change of writing style. Professor Llewelyn had not been in touch, had not phoned, texted, emailed, skyped. Nothing from her at all—until 1 April. A phone message appeared on her voicemail. "Lucinda, its Professor Llewelyn here. I have news for you but would prefer to talk on the landline. Please call me on…" and left her number. Lucinda smiled and then having just realised – April Fool? – that the unanswered question was about to be answered, frowned. She was pleased that the professor had finally some news for her but dependent on just the nature of the news, it could have a devastating effect on her sister. During lunchtime, Lucinda found a rarity, a payphone in a local pub—she was at work after all.

'Professor Llewelyn, Lucinda Turner. You have news for me, I believe.'

'Lucinda, thanks for calling back. Yes indeed. I looked at the manuscript you gave me, studied it in detail, made notes, checked out previous books she had written, then our computer was employed to fine sift it for standard phrases, literary irregularities, possible plagiarism, etc.'

Lucinda was holding her breath. 'And...?'

'The book was, up to page 185, written by the author—'

'But from there on, it wasn't.'

'That is correct. A very sophisticated attempt at forgery but an expert and the right software can always tell.'

'So just to confirm, what you believe is that two people wrote this book.'

'Precisely.'

'...And you would vouch for that, would you?'

'Depends what you mean by "vouch". I spent three days of my own time and five hours of unauthorised computer time using RABID (the university computer) to analyse the book. I am 100% certain of my view, what I wouldn't be able to do is make any kind of public statement to confirm it. However, you now know that your suspicions have been proven correct.'

The academic had spoken. It was clearly a challenge she had relished and quite possibly had also wanted to put her computer through its paces. Brilliant people like her didn't have objectives like mere mortals and this had been an exercise in validation of a suspicion, possibly one she would use in lectures on the subject. Lucinda thanked the professor and hung up.

Lucinda Turner took a seat in the pub, ordered a sandwich and smiled. Mystery solved but what now? Didn't take long to answer that one. Lizzie Spector. This would be a severe blow for her sister, but it was a scoop that Lizzie and, who knew, even herself might benefit from. On her way back to the office, Lucinda pondered the discussion with the professor and in the light of her not wanting to be named as the expert, she debated with herself just what kind of information she would be able to give Lizzie other than some cryptic clues. It was either tell it all to her or forget it. She reckoned that it was a problem she would need to sleep on. In the meantime, she'd need to break it to Gretchen that evening. Maybe her response might give her a clue as to what to do.

Walter was still pissed off. After Ruby Latimer had signed his letter, he had expected that Arthur would have been pleased to give him a job as an editor, but he was still prevaricating. Truth was he had a full complement of editors and Walter was good at what he did. Walter, between work, writing and wanking, had nothing going on. He decided to diversify his talents and took up another side-line. It was one designed to be soothing, relaxing and might be popular with women. He started night classes and after a few weeks, he was getting quite good at it. All he needed was to get a few people to practice on. He invested in a collapsible table and various items necessary to ply his new trade—oils, creams, incense and a small ghetto-blaster. He thought he could put his disappointments on the backburner, which, of course, he couldn't. He would offer free sessions, loss leaders, to all and sundry. The problem was that most men wouldn't let this scrawny guy near them, men preferred women to do it, go figure, and women found his offer somewhat sinister. Nevertheless, he practiced on family members. His younger sister was very happy for him to do it; after all, it was free. However, he needed to think about how to break into the market. Of course, there was his answer—the authors!

Gretchen was home as usual when Lucinda came in. Lucy would wait until after dinner to discuss the thorny matter of Professor Llewelyn. Dinner came and went, and Lucinda dragged Gretchen away to tell her something. Having told her in a calm and clinical manner, she expected any one of several reactions, fearing the worst. Gretchen took it all in, having multiple contradictory feelings about her fake of an author, one she had invested years of personal time and capital in. Maybe she was just growing up. Maybe it was her awakened libido. Maybe she cared a lot less.

'I'm not in despair. I'm not.' She was crying though. 'I'm just disappointed, fucking angry, but I want some closure on this shit. I can't just let it go. I'm going down to see her tomorrow.'

'No Gretchen! Bad move. She'll just deny it, then freeze us, you, out. There's a better way to do it.'

Then Lucinda told her about Lizzie Spector, her old school chum (of sorts) and how she was an investigative TV reporter. Gretchen was still fizzing, still angry, and oh so disappointed but was prepared to let her sister run with it. The RLFC had eaten up a fair chunk of her young life and now her doyen was just another phoney. The least she could do was let Lucinda on board, getting this woman exposed.

Lunchtime the next day, Lucinda and Lizzie were having a pub lunch at one of their favourite locals near work. It wasn't very busy; Easter weekend was in the offing.

'Lizzie, you looking for any stories? I know, silly question. Always on the lookout, aren't you?'

'Got something?'

Lucinda filled her in on the entire background, the Fan Club, the novel, Gretchen's mysterious email, self-deleted but at least Gretchen had been quick enough to capture it, and finally, the professor's analysis. 'And you say the phone call you took from her, to her, was yesterday!'

'It's no April Fool, Lizzie. No way. She's an Emeritus. No kidding. Look her up on Google if you don't believe me.'

Lizzie just smirked. 'Gotcha!' and they both giggled. Lucinda, after some soul searching, had lit the blue touch paper and the rocket that was Elizabeth Spector, TV reporter on "Secret Society"; Lizzie was engaged. Ruby Latimer had trouble coming her way. Big trouble from the person who already had a grudge against her.

Chapter 23

Empire Building in Orpington

The Grisham Corporation was now fully in control of their part of Orpington and were just starting out. Bold Bob fantasised from time to time of following in the footsteps of his idols, the Richardsons' and Krays' of the 60s. He'd seen the films and had thought they were pussies compared to what he could achieve. He now had a funding stream consisting of seventy shops, eight bookies, eleven pubs, three factories, four chemists as well as various people in the "Black Economy" who paid just to keep them at bay. From time to time, someone would give one of them lip, claim to be struggling, even downright just refuse to cough up. Bob didn't believe in warnings. He had a "one-strike policy". You paid. If not, the next time that proprietor was seen, they would either be left without working premises or left with lifelong injuries. 'Harsh but fair,' crowed Bob. Extremely harsh but to show any other side would scream "weak" and others might try it on. It seemed to produce results. Most weeks, they had a one hundred percent collection rate. Bob looked at expanding the Corporation's patch, which was already three-square miles. He had a plan.

The plan was simple. Stage one: consolidation. Wait for six months, and when he was sure no one would cause any trouble or renege on payment, they would move on, appointing one of the family as the managing agent. Stage two: scout adjacent areas for similar types of businesses, possibly garages and repair shops, second-hand car dealerships, etc. They were not involved in drugs, mainly because of not just being able to find a wholesaler but also because of apprehension of ending up on the police radar when things were going so well below it. Stage three was open-ended. Bob was a canny operator and he had Marilyn who had developed some useful business skills. He thought Franny and Marilyn might be able to hold the fort, continue consolidation so that he and Tony might be able to start their expansion programme. Bob thought like a businessman, acted like a thug and was capable of anything. Meanwhile, money continued to roll in and Marilyn as banker continued to launder and stash away their ill-gotten gains until it came to the point that clearly the amount of cash was becoming a problem. They would need to do something positive with it. The proverbial mattress was getting too lumpy!

All this time, what of Mr and Mrs G? Well, they had spent a lot of time trying to sort out Pete in the hope he didn't go down the same road as Alf. Pete had drink and drugs addiction issues, but Alf had been so out of control, he'd been kicked out, probably the reason drugs selling wasn't part of their list of misdemeanours. Bear and honeypot. Bob had no time for either of these wasters and only Linda was prepared to do anything. Linda was still living at home but hoped to move out soon as she was getting to that age and wanted a guy to, as she so delicately put it, "knock her up"! Ah, true romance! Bob hoped she'd hurry up and move out as well. They had accrued enough money to buy several properties and it would be a good way to offload an amount by buying his younger sister a house, despite her going over to the "dark side", working at a Funeral Directors. She knew fine well how the family made its dosh and had resisted benefiting from it up to that point, but her biological clock was dictating to her that a sprog was desired, so having been talked to by Bob, she relented and accepted his offer. She insisted it was a loan, payable back at a monthly amount but that just wasn't going to happen really was it. In two months, Linda was gone the Grishams' bank balance was reduced by £275,000 and Bob had acquired a room from which his sister could do the family accounts—encrypted, of course!

The Grisham house still contained their parents, Bob, Tony, Marilyn, Franny, Mike, who kept well clear of everyone, Pete when he wasn't serving at Her Majesty's Pleasure and, at that point, Linda. All owned outright, even incorporating the attached four-bedroom property, making eight bedrooms, it still felt at times stiflingly full. Ray and Alf no longer lived there—Ray shared a flat with an old school friend and Alf, occasionally in a squat, sometimes on the streets, sometimes home for a handout, but always seen OK by Mrs Grisham; after all, for better or for worse, he was still hers. A most dysfunctional lot, kept together not by the parents but largely through Bob and to a lesser extent, Marilyn.

For the family, money was never an issue. Bob "made" it, Franny and Tony collected it, Marilyn "banked" it, they all spent it but in small amounts so as not to raise any suspicions. As far as love lives were concerned, outside of work, they all had one of sorts, mostly of a casual nature. Bob acted as some sort of quality controller of whom any family member's friends and anyone remotely connected with the law was *persona non gratis*. Tony had a girlfriend who wanted him to move in with her. Bob scrutinised the woman, who seemed not to be a threat so that would be OK. In truth, Tony would have just done it anyway but since he would get a £25,000 "dowry", he thought telling his big brother to take one might not have been smart. Anyway, in another four months, another room at Chez Grisham had been vacated.

Bob was a "casual sexer". By that was meant he wouldn't fall head over heels for any bint—far too dangerous—but sex was OK. The last one he'd bedded was some little scrubber called Kirsty or something, not a bad shag. She lived fairly local and he expected to bump into her again. Her sister was a bit too intellectual for him. Franny, his brother, liked her but told Bob she wasn't great at fucking. Kirsty, on the other hand, seemed to give it a go great style and encouraged him all the way home. She was loud as well. Loud was Bob's type. Anyway, if they met again, who knew what might come up in the conversation!

Bob was too preoccupied with bigger things, like the expansion of his territory. He thought about other activities but at the moment just wanted to concentrate on his main line—extortion. He was getting more and more convinced that Franny and Marilyn were on top of their existing patch, money was coming in nicely, no one was acting up, superb. Then Alf! Arsehole of the family was found in a coma in a local dosshouse, drugged up to his eyeballs and ended up in intensive care. Everything was put on ice whilst this family dickhead was hovered over by his mum until the danger was past, then he discharged himself and disappeared. Such an ungrateful cunt. Found again in a couple of days, Bob dragged him home, locked him in one of the vacant bedrooms and forced the prick to go cold turkey. His screams could be heard blocks away for days, but no one reported it, did they! As if they would. Bob was a retributive bastard, he was.

Keeping track of the Grishams was like trying to corral a box of kittens that were flying in every direction. A holiday was needed. Marilyn booked them a large cottage. It even had a pool. Off the whole bloody lot of them went, only thirty miles away in Sussex, but it was needed. The poor owners didn't know whom they had rented their precious home to. By the time they left to return to Orpington, the place was wrecked. To shut up the owners, Marilyn left a tip of £2,000, just in case.

On their return, however, there was trouble. The old saying, "whilst the cat's away, the mice will play", was writ large. Some of the proprietors said that some other lot had been around saying that the Grishams had retired and they were taking over. Panic stations! Who were these cheeky fuckers? Bob had a plan to visit all his customers and see if these "new kids on the block" could be identified. It didn't take long. They were from St Mary's Cray and were called Ellis. An address for them was acquired and retribution plotted. The male members of the Grisham Corporation in two cars, plus some reinforcements—locals who owed the family—piled into three cars and headed for the address of the Ellis' lot. 6 am. Knock, knock, then bang bang! No one was killed but the discharge of firearms at close range, the appearance of ten leather-jacketed thugs terrorising this family with the parting words, 'And if we hear you've been within a mile of our patch, it won't be your fucking ceiling full of buckshot!' That was the last time anyone called Ellis was seen in that part of Orpington. Police did interview the Ellis dad, the shots had been reported, but no charges were filed, he claimed not to know the assailants. Given their colourful reputation, pot and kettle came to mind.

So, an emergency had been averted. Equilibrium restored. Grisham vengeance was often swift and brutal as in the case of the Ellis interlopers. Bob thought maybe another string to their bow was required. In reality, there was himself and five others he could rely upon. Two of his siblings were wasters, two half-alienated and one braindead. He needed a "consigliere", a fixer with eyes in the back of his head. Not exactly going to get one on eBay! Couldn't exactly advertise for one. "Wanted—minder of criminal family. Job description: frighten the shite out of competitors and protect area from anyone trying to muscle in on patch. Qualities: ferocity, gratuitously violent, sadistic. Pay: by results. Conditions: flexible working." Marilyn was thinking about it as well.

'Heard of the "Dark Web", have you?' Bob looked puzzled. 'Where you can get people like that.'

'You can? Fuck me! Amazing.'

So, Marilyn showed Bob how to access it and left a message, not expecting anything, but lo and behold! The next day, there was an encrypted response. They could be in business. They were in business!

It was like something from a Bond movie. Bob and Marilyn, in the family motor, arrived at an appointed rendezvous. A Merc in the distance approached

129

and flashed its lights at them to follow, which, of course, they did. They followed until they arrived at a deserted retail park.

Sitting in the backseat of a blackened-out Mercedes saloon, Bob talked to this man about the problem, their requirements, how often, what action and, most importantly, how much the person would be paid. The person had Armani sunglasses and spoke in a whisper; strange given it wasn't sunny and the driver had gone for a fag.

'I've worked for them and now it's my turn,' Armani whispered.

Bob demanded, 'Just who have you worked for? Who are they?'

'I'll mention two names, you check them out and see what I mean,' and he whispered the names to Bob. They left and the man, Brad—possibly not his real name—would call at noon the following day to get their answer. Getting home, he asked Marilyn to do an internet search. She went onto the "Dark Web" again and came back and said, 'Which first—good or bad?' That could only mean one thing, they were about to be up to their necks in all kinds of shit.

'The good news is that your man is who he said he is.'

'…And the bad?'

'Out of our league. Way out. I've checked up those names. Grigor is Grigor Sivkov, a Bulgarian hitman, and Boris is Boris Ulyanov who runs things in the West End. I guess your guy wants his own independence. When he phones, what will you say?'

Beads of sweat were running down the now not-so-bold Bob's face. On one hand, he was entering a dangerous place where people just "disappeared", but on the other hand, he would definitely keep those Ellis scum and other hyenas dead busy, if not just dead.

'Let's just fucking go for it.'

Chapter 24

The Mouse and the Cat

It was early May. The shortlist for the prestigious book award—AFC Scimitar—had been announced and as expected, *Heavenly Hell* was on it. A small reception was held, organised by Laurel Publishers, to showcase the book and allow the media to do their thing and gain it some possible free publicity and extra sales. The press, radio and TV were all invited but most sidestepped this blatant attempt to influence the outcome. Appreciating this and the perception that might be garnered, Greville invited other folk such as editors and staff from Arthur's office to make it look like there was interest. Ruby Latimer was due to show up but in truth, she felt a little uneasy. Part of the event would be a short Q&A session and whilst she was an expert in fielding awkward questions, her Achilles Heel was obvious. There were about a hundred people there, supping sherry, champers, eating *vol-u-vents*, finger food and so on. Ruby Latimer still wasn't there…then she was, amidst flashing cameras, mics and the like, most wishing her well, some just wishing. Ruby was looking around to see if they were all friends or was there some foe lurking. All she could see were friendly faces.

Ambreen, Lizzie and Lucinda scurried out of the black cab and flew into the boardroom of Laurel Publishers. The invite had gone to Nick, the arts interviewer, who had been deserted by the author a few months previously. He wasn't going to bother but administration had passed on the notification and invites to Ambreen, who had dropped everything and scooped up the two young women, using the line, 'Come on you, Ruby Latimer, free food and drink. What more can three girls ask for?'

The three arrived slightly late, just as Greville was thanking them all for coming on that auspicious occasion. They grabbed glasses, sausage rolls and listened to what was being said. Ruby was asked to say a few words, which, in her usual, somewhat acerbic way, expressed gratitude to those who had made the nomination possible. Three editors there flashed each other knowing looks. One was missing, "elsewhere occupied" in a manner of speaking. Greville thanked her and announced that there would be ten minutes at the end for questions. The three C8 women refilled their plates and glasses and circulated.

'And what do you do?'

'Oh, I'm an editor, the three of us all are.'

'Ever edited any of her books?'

Back came the reply, 'Yes, we all have from time to time.' Lizzie was working up to the big one just when, 'You can now ask the author, Miss Ruby Latimer, those questions you've been storing up.' Greville ushered Ruby forward, like she was reluctant or something, to the one mic set up for this in what was now seemingly not a big enough room, packed full of staff members and a few reporters.

'Where do you get your inspiration from?'

'Where can I purchase a weather balloon? I'd like to tie my news editor to one.' Loud laughter.

'Is it getting harder to find new subjects?'

'What do you think of your chances of winning? It's a very strong field you're facing.'

Ruby was batting them out the park left, right and centre. None of the smarty-pants big bears had appeared or if they had, they were too full of drink to be arsed to ask her anything too difficult until—

'Elizabeth Spector, Channel 8. It's a great novel, but I was concerned that it is such a departure from any of your previous novels, both content and style, that you must have some amazing researchers to get you to that brilliant ending.'

'Sorry, was there a question there? I do all my own research. I always have.'

'So is that why the publication was delayed a year? Were you having problems with that research then?'

'Sorry, I don't like this line of questioning. Who did you say you were again?'

Lizzie, it appeared, had her on the ropes. She had come a bit prepared, saw no one to threaten her and dropped her guard. She was then sucker-punched by this young reporter, not for the first time either! The event was drawing to a close, but Lizzie still had some work to do.

She went back to talk to the three editors but by this time, only one of them seemingly still there, drink in hand.

'Rebecca Letts. Becky if you like. I can't say too much. My job and all that. Marion is the one who has, how would you say, grounds for suspicion, I can only say that. She's away now but you may well want to give her a call. Here's her number.'

Meanwhile, Lucinda came across to Lizzie with a young guy.

'Lizzie, this is Walter. He works for the author's agent.'

'My first thing like this. Don't really get invited. Too low down on the food chain for it, I suppose. I heard not many people were going to attend so Mr Newell asked me if I wanted to go.'

As they continued, Walter took the bull by the horns. 'I'm starting up my own massage service. I'm looking for people who want a free massage. I need to practise as I've just qualified.'

All the women smirked, supressed a giggle, but nevertheless said they'd love to try one, so he gave them a card each. Things might be looking up for Walter's little venture.

Meanwhile, Ruby Latimer had been well and truly rattled. She was beyond incandescent and had berated Greville about the invites.

'Who invited that bloody obnoxious woman? Every time we meet, she insults, provokes or tries to trap me.'

Greville attempted, mostly unsuccessfully, to supress a smirk. *Pompous arse*, he actually thought. *She needs a good fuck, that would sort her out.*

'Don't you dare,' snapped the irate author at her beleaguered publisher who, she sensed, was in judgemental mode. 'This is serious, I should have you know. I want that channel banned from covering my events.'

'Ruby, my dear child, Channel 8 was the ONLY terrestrial channel here.' Ruby did a double take. She was loved, wasn't she? Adored?

'Well, whatever, keep that bitch away from me.'

Unfortunately, the unseemly spat had been within the earshot of Abigail.

'Wow, so that's the REAL Ruby Latimer, warts and all. She was lucky most people were away, or it could have been another PR "disarster darling" for her.'

Lucinda was the object of Abigail's revelation and had heard snippets of the outburst. Ruby had let her seemingly impregnable guard down and would be lucky to escape without any damaging consequences. Like most of these things, a series of apparently unrelated events had come together and the results could end up with public revelations that could seriously damage reputations. Luckily for her, most of the news agencies didn't think it had been an event worth turning up to.

If you thought Ruby was beginning to smell a whiff of danger about her "ghost-writer", it was nothing compared to the whiff of an entirely different kind that Bob was smelling. Danger yes, but more anal than that. Bob had just been in contact with a hitman with proper links to, if not The Mob, then definitely a Mob, and now he had serious regrets. He and the Grisham Corporation had been doing reasonably well, had been turning over a seven-figure income—tax-free, of course—but things had begun to close in from competitors so he had thought about taking on a "hired hand". Through young sister Marilyn, he had met Brad who had impeccable references, if you wanted to call Grigor and Boris thus. He had rashly shaken hands and that was his contract. Bob had told him he'd be in touch, almost hoping he would have no need to do so but as with these people, Brad was the one who would be back in touch and sooner than he had thought, seeing what assistance he could give. A somewhat tetchy conversation took place and afterwards, Bold Bob was less bold than bricking it. The guy wanted a retainer as well as a kind of "call-out contract" money every time he was needed. The £10k retainer was duly paid and thereafter, Bob would use this guy as sparingly as possible. Brad, however, was keen to show he was good at what he was employed to do.

Another lot of scum, similar scum to the Grishams themselves, had been nosing around the patch, asking questions, making Grisham "customers" unhappy. 'Not bloody paying another lot as well as you,' was just one comment. Bob had his brothers but lacked the numbers to control everywhere and this mob were crazy. Reluctantly, he contacted Brad, explained the problem and negotiated a fee for his involvement. One week elapsed. One house fire, four dead, two badly burned. Problem solved. Fee paid. You could see from this that Brad was differently "calibrated" to Bob and the rest of the Grishams. Bob was, comparatively speaking, a petty gangster who would most certainly hurt someone, but Brad was a gangster who saw the problem in shades of black and white, with the only answer in the total elimination of said problem. He used his links to find the opposition, then got their place torched making sure the house was fully occupied and the inhabitants asleep. In the space of twenty minutes, the task was complete, his fee earned. It was, of course, just an electrical fault! Bob had to compute what had happened and just accept that was how Brad operated. He hoped he would never have the requirement to call upon his services again. An erstwhile hope if ever there was one. Brad actually gave Bob a small refund on account of the two survivors. 'Sloppy work. Very sorry.' The two died of their injuries a week later.

Back to the aftermath of "Rubygate"; the three women from Channel 8 were riding back to the office at just about three in the afternoon, chirpy and full of shampoo. They had started a process that might lead somewhere but it would depend on what they did next. Lizzie had been told the results of Professor Llewelyn's study and whilst she was encouraged by it, she thought she had better put that side on the backburner pending other investigations as the professor could find herself in serious trouble for the misuse of university computing facilities.

'Where do we go from here, Ambreen?' Lizzie enquired. 'Lucinda needs to find out where we would stand legally if we get this wrong. Personally, I'd let the bitch have it both barrels, but we need to be sure. What about that editor? What about Walter? He might know a thing or two.'

'He was looking to use us as massage guinea pigs. Might be a way to get some info if he knows anything. What do you think then?'

'Thought he was slightly creepy myself. Wouldn't like to go on my own but I suppose we could book an afternoon, safety in numbers and all that,' said Lizzie.

'Not into all that stuff, girls,' said Ambreen. 'You two could do it and let me know what you find out.'

And so, a plan was hatched. Walter would get oiled up, stroke, rub and caress three almost naked young women, whilst they subtly asked him questions about Miss Ruby.

Chapter 25

Lizzie – Her Search for the Truth

Things seemed to have hotted up indeed! They certainly had in regard to Grisham transgressors. In other ways as well, they certainly had. Ruby Latimer, by her almost but not completely out of hearing range tantrum, had set tongues wagging and these tongues had just reached the ears of her tormentor. Lizzie Spector already had certain information that *Heavenly Hell* had been completed by someone other than the author, but needed to see if this could be corroborated, which was not an easy task. The problem was the same as ever. One person of substance being in a rarefied position of influence and with a certain degree of power, if accused of something underhand could either deny it completely, threaten legal action or close ranks on the accuser. If that accuser was a journalist, then the stakes were high. It was inevitably reputations on the line, so any journalist had better be bloody sure of their facts.

The one thing Elizabeth Spector had learned in her career was that it was vital to keep meticulous notes and be able to access them whenever they were required. This was one thing she'd learned from her QC father. She would have given a king's ransom to have recorded the outburst, but she only found out about it after the event, more was the pity. What she did know was that an eminent university professor had analysed the novel and corroborated her opinion using university computer power. This verdict, however, was not for publication in case the professor was outed, something she was afraid of for several reasons, the least important one being the unauthorised use of the cloud.

Lizzie had started work as an investigative reporter on the new C8 series, "Secret Society", which, as the title hinted at, sought to shine a spotlight on goings on not in the public's full gaze. Other reporters on the programme had been working on other stories. Some were to do with criminal gangs, but mostly up north. Reporters sometimes got badly hurt in the pursuit of a scoop, but this was quite rare.

Unknown to Lizzie, and she would have been mega-pissed if she'd known, Craig had spoken to Ambreen and suggested to her that *Heavenly Hell* might be a safer story for her to cover. He might have done it out of love and concern for his fiancé, but it could have seriously backfired on him if she'd found out that he'd been manoeuvring behind her back. She might have been a redhead, but her temper was all redhead! Lizzie was happy to follow up this story even though she now accepted that she'd more than a healthy degree of emotional collateral invested in it. She had a word with Lucinda, her co-conspirator, about the professor but decided to leave that line of enquiry for the time being.

Who knew what? That was the first question she posed herself. Whoever had edited the finished article must have had some suspicions about it surely. It was expertly written, and the finished product looked convincing enough to the untrained eye but surely the last person to edit it must have smelt some sort of rat? Marion French! Of course! One of the editors had given Lizzie a card with Marion French's mobile number on it. She would start there.

Lizzie phoned her. 'You have reached the phone number of Marion French, book editor at Arthur Newell Agency. I'm not available. If you leave your name, phone number and reason for calling, I'll get back to you.'

Lizzie hung up. What could she say that wouldn't start alarm bells clanging? She needed something subtler, but what? She could, of course, lie and say she wasn't who she in fact was. Such a bad idea. She sat for a few minutes, pondered the proposition. She could text her but again, same problem. Then…the phone rang. She could see from the number it was Marion calling back. Most people didn't return calls from people they didn't know but it seemed Marion wasn't one of those types.

'Marion French. Who's this?'

'Hi, Marion. We chatted at the Ruby Latimer do a few days ago. You may remember?'

'Yeesss?' Marion moved into a guarded tone. She had twigged who she was talking to and her guard was on its way up.

'It was just that I had a chat with Rebecca who thought you'd be interested in what work I'm involved in.'

'…And what work might that be?'

'Doing a short history of the author. I understand you might have edited some of her works. It was just to try to get a better insight into her writing.'

Lizzie knew that was a croc of utter shit, but it had been the best she could think of at that kind of notice. Maybe she should have dangled an incentive in front of her, like cash. She also reckoned that this Rebecca person would no doubt be getting an earful from Marion French as a result.

'I'm not sure. Miss Latimer, I presume you are talking about. Is that the author in question?'

'Yes. Just that my network is thinking of doing a programme about her and thought you might be able to add something to it. I'd be very grateful to meet up for a coffee if that would be possible.'

The phone on Lizzie's ear went silent for a few seconds.

'I'm meeting up with my editor friends next week. I'll need to ask them but if they don't mind, I could invite you to meet them. They have edited some of her books as well.'

Lizzie gave herself a big thumbs up. The next day, Marion called her back to say that the others were fine with her joining them for a coffee. She could pay, of course. Marion thought that any publicity would be good publicity—had she been living in a cave? —so thought that she could talk candidly. She had, however, no intention of being trapped into revealing her suspicions. Such naivety.

The following Monday morning at a coffeehouse at Charing Cross, Lizzie entered to see three women sitting and chatting. Lizzie wasn't alone. She had brought Lucinda in case any of the comments needed to be corroborated. First of all, they introduced themselves and stated what they did. Normally, no one ever remembered the name of someone newly introduced unless it was an unusual name or that of a celebrity. In the company of a journalist and lawyer, this wouldn't exactly be the case.

The discussion started with Ruby's early books, the Mormon Trilogy, subsequent books, the possible film etc. All this put her at ease. Another round of coffees and a toilet break as L&L went off. In the empty Ladies, into adjacent cubicles.

'Going well, Lizzie?'

'So far so good but must try to introduce our agenda. Can you…' They heard the door open and a couple of women come in. The two in the cubicles held their breath. In another couple of minutes, they heard the toilet entrance door close and all was silent once more. The cubicle squatters both exited to wash their hands.

'Can you, can you—'

'Ask them about their editing knowledge and techniques so I can get them to return to that bloody book.' So, it was agreed.

Back at the coffee table. 'That's better. Rebecca—'

'Everyone calls me Becky, Lizzie.'

'How long have you been doing the editing thing then?'

'Oh, I don't know. I was young when an auntie asked me if I wanted to try it. Arthur is dead nice, so I just stayed. Must be seven or eight years now.'

'Did you edit *Heavenly Hell* then?'

'No, that would be me,' interjected Marion.

'Oh, sorry, I thought you told me you had done the editing on it last week. So sorry.' Marion gave Becky a cold "I'll see you later" stare.

'Marion, now that the book is published, I just wondered how you rated it compared to…say, "Harvester Hill". That one I thought was a bit bizarre.'

'Not as bizarre as this one,' piped up Becky. Abigail, who had said very little, cleared her throat and looked at her watch.

'Sorry girls really must dash. See you next time,' She left the four. In reality, Abigail felt almost excluded from the conversation, which was her real reason for going. The others continued their chat.

'Her writing style had been consistent over the years,' Lucinda, the actual expert at the table on Ruby Latimer, offered as her opinion. 'All writers' styles can alter depending on the subject, can't they?'

'Sometimes.'

'Not by the amount *Heavenly Hell* changed.' Lizzie was now in combat mode. 'If I didn't know any better, I'd have sworn blind it had been finished off by another writer.' Lizzie was not exactly beating around the hedgerow here. Marion half stood up but thought twice about it, slithered back into her chair, looked at the two strangers, sighed and just remarked dejectedly, 'I agree.' Bingo.

'You agree! You think it may have been a ghost-writer finishing it off then!'

'Quite possibly.' The cat seemed to have exited its bag.

'Lucinda here is, just in case you don't know, chair of the Ruby Latimer Fan Club and her sister is the secretary. They have evidence that proves what we have been suspicious of. Would you like to appear on our programme?'

Marion was utterly gobsmacked. She had been unwittingly ambushed, snared like a bloody fox and now she had absolutely nowhere to escape. She realised it had all been a setup but…well, there it was. It was obvious she was profoundly unhappy at that juncture, but at what? Her author's dishonesty or her own, up to that point, tacit complicity in the deception? Probably both.

'You two don't understand, do you? I love my job, my friends, my life. If I do this, act as a…whistle-blower, I'm screwing myself in this profession. I can't do anything else. I won't get the chance.'

'We could disguise your identity, if that would help, for filming.'

'Can I at least think it over, please?' They agreed to contact her the next day with her decision, very much Hobson's choice, it would have appeared.

The two TV people left their cards with Marion, leaving her and Becky to ruminate over what had just transpired. No doubt Becky would be getting a right earful. What had just happened could change Marion's life permanently, it could put money in her pocket if she wished but it also would do one other thing—it would give her a clear conscience. It had been bothering her for quite some time, ever since she had drawn the conclusion that smoke and mirrors had been in play, so this could be a chance to exorcise that particular ghost. Becky was almost as shocked as Marion. She had thought it could all make quite a good book in its own right, but people would think it too far-fetched. Nevertheless, it was quite an experience for her. Marion was undeniably upset, Becky did her best to placate her, but she just wasn't in the right frame of mind for placating.

'So, what are you going to tell them tomorrow?'

'I don't have a bloody clue. Maybe tomorrow, after a good night's sleep, I'll see things clearer.'

Good night's sleep! Fat chance. After twenty minutes and yet another coffee, the two of them upped anchor and went their separate ways. It was the start of a rollercoaster ride and the brakes on it were faulty. Hold on, everybody!

Chapter 26

Walter's Healing Hands

It was the very thing Marion and possibly Mary could have done with. Mary had been absent for some time from the group and hadn't kept in touch, which was unusual for her. Walter had offered to practise and hone his newly acquired skills as a masseur, albeit an occasional one, and had offered free massages to the ladies at the book event. He had been given their business cards, or at least some of them; he had given Lucinda a call. She talked to Lizzie and a date had been set, the last Saturday in May at Lizzie's flat in Greenwich. Lucinda would come along and bring Gretchen, so Walter would get three for the price of one.

Massaging was quite strenuous work so he would need half an hour between each one to allow his hands to recover. The sisters travelled by train and brought Prosecco! Something to drink whilst waiting for the pampering session. Gretchen also brought a holdall full of stuff. Apart from a bikini, she had oils for massaging her own feet, and indeed anyone else's who wanted it, towels, a foot "grater" and other girly stuff. She obviously intended to make a day of it. They arrived at 1 pm and Lizzie was already prepared. All that was missing was the man himself. They spent the few minutes before his arrival questioning how wise this all was and agreed he was a harmless young man trying his best and the worst thing that might happen was him getting a stiffie.

One-thirty, the doorbell rang and there was Walter, huffing and puffing in with his fold-up table and his bag full of equipment. He, with some effort, had gotten everything up the fourteen steps to Lizzie's flat, a flat she would soon be putting on the market in order to find a place to live with Craig.

'Hi Walter,' shouted Lucinda as he entered. 'This is my sister, Gretchen. Hope you can handle three women in one day.' They all laughed, all that was except a slightly sheepish, red-faced young guy. Walter, for a minute, wondered what he'd gotten himself into and began to regret his somewhat rash offer a little.

Women together could be such bitches, such teases, particularly when they thought the guy might be a virgin.

Walter put up the table behind the couch near the kitchen entrance and emptied the contents of the bag. He obviously took this new venture very seriously and hoped to get some recommendations as a result.

'Would you like a Prosecco?'

He shook his head. 'Not a good idea for either me or you until after the massage. Dehydration and all that. You need to drink water before and after the massage.'

The girls promptly ignored this medical-based recommendation, opened the bottle and poured everyone a glass. 'Thanks for the advice, Walter. We'll take it under advisement,' said Lucinda as the three clinked their glasses in a *Salut*.

Meanwhile, Gretchen had been into her own bag and pulled out her accoutrements. She then went into the bathroom and came out in a dressing gown, hiding her bikini and wearing flip-flops. 'All set are we, then?' smiled Lucinda. 'Lizzie, you go first. Your place, after all.'

Walter considered which of the essential oils to start with. Each massage would take around forty minutes with a half hour recovery for himself. Lizzie also changed into her bikini and then Lucinda followed suit. If Walter's pulse wasn't a little racing, he mustn't have had one or he was gay. Walter knew fine well about his sexuality, he was definitely straight, and definitely his pulse, at the sight of three bikinied young women whom he was to fondle in a totally professional way (more's the pity, he probably thought) was not meandering along.

The TV was on with a low volume. Lizzie stood up and climbed up onto the table.

'What first, front or back?'

'Lie stomach down please.'

So, she did with her face over the blowhole.

'Don't be gentle with me, I quite like it rough!' Lizzie said, smirking, knowing how such innuendo would be playing out with this young guy. It was just playful banter, but she actually did prefer rough, deep massages rather than the beauty "tickles" that masseuses were inclined to give. Quite in character for Lizzie Spector.

It was quite hard to do small talk when you were getting pummelled on a massage table, but Lizzie did her best. Normally, after five minutes or so, it was done in complete silence except for the sisters gabbing away. There would be plenty of time to talk between massages. Pizza takeaway for lunch after her massage, she thought, and everyone was in agreement.

'I'm using sandalwood oil, by the way. Hope you like the smell.' They all did. They all could smell it. After finishing Lizzie's legs and feet, he moved up her back and shoulders.

'Oh, your back, such lactate lumps. You must be awfully uptight about things.'

That would be a first, Lizzie Spector tense! Maybe it was the job of trying to find out information about Ruby Latimer's ghost-writer or the impending nuptials. Probably a combination of both, or maybe that was just her natural state.

'It's this case. You know a lot of people in publishing, I expect, given your job. Have you ever come across any that uses someone else to finish off their work?'

Lizzie felt a distinct change of pressure in Walter's hands, if only for a couple of seconds.

'You mean a ghost-writer?'

'Yes, a ghost-writer.'

'Can't say that I have. Are you thinking of anyone in particular?'

Lizzie thought twice about prematurely dropping the name of Ruby Latimer. There was still over two hours of time to do so.

'No, just wondering. It must happen though.'

'It does. Why, just the other day…' and then he said, 'All finished.'

'That was awesome,' sighed Lizzie as she slowly stretched and then attempted to sit up on the table. Meanwhile, the sisters were listening, sipping and generally just chilling. Lunch.

Next up was Gretchen. The three girls were all lookers but Gretchen! OMG! No wonder George had a thing for her. Before Walter was finished with Lizzie, the sisters had been chatting between themselves and it was clear that Gretchen hadn't been briefed by her sister entirely about the ulterior motive in having the massage, that ulterior motive being to surreptitiously find out if the boy could shed any light on the Ruby Latimer ghost-writer, or maybe neither sister was a good listener. Anyway, as the ritual of wiping down the table, cleaning up, etc. before his next "guinea pig" was taken, the pizzas arrived. Walter joined the other three and as they sipped water and ate Hawaiian—Lizzie was paying and she liked it, so there! Small talk ensued.

'Nice place you have here, Miss Spector, Lizzie. Nice part of the Capital, Greenwich is.'

After five minutes of boring them, Lizzie asked him, 'Do you enjoy your job then? Sounds as if it must have its good points.'

'Job? Oh, you mean working for Mr Newell? It has its good points. Not really what I want to do for the rest of my days though.'

'And what would you like to do, be a professional masseur? You're good enough, you know. Got a firm touch and lovely moves.' Lizzie was trying to wind him up a bit downstairs, but she needn't have bothered, Gretchen would be doing it.

'I want to be a writer, but first of all, I need the experience, so I thought about editing.'

'Will you be doing that then?'

'I want to if I can persuade Mr Newell to let me try it out.'

The crux of the matter was that Walter was in a rut and wasn't likely to be getting out of it any time soon. The masseur thing was just another way of dealing with disappointment. It might also have been a way to meet women and then, who knows what. More hands on than the Valentino Dating link. He ate his pizza surrounded by three young women in bikinis and chatting. *It's a hard life but someone has to do it*, crossed his mind.

'Who's next then?' Gretchen smiled, stood up, stepped out of her flip-flops and walked towards the table. She had been talking quietly to her sister whilst Lizzie had been getting the works and had been talking unguarded about the "bogus book", which Walter must have heard her say. He couldn't have really missed it as at that juncture, he had been changing Lizzie's essential oil for another one and they hadn't been conversing. Gretchen was the best endowed of the three and Walter, unless he had ice water circulating instead of blood, could hardly have not noticed. He was a bit more enthusiastic about massaging Gretchen.

'I'm going to use eucalyptus and lavender, you happy with that combination?'

Gretchen, lying face down, just sighed a slightly erotic, 'Yes please,' and off he went. Lucinda and Lizzie sat, one looking forward to her shot and the other listening intently to the two behind her for any dropped nuggets from Walter who was as relaxed as his subject.

'So, what's a beautiful girl doing in a place like this?' He gave a slightly embarrassed giggle. 'No, really, what is it you do?'

'Not a lot. Looking for something interesting.'

'What do you like doing? Sport, dancing, computer games?'

'I read a lot.'

'So do I! Funny that. I love history and fiction. What do you read then?'

Lizzie listened to the conversation in the hope it might lead somewhere. In her three quarters of an hour, she had found that getting Walter talking had been a bit akin to pulling teeth. Maybe it was her sparkler that he had noticed and presumed that she was spoken for so was keeping his powder dry for a more promising candidate. The conversation behind her was starting to go somewhere interesting maybe. She looked at Lucinda and mouthed, 'Listening?' Of course, Lucinda was.

'For my sins, I'm the secretary of an author's fan club.'

'Which author?'

'Ruby Latimer,' and she could feel a difference in his massaging intensity on her back. 'That was why I was at that do last week held by her publisher.'

Gretchen sensed that something defensive had just happened from her masseur. 'Oh!' she groaned.

'Sorry, too hard then?'

'No, lovely. I like it hard, just how I like my men,' and giggled. Through her blowhole, Gretchen saw his crotch was full so no doubt it was just what happened when sexual innuendo came into play in such circumstances. In a few seconds, the swelling had disappeared.

'What do you think of her then?' Gretchen enquired.

'I like Miss Latimer; she's been good to me recently, very friendly.'

Lizzie was busy on her phone. She was sneakily recording the conversation and also texting Lucinda—yes, the person who sat next to her on the couch—follow-up questions when she finally got to get her massage.

"Might just find something useful. Guy knows RL." Behind them on the table, the conversation had turned to what Lizzie had been hoping and praying for—that book.

'Gretchen, how well do you know Miss Latimer then?'

'Well, I get to go to all kinds of things where she can turn up at (a bit of an exaggeration) so I suppose quite well.'

'I was wondering if you could do me a favour some time then?'

'What type of favour?'

'Could you ask her to mention to Mr Newell about me becoming an editor?'

'Who?'

'Arthur Newell, my boss.'

'Oh, OK. Will do if I get a chance. What did you think of her last book then? Kind of a strange way to end it, didn't you think?'

'I liked it. Quite good. Not her usual…'

'I didn't think it was like her normal thing either. If I didn't know better, I'd have said she hadn't—'

At that very moment, Lizzie shouted, 'Got much longer to go, you two?' in an attempt to forestall any drifting into that subject. She was successful.

'Just finishing up. What was that you were saying, Miss Turner, I mean, Gretchen?'

'I've lost my train of thought. Might get it back.'

And then the massage came to a relaxing end. Gretchen lay for a minute and then slowly sat up whilst Walter handed her a glass of water.

'Important to drink lots of water. Need to keep hydrated,' Walter said with the full authority of a novice but also of a young man who had definitely seen something that had taken his fancy. Gretchen went into Lizzie's bedroom to change back into her clothes. Lizzie followed her in and closed the door. Lucinda was busy offering Walter a cup of tea and chatting, distracting him from the whispers going on in the bedroom. Lizzie had set some questions for Lucinda who would be following up the line of enquiry Gretchen had quite accidentally begun.

A half hour later, Walter was set to…well, "set to" on Lucinda, who was every bit as pretty as her younger sister, but she was dark, not blonde, and smaller in other obvious ways as well. Men always seemed to be attracted to big breasts. She was less voluptuous but still drop-dead… Lizzie had texted her some follow-up questions emanating from the discussion her sister had inadvertently begun.

'What do you do…can I call you Lucinda?'

''Course you can, I'm a lawyer at Channel 8.'

'Oh! Interesting, is it?' and so the small talk continued. 'I'm chair of the Ruby Latimer Fan Club, but not for much longer.'

'Why's that?'

'Job is getting busy but not only that.'

Walter was massaging peppermint into the sole of Lucinda's left foot. Pretending she had heard him say something, 'Oh, because of that last novel. I'm not convinced it was all her own work. Nor is Gretchen, are you?' Gretchen nodded from the couch.

'I must admit that the last two times I saw Miss Latimer, there was a great change in her. The time before was at the start of the year and she wasn't very nice, but the last time she was very hospitable, made me tea, chatted, that sort of thing.' Ears on the couch pricked up.

'Have you read the book, Walter?' He nodded and tried to remain poker-faced.

'Do you think it was her?' Walter was still massaging Lucinda's feet and legs and felt her wince.

'Sorry, was that too hard? Feet can be sensitive. I recommend people going barefoot as much as possible, makes the feet receptors less...well, sensitive.' This was an obvious attempt to change the subject. Lucinda had no idea what he was on about.

'Walter?' Lucinda's pain had quickly subsided, and she was back on the case.

'It could have been, I suppose. She did seem to have been struggling with it and then, when she had come back from holiday—Switzerland, you know—she seemed happier, content that it was finished.'

Walter himself must have suspected something had changed. Her demeanour change must have alerted him to question her newfound inspiration. He might have put it down solely to the holiday. It must have been some vacation! It, in fact was, but for entirely different reasons.

'Did she say just where in Switzerland?'

'Davos, Lenovo something, I remember her saying.' That was a good lead. Something to go on. The massaging finished, and Walter packed up his things ready to leave.

'You're not leaving without this...' and £80 was placed in his hand.

'I can't, this was just practice for me, after all.' The women insisted.

'It was brilliant, you have expenses. If you give me your card, I'll see if anyone in the office fancies one.'

He gave each of them a card. Gretchen took it and took his other hand, saying, 'Wonderful hands you have, Walter. Why don't you give me a call and we might arrange another one sometime soon?' Gretchen was clearly attracted to this young man. Maybe he thought she was just being kind—she gave him her card as well—but who knows where these chance meetings could end up? The girls sat down again as the front door closed behind Walter.

'Davos, Lenovo…Hotel? Let's see what we can find out, shall we?' The game was definitely afoot.

Chapter 27

Kirsty Gets it On

Alf Grisham. Even by the rock bottom moral standards of this criminally dysfunctional lot, Alf took some beating! He had been locked up in one of the recently vacated Grisham family bedrooms three days previously in a state of utter "out your head" oblivion, drugs of one nature or another. The Grisham Corporation by design didn't deal in drugs, not through some high ethical principle, just that they were usually the domain of middle-class areas and users and their part of Orpington was distinctly working—and not working—class. God knew where he got the money for them, never mind who his supplier was. If Bob found out who that fucker was, it would be his last day breathing, let alone dealing.

The screaming and pleading had died down from the ear-splitting variety to low moans and despairing cries for water. His mother persuaded Bob to let her go and see him with bottled water and oh, what a sight! A grown man, dirty, smelly, bearded, red-eyed, clothes tattered, clearly in need of new trousers as his were soiled. A bucket had been left for him to defecate in but he hadn't bothered using it. His mum spent an hour with him, gave him liquids but no solid food as he might choke on it. After that, the waif was escorted downstairs to use the loo. Mrs Grisham went to make him a cup of tea but when she came back, Alf and £120 that had been sitting on the kitchen table had both legged it. He was a lost cause.

Bob was doubly enraged. It wasn't just about the money; he wanted Alf to tell him who the dealer was even if he had to beat it out of him. Brad might be of use after all. No doubt the man who could be laughingly called the Grisham black sheep would be found in the local pub toilet's cubicle with the dealer, buying £120 worth of something.

'That's the last time, Mum. He doesn't want or deserve help. He's had it.'

Mrs G was tearful. 'But he's our own flesh and blood. He's one of my babies.' Bob thought he more properly resembled skin, rags and bones. He thought he'd better leave it as he would only make matters worse. His idea of getting the dealer done over had a major flaw, several actually, starting with if the offending dealer was found and "dealt with", Alf would just find another one. Also, if the dealer was working for someone else, the whole thing could escalate. Bob decided to put it down to experience and get back to the business of extortion.

Kirsty Letts was walking up the High Street in Orpington when she noticed up a lane, something that vaguely resembled, in the widest sense of that description, a human being. It had legs and was lying near a couple of those big double-sized rubbish bins, sprawled over several full black bin bags. She recognised the person as Alf Grisham who she knew from some time in the past. He was clearly under the influence of something, drink or drugs, both most likely. She went over to him and smelt him. Dear god, what a fucking pong! His breath didn't smell of drink, so it must have been the other thing. She had been given Bob Grisham's mobile number after their last shag in the likelihood that he'd want to do her again. She thought out of courtesy (uh-huh), it might be a thought to tell him where his brother was.

Kirsty phoned Bob. Twenty minutes later, down he popped, picked up the deadbeat, stuck him in one of the Grisham cars and was off. He did something totally out of character then—he called Kirsty back to thank her for letting him know about his brother. It was Saturday and sister, Becky, had invited her up to her flat to have a few before they went out after nine. Becky wasn't any better at holding her drink as she was her tongue.

'Guess who I did today; only got a million brownie points from bloody Bob Grisham. Found his fucking brother up a lane, scooshed. Phoned him and he collected him. He owes me now.'

'His type never owes anyone; you should know that.'

'Yeah, but I think he might fancy me.'

'Fancies your fanny more like. His type? Only interested in humping. His ty—' Becky was already a bit advanced, drink-wise, and needed to sit next to her sister.

'And how did your meeting go with your literary lot in London? Thought you were at some do or other. Book launch or something.'

'Not a book launch, promotion. Ruby Latimer was up for an award and was just celebrating it, that's all.' Now Becky was about to say something that she would live to regret for the rest of her life.

'Bitch is a fake. Didn't write that book. Kidding us all on, she is.'

Kirsty's ears were now fully switched on. Becky recalled, blow by blow, the whole tale, the scene and the subterfuge over the very late book. Kirsty was a criminal novice, not having done much apart from shoplifting, but knew an opportunity when it presented itself to her. She listened intently to this story and reckoned that she may have something yet to discuss with Bold Bob, who was busy "interrogating" brother Alf about who sold him the drugs, and this time he wasn't getting out until Bob found out who the bastard was. Bob wanted to rid the borough of one particular drug pusher using his hired hand, Brad, to do so if necessary. It was both honour and business, honour in a vain attempt to save his brother's life, and business—drug pushers had a negative effect on his extortion business.

Meanwhile, sly Kirsty had already begun, in her mind anyway, to perfect a way to get money from a famous author, a way that would protect her from public exposure and disgrace. It would involve a partner and that was Bob Grisham. Off they both tottered, or should that have been tittered, to the pub. Becky was already well-oiled; Kirsty had the constitution of an ox as well as an agenda. Would he be there? No, he wouldn't.

Ten fifteen and there they sat alone, Becky and Kirsty. Usual scruffy lot, a few suits but mostly shirtsleeves. A couple of young guys came and sat next to them, trying their best to chat them up. Becky was well past that point, Kirsty distracted in the erstwhile hope that HE might still appear. The two lads looked up, went white as a sheet and stammered, 'Ju…just keeping your seat warm, Mr Grisham.'

Both scarpered in quick style. HE had arrived. On a chance meeting weeks ago, good sex, surprising gestalt and extricating brother Alf once more from the gutter, Bob thought she just might be there—and she was. He thought all he was likely to get that night was his leg over, but she had more to gain.

Just before chucking out time, the three of them left in a taxi back to Becky's place. Back at her flat, older sister slumped on the couch and was soon out of it. Kirsty was determined to do business before pleasure with this man, not "her" or indeed anyone's "man", just "this" man. Kirsty knew exactly what Bob had in mind, could feel what he had in mind but she wasn't to be deterred. First things first.

'Sis told me something that could be a real money-spinner.' She explained all about the author, her book written by someone else, portraying it as her own work and so on. 'Have you ever considered blackmail then?'

Bob shook his head. 'So why do you need me? Not really my scene.'

'Backup. She's loaded, and we could make a hundred grand or more. Might need your powers of persuasion.' Kirsty's "powers of persuasion" were not at all bad either. He was anxious to seal the deal in bed. Kirsty was as good to look at as she was with men coitally. The conversation continued with some amount of groaning, 'that's it, big boy', 'fuck me hard' and 'oh god, yes'. Kirsty got her desire and so did Bob. Meg Ryan knew a thing or two about faking it and so did she. They were going to blackmail Ruby Latimer out of £100,000 to not let the world know that she was an out-and-out fraud.

Kirsty had lifted her sister's phone, identified and captured the author's details to her own mobile. She would see Bob again soon and he had rather enjoyed the extra-curricular activity and would soon be branching out into blackmail. This would be a new venture for him, but it looked as if his new partner, whilst lacking somewhat in formal qualifications, was sly enough to work up a plan. Maybe Marilyn needed to become involved. It would be necessary to cover their tracks, work out how to deliver the ultimatum, arrange for payment, etc. Little did they know at this juncture that elsewhere, others were also busy gathering evidence to show up this devious woman. Both Bob and Kirsty individually lacked…well, class but together, they looked as if they might be able to pull it off. That was unless some others thwarted them by a public expose.

Lizzie had a plan. Lizzie was always planning something. Occasionally, she might share it but not often.

'Craig darling, can we have a break away?'

'Where would you fancy?'

'What about Davos in Switzerland? Supposed to be nice this time of year. You could learn to yodel.'

Chapter 28
A Busman's Holiday for Lizzie

Craig Endoran knew his fiancée well enough by then to suspect that the Davos trip might have an ulterior work-related undercurrent. Nevertheless, he thought it was a good idea. He'd never been and it would be good to get away for a few days. Lizzie, as you would expect, knew exactly where she wanted to stay and at that point, only she knew exactly why. He, as he would soon learn to understand, would find out things on a "need to know" basis. Need to know! He was the boss, for God's sake. He would be her husband soon and, with her express permission, the father of her babies. Nevertheless, she didn't want to reveal too much in case it all failed to live up to the promise she hoped for.

Lizzie had a game plan: talk to someone at the hotel who might remember Ruby Latimer and what she'd done there, who she'd talked to, etc. It could just be possible that there was a connection between the holiday and the ghost-writer. It was a jigsaw and she needed to find several missing pieces of it. The C8 couple travelled business class, got a taxi to the hotel and checked into their room, not a suite like the author had done. Lizzie wanted to start off investigating straight away.

'Just want to check out this fab hotel.'

Right. Craig, there exclusively on holiday, wanted to fool about with his fiancée a bit. She relented. She had taught him about his mouth and she certainly knew alternative uses for her own, not just for eating.

After an hour of fun, Lizzie got off the bed, walked into the bathroom to brush her teeth, put her shoes and knickers back on and said, 'Craig, why don't you have a bath? I'm away on a walk to see what they have here.' What she really wanted to do was go to reception to see if anyone could tell her anything. Receptionists, all five of them, and not one recalled a Ruby Latimer, author, having stayed here in February, even though it had been only a few months before. The hotel attracted many more famous celebs. Disappointed, she entered the swish bar, swish, Swiss bar! To have a cocktail and ask one of the staff members if they remembered Ruby. One did but it wasn't a lot of good.

'The lady was never here but I remember that she liked the spa. Someone there might know.'

Lizzie thought to go there but having looked at her watch, an engagement present from Craig, she thought that maybe she too should have a bath and dress for dinner. She had time to find out more throughout the week. At least it was the right hotel.

'When will you tell me the actual reason we're here, darling?'

Lizzie was going to once she had a lead. Craig was a good man, her boss as well as lover but she had a certain, secretive way of operating, mostly down to her time at Squawk FM and the clandestine background to that famous super injunction. She just couldn't change overnight to the more open culture of C8 but would definitely need to try. A marriage needed one to not hide behind lies and indiscretions, so she recognised that she'd better change and soon. Noted. She sat him down and explained to him what was going on.

'You're a strange one at times, Lizzie love. I'm not going to stop you doing great work for our company, am I?'

Lizzie just knew she'd made a terrible miscalculation not confiding in him. It, in different circumstances, could have led to real ructions but Craig wasn't that type of man.

'I'm sorry but—'

'…But you fancied a jaunt to Switzerland. You could have just come anyway as part of the job.'

'—But I was concerned about setting off alarm bells here and a wall of silence descending. This way I, we, can have a lovely time and I just might crack open the "mystery of the crooked author", or something like that.'

Craig at last saw the logic of where his cute – in more than one sense of the word – partner was coming from. It was for reasons like this that he'd fallen for her hook, line and sinker. He thought how much better suited they were compared to him and his ex-wife. Another passionate kiss just for good measure with him saying, 'Don't do that again,' and her saying, 'So sorry if I hurt you.' It would not likely be a marriage of equals; Elizabeth Spector was equal to no one. It could be a good one though.

After dinner, it occurred to Lizzie that maybe the staff members she'd talked to hadn't been on duty when Ruby Latimer had been around. If it had been post-World Economic Forum, it could have been that some were now on leave themselves or had been taken on purely for that week. She thought to herself that it was still worth looking around. She asked a waiter if they had staff away on leave after the event and he told her some but not restaurant staff. Had the author dined alone in their plush restaurant? It appeared she had. He remembered because she'd tipped well. Who else would have been about? Possibly Michelle in reception, most of the domestic staff had only been there for the event but senior ones were permanent. Lizzie was now hot on the trail. Michelle in reception was a smiling late-twenty-something, immaculately suited with manicured hands and straight auburn hair and red lipstick. The Swiss could be a mixture of lineages—Italian, German, French—but Michelle, despite her name, looked Italian and spoke immaculate English, which meant Lizzie didn't have to use her somewhat rusty French. Lizzie spoke all three languages plus Spanish. Michelle smiled at her.

'Yes, Miss Latimer, Room 509, I remember, one of the hotel's best.'

Michelle was tempted to ask why all the interest. Lizzie had an answer. She was president of the Ruby Latimer Fan Club and wanted to tell the RLFC Convention (!!!) that she had seen where their author had stayed. As good a fib as any.

Lizzie now knew that the author had, in fact, stayed here, had been in Room 509, had been to dinner, possibly had the same room staff as then. She determined that the next morning Craig could go do the spa whilst she camped out outside Room 509, hoping to talk to the maids to see if they could tell her anything about…well, anything.

After breakfast, they went back up to their room, he got his spa stuff; he'd also packed gym stuff as he had noted on the website that they had a great one and he did run occasionally. He also thought that as his lover had quite some libido, he'd need to get fit! Meanwhile, Lizzie went up to the 5th floor from their room on the 2nd to see if there was any activity. That was the floor of the deluxe suites. Certainly, there were linen-laden trolleys and wicker baskets with used silk sheets in them as well as some white uniformed women in white plimsols. Lizzie stopped one to ask her, but she only spoke French. In her best French, Lizzie explained her interest and wanted to know if she could take a couple of photos of the room, now empty and awaiting its next inhabitant. Having done that and thought, *Bloody massive compared to ours*, she asked the girl about Ruby Latimer. The girl had been on other duties but pointed to her co-worker who had serviced the room that week. Lizzie Spector closed in.

Lizzie hightailed it back to reception. Out of the lift, she slowed down, got back her breath, went back, waited for one of the receptionists to be free and asked her, 'Can I please get a massage?'

'The spa has its own bookings.'

'I was hoping to get someone called Lars. He comes in from outside. He was here for Miss Latimer. I would love to be able to say I got a massage from the same hands that massaged Ruby Latimer.'

The receptionist raised an eyebrow, thought this a bit obsessional but shrugged her shoulders and asked her, 'When would you like your massage?'

Lizzie decided it would cause too much suspicion if she seemed keen to have it too soon. As it was Monday and they still had six days left, she decided on Wednesday at 3 pm. Phew! That'd been hard but it looked as if she was getting a result after all. Her next move would need to be subtle if she was to get any info out of Lars. He may have known nothing. It might be a wild goose chase. At least this guy might get eliminated from her enquiries. *Right*, thought Lizzie, *my turn to get some pampering*. She got her stuff and headed for an hour and a half of swimming, Jacuzzi, steam room, general rejuvenation after a busy morning and a most productive one.

Lunch. Craig and Lizzie hit the restaurant. Both were famished from all that exercise and Lizzie was desperate to tell him about what she had found out.

'But darling, you've no evidence to say this Lars guy had anything to do with it. He might just be a masseur.'

'Call it intuition, darling.' *Sauce for the goose*, she thought, returning his endearing term. 'I just feel I'm on the right track. Anyway, Wednesday.'

The next two days, up until lunch on Wednesday, were spent chilling, having fun, great sex, just wonderful. Craig had now realised that sex was about pleasing his woman not himself. However…Lizzie was a difficult person to relax so she spent some time on considering her approach to culling information from the masseur. Just like her and the other two girls had done to Walter, there would be a way in to find out the source of the ghost-writer.

It was Wednesday, a quarter to three. Craig made himself scarce and left it all in Lizzie's more than capable hands. On the dot, the doorbell rang and there he was.

156

'Lars?'

'Yar. Mrs Spector?'

'Miss Spector. Please, just Lizzie.'

'Have a questionnaire before we start. Some medical questions,' and so Lars went through a list of questions.

'Are you pregnant or intending to become pregnant this year?' was one of the questions.

'No and definitely not,' Lizzie quickly responded indignantly, with her fingers crossed for good measure. She was always cautious. Some year maybe, but not yet. Questions about diabetes, heart disease, asthma, etc., all of them negatively answered. She was pretty healthy. The break was helping as well.

'So why did you request me to be your masseur?'

If Lizzie told him about Ruby Latimer, even if it was the big fib about the fan club, he would be on his guard. She had to improvise.

'I wanted the massage up in my room and the spa only did them downstairs. Michelle had mentioned you. Hope you don't mind. All those people staring. Ugh.'

Lars bought it. The massage was half over before Lizzie thought of another line of enquiry. 'Do you play any sports?' she asked.

'Table tennis. I'm quite good.'

This was an observational question as she had spotted a small table tennis bat-shaped cover in his masseur bag.

'So's my partner, fiancé, Craig. He'd love to play you, I'm sure.'

As it happened, apart from work and Lizzie, Craig did play table tennis so this one wasn't a lie. He played in a club in South London, Honor Oak Park. He was pretty good as well but his opportunities to play had dwindled somewhat due to work commitments; nevertheless, Lizzie pressed Lars.

'There are tables here, but no one seems to use them. Could you possibly spare time to give my fiancé a game after the massage? I'd appreciate it and would also like another massage on Friday if you are available.' Lars checked his diary on his phone.

'Same time on Friday. I've got some time now so if Mr Spector…'

Lizzie knew what to do next. A plan was coming nicely to fruition.

'Mr Endoran, Craig.'

'If Mr Craig wants a game now, I could meet him at the table tennis room in ten minutes.'

'I'll give him a call to let him know to meet you there.'

Lizzie phoned Craig to tell him the "good news".

'He'll meet you there. If you want to leave your stuff, table and the like here, you can get them when you're finished.'

Lars went away, leaving everything. Lizzie closed the door behind him and urgently phoned Craig.

'He's on his way down. Keep him busy. I need to see if he's got anything of use—searching his property? Course I bloody am! What kind of a journalist do you think I am? Ethical! If I turn up anything, I'll capture it on my phone. Keep him there as long as possible and text me when he's beaten you... He will beat you; I think... Yes, I know you're quite good. Bye, lover.' And with that the hunt was on for something, anything, that might be of use.

Lars had left everything in Lizzie's room except his table tennis bat, intent on returning after crushing Craig. As soon as he'd left, she locked the door and searched his masseur bag, but it was just oils, towels, talcum, etc. He had a man bag that she searched but nothing. Her Swedish, or was it Swiss, wasn't really much to write home about, so finding something of use might be a translation nightmare. She photo-captured what she could in the hope it might lead somewhere. Surprisingly, he'd left his phone. Lizzie noticed that he'd failed to lock it as well. She leafed down his phone numbers, capturing them. There were over one hundred, so some work was required. She went back to the man bag once more just as a text came through, "He's on his way back".

Lizzie was in a panic. She put everything back as it had been, left his phone exactly where it was and was doing the same with the man bag when she noticed a zipper to a pocket she'd missed in her haste. She opened it and a dozen business cards were inside. She took out one, photographed it, turned it over and did the back, put it back and just then there was a turn of the door handle, then a knock on her door.

'It's Lars.'

She opened the door. Everything had been put back exactly where it had been.

'Who won?'

'Oh, I did. Your lover is very good, but I play a lot.'

Lizzie had only heard one person describe Craig as lover before—herself. Swedes were so unrestricted. He packed up and left. As he was out the door, she closed it behind him, turned her back, leaned on the door and slid down it, feeling the full effect of the adrenaline rush. There was a knock at the door. Lizzie jumped, startled. 'Lars again. Forgot something,' and in he came to collect his man bag. 'See you on Friday,' and this time, he was definitely gone. Lizzie had some work to do.

Lucinda had left work for the day, but Lizzie called her up to give her the tasks for the following day.

'I know that you're busy, but this is a priority. I've phone numbers and a card that might unlock this whole bloody fiasco.'

This all was putting a bit of a strain on a burgeoning relationship but luckily Lucinda rearranged some copyright document proofing and allowed herself to do Lizzie's work. It was a matter of getting information checked on the Internet, but it would take time and knowledge of where to look. Lucinda had gotten information on over eighty of the numbers but the most interesting thing she had was the card. "GW" was on it in big letters on the top left-hand side of it and a phone number, which, if traced, could reveal a mountain of information if only GW meant what she hoped it might. Lucinda was speculating whether to give the number a call but if it was who Ruby Latimer had gotten to finish her book, it could put them on their guard, have them change numbers and alert customers of a security breach. The number had been put through their database, but the result had been negative. Some international numbers could be bounced all over the planet and this was just such a one. Lizzie might need more information on Lars. If that was what was needed, then so be it.

Chapter 29
Massaging Out the Truth

It was the start of June. Time for another sojourn to their favourite coffeehouse at Charing Cross. It wasn't normal for there to be a meeting of the "Post-Rowlingite Sisterhood", which was as good a name as any, Abigail thought. Anyway, the reason for the meeting was that by her calculations, pregnant Mary was due fairly soon and just couldn't get her on the phone. Abigail was the most "mumsy" of all the women, being in fact the only mum of the lot of them, so thought an extraordinary session of PRS was needed.

Mary had been called, texted, no response. Her friends were keeping their fingers crossed for her and the baby boy she was so unexpectedly carrying. It was as if she didn't want to keep them up to date. Maybe something dreadful had happened. Maybe she had miscarried or was dead! Oh God, what a thought. The reason a very worried Abigail had called them together was to see if anyone had any information on her or knew if there was a contact address. They knew she lived in Windsor so that was a start.

'That guy, Walter, might be able to help. He works at the agency, so we could see if he could get us her address.'

'That old bugger Arthur won't,' Becky retorted, now in a fun-loving mood, something that happened in the warmer weather apparently. 'And how do we contact Walter? Telepathy?'

'Phone,' and Becky got out his business card—Walter Sims—Masseur.

At the Ruby Latimer reception, Walter had been trying to get women to be massaged by him as a freebie for some practice. None of the editors had bothered to phone but now they had a reason. A case of "you massage my back and I'll scratch yours". He could get Mary Callan's address in return for massaging one or more of the women. He'd have actually done it without the massage bit but, hell, if they were offering. Becky called him up, explained about what they needed, fixed a date for him to come out to Orpington and that was that. Abigail was the least keen of the three, Becky the keenest and Marion somewhere in between. Abigail had never been massaged in her puff, not even a foot massage. You'd have thought her hubby might have obliged at least once but no, she hated being touched, especially on her feet. Becky actually loved it and thought she'd ask her sister if she fancied it as well. Fate was now in the building.

That weekend, Walter huffed and puffed into Becky's recently spruced up flat in Orpington with all his paraphernalia to be met by three women—Becky, Marion and Kirsty. Abigail, true to form, had been a no-show. The massaging had been fairly uneventful. Becky and Marion had gone first and second. Walter was starting to get the hang of it all and would start to charge in future. After Becky was done, he gave her a bit of paper with all the details they would need to find Mary Callan. Kirsty, however, had been listening to the small talk of the other two and had worked out that this guy knew Ruby Latimer. They all seemed to. She got her chance and decided to vamp it up a bit in order to see if she could excite the young man who in turn may be a fount of information.

'So, you like women, do you, Walter?'

'Oh yes, I do actually,' he replied without even a hint of a blush.

'You like touching us, rubbing us. We like men doing it to us. It's so sexy.'

Walter found this line of conversation a bit disconcerting and made it hard for him to concentrate. The other two women returned from the kitchen with cups of tea.

'I'm…I'm just learning a new skill, that's all.'

'Bet that's not all eh Walter,' Kirsty said and giggled. He thought it was just because her soles were sensitive. This was just self-delusion. He needed a glass of water as he had started to sweat. He now had a proper boner that Kirsty was fully aware of as he massaged her neck and she could hardly not notice it through the blowhole.

'I just need to go to the toilet for a minute,' and promptly went there. He was several minutes in, during which time both Becky and Marion remonstrated with Kirsty not to taunt him, he was a nice boy. Kirsty was planning to use her undoubted attributes and talent for information gathering. Walter returned, smiling a certain relieved smile, trousers now back to normal—as if they didn't know what he had been doing in there—and continued the massage. As he finished off, tidied up and was about to leave, Kirsty said to him, 'My number, give me a call if you're not too busy.'

He looked surprised but took it and in a spirit of reciprocation, he handed her one of his business cards. He began to think he was attractive to women after all. He now had contact with two!

Walter Sims, still a virgin, just, had been given the biggest "come on" he'd up to then ever experienced. He was still shy and awkward in their presence. Some women warmed to this type of guy. In Kirsty's case, however, she saw an opportunity to get info from him about Ruby Latimer. He was always a racing cert to phone her. He called her the next day. He saw her on Wednesday. He lost his virginity that day whilst Kirsty Letts got the address and phone number of Ruby Latimer in return. For her, it seemed a fair swop; for him, he'd have given her the entire Central London phone book. Mind you, given his lack of sexual experience, she did give him extra time to let him get all those years of sexual frustration released. After that, he would have done anything for her. If she'd have said, "kill such-and-such", he would have. Sex was such a powerful weapon at times, particularly when in the wrong hands. Kirsty's hands had been full all night and she now had the information to do to Miss Latimer what Walter had done to her several times that night.

Unknown to Becky Letts, her sister was proceeding with a plan to blackmail their "favourite" author. Becky, Marion and Abigail had their own agenda: to see whether their pregnant associate was OK. Had she given birth yet? If so, were she and her new-born son doing OK? The lack of contact was worrying. Mary had been so joyous the last time they had met her. They hadn't expected to see her at their last meeting but no contact at all was out of character. Marion called Abigail and the two arranged for a visit to Windsor to see what they could find out. Abigail drove down from Eynsham on Saturday morning, picked up Marion from Windsor train station and then, using her Satnav, drove to the address Walter had given them—18 Orchard Drive.

They arrived at the house about noon. It looked deserted, possibly because it was. They rang the doorbell and knocked at the door for a full ten minutes to no avail. Abigail's mind began to race. She imagined the unimaginable, that Mary was dead along with her unborn child. A neighbour heard them and came out to see what they wanted. Marion went over and talked to her. George and Mary had gone to the local maternity that very morning. Maybe Abigail had jumped to the entirely wrong conclusion.

Twenty minutes later, the two arrived at the maternity unit. Marion went to reception.

'Has Mary Callan been admitted?'

'What for?'

'Having a baby!'

Marion had to control herself as given that it was a maternity unit, it would be hard to be admitted for an ingrown toenail! A quick check of the records and there it was. Yes, she had been admitted at 10 am. No, she hadn't had the baby yet. Yes, she had started labour. No, they had no idea when she was likely to give birth or even indeed if she had. The women were in a quandary. Abigail knew that the act of giving birth could take hours, even days. As a first-time and older mum-to-be, Mary could be in labour for quite some time and there might be complications. One thing was certain, they wouldn't be seeing her that day anyway. Abigail went back in herself, and after talking a while with the woman at reception, came out having got a ward telephone number and writing out a message for Mary to phone her when it was convenient. She remembered having her own kids and how it was never bloody convenient. Thwarted, the three decided to call it a day and returned to Windsor Station to get their train and Abigail returned to Eynsham. A quick coffee in the station was called for, first of all.

'I still don't know why she didn't call us back,' sighed Abigail. 'I mean, it wouldn't have taken much to tell us how she was doing.'

'Maybe George had her in confinement,' suggested Marion.

'Confinement! A bit OTT for these days,' Abigail scoffed whilst Becky just looked confused.

'What's confinement?'

'In days gone by, women would spend the last month of their pregnancy in bed. They thought it a good precaution. George might have insisted she do something similar and who knows. She might not even have had her mobile turned on.'

This explanation from the older woman did the trick and reassured everyone, including herself, that everything was in order. They would try contacting Mary again in a week or so.

Kirsty sat on her bed in the dilapidated HMO (House of Multiple Occupation) in a rundown part of Orpington, which she seemed to be destined to inhabit forever, that Wednesday after her "guy", Walter, had departed with a smile wider than the Thames. He was no longer a virgin and oh, how much of a relief that was. He was infatuated with this Kirsty Letts, he thought, but it was in fact nothing more than the result of their congress and his, as it transpired, misguided thought of love masquerading as sexual attraction. He thought she returned his love when she was intending to turn him and his author over.

Kirsty sat on her bed, put the spent condoms in a bin and hoped that no one had been around to hear them for the last hour. All the time Walter had been doing her, she had been imagining how much her share of the blackmail money would get her. At least she would be able to move out of this grubby little shithole, room and shared kitchen, toilet and filthy communal shower. The information he had given her in between rumpy-pumpy and random snippets of stuff about Ruby Latimer had been surreptitiously recorded on her smartphone, unnoticed by Walter. Kirsty thought to delete the sexually explicit bits, but on reflection thought it might be able to be used in some instance, maybe to "encourage" Walter to get more information for her. She knew she had him hooked and he knew he was. Poor Gretchen. She who hesitates…

Meanwhile, an invite had arrived through the Hounslow letterbox of Ruby Latimer. "AFC Scimitar Annual Awards. Miss Ruby Latimer plus partner are cordially invited to be present…" PARTNER! Ruby had no intention of bringing anyone with her. She had never done so in the past, although this was the first award nomination she'd been to as a real contender for the prize for a decade so just maybe she should consider taking—the doorbell rang.

'Walter! And to what do I owe this pleasure?'

Chapter 30

Slave to the Rhythm

'Miss Latimer, I was asked to deliver this envelope to you. I have no idea what it's about.'

Ruby opened the letter. It was another invite to the AFC Scimitar event.

'Oh, I just got one of these just now. Must have sent it to Arthur as well as myself. Naturally, I'll be going. Thank you.'

Ruby wasn't a spontaneous person, at least, she never had been much of one, way too calculating.

'Mr Newell said that Mr Walsh would appoint someone to chaperone you to the event.' Wrong words, wrong time. Just plain stupid. Ruby was unhesitatingly on the blower to her agent.

'Arthur, what's this about me getting a bloody chaperone to the awards ceremony? It's as if I don't know how to behave. I'm not having it. This is MY invitation, MY plus one and MY choice. Tell that...that...that man I'm taking...taking...' She was taking just who? 'taking...Walter?' ('What's your bloody other name, son?' she whispered.) 'Walter Sims as my...my fucking chaperone.'

She hung up as you only could do with effect on a landline. Walter was, if anything, more shocked at this side of the author than the author was at her presumption that she could just click her proverbial, and actual, fingers and he'd come running. It was all too much. Walter was red in the face. He was being used as some kind of pawn in a test of strength. Inwardly, he was enormously flattered, of course, but he then thought it might not do his career chances at his place of work a great deal of good if it was seen that he was Ruby Latimer's "pet poodle".

The strength of her adamantine response and of Walter's clear embarrassment at being the rope in a tug of war was appreciated but ignored by

Ruby Latimer. She only saw that this was HER award ceremony and she would decide who accompanied her. End of. Her phone rang again.

'Ruby darling, Greville. Sorry to hear you don't want Dave Scott to go with you to the AFC. He was really looking forward to it as well.'

'YOU FUCKING…ASKED HIM BEFORE HAVING THE FUCKING…COURTESY TO TALK TO ME!'

And so, the conversation, correction, one-sided shouting match, correction, castigation continued with more expletives raining down from Ruby Latimer's mouthpiece. Greville was trying to explain that he didn't know that she had anyone to go with her so out of consideration he had…oh dear. When you were dealing with an ego the size of a planet-killing asteroid, then you needed to be somewhat more diplomatic than Greville had been. Walter was her plus one and that was that. By this time, the young man had just about had enough. He was the one now who needed a massage, let alone give anyone else one. Out of misplaced gratitude, he said the words he would mull over from time to time, interspersed with the expression "stupid fucking bastard", topping and tailing it.

'Miss Latimer, you are really tense. You need a massage to relax you. I have just…' You could guess the rest. 'I'll be back tomorrow with my massage table.'

Despite all appearances to the contrary, Ruby Latimer wasn't out of control. She was now in the prime of life, highly successful, about to win a major literary award, or so she expected, what could be better. Sex? She thought long and hard. She was in that age bracket where women were usually looking anxiously at their fertility and either giving conception a final fling or a first go. Some women had no interest in it at all, or so it was said. Ruby thought about being responsible for someone apart from herself, partner or offspring, and thoroughly rejected it— until that phone call. It had hammered home her self-imposed solitude in life. She was asking a twenty-something she hardly knew to what was about to be a high point in her career—receiving a prestigious award. He was a nice chap but in reality, almost a total stranger. She had now made her bed and would have to lie in it. She thought to herself, *I hope he's good at massage. Oh Lars!* She looked at the little compact and the gift he had given her. She mused.

Walter would be back on Friday after his work and whilst he was still living at home, like most young men, he hoped to be independent, but London flat prices! Ayeyiyi! Totally, completely, out of the question. Even renting was out of his range. He was now a fully-fledged "man", thanks to the tender, actually pretty rough, ways of Kirsty Letts. He knew, or thought he knew, the mechanics of intercourse but then didn't all men think that! He knew that he would be laying hands on this precious, glamorous, famous woman and didn't want to disappoint her. *Condoms?* he thought. *Better take a couple just in case.*

It was now a week before the award ceremony. Walter was always well-dressed but depended on his folks for his suits, shirts, ties and shoes. When he was doing his masseur thing, he would have a change of uniform in the boot of his old car. It was the day he had promised to massage Ruby Latimer, the day after the telephone battle-royal during which she had taken no prisoners. Ruby was, by the early evening of that Friday night, back in control of herself, thoughts of men, sex, procreation back in their box, only thoughts about the one person in her life that really mattered a jot. Walter rang her doorbell. She was already ready and waiting, robe, slippers and so on. Walter started to fantasise about just what he might be going to find under that robe, then pulled himself together. This was a pro bono professional consultation and treatment session. He started with the usual question about her heart, diabetes, asthma, etc.

'Are you pregnant or intend to become pregnant?' Wrong bloody question. She did actually seem to momentarily hesitate before answering in the negative. It appeared a massage posed no health risks.

'Can you make it a hard, sports one please? Yesterday was draining.' A hard, sports one it would certainly be. So, there they were, Walter in the bathroom putting on his masseur's "whites", having laid out the table and taken out his essential oils. He was ready and when he emerged from the bathroom, apparently so was she!

Lying on the table on her stomach, her head through the blowhole, was an inspiring sight of some real beauty. Walter was sharp-eyed, he'd noticed something straight off. She was completely naked. This for him was almost a first experience of seeing a woman totally naked like this, let alone a famous one. Kirsty Letts, OK, but she hadn't been on his table. Well, come to think of it…never mind. Yes, he'd massaged others, but they'd worn bikinis. This was a woman on his massage table, without any encouragement, starkers and still. He gulped. And famous. Why? This hadn't happened before. Maybe it was normal for the famous to be uninhibited.

Walter hesitated for a few seconds, then he began. He did his usual massage, starting on the back and neck—her shoulders had Matterhorn lumps, Switzerland had a lot to answer for—moving down to her feet and legs; the bits that were freaking him out a lot were the parts in between! He partly felt like saying to her, Right, Miss Latimer, that's you done,' but he knew she wasn't and so did she. He fumbled about in his bag for some bergamot essential oil.

'I trust you're going to give my arse a good seeing to,' she mumbled quite audibly.

Fuck, he thought, *what have I gotten myself into here*? He was about to lay his hands on this woman's firm, white, naked buttocks, the rest of her being bottled bronze. He began, a bit gingerly at first, but she then mumbled something about, 'That's nice but I want it harder. Give a good rumble up. I can take it.'

So, he did what she asked. He was sweating more than she was by now. He was getting more perturbed, not a little aroused, and very aware of how she seemed to be manipulating the situation, one where he had no option but to continue.

Walter was no longer a virgin, but as someone about to go "where no other man had gone", well, not presumably for decades anyway, he was in that respect still a virgin.

'If you go into that pink bag on the table, you'll find something that might be of use.'

Walter was having palpitations; his particularly sweaty, bergamot-scented hands opened the pink bag and picked out this small pink device. He wasn't that much of a novice not to recognise it and what women needed it for.

'I just need to go to the toilet for a second.'

He did, placed his back against the door and pondered what to do. If he refused, it could go badly for him; if he didn't, he would be hers to do what she pleased with him thereon in. Rock and a hard place, metaphorically speaking. Maybe not so metaphorical!

'Just putting on more essential oil.' Walter had decided. He would go where "no man had gone recently" and take the pink thing with him! The rest was what she needed to get over the day before. He heard her mutter 'Oh Lars' once. Clearly, whoever this Lars was, he had done it to her as well, could possibly have even given her the toy. After ten minutes, where she had clearly gained something missing in the orthodox massage, he slapped her backside hard and said, 'Now, please turn over.'

This she did. He could hardly believe he'd just slapped the butt of a multi-millionairess. This woman was so well preserved, he observed.

Walter admired her at close range, purely professionally of course, before pulling himself out of the mental kamikaze death dive and concluded the massage and that little "requested" extra—like he had a choice—with a little detailed instruction from the recipient. He had "finished her off", in a manner of speaking. She obviously must have known the state of sexual excitement she'd created and left this young man in without relief. Surely. Tough.

'Walter, do you have formal dress for next Saturday?'

He'd completely forgotten he needed it and shook his head. She gave him a card for a gentleman's tailor where he could rent the whole package. She told him to tell them to send her the bill. 'Now I need to run a bath,' she said. 'Could you put "that" back where you got it?' She went into the bathroom and he could hear water running. He went to put the toy back and on opening the small bag noticed a card inside it. He took out his camera and photographed it and the bag it was in. The card said "GW".

Walter left and was in need of some urgent, serious sexual release due to the entire event. He thought it would have been done for him by the author but obviously, it had been beneath her to do so.

'Kirsty, are you busy tonight? You are! Oh well it was just that I have something to show you…on my phone, of course.'

'If you make it quick.'

He'd every intention of making it quick. He drove from Hounslow to Orpington like Lewis was behind the wheel. He got there. She opened the door to her bedsit. 'Please,' was all he could say. She sensed desperation and felt it in his trousers. She just let him. He didn't speak for ten minutes. He had a lot to unload, literally. She knew something must have sparked it off and just closed her eyes and thought… When he was done, she said, 'Wow, I take it you needed that. Hope it was worth it.'

'It was. Look what I got for you,' and got out his phone. She saw it, the initials and the phone number and hugged him again. Her lack of formal education hadn't deprived her of the power of observation and deduction. She knew instinctively what it must have meant. She captured it on her phone. Phone to phone made it a bit blurry but it was readable.

'You're some fucking guy. Can you text that to me just now, image didn't come out too well.' This he did. Walter wasn't sure he'd done the right thing, given it was spontaneous and borne out of a huge sense of sexual relief and the need to justify himself being there. Kirsty had places to go that night, one being a rendezvous with Bold Bob. She was now quite raw downstairs, due to the unexpected seeing to she'd just had. Foreplay hadn't been on Walter's agenda. It wasn't rape because she hadn't said no, not that she'd been given much of an alternative. It had been much brisker than the first time when she had led the charge. He'd made her bleed just a bit—and no protection this time. Lucky she always protected herself. Satisfied, his breathing returning to normal. As Walter prepared to leave Kirsty asked him if he was about the following weekend.

'No. Didn't I tell you, off to this big award do with Ruby.'

She contained herself until he left, then did an almighty raver dance to thank whichever god seemed to be looking out for her. The plan was moving ahead.

Chapter 31

First of All, I'd Like to Thank...

Walter mused whimsically to himself, *One woman I really like but don't know well, one who is great at sex and another that I'm now more or less the sex slave of. Oh well. Isn't life bloody strange!* Life had taken a turn for...hard to say. Opportunities were presenting themselves left, right and centre, but were they the appropriate opportunities? What did he actually want from life? Did he know? Walter Sims had started out as mild-mannered reporter Clark Kent and had now morphed into bloody Superman, minus the cape. Women needed him, it seemed, for sex maybe, being pleasured apparently, who knew what would be around the corner! After the AFC Scimitar Awards, what would happen between him and Ruby Latimer? What if she won? What if she didn't? He could see himself in a predicament. What about Kirsty? What about Gretchen? Gretchen Turner would be an oasis of normality compared to the sexual madhouse he'd experienced. Funny old world!

It was Monday morning and he'd just arrived at Arthur Newell, literary agent's office. He'd no more than walked through the door, hadn't even had a chance to take off his coat, when Arthur's secretary said, 'He wants to see you—now!' Very ominous it sounded. Now, in a virgin, unsure of himself, this may have fazed him. Things were different now. He had a confident spring in his step that could only come from his change in sexual experience status. Walter kept on his coat and went in to see Arthur, certain in the knowledge that he was about to be fired for...well, whatever he'd been doing with Ruby Latimer.

Arthur was in his seat at an angle to the young man, smoking his favourite cigar which he did only on special occasions. Walter wondered if firing an employee was one of them. 'Sit,' he instructed the lad—Walter would always be a young lad to Arthur. 'I hear you're going to the awards on Saturday.'

Walter nodded, expecting the next words to be, "not on my shift, you're not. Collect your cards on your way out".

'I'll see you there then. Ruby will be coming by limo and you'll be in it. Don't know how you did it but, champion lad.'

Walter had forgotten the private rivalry, even when making money, between Arthur and Greville, though neither would ever admit it. Arthur looked at it thus: Walter, his employee, had...well, for lack of a better expression, "pulled" Ruby Latimer, and that had pissed off Greville. Arthur cared not a jot how or why, it was a coup and that was that. 'Thank you, Mr Newell,' and then, 'Have you reconsidered about me becoming an editor at all?'

Arthur puffed on his Havana, deep in thought. 'As it happens, one of our editors is missing in action. If you fancy a trial period, you can take over her roster. Want to give it a go?'

Walter smiled and, completely out of character, stood, went over to his boss, took his hand and said, 'You won't regret it, Mr Newell.'

'Better bloody well not, sonny. Will get one of our veteran editors to show you the ropes.'

Life just gets better and better, Walter thought whilst he considered immediate retirement from massaging. It was too complicated.

The AFC Scimitar Awards were very prestigious. Only the good and the great were allowed to attend. They pre-dated Man Booker and were considered by some the "Bentley" to Man Booker's "RR". Walter was going in a Bentley limo with his famous author, her in a Stella McCartney, him in a very smart dinner suit, bow tie, great cut, patent leather shoes, silk socks. He'd even gone to get a more appropriate hairstyle, courtesy of the author.

Saturday was less than a week away and he hadn't had time to figure out what Kirsty had wanted that information for. He realised that he may never know. Kirsty was more than a memory; she'd shown him how delightful the physical side of a relationship could be—he still harboured the illusion that they were having such a thing. Now he'd fulfilled one objective with her and seemed to be on his way somewhere. He now appeared to be under the tutelage of Ruby Latimer. This was also an illusion. Both women had their own, very different agendas, in which he was playing a supporting role, one a spy and one as...well, masseur! It was like being a double agent. Both had gotten something out of him whilst he had gotten some sort of advancement as a kind of quid pro quo. As Saturday approached and he kept remembering Kirsty, he thought he'd better try to see her before the event. He phoned her and arranged to pop over on Thursday night. He apologised if he'd left her sore after their last encounter. She told him to forget it, she'd already gotten over it. He did pop over. They did it again. He did need it. After all, he was a man!

Friday night, Kirsty saw Bob and this time it was truly only business.

'Had that creep Walter over again. He's very useful. He'll do anything I ask. I've got this author, Ruby Latimer or something, fiddling her readers, getting some other tosser writing her book for her and kidding on that it was her all along. I've a copy of a card he found with the phone number of the guy on it. Now we strike. A hundred grand split down the middle. He's delivering the note to her at some fancy fucking do they're going to tomorrow. I've worked it all out. She'll be shitting herself when she reads it.'

This was quite a departure for Bold Bob who didn't feel at all at home doing something that didn't involve threatening or injuring someone. Money gathering shouldn't be that easy. It was a bloody crime but not as he normally committed it! Kirsty had showed her acumen at robbery. She'd planned it all out. Where to get the money, how to remain undetected, what to do with the cash, money laundering, etc. She was so good she could have been a Grisham. Not all Grishams. Bob resolved if it came off, he'd break a golden rule—again seemingly—and involve someone not of the family in their doings. He'd forgotten about Bradley.

'How's the note to be delivered then?'

'The guy. He hasn't a clue what's in it, just that she should get it once they are at the award thingy, and not a second before.'

'And how do you know he'll do it?' Kirsty put on an expression that he had seen on his young sister Linda. If it meant the same thing, it was connected to sexual power over a man and that the guy knew what he wouldn't be getting again if he messed up. 'Oh. I get it,' he said.

Saturday arrived. 6 pm. Silver Bentley and chauffeur, complete with a stunning Ruby Latimer, drew up outside the family home of Walter Sims. Out he stepped, complete with a large-ish bouquet of roses…well, what else, for his hostess. In he got and the Bentley set off, destination: Guildhall. They exchanged small talk, him complimenting her, her saying nothing reciprocal, apparently having returned to her default. She was more likely thinking about the acceptance speech she had rehearsed.

Her chances of winning were by all accounts pretty high and she was the bookies' favourite, if only slightly. The car pulled up and the chauffeur opened the door. Out she stepped, dark blue chiffon dress, matching blue shoes, hair immaculate, sunglasses. You'd have thought it was a film premier, not a book award event. Then out came Walter. The paparazzi had been taking photos the second she had emerged, then out stepped…who? They had expected someone they knew. They got Walter Sims. He was totally uncomfortable being in the spotlight but reckoned he could handle it. After all, her was her handsome toy boy. He'd had a pretty good week so far and this was the culmination of it.

They went, arm-in-arm, up the impressive stairway, then off to a large anteroom where champagne was handed around whilst "dahling", "fab-u-luss", "rarthur" and other hoity-toity expressions abounded the place. The only thing Ruby did was to whisper in Walter's ear, 'How should I introduce you?'

'What about literary associate?' he suggested.

'Literary secretary sounds much better,' and that was who he was for the evening. She talked to several other authors nominated in minor prize categories, children's author, best short story, etc. She was as nice as ninepence to them whilst secretly despising most as lesser beings. Occasionally, she would deliver a backhanded compliment, 'You're looking well after that messy divorce', 'Can I get the number of your plastic surgeon?' Comments to which there was little to come back at. 'Just softening them up for their big disappointment later,' she whispered. Then she saw Arthur, Greville and their wives.

Dinner at the Laurel Publishers' table with sixteen of them, including Greville and his wife, Arthur and his wife, Ruby, masseur—sorry, literary secretary—plus other senior management from the publishing group. Gretchen Turner, despite major misgivings, as the secretary of the Ruby Latimer Fan Club, had also made up the numbers, seated four seats away from Walter. As the saying went, Gretchen scrubbed up well. She had missed the drinks and had been the last to take her seat, sandwiched between a couple of old codgers who by that time were pretty merry.

The first course of five came and was consumed, the champagne, likewise. By the time of the final course, they were all stuffed, quite a few were also pissed. Just then, Walter remembered. 'I was asked to give you this, Miss Ruby,' and handed her the envelope, which she looked at before opening. She read the short note with cut-out letters and a photo of the card on it. She went extremely silent.

'Excuse me all, will you?'

Ruby went to the toilet with the note clutched in her hand. Twenty minutes later, she returned, still silent.

'So, what was it about then?'

Walter may have delivered it, may have sought information to give to Kirsty, but still had little appreciation that he had been used in a less than sophisticated blackmail attempt. By then, it was about time for the ceremony to begin. Her award would be the last presented. She tried hard to concentrate on the business in hand. It took some amount of concentration! Five other awards were given, then it came to "Outstanding Contribution in Fiction Writing". The nominees were read. The envelope was opened.

'And the winner of the AFC Scimitar Award for Outstanding Contribution in Fiction Writing is…Ruby Latimer, *Heavenly Hell*, Laurel Publishers.'

The table erupted. The whole place also erupted, with the odd notable exception sitting down, presumably those who either knew what she was really like suspected that something wasn't totally kosher. Gretchen Turner politely clapped, remained seated. Ruby was backslapped, not that she liked it, and shook hands all the way up to the stage, accompanied by Greville. Getting kissed by the famous co-host and a wannabe actress who was presumably "friendly" with the owner of AFC Scimitar, Ruby was presented with the trophy in the shape of an open book in gunmetal and a cheque for £40,000. A good down payment on the blackmail. Taking the prize, Ruby forced a smile and took the mic.

'Thank you, Bernard, thank you, Rachael. I have been waiting many years for this moment. I've been writing for over twenty years and this is so sweet. Writing is a gift, but it's also a challenge. It challenges you to continue to come up with innovative storylines, epic adventures, heart-breaking relationships. I'm so lucky that I've always managed to find that ending. *Heavenly Hell*. Believe me when I tell you it was hell to write but now I'm in heaven. I hope that my next book will be better still. Till next year, thank you from the bottom of my heart.'

She was done. Inside, she wasn't close to being done. She hadn't started but then there would be the interminable photos and finally, the press conference. She was fine with the paparazzi. She had always been fine in that situation. Whilst Diana, Princess of Wales, had hated them, Ruby, Princess of Tales, loved 'em.

Then the media departed to get to their paper editors. It was at the press conference, with her Pretorian guard of Arthur, Greville and Harry Chase, Laurel

Publishers press officer, that Ruby, she now knew that someone was on to her, felt ever so slightly vulnerable and exposed. Every question from every angle was met with an uncommon wince. She was fully expecting that young fucker from C8 to pop up with a beezer of a question, just to force her hand. Elizabeth hadn't been there on account of the time of the month, sitting at home with a hot water bottle and paracetamols.

Whilst the press conference was on, Walter sat in the chair vacated by Harry. Gretchen seemed less happy than you would have expected.

'You do know that we all know she's a fraud.'

Walter, in his heart of hearts, knew it too. He'd been infatuated by the power, privilege and influence of her and her circle, but Gretchen had grown up and now realised that *Heavenly Hell* had not been all Ruby's work. 'Lizzie Spector is doing a big expose on her, something called "Secret Society". You might want to distance yourself,' she advised him.

'Thanks for the advice,' he told her, 'but I can look after myself.'

He was very fond of Gretchen and despite only having met infrequently trusted her judgement. She wouldn't make such accusations without knowing something tangible about the book. He still had the journey back to Hounslow and this would prove eventful.

'Driver, could you close the partition, I need a private talk with my friend.'

It was the inflection Ruby used on the word "friend" that must have hinted to Walter that something untoward was about to happen. Even though she was sitting next to him, it wasn't close enough. She sidled up to him, placed her left hand over the side of his face, bringing his ear as close as possible to her mouth.

'Now, you little fucker, listen good. I know you think you're smart but believe me, you're not near smart enough for me. Your blackmailing scum fucking friends will end up in the morgue if they try to fuck me over.'

Walter was at first unsure what she was talking about and said as much.

'The letter, the one you gave me. £100k. I'll take out a contract on you all and use the fucking £100k to bury you all.'

Now it dawned on Walter. He had been a prize plum, used by almost everyone. He needed a way out. He used his ace of trumps.

'It wasn't me. I didn't know—still don't know—what was in the letter. There's a TV programme being done on you to say you didn't write *Heavenly Hell*, did you know?'

And she let go of his head and slumped back in her seat. She was stuffed, or so she felt for a few seconds. Then she thought of a way out of it.

'Do you know who gave you the letter?'

Well, of course he did.

'I want to see them, not for £100k, for £500k. I've a job for them.'

Walter now knew what was going on. He was an unwitting conspirator. He had just been bloody well used as ever. He'd never seen the content of the letter but presumed it was short in words, long on threats.

Chapter 32

Lizzie Closes in on Her Prey

Super-sleuth, Miss Elizabeth "Marple" Spector had the bit between her teeth and armed with fortitude, determination, female intuition and…well, a few minor facts, was determined to get another scoop. She knew there were some corroborated suspicions that Ruby Latimer's latest book had been completed by someone else. Lizzie had photographed a card with "GW" on it and a phone number, not called but was being checked out. She knew a university professor had confirmed their suspicions. However, this was all circumstantial and Ruby Latimer continued to absolutely refute any suggestion. Even ghost-writers who offered their services via the Internet were extremely circumspect in being prepared to come clean about just who they were and just who they had done work for, the difference was that given a technically proficient individual, at least the former could be traced. The cloak-and-dagger nature of the Ruby Latimer "ghost" made tracing the person virtually impossible but what could be proved was that someone had faked her ending. Lizzie and Ambreen sat down to work out a game plan and see where it would take them. A cameraman was booked. The script for "Secret Society—Exorcising a Ghost" was drawn up and Lizzie started to dictate something on her smartphone. First thing: talk to those who suspected foul play.

Gretchen was first. Pretty much standard stuff but it was from the viewpoint of an avid fan. How much more of a "fan" could you get than the bloody secretary of the author's own fan club? She thought to keep Lucinda out of it as, being a C8 employee, it could be viewed somewhat iffy. Next, she had a choice of one of the editors or Walter Sims. Gretchen had given Lizzie his number. He was at work. Yes, he would see her, would Gretchen be there? Lizzie said she would. White lie. Gretchen knew about the meeting, was keen to be there as she liked Walter but was unsure if she had the time that evening. Nevertheless, Lizzie set up the meeting at her favourite Central London pub, the Red Lion, Whitehall.

Walter appeared dead on seven; Lizzie was already there. After a G&T for Lizzie—Walter, nothing alcoholic as he was driving—Lizzie launched into it.

'I take it you know that suspicion about Ruby Latimer not only not having completed *Heavenly Hell* is starting to circulate but given her flat denial to me about the accusation, we, C8, are doing a story on it. She may be your pal, but she's also a literary cheat. Could be if you stick with her, it might reflect badly on you.'

Walter just sat and shook his head. 'She's not like that. She's honest.' He was in a state of denial. 'Where's Gretchen then? You said she was coming.'

'Delayed by traffic, I expect.'

'Not saying anything more until she arrives.'

'I'll phone her.'

Lizzie was, very unusually, a little anxious that Gretchen should be with them soon. As it happened, she actually was stuck on a tube train but should be with them in twenty minutes or less. Stuck with a silent man, Lizzie decided to try small talk.

'Walter, she won't be long. How long have you worked at the agency?'

'Been there over two years now.'

'Do you like it?' The almost "yes" and "no" conversation, with many pregnant pauses, continued for what seemed an interminable amount of time. Lizzie hit upon one thing she'd learnt though: Walter was to be a temporary editor, something he intended to prove himself good at. He'd done his apprenticeship, now it was time to step up to the mark. Lizzie as ever was storing every word for future reference.

'One of the editors is off having a child. I'm just filling in but who knows for how long.'

Lizzie had met the editors at the book bash a few weeks earlier for coffee. None of them had looked even slightly pregnant, so it must have been another one. Maybe she knew something. Lizzie was apprehensive about talking to the others as it might lead to "shutting up shop" but this other one…well, just like hyenas separated that solitary wildebeest…Lizzie also filed that in her "later" mental folder.

'Gretchen! At last the—' Finding a description adequate for the moment was difficult. Walter had the hots, bigtime, for her, so much that he was tongue-tied in her company. He was never tongue-tied with Kirsty. He was always too busy! Gretchen was a different kettle of fish. At some time in the future, they might "get it on" but Walter saw it as a bit more, he saw her as possibly "the one". Gretchen arrived and Lizzie, sensing the sexual chemistry between them, went and got a drink for them all at the bar, giving the couple a few minutes for small talk.

'Now Walter, can we continue? Gretchen, tell him what you know about Ruby Latimer and that book.'

As Gretchen unfolded a tale of deceit, compounded by skulduggery, Walter realised he'd been played bigtime. Then the *coup de grâce*— 'My sister, Lucinda has evidence from a university professor that the end of the book wasn't written by her, Miss Latimer.' Walter put his head in his hands.

'This is awful. She's so nice,' conveniently forgetting the little episode in the limo the previous night. Misplaced loyalty.

'You see, Walter,' Lizzie clasped the poor guy's hand in a sign of understanding over what he was going through 'the best thing for everyone, for the public interest, would be for me to run this programme, asking her to give her side, of course. It can't go unchallenged. It just can't.'

'So what do you want?'

'All I want is for you to say on camera what you know.'

Walter, though reluctant, sighed and nodded.

'Tomorrow night. I'll get it filmed.'

Gretchen sidled up to him, being on the other side of him. She grabbed his hand. She knew he was hurting and did what she could to comfort him. Whilst it wasn't untrue that she would like more than this from him, this would do for now, given his state.

There were things Walter would tell Lizzie and things he wouldn't. He would tell her that it was more than conceivable that her information was correct, that Ruby Latimer had been behind a deception allowing her not only to have her book completed but also sell a million books and get that award. He would never tell her about the conversation in the back of the silver Bentley on the way back from the awards. Even thinking about that deeply malevolent, singularly egotistical look was enough to make his spine tingle. Ruby Latimer was persistent in her desire to survive whatever and survive she would. Walter had given the author the phone number of Kirsty Letts. The phone conversation went thus.

'Yeah?'

'You little fucker. Never mind a hundred grand, how about half a million! Meet me tomorrow.'

And with that and the address at which to meet, the very short, sharp, one-sided conversation ended. Totally focussed on taking out whoever wanted to expose her to the press, blackmailers were such pussies in comparison. Ruby Latimer wanted to have them rid her of all these pests, who she would identify and eliminate. This was a side of her that the public was never ever likely to see. Walter had felt it on the ride back from the event but didn't realise just how vicious she was capable of being. He wasn't consciously doing so, but in reality, he was betting on both sides. He was involved. His meeting with Lizzie and Gretchen finished, Walter Sims headed home. He had been trying to pluck up enough courage to ask Gretchen out, but his courage had failed him. He was kicking himself as he left, hesitated for a second then strode on and promised himself to phone her.

The Crystal Palace was a pub that Ruby had frequented before she had become famous. Even though she had been well known then, it had been a long time ago. Despite getting a few "is it, isn't it" glances, she wasn't recognised. Kirsty came along on her own. Both exemplified unbridled determination, one to stay up that greasy pole a bit longer, the other to start up it.

There was an interesting beginning. They sat in a snug booth and Ruby had a port and lemon, Kirsty, a whisky and coke. It was tense but rather than let the author have the initiative, Kirsty kicked off.

'We know you cheated. We can prove it. We want money, lots of it.'

'Darling, first of all, you have nothing. You have what the courts would call circumstantial evidence. You can do what you want. They will just fuck you over. You're not fucking me over. In any case, you're not the problem. I've a bigger one. One that may well join up all the dots. You can deal with it.'

And then Ruby Latimer regaled the expose-in-training with a certain TV company, a certain reporter, certain other people and a lot of bastards needing to shut their mouths. The way she talked it wasn't about a slap on the back of the hand either. Ruby Latimer was looking for a permanent end to this monstrous invasion of her privacy that only one thing could put an end to. She hoped that this girl was the answer.

Walter had told both of them separately about the other. It was the background of Kirsty Letts that made Ruby Latimer think that maybe she had the kind of contacts that were in the business of "problem-solving". Kirsty had never considered this. It would take her well beyond the limits and ability of her present ambitions. She would need to talk to Bob about it.

Ruby gave Kirsty an envelope as they were about to leave. She then left and on opening it, Kirsty discovered £5,000 in £50 notes and a list of names and where they could be found, people who were risking Ruby Latimer's future and whose future existences were all at risk. Kirsty had never seen or held such money in her entire life. Yet it was only a 1% down payment on what she hoped would see the end of this problem. Her conversation with Kirsty, to find out who she knew and what they were capable of filled her with hope. She went home satisfied and with an expectation of results.

The next day, Kirsty texted Bob Grisham.

'News! Must meet ASAP.'

They linked up and she told him about their conversation and what she was wanting for half a million. Ruby Latimer wanted executions! Bob had been violent, yes; very violent, oh god yes; but he'd never yet killed someone. He reckoned he might be capable of it in the right circumstances and for the right reasons, but it would depend. Kirsty showed him the list. He knew that they would all need to be "done" separately. He thought about it. He wasn't sure. He would need handers. He went home to think about it.

The next day, he met up with Kirsty again to work out a game plan. He would do it. They would all need to "disappear". Then they would need to be disposed of. He thought that it would be possible to abduct two of them together whilst the others could be taken a day apart each. This was a job for Brad.

Brad was called up and they met. Brad thought about their contract. He eventually settled on £12k per person. There were logistics to look at. How to abduct, how to kill, how to dispose. Brad had worked with the best at this so wasn't particularly fazed, but he expected Bob's lot to do reconnaissance, bring photos, etc. He knew the perfect "final resting place". They looked at the list and the one on top of it was Lizzie Spector.

Chapter 33

Fun with Bob and Kirsty

Bob was in Kirsty's bedsit at 11 in the morning. The place was empty except for them.

'My guy will do the job. The money will be payment by result. He needs us to get information on the targets and arrange for them to be "collected". It might take a week or longer but the sooner we get him the information, the sooner the job's done and the sooner we get the money. He needs something else...'

Bob Grisham and Kirsty Letts were of the criminal fraternity but were rank amateurs when it came to the sorry business of execution. Bob lived in the family house, which had, at that time, two spare rooms. Out the back of the former two-knocked-into-one ex-council, there was a large, for lack of a better description, shed, really a one-time garage. It would play its part in the plan. His parents turned a blind eye to the comings and goings at the house, living in a virtually self-contained one-bedroom en-suite part of it, only being around the rest of the house at mealtimes.

The first phase of the plan was to get photos of the intended victims. They weren't too difficult to obtain. Once known where they worked, a car containing Bob and Marilyn parked and took numerous snaps. Brad also wanted information on their regular movements to see their patterns. This would allow him to draw up an abduction plan. The victims would need to be followed, times noted and so on. At the end of the week, all the information had been gathered and a meeting with Brad had been arranged. It was only then that he explained what he intended. The victims would be taken one at a time. They would be restrained, killed and their bodies would be disposed of together in a special place no one would ever suspect or find. However, Brad required more from Bob.

'Linda, it's Bob; you free to talk?'

'Well, I'm busy at work, what is it?'

'Call me back then, need something from you.'

Linda, Bob's younger "straight" sister, had escaped the clutches of the Grisham Corporation but still owed them. Bob had gotten her a house, quite a nice one, not one she could ever have afforded on the pay of an administrator at a funeral director's place. She was living at the house with her boyfriend who she hoped would propose to her before the year was out. Bob still owned it but her staying there free gratis had its advantages, it kept the place clean and heated and no council tax for him to pay. It was also something that he could use as a bargaining chip if he ever needed a favour. He had never needed one thus far, but one was now required.

Lizzie Spector had a bit more to go on, not for one moment imagining how high the stakes had just escalated. She was now in terrifying danger of abduction and murder. Walter hadn't the faintest idea that it had gotten so deadly serious. He had thoughts to maybe warn her that she should proceed with caution. He arranged another meeting with her. It may have been to salve his conscience but if that was all it did, more to the good. He was now also having some darker thoughts about just who Kirsty Letts was and who she associated with.

Walter went to see Lizzie at her work in his lunchbreak. It had only been days since their last meeting, but she was keen to meet up anyway. She was still attempting to get him to do an on-camera interview with him but had experienced logistical problems. Walter told her of the one-sided whispering conversation he had in the back of the limo and the overt threat about spending mega bucks to get rid of the problem. It may well have been the shampoo talking but forewarned was forearmed. Lizzie listened with a fascination combined with a fair degree of supressed horror. She was by now a tough little cookie. Maybe she wasn't yet a Kate Addie, but she knew that there were dangers in investigative journalism. Maybe she should report it to someone. She thought about it.

Just as he was finishing up, Lizzie asked Walter if he remembered anything else that might help her.

'Didn't I show you the card?' He knew fine well he hadn't. She looked bewildered. He took out his phone. "GW" and the phone number. Now it all started to make sense. Lizzie had the exact same thing on her phone. Bingo! Problem! From past memory, these kinds of things were not easily accessed. First of all, if you called and they asked you for, say, a codeword or suchlike and you got it wrong, it was "hasta la vista, baby", cover blown, end of lead. Walter looked as if he wanted to say a little more. Lizzie gave him a doe-eyed look and that was enough.

'Just, when I gave her, Miss Latimer, Ruby, a massage, she mentioned a name.'

'Name?'

'I think it was Lars, sounded very much like Lars.'

'Did she say anything else?'

'No, just "oh, Lars" and that was it.'

Lizzie was now getting the context of this name and its significance. Was Walter that good at massage or…Lizzie decided to leave her thoughts there. She had more bits of the jigsaw, not the full picture but enough to make out what she was looking at. She imagined phoning the "GW" number as Ruby Latimer had done. 'I need help.' 'Your name and (just maybe) contact name?' If she answered as Ruby Latimer and even gave "Lars" as the contact, she still might not make it. She needed to be cleverer than that. It was, however, undoubtedly a break.

Lizzie went back to work satisfied, a little bit scared, but with a quandary about just how to proceed. She talked to Ambreen. Ambreen said nothing. It was all getting exceedingly heavy. There were some known unknowns. Where was "GW" from? How did he or she recruit ghost-writers? Would they have many Lars-type salespersons out there? And a lot more. The whole *raison d'etre* of the organisation was not just making money but total secrecy. Maybe rather than a programme exposing Ruby Latimer, it should now widen its scope to be about an international fraud. It could be an entire clandestine criminal service industry. It would, of course, include the Ruby fraud but only as part of the overall deception. It could be that many books were now being written using famous authors to sell them when they weren't written by them at all. Food for thought. Fake authors. Was anything genuine anymore? Would you buy a Rolls Royce made in Pakistan? You'd want to have proof of its authenticity. So maybe the whole investigation might end up being knitted into a larger tapestry of falsification. Just how to get acknowledgment of this was indeed the problem.

Gretchen. Lizzie might be able to use her. She was really growing up and might make a journalist herself. No harm in asking her. Possibly time for another drink in the Red Lion. She would let Lucinda arrange it. And so, a drink was arranged for a couple of days hence. Given that Gretchen was now thoroughly disillusioned with the woman she'd idolised, asking her to come clean that it was all a lie would still be a big ask but she would ask anyway. That was the purpose of asking Lucinda, who'd been out of the office all day to meet her sister and accompany her to the pub. Fridays were always busy in Central London.

'Doll, (Bob only called Linda this when what came next wouldn't be something good), I was wondering; see, your work…'

'Yeeesss?'

'Well, you use body bags, don't you, for the stiffs and the like?'

'Don't know what "the like" is but by "stiffs", you mean the recently deceased, only when they come to us from the police mortuary. Why?'

'I was wondering what happened to them. Do they get cremated or what?'

'Actually, they are normally emptied, the body is cremated, and the body bag is either destroyed or cleaned and returned for further use if it is in good condition, but mostly destroyed. Just where is this line of questioning going?'

'I need some body bags for something coming up.'

Linda wasn't a wuss. She knew her brother was a wrong'un. She knew that a body bag was for, well, containing a body. She also knew not to ask too many questions. She could end up homeless.

'How many exactly?'

'Don't know how many. Do you think you could get us, me, a bundle?'

The conversation finished with Linda agreeing to get some body bags. It was Thursday and the "uncrems" (unknown cremations) normally took place late on a Friday. There could be as many as seven or eight, dependent on what kind of week it had been downstream. Lots of suicides, normally fished out of the Thames, with bodies of "John Doe" and "Jenny Doe" cleared out to make way for more of the same at the police mortuary. They were removed by fully protected staff with masks, some in appalling states and eventually cremated, the body bag placed to one side to become part of the weekly rubbish, although they were hermetically sealed to ensure no infection or contamination could take place. Linda didn't normally have anything to do with the business side of the parlour but, coincidentally, did collect the body bags. Bob and Marilyn went over to Linda's that night and picked them up. Not a word was exchanged. Hard to know what line of conversation would possibly have been apposite in the situation.

Lizzie sat and waited and had another drink, looking at her watch. She had expected to see Gretchen and Lucinda by then. She thought she'd better phone them. She just got their answerphones. Not getting one, given it was Friday, was not unusual. She texted and waited…and phoned and waited. After an hour of repeatedly trying and failing, she left one final voice message. 'Don't know where you are, Lucinda. See you on Monday.'

Chapter 34

Lizzie Searching for Wild Geese

It was a Sunday morning. A long lie-in for Lizzie, but not long enough as far as Craig was concerned. Ever since their engagement, Craig had found himself in her bed most weekends. You could call it preparation for the real thing. On this occasion, whilst sex may as ever been foremost on his mind, he was a man after all, it hadn't been on Lizzie's. Try as he could, she just wasn't capable of arousal that morning. He gave up, his head appeared from under the sheets and asked, 'What's up?'

'I'm worried. Lucinda and Gretchen were due to meet me for a drink in the Red Lion Friday night. They didn't show up. It's so out of character for Lucinda. I've tried and tried but I can't get them on the phone. No reply from her or Gretchen.'

'So?'

'So, can we drive up to Bishop's Stortford to see them? It would put my mind at rest.'

'I can see you're uptight. I know how to...' But it was clearly not the time, so Craig shrugged his shoulders, got up and made a coffee for them both. He could arouse her maybe later.

'Can we go soon please? I'll fill you in on the way. It's to do with the story.'

They had a quick breakfast, a quick shower, together so it wasn't a total loss, and left at ten for Herts. On the way, Lizzie told him the developments and how it was still circumstantial until they could get an expert to verify what the professor had told Lucinda.

Lizzie had the address and the Satnav on her phone got them to their destination. It was a big house alright. The girls' daddy was loaded. It would have been a wonder if they ever intended to leave home. They got there at lunchtime. The house seemed empty at first. Lizzie rang the doorbell and a smartly dressed woman in her mid-forties answered.

'Mrs Turner, I'm Lizzie Spector and I work with Lucinda. I was due to see her on Friday night, but she never showed up and I've been calling her and her sister, Gretchen, but there's no answer. Have you seen either of them?'

'Sorry Miss Spector, Mr and Mrs Turner aren't at home. They left on an extended walking holiday, Southeast Asia, yesterday. I've not seen the young ladies recently, which, given their high social life, is not so unusual. I can go for days without bumping into either of them. The girls eat in their rooms or occasionally come down to eat. I'm off duty at six every evening, so may well not see them if they are late in. They make their own beds, boarding school training I expect. They're always off doing what young people do these days.'

The woman glanced over Lizzie's shoulder at the driver of the car.

'Oh, my fiancé, Craig.'

The housekeeper was not overly concerned about the young women and thought that their parents would contact them from abroad. Such a pity that Lizzie had no such facility. On the way back, Lizzie felt and looked terrible. She just loved what she did, but thoughts of what Walter had told her couldn't be put out of her mind. Was this author just all wind and water or was there real menace in her? Descriptions of how Savile behaved when no one was watching came to mind. Ruby Latimer might have had such an alter ego. Maybe she'd become like some of her characters. Maybe she—

'Go to the police.'

'What? Lizzie, we can't, what with? They might be fine. Housekeeper seemed unconcerned.'

'Put my mind at rest. Let's stop at a police station.'

On the M25, they googled where a local police station was and headed there. A young PC took down all the details and boy, were there plenty of details, and filed a report. He wasn't sure how much of it was fact and how much pure fiction. Lizzie had the sisters' mobile phone numbers, their home address, Lucinda's work address and that was about that. There was a selfie of the three of them taken some time ago which the police took a copy of to circulate.

After that, Lizzie and Craig continued home, her home, and spent another sex-free, tense day. Craig would not normally have spent Sunday night there, it was one of those things about employees coming in to work from the same car, office relationships being what they were, but felt in the circumstances that his fiancée needed him. He popped home to pick up some clothes and was back in an hour and a quarter. This time, using his key, he entered Lizzie's now empty flat.

Craig thought, *Strange, must have popped out for something.* He rang her mobile. It rang on the coffee table. He was now exceedingly concerned. Lizzie never went anywhere without it, not even to the toilet. Turning around, he strode back down the stairs to look outside. Sunday early evening and the road was deserted. He was then outside in the cool evening air, thinking of all the places she could possibly be. He walked to Cutty Sark, the Tube, the now shut market. No sign of her. After forty minutes, he came in and sat down. He was now becoming frantic. This was so out of character. She was a creature of habit. She wouldn't have just gone out without—there was the noise of a key in the lock, footsteps on the stairs.

'Where the hell were you?'

'Didn't you see the note?'

Lizzie had left it next to her phone, but it must have fallen on the floor.

'I needed time to think and without distractions. I went up to the park to think. This is so unusual and not in a good way. The girls are missing. I don't know where they are, but I need to do something.'

'We've already alerted the police, what more is there to do?'

'I know, frustrating. That's what I was walking for.'

'If there's no sign of Lucinda at work tomorrow, I think we will need to go back to the police. Our newspeople might be able to put out an article on it.'

'They still could just reappear you know, like the proverbial bad pennies.'

'I hope so but...' Lizzie tried their phones again with the same response. Then, remarkably a text came:

LOL. SORRY BEEN BUSY SEE YA SOON

'Looks like Lucinda's OK then,' said Craig, looking at the phone. Lizzie's first response was of total relief, her next of total confusion. She looked back at some other texts from her friend over the past weeks. She never used "LOL", always punctuated and NEVER used capitals. And as for "YA"! She tried to phone again but only got the answerphone. Oh, how very, very wrong this all was.

Lizzie's idea of waiting until the next morning had gone completely out the window. She put her coat back on and said to Craig, 'Coming?'

'Where?'

'Police, of course.'

This time, Lizzie was in a different mindset. She had seen a crude attempt to divert her focus from the concerns of a missing colleague and now wanted real police action. It was after six on a Sunday evening in late June. It was soon to be the second week of Wimbledon. They got into Craig's car and drove to Greenwich police station. It was closed, permanently, so they headed to the one at the Isle of Dogs. They were unaware that they were the subject of interest by others, following at a distance. However, when it became plain about their intended destination, they backed off for another time. Whilst Craig sat tight in the car, Lizzie bolted through the side entrance.

Serendipity! At the front desk was an old face. PC Ronnie Forbes. Ronnie Forbes had been a DC. His at-that-time partner, DC Angela Peake, had been on a case trailing a stalked woman when she, DC Peake, was abducted by an organisation called "Achilles Heel". She had survived and spent several months in hospital recovering her memory. As her partner, Ronnie had taken the fall, even though it hadn't been his fault. Blackballed for advancement, Ronnie reverted to the uniformed branch. Lizzie knew him from her time at Squawk FM. They looked intently at each other then...

'Lizzie! Lizzie Spector.'

'You're...Ronnie, isn't it? Uniformed now. How?'

'Long or short version?'

'How's Angela?'

'Still struggles a bit but back on duty, not the same as she was but Michael, DS, DI Madison, is helping. They're engaged now.' Lizzie shot a smile and waggled her left hand in front of him.

'You too! Must be something in the water. So, to what do I owe this pleasure?' Lizzie retold the whole sorry tale.

'...And I did report it to your guy in North London, Cricklewood, but now I'm getting seriously concerned.' She showed him the text and showed him other ones.

'I don't think she sent it. It's just not, well, her, is it?' Ronnie went into detective mode and captured it on his phone.

'If it's still on, our guys might be able to use the location finder to pinpoint where the phone is.' Lizzie thought that Achilles Heel, that underground stalker buster group, would have the technology to do it super-fast, but no one could ever find them—too busy stalking stalkers, she presumed.

'I'll have a word with Michael. He's now DI. Busting that paedo ring helped.'

Ronnie was a sincere, if one-paced, copper but he knew that Lizzie was both sincere and concerned for her friends, so he agreed to get it up the line, as a special favour.

'Brian excited at the wedding then?'

'Brian... Oh sorry, Brian. Me and Brian split up. I'm marrying Craig Endoran who's now at C8 along with me.'

'Following you about, is he, or is it you stalking him? Hehe, just kidding.'

Lizzie wasn't in a jokey kind of mood. *Moot point*, she thought, then dismissed it. She left the Isle of Dogs police station in a much better frame of mind than when she had entered it. She even gave Craig a most passionate kiss, which he reciprocated. He would stay over at her place that night, which, he hadn't realised, could well have saved her life that day. Lizzie still wasn't feeling horny, even though men normally were, pretty much permanently so. She did, however, ensure that night that Craig got some relief.

The next morning, they both went into work and, as expected, there was no sign of Lucinda in her legal office. She had Ronnie's number and called him to let him know. If she'd had the merest inkling of just how close she'd been to mortal danger... When she'd been walking alone in the park, Brad, Bob and Franny had been trailing her, just looking for that chance. She had gone up to the Royal Observatory, but it had been quite busy even then. Other fleeting opportunities had come and gone, then she was back home. Abducting someone in broad daylight was tricky at the best of times and two of them had only done it once and that had been a couple of nights before. They had used Brad's Jaguar Chelsea Tractor, which he'd gotten from Grigor once it had been altered— number plates, colour, engine number, etc. Getting the two girls in a back lane near Exhibition Road had been a stroke of luck but now they had work to do with them.

Lucinda Turner woke up, totally disorientated, with no idea where she was and what had happened to her. All was black with only the slightest sliver of light. She tried to move. She couldn't. Her wrists and ankles were bound very tight. She tried to scream but she couldn't. Something was preventing it. Then she heard similar muffled noises just next to her. Lucinda Turner was helpless.

She felt something fall on her. Then…oh dear god, that smell. It was the putrescent odour of death. Then, something on her face that was cold and metallic plus simultaneous pain coming from between her legs, not just like she'd been kicked by a horse but a burning pain. No, it was more than just a kick. Then she remembered! She writhed in sheer blind panic but to no avail. She tried to open her mouth, but it was sealed with something. Apart from the smell of death, she could also taste and smell glue, hardened superglue. Then she remembered!

With Gretchen, relaxed, laughing and joking, walking to South Kensington Underground, they'd thought about taking a shortcut down a lane they knew. Fatal error. A four-by-four had blocked their exit. Three men had quickly caught them and bundled them into the car, holding chloroform rags to their noses. By the time they were in the boot, they had both been out of it. The gang took them to Orpington, where they were unloaded and quickly removed to the shed. Both girls then had their shoes removed—stiletto heels could tear fabric—wrists tied behind them with cable ties, ankles tied. Lips duct-taped before Brad had them all held down whilst he applied superglue to each of their mouths. Then both were placed in a body bag and zipped in. They weren't the first "guests" in the shed that night. Brad had been a busy bee.

Chapter 35
From Orpington to Eternity

Lucinda remembered. She and Gretchen had been taken captive. It was still a bit light, maybe dusk, so they must have only been there an hour or so. She had been drugged and remembered little else. She had seen her sister directly opposite her. Both could see the other, both bruised on their now bare legs, a result of the struggle to get them into the car. Both had duct tape on their mouths but were able to sit up slightly. It would be preferable to what Brad would be replacing it with.

There were three men there, in the shed.

'So far, so good, eh Brad?'

'For fuck's sake…oh, it won't matter, will it?' He checked the ankle and wrist restraints on the inhabitants of the shed. Brad had made a zipper sign over his mouth and mouthed, 'No fucking names,' to Bob.

'We'd better get the bags from Linda then. She has them in her car. Shouldn't be too long, Franny. Oops,' as he accidentally kicked one of the girls. So much for no names!

'Never mind. You look after the shop till we get back.'

Bob was about to learn a new skill, that of murder. He would take to it like a duck to water. However, an act of pure folly, as it would turn out, would be to leave Franny alone with young women incapable of stopping him from doing anything! It had been asking for trouble. Franny had two things, no scruples and a rampant sex drive.

The other two left Franny on his own, what you could have laughingly called "in charge". He didn't do anything for about ten minutes. All that time, he had simply been looking at them and thinking, *Eeny meeny miny moe.*

'And the first one will be…you!'

Lucinda screamed, a muffled duct tape kind of scream as he came over to her. She tried her best to resist in her extremely tethered state, but he just turned her onto her stomach, pulled down her pants to her cable-tied bare feet and… After he was finished, he pulled them back up and thought of having a five-minute break to decide who was next. He liked doing it dry, regardless of what damage it might do.

After that one there, I'll do that one there last, he thought. Franny was a sexual predator, a beast. Franny liked his sex any way he could get it. To him, they were just three bits of meat with convenient orifices there for his pleasure. He then did the one who had been the first to be deposited in the shed, before the arrival of the sisters. That one was still completely out of it so no resistance there. Franny finally turned his attention to the other sister. He was running a bit low on you-know-what but still had a supply for her. She also tried to fight him off, but it was useless. He straightened them up and left them just as they had been.

'Won't be long now, folks.'

It was said in a chirpy, friendly voice but what would be happening wouldn't be at all friendly.

Lucinda had very little sexual experience. She had just been subjected to the most brutal of sexual assaults. She'd been badly mutilated and traumatised, still utterly helpless. She started to cry. Franny, psychotic lad, tried to comfort her, 'There, there, soon be all over.' All over! What would be all over? Was that supposed to comfort and pacify! Just then, in came Bob and Brad with a load of body bags and threw them in the corner.

'What's up with her? You been tormenting them? Right, let's prepare these ones. I've got the perfect place for them.'

Squeals and violent headshaking were heard and seen. Panic in triplicate.

'If you hold them, I need to…' He produced a tube of superglue. 'Hold her,' he told Franny and he ripped off the duct tape, squeezed her lips and applied it. After holding her for a minute of writhing, he moved on to do the other two.

'Right now, the bags.'

'They'll wriggle like fuck.'

'Not when I do this,' He kicked one with force between the legs, who fell flat on the broken concrete and wooden floor. The anguished body was put into the bag and zipped up. The other two, even though they didn't resist, got the same treatment with the same venom and result. Brad was such a gent but when money was concerned, he always reverted to animal mode. He inflicted pain as part of his "day job". The three now severely damaged captives were left next to each other in the shed as Brad, in a jaunty voice, said, 'Cup of tea, men?'

'Fucking beer would be better,' grunted Franny.

'We'll come back when it's totally dark.'

The three body-bagged victims had been there for two days without food or water, restrained, in excruciating pain and terrified beyond imagination; they just lay there, life slowly ebbing away.

Lizzie got a call from DI Michael Madison to find out some background on the two missing persons. He had always rated Lizzie Spector and believed in the close collaboration of police and media to unearth and expose criminal activity. What Ruby Latimer may or may not have done wasn't criminal, just unethical, improper and deceptive to her millions of fans. However, two of her one-time supporters, now critics, were missing, and Lizzie had been told by Walter of a very unsavoury one directional "conversation" he'd been subjected to and the threatening nature of it. Would Walter Sims be able to shed any light on these disappearances?

The girls hadn't been formally declared missing, but they most definitely were. The police needed to talk to anyone who might have information. Lizzie got out her phone and called Walter. His mobile rang, then immediately went to voicemail. She left a message for him to call her. She called DI Madison back to tell him and gave him some phone numbers. There wasn't much more that could be done. Anyway it was way too early for anything to put up for "Crimewatch UK". Lizzie had other work to get on with. She seemed to be losing all the witnesses to the subterfuge. There were always the editors. Lizzie had the phone numbers of them all, but looking at the various phone numbers thought that Becky was the nearest. She called her to see if she was around and as she was home decided to whip down to Orpington to talk about things.

Lizzie arrived at Becky's at two that Monday. Becky was in a talkative mood. She made Lizzie a cuppa and both made small talk before moving on to the real reason for her visit.

'We think there is proof that the novel *Heavenly Hell* by Ruby Latimer is partly the work of a ghost-writer.'

'Yeah, I know, we all do.'

'All?'

'All us editors who've done stuff for her over the years. Snooty bitch. Anyway, my sister, think you may have met her, Kirsty, was asking about it for some reason and I think I may have just overegged it a bit. Anyway, not sure how much more I can tell you.' Just then, the phone rang.

'Hi. Becks here, can't talk, got someone here. Think you met her, Lizzie Spector. Do you…funny, phone went dead. Anything else I can do? Think she may be going to pop around if you want to talk to her.'

Lizzie declined and thought she needed to contact the other editors.

'I've never met Mary. What do you know about her? Do you think she might know something?'

'Might, but she might be busy. Late baby and all that.'

'OK. Fine. Need to fly.'

Lizzie drove off and just as she did, a Chelsea Tractor rounded the corner almost on two wheels as she disappeared onto the dual carriageway. A woman got out of the car and rushed into Becky's house and returned in under a minute to the man waiting outside.

'Just missed her. Fuck.'

The driver shook the wheel, shouting, 'Fuck, fuck, fuck.' Bob, Brad and Kirsty had just missed out on a glorious opportunity to get another for the body bags. Brad was a little peeved, given it was worth £12,000. Lizzie had escaped again. Her nine lives however were dwindling.

The victims had been given a 24-hour stay of execution. Having been packed in the back of the four-by-four and driven into the country, they found that a gypsy camp had taken up residence half a mile away. They turned back in the certain knowledge that by the next night in early July, they would have upped sticks and moved on. The victims were now in a very bad way indeed. The heat in the body bags was stifling and the smell of corpse residue must have been pungent. They drifted in and out of consciousness. At least unconsciousness was painless. That same day Lizzie had escaped their clutches by seconds, the large vehicle with its deadweight in the boot set off with Brad driving, Bob next to him, Franny and Tony in the back along with Kirsty there just for good measure. There was banter from Franny, still not realising that his "calling card" had well and truly been left on, or was it in, the boot "passengers" and the conversation was on phase two once these had been disposed of.

They knew they were off to Kent but just where about and, for God's sake, why? They turned off a B road and headed up a dirt track. Brad knew exactly where he was headed, an old abandoned well near the one-time mining village of Cobham. They arrived and started to prepare. All the body bags were in the boot, not just the ones that were full. Whilst Brad left the car lights on and the engine running, Franny and Bob dragged out the three full ones and, in the powerful headlights on that moonless night, dropped them at the outside wall of the well. Brad had been there before, hence his reason for going there. It was even programmed into the car's Satnav. There was definitely a whiff in the air and it wasn't just coming from the body bags either. Only Brad knew the reason why.

Half an hour later, it was Bob driving, utterly stunned by what had just occurred, numb at the consequences, but also that their money cut had just increased considerably. Kirsty, shocked, shaking, furious, sat next to Bob in the front. They were short of one. Twenty minutes earlier, screams uttered could have been heard in hell itself. Brad had been standing near the body bags, which twitched and groaned, and had been talking to Bob about how unlucky they had been not getting that Spector bitch.

'She'll run out of luck, third time lucky, you just wait and see. Anyway, phase one almost done, phase two starts tomorrow.'

'So, who is that to be then?' enquired Franny.

'All those other editor bitches and some professor in Bristol. Clear them all out.'

Kirsty had just computed something in her head.

'No, you…fucking well won't.' Brad fell to his knees and keeled over, violently convulsing as if electrocuted, blood spurting from a huge dent in the back of his head from an old half brick that Kirsty had picked up and that Brad had just been quite literally brained with. Kirsty had double-handed him with it and blood was over her, Franny, everywhere. He wasn't just out cold; he was out dead.

Bob was shocked. Franny was shocked. Tony was shocked. Kirsty was shocked. Brad was dead. Kirsty had just killed her first, possibly not her last, person. Apart from multiple other feelings, she felt totally exhilarated. Now she was as good as anyone else there. It was her twisted, perverted badge of honour. The Killers' Club.

'What the fuck did you do that for?'

'My fucking sister's one of the fucking editors. He was going to kill her as well.'

'No, he wasn't. He could have done that today. Said you being her sister and all made her safe. Needed her for bait for the other women.'

'Fuck,' said Kirsty, 'really screwed up now, haven't I?' Bob examined the body. Brad had a gaping hole in the back of his skull and his brain was exposed. He couldn't have been any deader.

'Well, only one thing for it. Franny, boot.'

With that, Brother Frank went and returned with yet another body bag. The stiffs' count was continuing to rise; at least it would in a few minutes.

It was now 11 pm on a barmy summer's evening. So beautiful, so macabre. On one hand, having done a day's work and finished up, Lizzie Spector went home oblivious to the close shave she'd had on successive days. Ruby Latimer wanted her dead. In fact, she had been the main target, not just because she was an inconvenience but because Ruby Latimer was a vindictive, borderline psychopath who saw her, very accurately, as her nemesis. All the others were but bit players but Lizzie Spector was the dragon's head and without her, all investigations might cease. So far three, sorry, four people were in body bags ready for disposal. It was dark even with the car headlights on but that was irrelevant. They had a job to finish off. Who would be the first down? Had to be Brad. He was the only one actually dead so far...and a big fucker. The three others were definitely at death's door, but possibly could have been saved. Wasn't going to happen though.

Franny and Tony picked up the still limp pre-rigor carcass of Brad, sat him on the edge of the well and...down he went, making some almighty racket as he plummeted, striking what they presumed were the side walls and then a large splash. It was pitch black and none of them had a torch, save the ones you got on mobiles, fat lot of use they would be. Next was...dunno. They all felt pretty much similar, one being slightly heavier on account of...well, to be expected. Whilst Brad made a clatter and a splash, the next one clattered but failed to splash, more of a crunch, whilst the others didn't even clatter much, more of a dull thud. Three of the murderers noticed the pungent aroma wafting up from the bottom of the old well, thinking to themselves that those body bags really fucking stank.

Lizzie was at home, alone, post-ablution, settling down to watch the news, C8 News. Her phone rang. It was Craig.

'Stay put, I'm coming over.' No explanation. *Wonder why?* Forty-five minutes and the key turned in her lock. Craig bolted up the stairs and took a seat. Normally, his lovey dovey approach would start the moment he walked through the door. On this occasion, it was absent. He wasn't there under some spurious pretext, looking for sex. This time, it was serious.

199

'Had Special Branch on the blower. You need to be careful. Apparently, word is out that someone has put out a contract out on you and the Turner sisters, maybe others as well.' Despite driving, Craig felt the need for a stiff drink. With that news, Lizzie needed one as well.

'Who? How? Why?'

'Apparently on a need-to-know basis. I got a call from your DI friend. He thought it better if it came directly from me. God, Lizzie, you were wandering around Greenwich last night. Didn't you see anyone?'

She thought about it. 'Might have. Hard to say. Greenwich is always full of tourists. Anyway, still here, aren't I!'

'Where did you go today?'

'Nowhere much. Worked around the office and…went…to…Orpington.' A penny was beginning to drop. That speeding car. Maybe it had been after her! She decided another drink was the order of the day.

'Am I to get police protection then?'

'Never mentioned it but if they told me that, then maybe we should ask them for it.'

'Craig, I love you loads but I've got a job to do. I can't have cops following me about all bloody day. They'd get in the way. I need space to work.'

'It wouldn't be for long, just until they catch these people.'

'…And how long will that be? It's the Met we're talking about, after all. Do they know who's behind it?'

'If they do, they're hardly likely to tell us, we're journalists after all…' Craig had just realised the irony of this expression.

'And targets. This is getting more and more—'

'More and more what?'

'My god, no. It couldn't be.'

'Couldn't be…what, who? Tell me.'

'Ruby Latimer!'

The appalling possibility was beginning to dawn on Lizzie Spector. The word she had been searching for and had found was "bizarre". That was the word that had set the bitch off when Lizzie had used it in a conversation with her. It had lit the blue touch paper and poor Nick, the TV interviewer, had received the brunt of her ire. Ever since that moment, the somewhat paranoid author had gotten it in her crazed brain that Lizzie Spector was out to get her. Circumstances had contrived to compound this illusion until it was no longer just an illusion.

Now it looked as if she'd gone completely over the top and wanted her nemesis killed.

Unknown to Lizzie, part of Ruby's problem had just been dumped down a well in North Kent, keeping company with others who had met the same fate. One man had a hit list and she was on it. The hit list was in his pocket at the bottom of that well in Kent. That list included Lizzie Spector. That said, were there any others that needed similar protection—the girls, the editors? They couldn't protect them all, could they? For some, it was already too late. And where were the girls? Walter? Mary? Coming from the bottom of the well were the last audible noises from dying people, then it was silent. Lucinda Turner only had one final thought, *Gretchen*. Gretchen Turner had only one final thought, *My babies*. The other person was too far gone to have any final thoughts.

Chapter 36
Serving Up a Racquet

It was the middle of the last week of Wimbledon. The uniformed branch was out in force, apprehending pickpockets and confiscating the odd strawberry. Craig had been lucky enough to get a couple of tickets for Number One Court and there were some good matches. The weather was stifling and dry. Lizzie was still facing up to the shuddering thought that she was the target of a gangland contract and so it wasn't surprising that she was in a less than a relaxed frame of mind. However, Craig was insistent they have a day off for R&R, as if the distant memory of Davos hadn't been enough of that!

Craig also had another thought. Maybe Ruby Latimer might be there. Maybe Wimbledon would be a great place to hide in full view. He needed a bit of a break as well. They took their seats and saw a women's singles match. A bit one-sided but nevertheless entertaining. They went out to do some schmoosing with some of the other fans. Strawberry tea and a glass, almost compulsory. Lizzie was still a bit unnerved by how close she'd been to…the day out would help. Whilst there, she saw someone she thought she recognised. Lizzie had a memory for faces but not always names or context. This was someone from somewhere or other. Nothing else for it; with Craig in tow, he wasn't for one moment letting her out of his sight. She walked up to a bonnily dressed woman in a lovely floral hat, the type worn by people sitting right in front of you, blocking your view.

'Have we met? You look very familiar.'

'You do too, we must have. You're…?'

'Lizzie, Lizzie Spector. I work for C8.'

'Yes, you know, the one you met us at, of course. Abigail Roberts. You were the one to get right up Ruby Latimer's nose, weren't you? Lost her cool all right. Don't think you'll be on her Christmas card list somehow.'

'Or her on mine.' Lizzie hesitated to bring up the pertinent matter of missing people.

'You coming back tomorrow then? I've got a spare ticket if you want it. Off to try to see one of our elusive friends, a fellow editor. Should have sprogged by now. Couldn't find her last time. So annoying.'

'Did I meet her at the do?' asked Lizzie.

'Don't think so. Too far along then. Didn't attend our usual soirée either.'

'Soirée?'

'Yes, the four of us meet up every few weeks to discuss the world and our authors. Such good gossip.' Lizzie had another lightbulb moment.

'I'd love to interview you for a TV programme, if you wouldn't mind. Can I come to your next soirée? I'll even shout the coffees.'

Abigail hesitated, then agreed. They exchanged details to the frowns of Craig.

'Lizzie, just can't bloody leave it alone, can you?' Lizzie could never "leave it alone". Back to the tennis.

The Chelsea Tractor had returned home minus its owner. Its owner wouldn't be coming to pick it up either. The four of them had driven back from Kent in stony silence, some of which had been muted rage, some sheer disbelief, not at what they had been involved in—multiple murders—but at just who one of the victims had been and who he might have known. Bob Grisham was now reckoning that they'd bitten off so much more than they could chew that they could easily choke.

Bob had thought he was the brains of the family, having steered them from mediocrity to a burgeoning, successful criminal empire. He had masterminded the protection and gradual expansion of it when this young bird, Kirsty Letts, had come along with an attractive if somewhat hare-brained blackmail scheme, which had quickly developed into a full blown "hit", something he hadn't been up for but Marilyn had gotten someone who had been. That person was now dead, they had his car, would he be missed? Fuck knew. He had some very unsavoury oppos who might wonder what had happened to him. On the other hand, they might not give a toss if the schmuck was never seen again. Time would tell. The first question was what to do with the car.

In getting rid of Brad's body, like the rank amateurs in that context, they had made some basic mistakes. In their panic, they had failed to search him—he had carried the hit list. He also had a wallet with several hundred pounds, fancy platinum and gold credit cards, prostitutes' phone numbers, a fancy 24-carat gold chain and ring and, most important of all, a phone with so much on it that they'd just better hope he would never be found.

However, the car presented a problem. If it was his and his alone, no problem. The logbook in the glove compartment showed them that the "keeper" was Bradley Atkins, handy enough. If, on the other hand, it wasn't, who the fuck's motor was it? Had they known or even checked the logbook for the previous owner, one Grigor Sivkov, consigliere to Boris Ulyanov. The name would have meant nothing to them, given their food chain position. Grigor was one mean motherfucker but compared to Boris was a total pussy. Grigor had given the car to Brad for his "making" and he was now operating his own area. Brad did "homers", but his real agenda had been to infiltrate the Grisham Corporation and figure out their operation in order to take over. That plan had now fallen by the wayside just as Brad had fallen down a well.

What to do with the four-by-four? Beautiful as it was, it could be a magnet to allow Brad's "mates" to locate them. Sorry, but the car needed to go. Question was, just how? Burn it, canal it, break it up for spare parts? In the end, they decided to do none of that. The shed had garage doors, so they thought to stash it away and decide about its final destination later. This may prove not to have been the most sensible move, but it was nevertheless what they did. It wasn't even a thought, let alone an afterthought. Did anyone search any of them? Everyone thought the others had done the searching. Amateurs indeed. Down a well in the middle of nowhere so who would ever find them anyway.

'When we get back, you and Tony will need to power-hose out the garage before we put the car in it. Can't leave any evidence. Tony, Franny, take care of it.' The boys would "take care of it" in their own impeccable way. They forgot.

The Grisham Corporation minus Brad was on this matter a bit of a rudderless ship and it could be heading onto the reef. Bob had his, for lack of a better expression, strengths, but in many ways, the cool-headed one was Marilyn. Quite pretty, good personality, but make no mistake, this woman was no lady and would answer any question with a constructive answer. Only part of the contract had been fulfilled, the most important, Lizzie, editors and professor were still pending. The Grishams had various scraps of information, mostly from Walter Sims and Becky Letts, both courtesy of Kirsty Letts. It was now going to be trickier to bundle any more of these into a car and do them in, particularly Lizzie as she had been now forewarned and was on her guard. Lucinda Turner's now confirmed disappearance meant snatching Lizzie would be almost impossible and she was no longer staying in Greenwich as it was considered much too dangerous. She now stayed with Craig temporarily. Craig didn't complain!

Two of the editors were at "addresses unknown" but the Grishams had phone numbers for them, again from Kirsty. Lucinda had been the contact for Professor Llewelyn but as it was University College, Bristol, it wouldn't be too difficult to find the professor. "Emeritus" indicated she no longer was employed there but still had working links. Grishams had no idea what "Emeritus" meant. Franny thought it was some kind of VD.

Marilyn called a meeting. Bob, Marilyn, Tony, Franny and Kirsty, well why not, met on the final Saturday of Wimbledon. Bob outlined where they were.

'Shit situation, this. Thanks to her, (pointed at Kirsty) our man is dead. Four bods done, five to be done or it's all been a fucking waste of time. Marilyn has some ideas.'

Marilyn continued, 'Options. First option, forget it, cut our losses.'

'We won't get any money then. Fuck that.' Franny made a succinct point here. He just didn't realise it.

Kirsty wasn't a happy camper. 'Or we could do them one at a time. The editors should be easy meat.'

'What happened to the guy, Brad?' asked Marilyn.

'Kirsty fucking bricked him, that's fucking what. Thought he was going to do in her sister.'

Marilyn continued, 'Just fucking great. Well, we have phone numbers of these tarts so can I suggest we start with them, then the reporter, send someone to track down and do the professor. Tony, you've been quiet; what do you think?'

Tony was always quiet. He was afraid that what he would say would be shouted down as it usually was. A team player as long as he was a sub.

'Just call it off. What's the dosh for this, anyway?'

'Half a mil.'

'Fucking do 'em all!' So, it was unanimous.

A scheme was devised. Kirsty would see if Walter could find out where these women editors met and find out when they met. Walter's phone just kept ringing.

'Where's the wee bastard?'

Then it occurred to her—Becky, one of the editors! She of all people would know where they would meet next.

Kirsty turned up that night. Becky was skint as usual and not going out. Kirsty came with three bottles of cheap wine, sponsored by the Grisham Corporation. After three hours and a similar amount of wine and a few spliffs, Becky, who couldn't hold her own water let alone a secret, told her sister that the girls were going to meet the following Tuesday in Charing Cross. It was part chat but one of them, they presumed, had just given birth and they wanted to visit her in Windsor. Did Becky have an address for Mary Callan? Of course, she did. It was… With this info, Kirsty left and called Bob.

'Got great news.'

'Not on the phone, tomorrow at your place.'

So, it was becoming clearer that they could most likely nab them all in Windsor. They weren't to know that Lizzie Spector may well be amongst them. Lizzie was still hoping against hope that her friends would soon reappear like bad pennies from some foreign jaunt. It was, of course, just a mental ploy to keep her spirits up. Hope sprung eternal in the Spector soul. It was a fortitude that she may continue to require.

Chapter 37
Lizzie's Third Close Shave

Marilyn Grisham and Kirsty Letts could have been twins. Despite being both members of what was ironically called the fairer sex neither of them believed in playing fair. Kirsty was sex on legs only when it suited her agenda and may well have enjoyed it, did definitely enjoy it, but this was difficult to confirm. Her beaus were mostly "done" for a purpose or because of drink. Her chances of getting VD or HIV were not high as she believed in protection and kept a supply and used them as a matter of intercourse. Not a hooker, she was pretty bloody manipulative though, using sex to obtain all manner of things.

Marilyn didn't do the one-night stand thing. Nor did she have a significant other. Marilyn was nevertheless no virgin and had been known to get her end away when she felt the need for it and opportunity knocked. She was fussy about who she let into herself. She always kept whoever it was at arm's length—figuratively speaking—but it was normally only flirtations. She had her own device, devices, for keeping herself contented in that respect. The real area of common cause for both of them was making money. Marilyn had money, courtesy of the family "business"; Kirsty, on the other hand, survived mainly on benefits, family and generous men. Kirsty wanted more and had now seen the main chance to get it. Five live people stood in their way, her way. She would protect Becky only up to a point and what exactly that point was still had to be determined. Brad had been an unfortunate accident.

Another Monday at the office. Lizzie was ultra-cautious, never having been in the position of being alone and had been given a panic alarm by Craig for her own protection. Once she tried it in her office. Fuck! Deafening. Mental note—*Alarm works!* She needed to work out what to ask the editors the next day. Finding out what they knew or were prepared to tell her may be difficult, but she could use factors like the disappearance of her workmate and that person's sister to concentrate the minds without consciously pointing any fingers, at least not yet.

Living temporarily with her husband-to-be at his insistence to ensure her safety, lucky bugger, Lizzie was both grateful for his concern but well aware he couldn't wrap her in cotton wool, she had work to do. Monday night, they returned to his flat in Holloway after a good day's work for them both, him sifting through news issues, her preparing for talking to the women.

'I'm not going in early tomorrow. Stuff to do on the laptop. Be in a bit later, lunchtime-ish.'

Craig thought that there was no problem.

'Phone me when you leave, won't you?' She nodded and continued on the laptop. Physical relations had taken a bit of a downturn since all the commotion re the "contract" had started. It wasn't just Lizzie either. Both of them had clearly been affected in that region and it may take time for it to resume. Meanwhile, the fondling, cuddling, kissing, even foot massages continued. Better than nothing, both reckoned. Young love, eh!

Kirsty gave Marilyn the information she needed regarding her sister's phone. From it she was able to access her address list. Mary Callan was amongst the addresses. They would go to pick her up. That would be after they sent a decoy message to Abigail, telling her it was from Mary and they should go and see her immediately. Abigail had a car and always seemed to drive into London. That way, they could take them all at one go.

A fly in that particular ointment would, of course, be what to do with Becky. It would take an intricate bit of management. The plan was to send Becky a text to wait there as Kirsty was on her way in to see her, thus separating her from the others. Kirsty of course, would not appear as she would be in Windsor. It was a bit of a contrived "sticking plaster" type of plan but could work. The Grisham's who still had Brad's Jaguar plus their own cars would go up early, case Mary Callan's home, lie in wait until the car with the women arrived and then pounce. They still had plenty of body bags to spare. They would need an extra one.

CID. in the shape of Detective Inspector Madison had been alerted via underworld contacts that there was a live contract out for unusual subjects. Seemingly, someone—a snout—in the Crystal Palace pub had overheard more than a snippet of a conversation. Normally, such contracts were reserved for members of the criminal fraternity, taken out by rivals or informers. It was highly unusual for any to be taken out on "non-combatants". Quite often, unless in the case of informants where intervention would be mandatory, they may just delay action; after all, if scum wanted to kill other scum, carry on. However, this one seemed a little out of the ordinary. In the first place, the contract had been placed with someone they had no knowledge of. Only a City heavy, Brad, had been involved and they knew him, a junior mobster. It almost, but not quite, flew under their radar.

The disappearance of Lucinda Turner being reported to PC Ronnie Forbes and passed up the line was the action that started the ball rolling and other unconnected information clicked into place. All that was known at that time was that a live contract, taken out by person or persons unknown, was not in fact circulating but that Brad had been brought into the picture to facilitate its execution, both technically and literally. The missing girl and now her sister could have been the subjects of the contract. By deduction and detection, the possibility that Lizzie Spector may also be a likely target was brought to the attention of her fiancé who decided to let her know. The police were now taking an interest in matters but still had little to go on.

Tuesday arrived. Coffee place, Charing Cross. Abigail was always the first to arrive. After five minutes, Marion walked in followed a couple of minutes later by Becky. Lizzie arrived fifteen minutes later. Still no sign of Mary. Marion wasn't best pleased that Abigail had invited Lizzie for a second time, whilst Becky, a "hail fellow, well met" woman, had not much to say except, 'Do you know my sister? She just missed you last week.' Her and the travelling Death Squad, that was! Becky had little awareness of it—it would be a gross understatement to describe it as skulduggery. Murdered one and was accomplice in other murders, not exactly skulduggery, was it!

'I invited her. Met at Wimbledon last week.'

'Lizzie jumped in I'm fascinated in how you can take someone's work and make it compliant with what a publisher is looking for. You have a real talent.'

Lizzie was good at buttering up folk before moving on to what she really wanted to find out. Lizzie was now quite some scribe herself. She talked to them about the editing process, how it was done, what common problems they encountered and suchlike. She was working up to the punch line when Becky's phone rang.

'Hi love. You what? Oh, you need to tell me something…go on then…I'll hang on…now where I am now? I'll hold on for you.'

Becky turned to the others, 'You just carry on, need to stay until Kirsty arrives. Wonder what it's about?' Lizzie heard alarm bells ringing in her head and as she'd travelled by tube decided to make a quick exit.

'I thought you wanted to see Mary. I'm just about to drive up to Windsor. You're very welcome to come with us.'

Lizzie had almost forgotten.

'Yes, if that's all right. We can talk on the way.'

And talk on the way they most definitely did! It was Lizzie's unfettered opportunity to get acquainted with the two of them, particularly Marion, who she sensed had nagging doubts about *Heavenly Hell* now, along with other people who also had doubts. Lizzie gradually unfolded to her what she knew and had been told, hoping to get a response from Marion. Marion was sitting in the front seat next to Abigail with Lizzie deliberately seated behind the driver. As Lizzie told what they had found out, Marion went quiet. Was she just taking it in, deep in thought or clamming up?

Two cars were parked on the road outside the small house of Mary and George Callan. Nothing apparently stirred inside the property and there wasn't a car in the driveway, or maybe they didn't have one, or one or both of them were out. The parked car's occupants, three guys and two women, waited.

Kirsty called her sister again to say she wouldn't be long. She "innocently" asked how her meeting had gone, to be told that the others had left for Windsor.

'That woman you wanted to meet; she's going up with them too.'

Kirsty smiled and gave a thumbs up to the others, said bye and hung up.

'Seems like our reporter is coming to us.' They all laughed and Franny, chirpy as hell, piped up, 'The well will be filling up.'

Meanwhile, in Abigail's car, Marion was now concerned that Lizzie Spector wasn't just suspicious that Ruby Latimer may have "ghosted" part of her book but had been amassing evidence to prove it. She also felt that maybe she needed to talk about it. As she began to bare her soul on the matter, Lizzie's phone rang.

'Hi love, how are you?'

'Fine, Craig. In a car going up to Windsor to see one of the editors.'

'No! Stop! Don't! Madison says there is a contract out on multiple people.'

Lizzie asked how long until they arrived. Under half an hour.

'What's the address? I need the address.' Lizzie told him. They arrived at the villa in a leafy suburb but saw no sign of life. Lizzie got out of the car with the other two and walked over to the front door. She looked around, Abigail rang the bell, no answer. Lizzie, 'Shall I see if there's anyone around the back? Could be they didn't hear us.' Having walked around the back, she thought she heard a slight commotion from where she had just been, then the sound of tyres screeching to a halt and cars roaring away up the road. Lizzie walked back around to see Abigail's car empty, but two police cars parked behind it with lights flashing.

'Miss, are you Elizabeth Spector? We're here to escort you to the station. We think there's going to be an attempt at abduction on yourself.'

Lizzie breathed a deep sigh.

'Where are my other two friends? They were here a moment ago. That's their car.'

There were two policemen from one car, the second had just pulled up directly behind the first and another two officers got out.

'We'll do a circuit of the house. They may have gone around the back.'

They all walked around to the back garden and back to the front. No sign of anyone. Lizzie now feared the worst.

'Maybe we should try the bell again.'

They did. There was no sound. They knocked. Again, no sign of life. Then the door opened. A middle-aged bald man answered.

'You must be Lizzie. Your two friends are here. Come in. Oh officers, is there a problem?'

Lizzie's relief was palpable. There was Abigail and Marion.

'If you don't need us anymore, miss, we'll be off.'

Lizzie was not for letting them go.

'Can one of your cars stay for ten minutes? We need to just have a quick chat here. Won't take long.'

They agreed. One car left whilst officers returned to the other squad car. Abigail told Lizzie, 'Mary's had a wee boy. Both are quite poorly but improving. George's car is in the garage for repair so has been taking the bus to the hospital. He was asking if we could drop him there on the way back, if you don't mind. Says she's not well enough for us to see her yet. Maybe soon.'

Lizzie was surprised that the two other women weren't wondering what two police cars had been doing there. The two editors weren't at all fazed.

'Good to see the local police are so active in the area. Must be a lot of burglaries, I suspect,' never twigging it was something much more serious. Lizzie, Marion and Abigail got a police escort to the hospital to let George off.

Abigail thought this most courteous of them, Marion wasn't so trusting, Lizzie left nothing else to chance and decided to ask one of the cop cars for a lift.

Abigail was heading north to Oxfordshire and would let Marion off at a local station. Lizzie, in one of the cars, talked to the boys in blue.

'Miss, you need to be more careful. We know about your case. We'll take you back to London. Can we suggest you take up the offer of police protection?'

Lizzie said she'd think about it. A close shave if there ever had been one, not actually having realised just how close it had been. Everyone was still at grave risk.

'That was fucking close,' Bob stated the bleeding obvious.

'We should have nabbed 'em when we had the chance instead of waiting until they came out. Fuck it.'

The Grisham's had missed their golden opportunity to get most of their tally in one fell swoop. They had thought to wait until all of them had come out of the house, follow them, run them off the road and…think you can guess the rest. The arrival of two police cars had altered that plan. The family would need to look at doing them all individually, a right pain in the arse but still, money to be made. They started to think that they might need to be a little more cautious in how they went about things.

'Wonder where the bint they were up to see was?' asked Franny.

'Dropping a sprog,' suggested Kirsty.

'You never thought of having one, girl?' Kirsty looked at Franny as if he was both daft and coming on to her. From there on in, there wasn't much conversation.

On the way back in the police car, Lizzie's phone rang.

'Lizzie, it's Marion. I think we need to talk again very soon.'

Lizzie thanked her and agreed to call her back to discuss meeting up at C8. The phone call finished, she gave out a loud, 'Yeess', scaring the two uniforms in the front of the car.

'Good news, miss?'

'The best.'

Meanwhile, an impossible act had taken place. Maybe it had something to do with the position of a satellite hundreds of miles up in the outer atmosphere being in exactly the right place at the right time. Submerged at the bottom of a well in a body bag, with other body bags on top, with virtually no power left, a voice.

'Brad, Grigor.'

Chapter 38
What Lizzie Made Marion Do

'Ruby, Arthur here. I was just wondering, you haven't seen that young pup, Walter, on your travels, have you? … You haven't! We've not seen or heard from him here either. Pity. He's just been taken on by me as a substitute editor. Bit offhand for him not to have been in contact. His wages have been paid into his bank account on Friday and I was wondering…oh well. What I really wanted to tell you was some other news. You're booked into the Edinburgh Book Festival for two days, 14th and 15th August… Yes, wonderful. Greville…just told me. His lot will make all the necessary… Where will you be staying? Balmoral OK with you? Fine…be in touch soon. Other festivals coming up, I suspect.'

Arthur always got his priorities the right way round. He asked about a member of staff who had just been paid but was nowhere to be seen before letting the author know about something exclusive to herself. For her part, Ruby Latimer loved book fairs, brushing shoulders with the not quite so good or great as herself. They must be very grateful she'd deigned to attend their little event. She hadn't been told she was replacing another author there but why spoil her illusion of grandeur. She'd be staying in a very plush hotel and would travel first-class by train. It was still over a month away and no doubt there may be TV and radio stuff to do as long as it had nothing to do with C8 or that horrible Spector woman. In any case, her "friends" must surely have taken care of that problem by then. The "problem", unfortunately for Ruby, was far from being "taken care of".

Lizzie had been dropped off by the police car on that Tuesday. They had made damn sure that someone had been there to escort her in and when they were satisfied all was well, they then headed back up to Windsor. Her little heart had been doing a veritable foxtrot. She was still unaware how very close her and the other two had been to a forcible abduction and murder, literally seconds from that. No, Lizzie's heart was beating so fast because she now seemed to be on the verge of having a key witness to the almost certain literary fraud open up and tell her what she knew or suspected. She phoned Marion French when she got into the office.

'Lizzie, I've been thinking it over and it does bother me. I'd like to talk to you about the book.'

Lizzie had hoped that Marion would have spilled the proverbial beans in the car but, she thought, *better late than never*. Possibly for her ears only? It'd be Friday before she could see her. She arranged for Marion to come into C8 offices. Friday came and at the agreed time…no show! Lizzie thought she'd been given a dizzy. She phoned her to discover that her train had broken down but she'd be there soon. Lizzie had another coffee. Reception texted her, "Your person is here". Lizzie went down to meet her.

'So what changed your mind? No, let's wait and discuss it in the studio.'

Marion hadn't thought that this might happen. Lizzie hadn't mentioned it and now she was being reeled in by this clever young woman.

'I'm not sure about this. Will it be recorded?'

Lizzie just said, 'What do you take in your coffee?'

'Milk and one, thanks. You've not answered my question. I don't want a politician's answer, I want a straight yes or no.'

'Marion, I think you do want to do this. I think you know that something about that book isn't kosher. It's not just a case of deceit, it's about reputation, Ruby Latimer's. I think there might be things you need to be told, things that I've uncovered.'

Marion was apprehensive, nervous and started to wish she was somewhere else. It was much too late for that.

'Let's go in and talk.'

They both went into a small room. In it were two chairs facing each other, a small round table with a jug of water and two glasses and a TV camera that was pointing over the shoulder of whoever was sitting in one of the chairs. It would be facing over Lizzie's shoulder.

'I'll do the lead-in at the end. Just take a seat there,' pointing to the other seat, 'and we can start. Do you have any questions?'

'What's it for? Will I be recognised? Will I be able to get a copy? Can I get any bits I don't like edited out? Can—'

'Whoa, Marion, let me deal with your questions. This is for "Secret Society", the programme I'm working on; you'll only be recognised if you want to be, your face and voice can be disguised if you want, something we can talk about later; you can certainly get a copy of the interview, I'll arrange it myself, and if you want anything edited out, let me know and we can talk about it. Was there anything else?'

Marion started to say something. 'Sorry, I forgot what it was.'

'We will cover today's expenses and if we use you, we will pay you a fee, was that what it was?'

'No, but thanks.'

The interview began. The room was slightly warm but not unduly so. Marion took off her jacket and so did Lizzie, who also slipped off her shoes.

'My feet are killing me. Hope you don't mind.'

Lizzie's feet were actually fine; she thought this act might relax her interviewee a bit, informality and all. Ten minutes into the interview, she had established who Marion was and her role in the editing of the book.

'…And you had edited some of it before you saw the ending.'

'Yes, that's right.'

'And then you got the completed article. What were your thoughts?'

'It was difficult to put into words. When I read it at first, it seemed OK, a bit unusual, that was all. Then I read it again and began to harbour suspicions.'

'Like…?'

'Like it was something the author hadn't completed, or with which she'd had substantial assistance. Can we have a short break please? I need to go to the toilet.'

Lizzie clicked the handheld button, turning off the camera. Marion went to the ladies. Ten minutes and she hadn't returned. Lizzie thought she'd better go and see if she was OK.

'Marion, you OK?' No answer from the cubicle. 'Need any help?'

A slight sobbing was audible. 'No, just coming out.' In a minute, she came out, her face red, eyes as well.

'Lizzie, sorry, I just don't think I'm cut out for this, being a grass.'

Lizzie had tried diplomacy and gentle persuasion but clearly another approach was needed. She brought out her phone and scrolled to a photo.

'Marion, that's me in the middle and on either side are Gretchen and Lucinda, both friends, both officers of the Ruby Latimer Fan Club, both with the same suspicions you have and now, both missing. Something is going on and we need to get to the bottom of it. I want to see my friends again.'

Lizzie and Marion returned to the room. Marion had washed her face and re-applied her lipstick. She took in a deep breath and waited for the questions again. Lizzie played back the question on the camera.

'I talked about it to my fellow editors but didn't take it any further in case it jeopardised my job. I'm not naturally a whistle-blower but no one else had been credited with the book so I was a bit uneasy, still am.'

'And what did your fellow editors think?'

'They just listened. They trusted my judgement, I suppose.'

'Have you anything you want to add?'

'Young Walter from our agency thought the same as me. I wouldn't use that until you talk to him though.'

'Thank you, Marion'

Marion's ordeal was over. She sat for a minute and put her head in her hands.

'I really shouldn't have done it. I'm a bloody fool. Really.'

Lizzie, after all her efforts, was still on the verge of losing this valuable bit of recording. She still had one card left to play.

'You won't know this, and you can't tell anyone but Lucinda, my friend that's missing, took the book to a professor specialist in Bristol. She verified that the book had two different authors. Your suspicions are correct.'

Marion sat stone-faced. Lizzie still wasn't sure how she would react. She said nothing and put on her jacket.

'When is the programme coming out?'

'Can't say. Up to the producer.'

Just at that moment, the door opened and in stepped Ambreen. Lizzie did the introductions. Ambreen was an authority on body language and could tell immediately that there was a problem. Lizzie introduced them.

'Marion's still not too sure about this exposé.'

Ambreen was so good with people. She took Marion's hand. 'Marion, you should know that we have a reputation to uphold of doing what is right by the public and in the public interest. If you've any doubts about that, give me a call. We're not cowboys. We play everything with a straight bat. If this is a fraud, don't you think readers should be told?'

Those words seemed to help. Marion left with a mild smile and a much better disposition. Lizzie was smiling slightly but kept remembering that photo and thinking, *Where are they? And where's Walter?*

George Pope, Gretchen's Bishop Stortford friend had also been trying to contact Gretchen and had been having about as much luck as everyone else. He was neither faithful nor loyal, but he was a young man and he and Gretchen had got it on twice, the second time for a lusty, lengthy weekend. He thought she was really hot. It wasn't love, just sex, but wow! He wanted to know if she was "available". She didn't return his calls, not that she had much before, unless she was at times as horny as he was, and they could talk dirty phone sex to each other. He was hoping to arrange to see her. After several attempts and total failure, he thought about taking a walk up to the big house to see what gave. George went up to see a police car just driving off. He was in two minds about going up but as he was there, he rang the bell. A woman answered, looked him up and down and asked what he wanted.

'I'm Gretchen's friend.'

'I'm very sorry, she's not here. I don't know about her present whereabouts. You're the second young man calling for her. Popular girl.'

It was then that the housekeeper told him Gretchen and Lucinda were missing.

'Was that the reason for the police then?'

'Yes,' and shut the door in his face. George just shrugged his shoulders, walked away and lifted his phone out of his pocket.

'Helen, maybe Iris…'

Grisham's had now killed four people: two themselves, kind of; Brad had killed one, kind of; Kirsty had killed one of theirs, no "kind of" there. None of it had been sophisticated stuff, a brick to the nut and shoved down a well was not at all sophisticated, dropping three barely living human beings down, even less so. However, it had just been a day at the office. Brad's expertise had proved to be a serious loss in the killing side of things, but Kirsty had just gotten the hang of it and actually quite enjoyed it. The gang had a couple of close calls in getting two editors and that reporter. Surely, they would run out of luck soon, the only question being who would be the ones to run out of luck—the gang or their intended victims.

Kirsty thought it might be a good idea to give "her authorship" an update and see if she could get some money on account—on account of three fucking murders, Brad didn't count. Call him a dividend. Kirsty phoned to update her. She would meet Ruby in the same Crystal Palace pub as last time on a Monday going on towards the end of July. It was quiet and there was a snug, which was private enough for them to talk without anyone overhearing. A whispering conversation took place.

'We've done three so far and will get the others in the next week.'

'What three?'

'Two sisters and…I dunno. Never saw her. In a body bag. Our hitman did that one.'

'Hitman? And proof?'

'Proof!'

'Photos or something. How do I know you lot are up to the job? Evidence please!'

'You're joking! We have (in a whisper) murdered three fuckers for you. You want proof? Call this,' and Kirsty gave Ruby Lucinda and Gretchen's numbers.

'You'll get no answer 'cos they're down the bottom of a bl…told you too much already.'

'OK, I get the picture. I don't but I do. Just get the rest of the job done. I'm off on a book signing tour. When I'm back, I want the fuckers gone, have I made it plain enough?'

'We'll need money to finish off the job. Expensive business this.' Ruby gave Kirsty money.

'I expected you'd be asking for something on account.'

Ruby handed over a large envelope. Kirsty peeked inside it and almost spewed. Ruby mouthed, '50k.'

'Careful changing them. Just make sure that fucking bitch Spector is gone when I get back from Edinburgh, understand?' And with that, the discussion ended. Ruby finished her drink, got up and left. Kirsty sat on. The envelope she had been given was thick. It was amazing how only £100 notes could feel so bulky. Not counting it, Kirsty put the packet inside her jacket pocket.

A number, correction, a hundred, OK, fifty thousand things crossed Kirsty Letts' mind. She had expected maybe £50, not £50k. She had never seen money like that in her life, let alone had it nestled against her left breast. She knew it was just a fraction on account, showing her gang that Ruby Latimer meant business and what to expect when the job was finished. Her quandary was what to do now. The expression, "honour amongst thieves", was a meaningless throwaway phrase. There was no such thing. She could take the money and scarper. £50k would buy a lot of…well, everything. However, she'd then be a fugitive from the Grisham's, unable to stay at home, see her sister, live the life she'd become accustomed to. And there was the matter of the money. £100 notes would be a nightmare to change. What shopkeeper, bartender or bookie wouldn't check it out, rustle it, put it up to the light? Couldn't just pop into the office, say a bottle of Chardonnay and flash one at the counter staff. No, Ruby Latimer knew that it would take someone more skilled than KL to have that money laundered. In any case, Kirsty needed a bank account, something she didn't possess. *Let's think*, and she did, continuing to furtively flick through the notes like they were a pack of new playing cards. *Maybe just one, a bonus for me?*

Chapter 39

Unusual Business

Regardless of this now seemingly foolhardy and increasingly risky venture, the Grisham Corporation was still in full operation, the money stream constant, rivals now quite literally cinders. If you wanted to equate the family to a large business, Bob was CEO, but Marion was company secretary/treasurer. She took care of all the financial issues and money flow stuff, for example.

'Franny, such-and-such missed a payment last week. Can you pay them another visit?'

So, it was Marilyn who Kirsty went to visit. Almost two days after getting that envelope, Kirsty texted Marilyn, "Need to see you. Got something."

It was a Wednesday morning in July. Marilyn and Kirsty shared a few things in common, but the main common characteristic, apart from a hardness borne out of poverty, was being bitches. Some women had "bitch" hardwired into their DNA. It was a hard trait to accurately define but it was normally a distaste of one woman by another, just because they were the same gender, shown by attitude or deeds. The one thing, in fact, the only thing that held these two together, rather than rolling on the office floor and punching lumps out of each other, was naked greed.

Kirsty thought herself to be pretty streetwise until she met Marilyn. Marilyn was sharper in every way, but it had just been a matter of experience. Kirsty came to the Grisham "office" in a back room in their home. A bit grubby but everything they needed was there—computer, scanner, printer, phones, etc. Kirsty sat down and explained her meeting and what she had been given. Marilyn didn't even bat an eyelid.

'So, where's the money then?'

Kirsty handed over a clearly now unsealed envelope.

'I've taken out £100. Services rendered and all that.'

'GIVE IT BACK NOW!'

Kirsty learnt a basic lesson—Marilyn knew best. Marilyn was very smart at what she did and what she did was launder money and fence goods. Kirsty went a bit red in the face.

'Can't. Already been spending it. Ted, the landlord at the local, changed it for me.'

'That was fucking stupid. I could have laundered it, and no one would ever have known. Now it's fucking well out there with your tabs on it.'

Kirsty felt a bit sheepish. 'I was skint. I needed it. Sorry.'

'Too late now. We work as a team. You're now part of the team. Well done getting the money, but next time…'

Kirsty understood. Marilyn went into a cash box in a drawer and handed Kirsty a wad. '£1,000 OK to keep you in spliff and drink for a while? I'll tell Bob you did OK.'

Kirsty Letts had never in her entire life been so rich. Her Universal Credit, for what that was worth, did at least mean that she had somewhere to stay. The grand "fun money" she'd just gotten would mean no needing to be "nice" to arseholes for a couple of weeks and who knew what else. Kirsty was useless with money, saving it, that was, brilliant at spending it. She had mentally spent it five minutes after it left Marilyn's hand.

'When we gonna do the others then?'

'Bob's side of things. You need to tell him you've seen me and what you got. Expect he'll be working on it. Think personally after the last cock-up, we need to pick them off one at a time. Going for them as a job lot ain't working, is it?'

That afternoon, Kirsty saw Bob at the family home. He was staying there for the moment because his own flat was just a bit too far away to easily jump back and forth whilst all the Ruby stuff was about.

'That bedsit, you hate it, right?'

'It's OK. Don't want to stay much longer though.'

'Use my place. Here's the keys. We're going to pick up one of the editors soon. One at a time from now on.'

Bob wasn't telling Kirsty the whole truth. He knew that sooner or later, Kirsty's sister would need to be dealt with. She would be well down the list. Next one would need to be the French bint, Marion French.

Meanwhile, things had moved down a gear at C8. A slight hiatus existed over the "Secret Society" programme production. Other interviews would be forthcoming, but the lack of verifiable and corroborated evidence, a studio imperative, was stalling progress and until they could get someone, anyone, to validate the assertion of Professor Llewelyn that *Heavenly Hell* was a collaborative effort, then there was a large gap in their story. Lizzie searched the net for someone who might be able to do what Professor Llewelyn had, but there were no hits. Seemed she had been pretty unique. Lizzie thought about the phone number. Maybe they could set up a sting operation. Tricky but possible, but if Ruby Latimer had used "GW" to have her novel finished off, it must have been authorised by someone in that organisation. For all she knew, it could have been a bunch of kids with a cool network of other kids who were great at writing, or who knew writers or folk in the profession. Lizzie was getting a headache thinking about it. She looked at her phone and was tempted to call the "GW" number but hesitated. She had forgotten to ask Marion French. She gave her a call but just got her answerphone. She left a message for her to call back.

Two days later, nothing. By then, Lizzie had been listing all the writers' events Ruby Latimer would be attending either side of the Edinburgh Book Festival. She had a couple before it but apparently, the Festival was her last one. Lizzie put a note of the dates in her diary.

Kirsty meanwhile had moved into Bob's old place, and he had even gotten Tony to help her. Tony, Marilyn's twin, was a follower but was basking in the power and money that had accrued to the family. They all tried not to raise suspicions about their lifestyle but buying property was part of what Tony did. He had one in a tower block in Hackney, a repossession in Bethnal Green and was on the lookout for something nearer home. Once bought they did a lick and spit job and got refugees in, not ethical but what the fuck. It meant someone was there heating the place and money would be coming in. Win, win.

Tony had a quick shufty around Bob's place when helping Kirsty move her stuff—actually, three cardboard boxes and an old suitcase, Kirsty wasn't asset-rich, at least not quite yet. She wasn't cash-rich yet either having squandered more than half the cash and had less than a monkey left. It was a two-bedroom affair, modest but with a kick-ass TV and other nice stuff. Bob had a method in his madness. Kirsty didn't know it yet, but she was soon to be a chaperone to another "guest".

Grigor knew something was up. It just wasn't Brad's style to vanish unless he'd been "vanished". He knew some things about the work he'd been doing and as he was a free agent, that was fine. He knew the general area of London but not much more. He'd tried to call him again but this time there was nothing, the phone always went immediately to answer mode. He tried again to be told "This number is not operative". It had become increasingly annoying. Grigor had been training Brad to be an active spider in increasing the web that was the mob. He was working but also doing reconnaissance of the area. He should have been done and back but wasn't. Grigor phoned Boris.

Craig got a phone call. Michael Madison had some news that he couldn't give over the phone. He wanted Craig and Lizzie to come in and see him early next morning. He would send them a car. It sounded ominous. Lizzie wondered what it would be about. In her heart of hearts, she already knew. What she didn't know would shake her to her very core.

Chapter 40

Autopsies

Craig and Lizzie sat in the outer office at Isle of Dogs police station, waiting to see DI Madison. It wasn't usual, it was a special, unconventional favour, one that, if it got out, could have led to serious consequences for himself. He had information to give them and none of it was good news. He came out, greeted them looking suitably solemn and ushered them into the police interview room holding a document. It was the result of more than one post-mortem. He felt that they should know not only because of Lizzie's relationship with some of them but because they now knew that her life had been and still was in danger.

Lizzie read the summary report. She took a handkerchief from her handbag and wiped her eyes, shoulders now hunched and heaving. Craig put his arm around her shoulders. The report announced the death of no less than six people, two 21 months previously, four as recently as a couple of weeks before. Two of the people were recent friends, one she only recently knew, and three she had no knowledge of. Lizzie, a bit red-eyed, tough as nails, but not quite so tough now, had just read of the deaths of two sisters and one other, all of whom had one thing in common—their relationship with Ruby Latimer. Lizzie looked up into the eyes of a wholly sympathetic officer and asked, 'How?'

DI Madison sighed. 'All six bodies were found in a well in Kent. Are you up to hearing the circumstances? It will take a bit of time and is not surprisingly, harrowing.'

Lizzie had great fortitude and nodded for him to continue.

'A week ago, we got a phone call. The caller told us of something suspicious at an abandoned well in Kent. Our people, forensics and others, visited it and discovered several bodies. We recovered them and the post-mortems showed their identity and cause of death. The reason I'm asking you to not divulge information on this at this time is to allow us to inform their next-of-kin. Are you happy to do this?'

Lizzie and Craig both nodded.

'I presume you have questions to ask.'

Lizzie was still in shock. She had hoped against hope for her new friends to turn up but not in this way. Her first question was how did they die?

'Lucinda Turner, fractured skull, though she had other injuries that may have contributed to her death. Gretchen Turner, broken neck. Death wasn't instantaneous but sudden in her case and there were other factors. She was also pregnant.'

'Pregnant!'

'Twins apparently.'

'God,' was all Lizzie could say through floods of tears.

'We believe that the other one, from personal items on him, is a Walter Sims. We still need positive identification, which is why we need to not make this public just yet.'

The medical team that had carried out the autopsies had not had the most pleasant of times, even given their imperative of dissecting corpses. They were used to the occasionally grizzly case but to have so many at one time was rare. Samples would be required for toxicology testing and, given the number of bodies, the involvement of a forensic psychiatrist to speak to those who may have knowledge of possible motive. The fact that so many bodies had been found in one location and having been dumped there on two separate occasions many months apart would suggest a connection of sorts.

The team had started with the two not in body bags. Having needed to return to room temperature so as to be able to separate them, the ME (Medical Examiner) took Subject A and the diener had considerable difficulty undressing them. The ME proceeded with the necessary dissection and the report showed that Subject A, male, died of trauma, dehydration, malnutrition and blood loss. The subject was minus a nose and the chin had been roughly removed by a semi-sharp object. The contents of the still bloated stomach had shown little remaining evidence of any undigested substances. The bloodstream had signs of narcotics.

Subject B male, also died of trauma, dehydration and malnutrition but evidence suggests the subject had died after Subject A. The contents of the stomach also showed signs of bloating and the undigested remains of what appeared to be the nose and chin of Subject A. The teeth marks on the nose and chin were from Subject B. The ME could only speculate mentally on what circumstances would force one man to turn cannibal. Extreme hunger, desperation, revenge all sprang to mind. Purely speculative at that stage. Both bodies had been in a cold, damp environment for at least 21 months and the process of removing them from the well, despite due care and attention, had resulted in some damage to the integrity of the corpses, of which Subject B had lost his right arm, ripped from the shoulder socket by a combination of probably contact from one or more other bodies and a brick found at the bottom of the well. That was the interim conclusion of the coroner's report.

'There's more you need to know, Mr Endoran, Miss Spector, and this may help us in identifying a suspect or suspects. The women and the man, Sims, had been sexually assaulted before being thrown down the well.'

Lizzie took in this information and was just about on the verge of losing it. Craig held her as she sobbed. She thought to herself, *Girl, you must get a grip.* In a minute, she was back up with a smile of sorts, saying, 'Go on.'

'We have evidence of the assault in the form of semen from all three victims.'

'Three! But…' She could only imagine what kind of animal would rape as it transpired, two bound and gagged, helpless women AND a man. It was beyond her comprehension.

'So, will you be doing DNA testing to discover who it was then?'

'That's already away to the lab. Toxicology and DNA results can take a while, but the Kent Chief Constable and the Met Commissioner have fast-tracked these as a priority.'

Lizzie was not just in a state of grief and mounting anger, she wanted to know as much as she could to encourage and spur her on to find who had been responsible.

'Had they been drugged before…?'

'They had been bound with cable ties, their mouths superglued and were in body bags. We think all were probably still alive when they were dropped down the well. We also think the man survived the fall.' Poor Walter.

The ME had finished with the two cadavers and the diener returned them to the mortuary and the recorded notes were sent to be entered on file. He was now ready for the other four, but not until the next day.

Returning the following day, he started with a corpse described as "well-dressed, thirty-five to forty years of age, six feet". The contents of the designer suit and the corpse's jewellery had been removed. This one clearly was well off, judging by the Rolex, 24-carat chain and rings. He also had, in his inside pocket, a smartphone, damaged by water but still with possibilities for information retrieval, as well as a leather wallet containing several cards and £800 in large denominations. The cards, if they weren't stolen, identified that man. There were also a set of keys—one looked like probably house and car keys, the other with a Jaguar insignia on it. The car keys looked suspect, possibly the spare key.

The ME began the autopsy. He noted that there were several abrasions on the body, consistent with being struck by blunt objects. The ME had been made aware of the consistency of the well walls and noted that they could have been the cause. These were all duly photographed and measured. He examined the head and noted that, apart from a sizeable piece of missing skull at the back of the head, the face had been badly crushed, something that may have happened recently but not simultaneously with the other injury. He deduced that the cause of death had been the damage to the rear of the skull. He estimated that the body had been there in the well for approximately two weeks. In order to be certain, he began the process of removing the brain from the skull. The DNA samples had been taken prior to freezing so they were available, but a significant amount of crosschecking had not identified them as neither was on the police database. More investigations were needed at that stage, but given the plethora of evidence, identification was virtually certain.

Craig asked for a short break. Coffee was duly provided. This was clearly a murder investigation. Michael Madison asked what Lizzie knew of the victims' backgrounds and movements prior to their disappearance.

'I don't really know much about the man, Walter. Only met him a couple of times, I think. He gave us all, me, Lucinda and Gretchen a massage a while back. I was waiting in the Red Lion in Whitehall where I'd arranged to meet Gretchen and Lucinda, I think you know because it was that which prompted me to report them missing. I'm not sure where they were coming from when they disappeared. Sorry.'

None of them realised at that time that because of the sudden murder of Brad, some things that he was about to say to the others that needed to be done had been left unsaid, like, "we need to search them all for ID, mobiles etc, just in case." The changed situation resulted in all the bodies being thrown down the well unsearched and with enough information on them to make a 3D image of them all. Such professionalism. It was still morning at the police station and whilst DI Madison knew the identities, he was still waiting for more information on causes of death and other forensic information. Those phones, what a break!

The other man was next.

'Male, mid-twenties, five foot eight, noticeable upper body development.' He then examined the wrists of the corpse.

'Marks on wrists and ankles consistent with some form of restraint. It was necessary to remove cable ties from the corpse to allow this examination to proceed. These are now in the possession of the authority dealing with this case.'

The ME examined the body. 'Marks evident on arms and body also consistent with coming in contact with blunt force objects, entirely likely the well's internal façade. There is also considerable bruising in the anal region.'

He then examined the face. 'The mouth is sealed with some form of adhesive. I am now removing it and opening the mouth.'

He did this with a scalpel and examined the inside of the mouth, which had a layer of congealed blood on it.

'It would appear that the subject had been attempting to open his mouth by biting at the adhesive but only succeeded in biting his tongue and inside of the mouth. Not sure at this stage if this contributed to death. Orifices having been partially sealed plus corpse containment may have delayed or prevented blowfly inundation.'

He asked the diener if the report of the forensic recovery team had mentioned a blowfly presence in the well and this was confirmed. He examined the hands. Minute DNA samples, likely to be skin and blood of a person or persons unknown, were contained under the fingernails. He deduced it may be due to excessive moisturisation. The ME, assisted by his team, carefully turned the body onto its back. He noted other abrasions. He noticed discoloration around the anus. This was swabbed and sent for analysis. He deduced it was from a foreign object. The lab would be able to determine the nature of the matter, possibly putrescence, possibly something else. It now seemed confirmed that the body bags plus the cold temperature had protected the bodies from blowfly infestation. The samples were sent to the lab for DNA for differential extraction to determine the nature of the matter. The autopsy continued with the removal of internal organs and the brain. This body was different to the others in respect of the actual cause of death being less obvious that the previous one. The ME's judgement was that it was due to dehydration. Walter had died of thirst.

Madison was reluctant to speculate about his probable line of enquiry with the couple before him. It was truly a conundrum. There were at least two separate cases, those in and those out of body bags. He thought that it must have been a coincidence that the bodies had all ended up in that one place. Another DI was dealing with the "gruesome twosome", as they were now being called (not publicly). Their identities were not confirmed at that time. Suddenly, there was a knock on the interview room door.

'Gov, some information.'

He stepped out for a minute and then returned. The identities of the ones removed by cryogenics had been told to him. One was an Albany Lansdowne, third Baronet of Lansdowne, son of a member of the House of Lords. The second was a Rodney Sutcliffe, a businessman who had resided in Chelsea. There seemed to be no connection with the other four, the only nagging question being who knew about that location? Someone who put Lansdowne and Sutcliffe there must have known it to be a place to stash bodies with impunity; therefore, whoever put the first two there may well have been responsible for the others as well.

Madison went back to Lizzie and Craig to confirm the sisters' interests.

'They were officers in the Ruby Latimer Fan Club.'

'The what?'

'The author. Gretchen was secretary and Lucinda was honorary chair. We were working on a line of enquiry, sorry, story. Now they're both dead.'

God. Madison noted this down. *It might be important*, he thought.

'You may not be aware but other bodies were in the well. I know you knew of one, Baronet Lansdowne.'

Lizzie showed an expression of realisation of that name, which Madison immediately picked up.

'The Stratfordgate stalker. Of course, I knew of him.'

'There is only one common denominator here and it's you, Lizzie.'

Lizzie couldn't work out what was going on. It was a plot thicker than an Agatha Christie whodunit. Baronet Albany Lansdowne, exposed as the Stratford Stalker by the Achilles Heel clandestine group, had disappeared almost two years previously. He was thought to have travelled abroad to avoid arrest. Rodney Sutcliffe had been a drugs supplier to the Baronet for his high-ranking clientele, but when Stratfordgate broke, he had grown weary of his shenanigans and with help, had decided to dispose of him down that well. Unfortunately, his hired help,

Grigor and Co., also had an agenda, courtesy of McMafia boss, Boris. Sutcliffe had gone down the well first and then Lansdowne, both alive but bound. Only imagination could work out what had happened down that well.

The two young women were last. The ME did likewise with them but felt the causes of death—fractured skull and broken neck—were sufficient. He did examine all orifices and noted glued mouths, damaged genitalia, both externally and, from what he could observe, internally. He swabbed the lower orifices and sent the contents to the lab for DNA differential extraction. There was no need to do any internal forensic work. The post-mortems were complete. Conclusion of examinations: six homicides.

In the circumstances, the ME asked if the lab could fast-track their work as this could be the actions of a serial killer. Madison had just been informed of the valuables found on the bodies. He was particularly interested in the phones and the sets of keys, particularly the car keys. They knew one was Sutcliffe, cards had identified him. They would run a check on the key reference number to see who it had been sold to and get the registration number. It came back as AV17 HBC, a Jaguar F-Pace. The keeper of the original was confirmed as Rodney Sutcliffe, one identification seemingly solved. Whilst the other one had no ID at all as well as no nose or chin, he did have hands. After the length of time he had been in the well, it would be an extremely difficult job to get verifiable prints but with the use of state-of-the-art technology, they managed it, and the fingerprint database identified him as Albany Lansdowne.

Lansdowne had been arrested but released nearly two years earlier, the records showed this, and at that time, he had been fingerprinted, which was fortuitous as identification may have proved a problem. Facial reconstruction may well have been necessary but that could wait for now. So that was those two boxed off. The other four were rudimentary. All had ID of various types, not to mention mobile phones. These were being checked for information. Despite being down the well, only Brad had been fully submerged, and the body bags had been waterproof. Information came burling off all devices.

A forensic psychiatrist came in and talked to Lizzie. He wanted to get some background details about the people Lizzie knew in order to start to piece together what appeared to be a very rare case, where five out of six people had been deposited there still breathing. After an hour, he left to consider what information he had accrued. Lizzie was inch-by-inch coming to terms with not just her loss but also with what a lucky escape she may just have had. She could have ended up at the bottom of that well with her friends.

Lizzie Spector used a technique called mind mapping, a technique aiding recall and plotting events. She asked for a piece of foolscap blank paper and began to work. Several bubbles appeared, drawn by her on the page. In the centre of the page, she wrote "Lizzie" and drew a circle around it. She then drew more circles around her name and added the other names of those she knew, all of whom were dead. She connected up with lines those who knew each other. She then drew up names of other people who may have known about the murdered people. One by one, names were added on the outside of this growing circle of death. It was taking shape. The name Ruby Latimer was added, and her known connections joined by lines. It would, of course, be incomplete but at least Madison could see an emerging pattern. There were indeed questions waiting to be asked and answered by others, including a particular author.

The foolscap paper showed Lizzie in the middle surrounded by the others. Craig looked at it and said, 'No darling, I think you are wrong. She should be in the middle.' He took another piece of foolscap and filled it in, placing Ruby Latimer in the centre and reconstructed the mind map.

'God. I never thought. If this is true…'

It clearly showed connections to several people. What was still missing, of course, was the gangster element responsible for the murders but hopefully, forensics would divulge clues to their identity soon.

After about three hours, Craig took Lizzie back home, his home. She was shattered but he could see her revving up inside to "release hell". Until then, she needed to go home, chill out, switch off and he would help. He ran her a bath. His love and respect for his fiancée just grew daily.

Chapter 41

Lizzie on a Mission from God

The Grisham's had quite a few loose ends to take care of. Bob was not at all used to dealing with this level of virtually everything—violence, criminality, covering their tracks. He had been stretched so far out of his comfort zone that he was…well, bloody uncomfortable. He was an empirical, not a methodical, planner, his attention to detail totally zilch. They had gotten nearly £50k for what they'd accomplished so far but there was more to be done, others to be murdered. It would be worth £450k so it was a no-brainer. First things first though.

He talked to Marilyn and she agreed that the swanky car they had, which must have been worth at least what they'd gotten in cash from that bitch, was parked in their shed-cum-garage. It was safe enough there, but they thought twice about driving it around. Thinking twice about something proved to be a bit of a unique experience. Bob instructed Tony to go through the car with a fine-tooth comb, remove all of Brad's stuff and bring them so that he and Marilyn could have a look at it before destroying. Brad was a messy bastard and the car was full of all sort of stuff: beer cans, fags, used prophylactics—he must have had a right old time to himself—and various papers. They came across a logbook for the vehicle. It showed that it was registered to Brad. It also showed that it had been previously registered to someone with the strange name of Grigor. The logbook, of course, was a forgery but someone in DVLA had "assisted" in getting it and getting the car on their database. Bob wondered about getting it registered in one of their names. What about Butcher Mike? Surely, he'd not say no to such an opportunity. He'd fucking better not! The car had been in the garage for two weeks already. He thought he should give him a call.

Lizzie was now, the day after, thinking of getting back to her work. Work would help. Her and Craig had spent a fair time talking about the situation and the mounting but very compelling circumstantial evidence implicating Ruby

Latimer in the entire miserable dealings. She looked at the redrawn mind map and could see who had connections with who, and many led back to the author. She then considered who out there had knowledge of or might have played a role similar to herself. They all could have been in danger. The whole list: Ruby Latimer, Gretchen Turner, Lucinda Turner, Walter Sims, Craig Endoran, Ambreen Gubta, Rebecca Letts, Abigail Roberts, Marion French, Mary Callan, Professor Llewelyn. There could well have been quite a few more that she wasn't aware of, such as relatives, etc.

Lizzie went through the names of the living and thought it might be necessary, imperative, to warn them of…well, that was the question. *Lizzie, put your journalist hat on. You can use this to get information under the guise of concern for their safety.* She thought about who was the most at risk. Did Ruby Latimer know about the professor? Walter Sims was a key figure in knowing who knew what. It may well be that if there was a contract out, it was for anyone knowing or suspecting a fraud had taken place. Lizzie didn't know if this Professor Llewelyn was known to the unidentified assassins. If she was on the list, Lizzie would need to get to her pronto. She determined that she should go to Bristol.

"Someone" had been snooping, asking around Orpington about who the Mr Big in the area was and where they stayed. It wasn't long before a name and address was forthcoming. The police had up until then had a workmanlike relationship with the Grisham's. However, mass murder was a bit of a dealbreaker. They were still unaware of the Grisham's central role in the contents of the Cobham well. They would find out soon enough. The "someone" got all the information they needed. That afternoon, the "someone" made a surreptitious trip to the Grisham house and had a peek through the garage/shed doors. "Someone" took photos and left. His boss would be interested in what he'd discovered. That "someone" now knew a lot more about this family of, relatively speaking, petty criminals, but they had a car, a lovely Jag, and his colleague, Brad, was nowhere to be seen. "Someone" now had them on his list. He and his boss would now be listening into their conversations, courtesy of the three mini mics now attached on the walls and garage. "Someone" had gotten into the side door of the garage and placed a mini-tracker device under Brad's motor, just for good measure.

Ruby Latimer was on her way up to Scotland. She had a couple of smaller book festivals to attend in the Borders before heading for the big one. Having arrived in Edinburgh, she headed for her suite in the Balmoral. This hotel, one of the premier establishments in Scotland, was just the ticket. The reception clerk had a letter for her that she took up to her room to read. Whilst a maid was unpacking, she sat down, took off her designer shoes, made herself comfortable and read it. A film draft contract for *Heavenly Hell*! *Cracked it at last! Yeesss!* It was all she could think. It had taken longer than it had taken Murray to win Wimbledon, but it was there at last. She was told not to make it public, especially not to the Edinburgh Book Festival as many, many details were still up for discussion. Nevertheless, it was a red-letter day. She ordered a bottle of Dom and toasted herself, her good fortune, her sparkling rebirth and the soon-to-be deaths of those infidel accusers of plagiarism that plagued her so. Ruby was feeling indefatigable. She was possibly heading for yet another rude awakening.

Lizzie was now, in the words of Elwood Blues, *"on a mission from God"*. She had seen from the mind map that possibly several other people could be at risk. As long as the instigator of the purge of those in the know was unfinished, no one, including herself, would be totally safe. Lizzie looked again at the list and remembered something strange when they had visited Mary Callan—those screeching tyres. Had that been anything to do with this? She thought about phoning those whose phone numbers she had but to tell them what? Was that even her job? One thing did stand out: she needed to see the Professor to see if she would change her mind. If Ruby Latimer knew of her existence, she could well want her, and her evidence disposed of.

Lizzie was up and running, running to Paddington. Such an impetuous girl! She waited until she was on the Bristol train before calling Craig as she knew just how he would have reacted if she'd been face-to-face with him; he'd have gone spare with her on the grounds of personal safety. If she had been in the Middle East, she'd have been wearing a flap jacket. In Bristol, a raincoat would suffice. On a diabolically wet Thursday, she made her way from Temple Meads Station to the university, hopefully not on a wild goose chase.

The university, then in Summer recess, told her that, yes, they had an Emeritus Professor Llewelyn. She was partly retired, hence the term "Emeritus", but still did some lecturing; however, she was at home that day. They heard her abridged story about the fraud, not the murders, and gave her a telephone number. Lizzie called and introduced herself as a friend of Lucinda Turner. A hesitant Professor listened to the pleading of the young reporter and decided to take pity on her. She told her where she lived and to come over.

By the time Lizzie arrived at the Professor's rather grand Victorian front door, it was raining pretty heavily. She answered the door of this somewhat old-fashioned, terraced house and all she saw was this thoroughly drenched apology for a young woman, despite an expensive raincoat. Lizzie thought she could walk from the university up to the professor's—it hadn't looked too far on the map and it had been dry when she started out, and then the rain!

'Oh! You poor thing. You're soaked right through. I'll fetch you a towel. And get that coat off and those shoes.'

Lizzie did what she was told, possibly being one of the few times in her entire life that she had obeyed someone else! She came in and apologised for the intrusion. Professor Llewelyn was intrigued.

'How did you know about me?'

'Lucinda Turner told me. She also wanted you to be kept out of it. That's why I'm here. I think there's something very serious going on. Very serious.'

The professor took Lizzie's supersaturated coat and wet shoes, placed them near her Aga and offered her a hot drink. Having settled at the table, Lizzie took her designer leather bag—a present from Craig—and brought out various papers she had printed. She had a quick read whilst sipping on her tea.

'Lucinda Turner gave me your name and told me what you did for her. She was very grateful.'

'I'm very uneasy with her sharing that. I told her I couldn't get involved.'

From the expression on Lizzie's face the Professor knew something bad must have happened. 'Professor, Lucinda and her sister have been murdered.'

The professor was visibly shocked, saddened by this horrible fact. She sat down at the mahogany kitchen table.

'Why, how, just who would do such a thing?'

'Someone with a secret to protect, one Lucinda and Gretchen Turner suspected and one you confirmed it seems to me.'

For the professor, this appalling news was a game changer. She had wanted to keep out of the limelight. She had used university time and the university cloud to confirm that the origin of *Heavenly Hell* was two people, not one. Now she wanted to help.

'Professor let me be clear, the people who murdered those two young women, I believe, know about your involvement. We need to stop them and fast,' at which point, Lizzie produced her/Craig's mind map and other evidence.

236

Professor Llewelyn was now the one that was silent. 'I'm retiring properly before the next term. Not much they will be able to do to me then. How can I help?'

'I need a copy of your report outlining this fraud. Can I get a copy please?'

A studious academic, Professor Llewelyn went into her study and returned with a ring-bound document entitled *Heavenly Hell* and handed it to Lizzie, who took her vein-lined hand in a show of utmost gratitude. She needed to get back to Temple Meads and the Professor kindly offered her a lift.

'You need to be vigilant, Professor. If I'm in danger, then so are you. I know exactly what I need to do with this and the other evidence but first of all, there's somewhere north of here I'm needed.'

'Thought you were headed for Paddington?'

'Yes, but Monday next week. 15th August.'

'Something else I did you might be interested in…'

Lizzie listened and realised what she could also find out, but later. It might not just be Ruby Latimer being exposed.

'For fuck's sake, Lizzie, you know the danger. Why didn't you tell me where you were going?' Craig gave Lizzie a squeeze that told her she was his most precious. She was on tiptoes, still a bit wet, but she unravelled herself from his clutches and said, 'If you'd have known, you'd have tried to stop me. Darling, I do know the danger. Besides that, I now have evidence here,' patting her bag. They went off to Craig's flat. She was coming back to be that woman he had fancied and now clearly loved. They talked over a glass of wine about the situation and what to do. If they had evidence, then they would need to take it to Madison. However, the journalist genes kicked in and Lizzie had a better idea.

'Fancy a trip to the Edinburgh Book Festival? Hear Ruby Latimer?'

'You fucker, Spector, you wouldn't… YOU WOULD!' He knew what she had in her inventive, calculating little head. He loved it.

'I'll need a cameraman.'

'It's Friday night. You'll be lucky.'

'Fix it please,' she said with a determined, quasi-threatening, quasi-privileges withholding, quasi-pleading, quasi-womanly stare, one that would unnerve some not used to her ways. Craig had to do some begging, but he managed it.

'Phil will meet you at eleven on Monday morning.'

Lizzie would collect her overnight bag, take a train up on Sunday, have a look around, get tickets and work out what to do. She recognised that it could all go horribly wrong, but if it went horribly right…what a story! It would be an exclusive, a sensation. She would need the element of surprise on her side, so she told only Ambreen about it. "Secret Society" would be getting a scoop. She might also find herself dead. *I can handle it*, she told herself. She was certainly a one-off. Craig got his "reward" that night. He hoped she would be safe. It was Lizzie Spector, wasn't it? Stupid man!

The Grisham's plus Kirsty Letts were busy. Bob, Tony and Kirsty were still trying to reel in the editors, one at a time. They had been able to find out where Marion French lived and had staked out her home. Bob had an empty property in Petts Wood that he was going to let out to an Afghan family but hadn't done so as yet. Marilyn took care of that side of things and a multitude of other such tasks. The small flat was in a block of four that was all but empty save one where the tenant was a junkie and mostly so out of his head, he really wouldn't have known the time of day. A pretty perfect place.

Kirsty had knocked on Marion's door to ask if she'd seen her "imaginary" dog that had run away. Marion kept her at the door saying she hadn't and just as she was about to shut the door, Bob and Tony barged in, knocking her over. The men were getting adept at assaulting women, so this was easy. No superglue this time, only duct tape. Marion was secured, a quick look around, then thrown into the car and away. A wet Sunday in South West London in August. Another victim to be put to the proverbial sword. Body bags to spare. Marion would be another one for the trusty, fast filling up well. The police investigation had still been ongoing, and no public announcement had been given so as far as the Grisham's were concerned, it was just going to be a routine body dumping. They seemed to get some sort of sadistic kick out of the thought of live bodies descending that well and slowly dying. Thoroughly sick bastards.

Chapter 42

Marion Goes on a White-Knuckled Ride

Marion's phone rang. She couldn't take the call. She was a little tied up at that moment. Abigail thought she'd try to organise the usual gathering again but was having trouble getting in contact with any of them. Becky was on the phone and Mary just didn't answer. Abigail wanted to organise another trip to Windsor to see how Mary and the baby were doing. It was beginning to look like she would be on her own.

Marion was in a rundown flat on the edge of Petts Wood. The area was pretty well-heeled, but it had a few streets of not-so-elegant residences. The "buy the worst house in the best street" had become "buy the worst slum in the worst street in an upcoming area". Hence this lovely abode. It lacked...well, everything. It had bare boards, no furniture and electric lightbulbs throughout. No mod cons. As it was only to be a temporary home for an editor, soon to be retired...permanently. Marion, unlike Lucinda, Gretchen and Walter, had been conscious throughout. They had overpowered her, Kirsty had sat on her whilst the other two duct-taped her hands behind her back, tossed her shoes away and did likewise to her ankles, taped her mouth and having checked that the coast was clear, had spirited her away by car to their hovel. Having arrived, they quickly got her into the block of four through a non-functioning security door and into the ground floor flat. The street was partially demolished, but no work had been done there for months. They had a free run at it. They took the poor woman through the door and dumped her on the wooden floor. She was clearly disorientated and absolutely petrified. This was only the beginning of her horrendous ordeal.

Marion was the one who had set the hare running. She had suspicions about the book as she had edited it. She had voiced these suspicions to her editor colleagues and told them not to tell anyone. Gretchen Turner had received an email on her laptop that she captured on her smartphone, now in police hands, also raising questions. From a very small number of folk there were now a number who knew or at the very least suspected. The Grisham's, despite their list being at the bottom of that well—that list was now also in police hands— knew who their remaining targets were through Kirsty Letts. What they didn't know was that the police were piecing together a mosaic using phones, that list and identification of the bodies. They needed more evidence but there seemed to be a prima facie case building regarding the involvement of Ruby Latimer. They knew about the Professor, she was on the list but bottom. Marion French was second top. Ruby Latimer was positive that Marion, as the editor of *Heavenly Hell*, had to know what she'd done. The deception was unravelling. It needed to be stopped. Meanwhile, Lizzie was on her way to "Auld Reekie". She needed tickets for one of the speakers at the Book Festival and it wasn't hard to work out which one.

The police knew the ID of the bodies in the well. They weren't making them public until all their next of kin had been informed. Mr and Mrs Turner had gone on an extended walking holiday to Malaysia and couldn't be contacted for at least ten days. It was thought best to await their return. Albany Lansdowne's father was gravely ill in a hospice. The nursing staff thought it would be wise not to tell him as it could finish him off. He had dementia. Would he even remember he had a son? Nevertheless, the police decided to take that advice.

Walter's family had been informed. Clearly, they hadn't rated their son who had followed his own path with little help or encouragement and unbelievably, his folks hadn't even reported him missing as he was hardly ever about. His old car was later found parked in a side street in Bishop's Stortford, laden with massage equipment—he no longer practiced massage as he was to become an editor—and had several parking tickets on it. These would prove useful in fixing a date when it had been parked there. It was thought that Walter might have been in Bishop's Stortford to try to see Gretchen Turner. Brad, presumably, had intercepted him there. The police knew about Brad, though he had never been convicted of anything. He had been, as they said, connected. More like protected. His car had been passed on from Sutcliffe to him via Grigor. He had enough identification on him to save them a lot of trouble. They most definitely weren't about to contact his next of kin. They had no note of who they were and could quite well guess what kind of people they would be. The police also thought that given his antecedence, it might start something very nasty in the criminal underworld. They would wait until the Turners got back and inform all next of kin simultaneously. This delay would prove to be once again something that the excellent Law of Unintended Consequences would play a big part in.

Marion, who was of average height, slightly overweight but not obese, was conscious, having circulation problems in her hands and feet, difficulty breathing through only her nose and in truth, she was experiencing terror and pain in equal measure. Bob had left Franny in charge whilst he had gone to fetch Kirsty and Tony. He had now grown to consider Kirsty Letts virtually one of them. Sure, they would continue to have great, loud sex occasionally, but his real reason was that she had proved herself to be as mental as himself, given the motive. He loved mad birds. Maybe after they stuck this latest one down the well to join the others, he'd give her one.

So, there was Franny, "in charge" of Marion. He remembered the others and began to think. He walked around her in the middle of the wooden floor. He knelt down and kissed her face. Her terror just increased. His hand slid down from her face to her breasts and continued down. He sensed a sudden smell of ammonia. 'Hell,' he said and stood up. It was obvious this one wasn't getting shagged by him that day. The others came back and Franny, all innocent, said, 'I think she's fucking pissed herself.' It had permeated down into the floorboards. This mob had heard of DNA but had no idea that it could involve urine as well as blood.

'Right darling, time to drop you off.' Bob smiled at her. Marion was now in full panic mode. Then she saw the body bag. It took all four of them to get her into it. It must have taken over twenty minutes of struggle to get her in, despite the tactics used with the others of booting her in the fanny, Kirsty being the most vicious kicker of them all. Eventually, she stopped, no doubt badly injured, virtually unconscious. And the light was beginning to fade.

Abigail went to Windsor. What a difference! Arriving at the Callan house, the door opened and there was Mary and little baby George. Mary had just finished breastfeeding the little guy and he was about to go to sleep. For a while, they talked about the baby.

'We phoned, texted, even drove over and you never got back to us.'

'I blame George. Because the pregnancy was so utterly unexpected...he called it confinement. No excitement, no stress, my blood pressure was sky high at one point. He was like a guard, stopping anyone getting in contact until after I'd had him. I tell you, Abigail, thank God that's all over. Thirty-one hours! Never again. Well, maybe just one more time.'

'Mary!'

'Well, George might need a wee brother or sister.'

'It often happens after the first one. I got pregnant again three months to the day after my first one. If you want another one, go for it.'

'So, what gives in the tawdry world of editing?'

'Ruby Latimer has ripped up the writing rule book, written a stonker and gotten the Scimitar.'

There was a moment's almost imperceptible hesitation on Mary's face, then just, 'Well done, her.'

'When will we see you again at the coffee place?'

'Not sure. Will bring the boy as long as they don't mind me feeding him there. Some small-minded sods still object as if it was something offensive. Bloody prudes.'

'I'll talk to Marion and Becky. They'll want to see him. Phoned Marion but she didn't get back to me. Haven't heard from Becky. Will try to fix something up.'

Abigail thought, *At least one of the girls was back. Now to get the others.*

Marion, now inside the body bag, bleeding badly from her vagina—not menstrual but the result of resisting being put into it. The bag retained all body fluids, not much use if it didn't. The Grisham Two, Bob and Tony, plus Kirsty had taken out Brad's motor—such risqué vanity—and with Marion in the boot were heading back out to Cobham, oblivious to what had transpired since they had last been there. Bob was fairly sure he could remember the route; he was good with such muscle memory directions.

At the Cobham well, all six bodies had, two of them with considerable difficulty, been retrieved and autopsied. There was a police presence as it was a crime scene, but it had been scaled down somewhat since the removal of all the cadavers. Nevertheless, there was still a low-level presence. The idea of criminals returning to the scene of the crime was bunkum; however, when the criminals were morons, anything was possible. Up the B road, then off up the hill towards where the well was.

The well was concealed from public gaze as it was on the downside of the hill, the other side from the road. It was almost dusk in that mid-August night and the three passengers in the Jag thought it was almost a game. The "passenger" in the boot may have other ideas. The car roared up the hill and Bob tried to get it skyward with all four wheels off the ground just to show off, but it wasn't going quite fast enough. The car came down with a jolt, settled on its expensive springs right in front of the well—and a dozen uniforms and three squad cars and a tent. 'Fuuuck!' was heard in triplicate. They screeched to a halt, reversed in a slightly muddy spot and hared off back up the hill followed in close order by one of the police cars, soon to be followed by the other two.

The hearts of all four, Marion included, must have raced as fast as their Jag. However, the police Subaru's were a match for it. They all scurried down towards the B road and headed off towards Cobham. The police had now put out a call for backup and phoned in the Jag details. A six-mile chase ensued. Bob saw a wood and turned off, followed by one of the cars. He took a bend and just missed a tree. Thirty seconds later, he did sideswipe a tree but carried on not realising his rear wheel had punctured. It was now only a matter of time.

'Next bend, you two jump and run for it. I'll see you back home.'

At the next bend, he turned off the lights and the other two, one in the back and one next to him, jumped out and disappeared. Bob kept driving until that tyre finally gave out. The car careered down a hill with him still at the wheel and came to a shuddering stop. Bob then scarpered into the woods. The car was abandoned, with a whiff of smoke coming from the engine. The police arrived half a minute behind to see the wreck. They approached it and as they did saw flames coming from the engine. They heard muffled squeals from the boot. A crowbar was quickly summoned, the boot opened to reveal a writhing body bag that was removed in the nick of time just as the car ignited. Marion was saved.

The three occupants of the car all went their different ways. Tony and Kirsty lost each other in the gloom and trees. Tony got a call from Bob to stay put, he was near. Bob made a call to Marilyn who arranged to pick them up. Bob tried to call Kirsty, but her phone seemed to be out of order. Kirsty must have made her way home, they presumed. She was lucky, tried to thumb a lift was taken pity on by a foreign-sounding gentleman in what Kirsty thought was a lovely black Audi. It was, in fact, a lovely black Mercedes Benz.

Chapter 43

Auld Reekie, Ruby's Rubicon

It was a beautiful Mid-August Sunday. Lizzie Spector had never been to Edinburgh before, never mind the Edinburgh Festival. She'd arrived in Waverley Station at midday. Edinburgh had been heaving with all sorts of visitors from everywhere on the planet. She wanted to get to her small hotel down in Leith. Edinburgh during the Festival was totally insane, as were its prices. Her wee hotel still cost C8 an arm and a leg but beggars... She got dropped off by the taxi, booked in, then decided to have a walk around, but she had to get to the Book Festival to ensure getting tickets for the Ruby Latimer Lying Circus the next day.

Ruby Latimer had two slots, that day and the next day, Monday. Lizzie was a little stiff from the train journey and wanted a walk. She would certainly get one if she intended to walk from Leith Walk to Charlotte Square. Off she strode, up Leith Walk, along George St, which was awash with people, stalls and theatre box offices. It felt so alive, vibrant, spontaneous, something she felt that London lacked. It took an hour, but she was almost at Charlotte Square, the residence of the Edinburgh International Book Festival. She was blown away when she saw the size of it, a massive public square transformed—marquees, bookshops, outdoor seating, food outlets, queues of people waiting to see and hear their favourite authors.

Lizzie went for a coffee and sandwich in the coffee emporium and sat outside, taking in the atmosphere. All of a sudden, there was a flurry of activity, cameras from everywhere, all seemingly for only one person. Lizzie brought her sunglasses down from the top of her head and hid her face in a large tuna salad sandwich hoping she wouldn't be spotted by her, but there was a fat chance of that happening when the author was too engrossed in talking to fawning fans, all of them clutching copies of *Heavenly Hell*, seeking the moniker of its venerable author, only for them to be told, 'Not now; after the session.' Such grace.

It still wasn't in the public domain that a major film company had an option on making *Heavenly Hell* into a film. It was clear though from the numbers of paparazzi that it must have been "leaked" because whilst some would have been there, the sheer volume of them just wasn't normal. Lizzie thought this might not be a good omen for her "August Surprise" and yet it might turn out to be to her advantage. As the rugby scrum swept past and the author was ushered away to the celebrity writers' area, Lizzie finished off her coffee and headed for the box office. She wouldn't announce that she was a reporter, she needed to continue the façade of just being "Josie Public" so as not to create any suspicion or alert the organisers to her sting. The episode of "Secret Society" that she was working on would be the first time her face would appear on TV, so she still had that incognito advantage, plus it was Scotland after all.

Lizzie got in the queue for tickets. She was so lucky! She bought for the next day two of the last eight tickets. The Sunday session had sold out ages ago and the two Lizzie got had been returns. She paid and had another look around. It was almost 4 o'clock, she had had a long journey and was starting to feel a little weary; however, it was Edinburgh, the Festival was in full swing, she was footloose and fancy-free. She walked up Princess St and headed up towards the Royal Mile. She knew that she had done her preparation on the train up to Scotland and, apart from a quick refresher that night, she was as ready to spring the trap as she possibly could have been. By seven, she was well done in. She got a text from Craig. Phil the cameraman would be in Waverley at noon on Monday. Lizzie would arrange to meet him at the station.

Ruby Latimer had been basking in the success of the bestseller and had gotten a great reception in the big marquee where she spoke, read some extracts, answered questions. It ended with rapturous applause. The queue to get her books signed was nearly a hundred strong. Then it was back to the Balmoral for a long bath, drink and lovely meal. This was the third and last book festival in a row and she would return to London after the end of the Monday session by first-class Pullman later that evening. She finished dinner—room service—and watched some quaint serial about some woman who had been spirited back to 18th century Scotland. Whatever. Her mind began to wander, thinking of how many of those nosey parkers and snitches were still alive and if so, for how much longer, particularly that awful Spector woman. Anyway, a nice G&T, then off to bed. *Pity about Walter. Good masseur.* She knew he was a gonner, just as she presumed the others were. She had not one iota of remorse. Her philosophy was "do unto others before they can do it unto you".

On Monday, 15 August, Lizzie was up and out for an early morning walk. She walked down to the Ocean Terminal to the Royal Yacht Britannia, stopped at a nice café for a spot of breakfast before heading for a little shot at the Festival itself. She got a bus up to Princess Street where all the activity was near the Scott Monument, that historic edifice known for its epic views and not a few suicide jumpers. She appreciated the truly cosmopolitan nature of the world-famous event and saw a couple of people she thought were a bit famous. She was stopped by a couple of leafleteers in full Scottish regalia, one she recognised from the TV show *Outlander*.

'You might have seen me in the first episode of the last season. It was at Culloden. I was the leading corpse!' What a chat up line!

By 12:30, she was at Waverley awaiting her cameraman. She knew Phil only a little bit, they were hardly a team. Off the train he came. Off for yet another coffee so that she could explain the cunning plan to him. They would not broadcast their intention to film the event but get there in good enough time to get a decent seat. The event would have a facilitator, in fact, a well-known author who was also a BBC broadcaster. Lizzie knew that in order to catch out the author, she would need to be lithe and nimble in getting the question out before she was shut down and possibly forcibly ejected from the event. She had rehearsed over and over again in her head what she would say. It was 2 pm, time to go. The session started at three so no time to lose if a good seat was their first objective.

Disaster! They arrived and the queue for the session was massive. Normally, as press or TV/radio, they would be prioritised, but they were masquerading as civilians. They got in and they were almost at the back row of this very big marquee enclosure. Phil would have had a difficult enough job as it was pretending to be a tourist with a small video camera, but at the back! He would just need to do what he could.

The session began. The facilitator did the usual pleasantries, self-effacing, suggesting even though she herself had books published she just wasn't in the same league as the great author and what a sensational book *Heavenly Hell* was. Then Ruby Latimer, to more ecstatic applause, did her thing, virtually identical to her "thing" since arriving in Scotland and Edinburgh. She finished to applause.

The facilitator asked for questions. Phil had decided to stand and move over to the side to try to get a better view. A large number of hands went up, including Lizzie's. One by one, they asked their questions, but Lizzie began to feel as if she was invisible. The session was drawing to a close with the facilitator being told to wind up.

'Any more final questions?'

Lizzie stood up and waved.

'Yes, the young woman at the back.'

'Loved the book. Only problem is that a university report,' Lizzie waved it at them, 'on it says it wasn't all written by you, but in fact you had a lot of help. Is that true?'

There was a decided buzz in the room as well as some audible comments such as "how inappropriate", "so disrespectful", "the cheeky…" and so on. The facilitator, trying to decide if she should allow the question, looked at the author who was seemingly caught completely off her guard, nonplussed.

'Would you like to answer, Ruby?' Ruby was for once lost for words.

Lizzie was on a roll.

'Many people are beginning to suspect this, didn't you know? Did you have a ghost-writer? Why have you taken full credit for someone else's work?'

For some in the audience, this was too much. A woman went up to Lizzie and tried to take the document off her, but Lizzie defended it as the session began to break up in disarray.

'Lies, it's all bloody lies. It was all my own work. I'll fucking sue you, bitch. She's been after me for months. Bloody Channel Hate.'

The session was definitely over. Normally, the facilitator would thank the author to enthusiastic applause and ask everyone to leave to allow the next author and their audience to file in. The audience had already headed for the exit, not in silence but apparently with bitter recrimination, both at Lizzie for disrupting the meeting and at Ruby Latimer who more than a few now doubted and who had very publicly lost her cool. Phil came over to support Lizzie who was getting a degree of dog's abuse off some leaving, some shouting at her, 'Not the way to do it, girl.' Lizzie stood her ground. She turned to look at the stage, but it was empty. The old bird had flown.

Book signings were done in the bookshop, adjacent to the speakers tents, after the sessions. Ruby had been escorted to the area, looking furtively around, and arriving at the signing table was faced with four people with books for signing. She hurriedly signed them, then disappeared. She wasn't going to be treated like that. She vowed never to come back to that sodding place. She got a cab and, even though it was only a fifteen-minute walk, was driven to the hotel.

Meanwhile, the Festival security people had been alerted to the incident and stopped Lizzie to ask her if she was indeed press and if so, why hadn't she declared thus, as her questioning hadn't been liked. Other press people played the game. They would have her card marked.

Lizzie had broken a golden rule regarding the festival and that was "play by their rules". People paid a lot of money to come to hear and question famous authors about their works. Lizzie had deliberately set out to rain on Ruby Latimer's parade to the obvious annoyance of many aficionados in the audience. A number complained directly afterwards to the stewards who called the manager. It was he who took down the details of Lizzie Spector. She may well be banned from the Book Festival for impersonating a human being! For Lizzie's part, she was partially satisfied with the result in as much as she was now in the driving seat on the issue and she knew how much the public were intrigued by conspiracy theories, this being only a starter for ten. The authorship subterfuge paled into insignificance in comparison to the attempts to "delete" all traces of the issue, including people involved or who knew the truth.

Back at the Balmoral, Ruby had just about enough of the bloody Edinburgh, bloody Festival and was now packing and checking her phone for a train back to civilisation. She called reception and asked them to get her a first-class seat on the next London-bound train. 'There's one at 7:36 tonight that gets in just after one in the morning. Would you like me to book it for you, madam? On your account?' Ruby confirmed this. Lizzie was also looking to get back with Phil as they had no accommodation booked and she was definitely feeling that she'd outstayed her welcome. Having some food, Lizzie had a look at the train times for a convenient one that would get them home before midnight. They went to the station to discover it was fully booked; many festivalgoers from abroad were going to London to catch flights home. They asked about the next one. It took longer but would at least get them home.

Ruby Latimer was still a bit unnerved but in recovery mode. In first-class, she felt at home as the train steadily moved inevitably towards King's Cross. It had by now just passed eleven that night and she would have really liked to have been home, but she would be in London in a couple of hours, then take a taxi to Hounslow. Occasionally, her mind would stray from that Spector cow to the prospect of her book getting made into a film. Her already substantial fortune may soon become considerably enhanced by box office and TV rights. And still that bloody woman, like some kind of spectre at the feast—Spector at the Feast, not funny—kept her from enjoying life. She thought she'd have been dead by now! Should be by now!!! Her so-called assassins needed a good bollocking. She tried to phone Kirsty but wasn't getting a good signal or Kirsty's phone wasn't switched on. Kirsty wasn't home either. Meanwhile, her nemesis was also trundling towards London not at that great a speed. Daytime trains sometimes took only four and a half hours; this one would take a full hour extra. It would be such an uneventful hour as well. Ruby Latimer ordered a bottle of red wine. Her inhibition of sobriety would soon change to that of inebriated belligerence.

Chapter 44

The Good, the Bad and the Desperate

There she was. Ruby Latimer, very comfortable in her first-class seat, a bit tipsy, blanket over her legs, curled up with an eyeshade. And there they were, away from a very cold carriage and upgraded to business class. Lizzie and Phil had talked non-stop about, guess what. Lizzie knew that she had pushed the author's "see red" button once again but it had been enough to start the process of recording a programme on the ghost-writer and who knows what else might come out of the woodwork. She found it hard to believe that Ruby had the kind of connections that could put her life at risk. And yet... For that, she needed further contemplation and a great deal of non-circumstantial proof. She would have gotten Lucinda to do some legal checking for her, but poor Lucinda was now in the mortuary. Phil had done a decent job at the Book Festival recording the questions and answers; he had thought it best to record the whole thing as opposed to just doing Lizzie versus Ruby. The two had reviewed the footage and it was very professional. It would almost certainly form part of the programme. Lizzie might need to return to Bristol for a Professor Llewelyn interview but as far as it went, with Marion French already in the can and the document, they had more than enough for a programme.

In a small forest in Kent, three people had abandoned a car, having been chased at high speed in semi-darkness away from a crime scene. The three, Bob and Tony Grisham and Kirsty Letts, had been there for, to somewhat understate it, no good. They had come upon three police cars and had scarpered, followed by the cars as well as Chief Inspector Gary Stevenson, who had coincidentally just arrived to see how his officers were going with the clean-up and well sealing. Tony and Kirsty had, at an opportune corner, jumped and rolled into the forest, gaining a few bruises on the way. Bob had deliberately crashed the Jag into a tree, but the airbag had operated efficiently and he too had been able to leg it.

What none of them appreciated was that their little escapade had been witnessed not only by the police. They would be the least of their troubles. Other criminal types, higher up the totem pole, sought the whereabouts of their associate Brad and would want to ask them a few questions, and those questions wouldn't be too long in being asked.

Bob and Tony did have a back-up plan called Marilyn who was on her way and would meet them at a main road. Kirsty's phone was out of juice, which would prove to be most unfortunate for the poor girl, most unfortunate. She saw a car coming, clearly not a police car, and hailed it. The driver asked her where she was going, and she told him. His backseat passenger made room for her. He wasn't going there, and neither was she. She had to answer a few questions first of all. She might scream a bit, quite a lot in fact and not as a result of fake orgasms this time. She would scream but she would also be very cooperative.

It was half past twelve. The train was almost a half hour late. Lizzie had phoned Craig earlier when they had left. She thought she should phone him again to let him know of the late arrival. Craig knew she was accompanied so wasn't particularly concerned. In total contrast, Ruby had had no such person to care about her in any way. The only person that cared to that extent about Ruby Latimer was…

Lizzie barefoot, walked to the toilet that Business and First shared. She phoned and pushed the button to open the door. As it opened, there was an almighty shove from the back. Lizzie went sprawling into the large modern toilet with its fancy automatic doors and collided with the wall next to the toilet itself. Suddenly, she was no longer alone. Oh no, she certainly wasn't. Her phone had gone flying out of her hand and had landed behind the toilet. She turned around. It would be some time before she would be able to fully recall what happened next.

The train pulled into King's Cross at quarter past two in the morning. An ambulance crew came on board as did British Transport Police. The exit nearest the toilet was locked and incident tape attached. A guard was stationed at the automatic doors separating the first-class carriage and passengers were directed to the exit at the other end. Needless to say, some complained about being inconvenienced. Passengers left in droves, so it wasn't at all possible to talk to any. However, there were CCTV cameras all over the train as well as in the carriages. After treatment in the place of the attack, the paramedics employed a stretcher and neck brace in case of spinal damage. A doctor had been on board and, having been alerted to a problem, had gotten her bag and attended to the victim, with one very worried Phil looking on, wondering if he had failed to protect Lizzie. As the ambulance men tended to her, she tried to indicate something to them. She pointed under the toilet. An ambulance woman put her hand under and retrieved her phone. It was still on. There was no one on the other end. Craig, who she had called, hadn't answered but instead it had gone to his answer service. It had been on for the entire time of the assault, recording every word, every blow.

Lizzie Spector was rushed to the Whittington Hospital for emergency treatment. The nurses in A&E were shocked to see the state she was in. It was like a victim in a road traffic accident, not the actions of a fellow human. She was given more pain relief and sent up to X-ray. Apart from her severe injuries, she would also run the life-threatening risk of delayed shock.

Phil tried to get Craig and eventually raised him to tell him the situation. He rushed to Whittington and waited. A doctor appeared and told them the extent of her injuries. The worst injury was a broken jaw. Lizzie would be unable to talk for a fortnight, something that in other circumstances might have elicited a quip but not that night. She was made comfortable and as there was nothing more they could do, the men left with Craig set to return a number of times.

Meanwhile, Ruby Latimer was in the minicab she had ordered just before the train had arrived in the station. She was still nursing a staved right wrist and a sore right knee. The CCTV tape had been reviewed. It showed what had happened outside immediately before the toilet door had shut. Company Privacy Policy meant as you would expect, no CCTV cameras inside the toilet. Later, they showed the toilet door opening, a woman exiting and clearly someone covered in blood sitting on the floor. The net would be closing in once positive identification had been established. Face recognition software meant that it might not be long before the assailant was identified, not too long at all.

It wasn't just Ruby and Lizzie in pain. A hog-tied Kirsty, prostrate on her stomach on a table, was in some considerable pain for entirely different reasons. She had been "prepared" for Grigor who had interrogated her in a fashion that would get results and also gave him that kind of pleasure only another sadist could fully appreciate. He was aware of the fact that Brad was missing. He also suspected that she and her Grisham buddies might know a thing or two about it. It had almost been a full day since he had picked her up at the side of the road near Cobham, but she hadn't slept a wink; not just because of his constant questions but also because of the exponentially increasing number of cigarette burns on the soles of her feet and between her toes which were so fucking sore, and every question she hesitated on answering had added another burn. At first, she had tried to say nothing, figuring it could ruin her chances with her newly adopted "family"; however, realising her predicament was way worse than anything the Grisham's could have had in store for her, she blurted out…OK, screamed out, that it had been Bob, then Franny, anyone except herself.

Grigor was unconvinced. He did know it was her, Franny, on the removal of his third fingernail, but why spoil his fun? He had thought about turning from cheroots to vaping on account of the health risks, but it was kind of hard to inflict pain with one of them. It also ensured that the chance of her doing a runner was academic, even if she hadn't been tied stomach down on a table. Standing up would be intolerable, not that it would be possible. Still seeking more information re who the paymaster was and having trouble finding any more spots on her feet, ankles or calves to burn her, he produced a bottle of industrial alcohol and an eyedropper. Starting between her toes, each application to her fresh cigarette burns drove her mad and increased her desire to cooperate. Now Grigor had what he wanted. He knew what had happened at the well; he knew who had all been there; he knew who had set up the contract; and he knew on whose behalf it all had been.

It was now 3:30 in the morning and a call had come through from his trusty informant cab driver who had just dropped off a fare that Grigor had been interested in. Kirsty could wait, hogtied and screaming. He had other plans for her. As he left the room, he heard her scream and curse…and vomit on the floor, a combination of everything she had experienced and what she suspected would happen when he returned. He would be back for her. He switched off the light. She was left in constant pain, complete silence and absolute darkness. Darkness and pain: Kirsty's own personal hell. He asked one of his minions to prepare her for his return. That would mean only one thing.

Chapter 45

Connecting the Dots

Ruby Latimer had been thinking about her rash outburst. Rash outburst! Better described as belligerent apoplexy. She had one regret: that she'd not killed the little fucker when the opportunity had presented itself instead of just inflicting GBH on her. Maybe she would die anyway. She should have been put out of action for some time, time enough for Ruby to concoct some sort of alibi; after all, she was full of fiction, wasn't she?

Ruby was almost home. She got out of the cab and into the house to see a note. "Been trying to get you all day. What happened at Edinburgh? Been on the news. Said you were called out as some sort of cheat. Think we need a long chat." It was signed "Greville".

Not more fucking stuff. Can't be bothered. Off to bed, she thought. The doorbell rang. *Who the fuck? It's this time in the morning.* She answered it. It wasn't the police. In an hour, another knock on her door, this time it was the police and this time there was no answer and no Ruby Latimer inside. The bird had flown. Had she been tipped off about the police wanting to interview her about the train incident? The recording had been viewed and she was certainly "in the frame" for it. A policeman was left to keep watch in case she returned. There was at least enough circumstantial proof to charge her, they reckoned. Police would also be required at Whittington, given what had happened and the possibility of another attempt on Lizzie's life.

Lizzie Spector by that time was at Whittington Hospital having had her injuries treated, badly bruised face, cracked ribs, jaw X-rayed and showing a clean break splitting her jaw in two in the middle of her chin. Lucky for her, it wouldn't need surgery, but it would require to be wired up. This would mean that Lizzie, in all likelihood, would be out of action for up to six weeks whilst it knitted back together. Her ability to speak at the very least would be curtailed, if not out of the question. It was imperative that her jaw remain shut and motionless. For a journalist and television reporter/presenter to be unable to speak for possibly six weeks was a disaster; for Lizzie Spector, it was unbearable. An unspeakable disaster!

Lizzie lay in her bed the next afternoon. She did something she didn't usually do—she felt sorry for herself. She thought that her "scoop" would now be gone, taken over by another from C8 or even another company. Her left eye was bloodshot and her lip had stitches in it. Lizzie Spector, victim. She thought it could never happen. The painkillers were starting to wear off a bit and her wired up jaw was aching. She buzzed for attention. A young nurse attended. 'You in pain love?' Lizzie pointed to her jaw. The nurse replaced the intravenous drip with a fresh one. The nurse noticed a tear rolling down her cheek. She felt cold to the touch. 'It seems God was looking after you. If that man hadn't hit you in the chin but the throat, you'd be dead. I know you're feeling a bit sorry for yourself but,' taking one of Lizzie's hands, 'it WILL get better. It will.' A tear ran down her other cheek and if the nurse had been able to appreciate it, a smile was painfully attempted.

Lizzie wanted to tell her the injuries hadn't been caused by a man but how did you do it when all you could say was 'Mmm...mmm...aaa!' She hoped that nurse would be back.

Lizzie saw Craig and Phil again that night. Ambreen also popped in with grapes! Lizzie was on a "nil by mouth" regime for obvious reasons. Craig joked, 'At last! I can get the last word.' She tried not to show any attempt at a smile. She was still not at all a happy bunny but all in good time. He'd brought her tablet, mostly for entertainment...well, that was his hope—as an older hospital, the TV was a good walk away and no doubt she wasn't exactly in the mood yet—but he expected her to use it for other things like communicating. She was still a bit groggy and uncomfortable but was feeling a bit cheered up. The three left. Ambreen mouthed to her, 'chin up,' then realised what she'd said and laughed. This time, Lizzie actually got the joke, tried to laugh a bit and groaned in pain. Another day maybe.

The tablet Craig had brought was the one Lizzie owned and had been on the train with her. Phil had collected it and given it to Craig. Her phone was in the possession of British Transport Police who needed it for evidence. Even if she still had it, what the hell could she have used it for? She decided to leave it until the next day when she might feel a little better. She hadn't seen her face and it was probably just as well. The Elephant Woman! It would take a week for the swelling to start to go down. Her bloomer of an eye stung but it too would improve as would her lip. She thought again about Gretchen. Had she known she was pregnant? Who had been the father? Surely it hadn't been Walter. They had never even…well, had they? Lizzie started to cry again at this thought. It just wasn't bloody fair.

Ambreen, Craig and Phil went for a quick coffee from the machine in the hospital before setting off back home or back to work. They quickly reviewed what had happened and just who had done this act. Phil hadn't seen it but given the folderol at the Festival, he suspected it to have been an enraged author. They all were incredulous that another woman was capable of acting like a berserker but then they seemingly were capable of these moments of blind rage. Luckily for Lizzie, she seemed to have been unarmed. Ambreen had to go back to the studio leaving Phil and Craig to talk a bit more. Some way into the discussion, Craig revealed something he had not been sure about.

'You know that me and Lizzie are getting hitched next year, I take it. Well, she can be so high octane at times, difficult to handle, and I was starting to have my doubts if I was the right man for her. Was. Then this. Phil, it's only when you're in danger of losing someone that you realise what life would be like without them. I really can't imagine mine without Elizabeth Spector. I can't. She, me, we belong. Funny as fuck when she's not even trying to be. Anyway, just had to tell someone.' Phil just gave him a knowing smile that seemed to validate Craig's comment.

Becky tried to call Kirsty. Abigail tried to call Marion. Neither got through. Marion was actually in hospital. Her ordeal had been horrendous. She had been duct-taped and in their efforts to force her into the body bag, all three of them had used the tried and tested brutal method of getting compliance from their captives by repeatedly kicking them in the groin. Kirsty in particular had participated in this. You would have thought that lady on lady…but no, Kirsty was definitely no lady. Marion had been badly injured and had been bleeding even when being slung in the boot of the Jag. Having been rescued from the burning vehicle in Cobham, she had been taken to a local hospital, then to another in Southeast London. Her genital injuries would require surgery. She was operated on. She and Lizzie would cross paths again but not quite yet.

Time had gone by. Bodies recovered from the well. Tracing of the likely perpetrators ongoing. All in all, this had been a harrowing episode but there were still many loose ends to deal with and the one best able to finish the jigsaw had a broken jaw. She was slowly getting better. Lizzie asked Craig—messaged him on her tablet—if he could bring her one of her folders that contained a lot of information on the disappearance of various people, papers, phone evidence, photos. Her mouth and jaw still hurt but nothing like they had, and her eye was almost normal again. Amazing how two weeks in hospital could do you a world of good.

Lizzie wanted to see if there was anything on "Crimewatch UK" about…well, anything. Still on painkillers, though the dosage had been getting steadily reduced, she could now speak a bit out the right corner of her mouth. Whether anyone could understand her was an entirely different matter. The young nurse who had comforted her when Lizzie had first been admitted, Eileen, popped her head around the door of the TV room to just say hi. As she did, she heard a "shoosh" from Lizzie. There was an item on "Crimewatch UK":

On 16th August, most likely in the early hours, an attack took place on the Edinburgh Waverley to London King's Cross train. A woman was brutally beaten about the head and body, suffering a fractured jaw. Police are looking for a suspect. A picture of the incident taken by a CCTV camera on the train and a video apparently shows a woman pushing another woman into the toilet, then shutting the door, followed by the door reopening, showing clearly the face of the attacker and the victim sprawled against the far wall, apparently bleeding. (A still photo of the assailant was then shown to the viewers.) All attempts to trace the attacker, believed to be Ruby Latimer, author, have so far proved to have been unsuccessful. She may be in hiding in the community or in another part of the country. Ruby Latimer hails from Hounslow, Middlesex. If anyone has any information regarding the whereabouts of this person, they should call us here. The number is on your screen now.

In another incident near the village of Cobham, Kent, an attempt to abduct a woman was thwarted after a police pursuit and the abandonment of a car. The car which hit a tree and burst into flames contained a person in a body bag. That person was rescued and required extensive medical treatment. Police are still trying to trace the occupants of the car, two men and a woman. The car, a Jaguar F-Pace, was found to have altered number plates. If anyone has information that could lead Police to these assailants, the phone number is also up on your screen.

Eileen could see the shoulders of one of her patients' tense, then move up and down and a kind of wail emanate from her. The reliving of that moment in Lizzie's head was just too much. Eileen knelt down and took her hand. She cuddled Lizzie's head on her chest. A couple of minutes later, she stood up. Her uniform was damp in the front. She had done a service to the young woman. Lizzie would remember this act of empathy.

Marion had also seen the programme. Her injuries were progressing, and she had spent a lot of time helping the police who were also piecing together just what had been going on. The mosaic that Lizzie had started to build weeks ago was steadily growing, piece-by-piece. The occupants of the wrecked Jaguar were still at large. Despite the fire there was a massive amount of evidence in the car. It was the kind of evidence that should lead to arrests. Marion told the police her story, but it was only when her job and the name Ruby Latimer came up that pennies began to drop. Dots were being connected and there were now plenty of them to connect.

DNA evidence taken from three of the body bag corpses hadn't come up with an exact match but had come up with a crosschecked matched suspect. As he had been convicted more than once, Pete Grisham had given DNA which helped point in the direction of Franny Grisham whose semen had been found in all three cadavers. Franny was not around. He was in hiding. The police had been at the family home looking for him. Bob thought he'd better find out why they were after him. He was holed up in the flat in Petts Wood.

'So why were the fucking rozzers looking for you then? Fucking tell me now. What happened to your hand?'

'Caught it in a door. Lost three nails, that's all.'

'So, the police? Well!' Bob could see from his younger brother's face that he was being shy about telling all. 'See, when we had those fuckers in the garage and I left you in charge, you didn't...' Bob knew. 'You fucking well did! You fucking plonker.'

'I never thought anyone would know or find them. You left me alone. I was bored.'

'So, you fucking bored them girls then.' Franny went a deep red. 'Oh, you fucking didn't. The guy as well? Fuck sake. Franny'. Franny lowered his head. 'Do you know what DNA is? It's what you did, and they can link us with the bodies. Fucking great. Just fucking great.' Franny thought he'd better get the rest of it off his chest as well.

'Bob, there's something else you need to know. I didn't actually catch my hand in a door. These guys came looking for you and you were away, you know, when you were dumping that other tart. They were looking for the bird, Kirsty, as well. I gave them her address. Told them she was out with you. They were looking for whoever had killed that guy Brad. I wasn't going to lose any more nails. Anyway, they took off. Don't know what happened after that.'

What happened after that was that simply the phone of Kirsty Letts had been tracked. The crash had seen the three of them scatter, Grigor had picked up Kirsty on a side road whilst the other two had gone home. Grigor now had all the information he needed. He didn't give a jot about the others down the well—he'd been responsible for two of them himself—but he wanted not only her but the person who had indirectly employed Brad and, in effect, had been also responsible for his death. He had one of them. Now for the other.

Chapter 46

Sisters in Survival

Lizzie's injuries continued to improve. Four weeks had flown by since the barbaric attack. Her eye was now back to normal as was her lip. Her chin was still black in parts, but the discoloration was reducing in size. Her wire would be out later that week. On Tuesday, she received an unexpected visit from an unexpected visitor.

Lizzie had once again, on her hospital bed, been laying out all the paraphernalia from the case. It was quite a spread. It painted a picture of mass murder, attempts at concealing these crimes, falsification by a best-selling author. The whole mosaic was becoming clearer and yet was it complete? Just then, in walked a woman, familiar to Lizzie, someone she had interviewed on camera about the Ruby Latimer book and who thought it wasn't all her own work. Marion French walked in rather stiffly, using a walking stick. It was as if she had just had a red-hot poker removed from her rectum. She was clearly in quite a bit of discomfort. They both smiled, both peculiar in their own way and for differing reasons. Lizzie could just about talk. She cleared the bed of all the stuff and suggested they go for a coffee. She was now off the intravenous drip.

'What happened to you, Marion?' Lizzie whispered with still some difficulty out the good side of her mouth.

'They tried to murder me.'

'Who did?'

'God. It was two guys and a woman, a girl. It was on Crimewatch.'

'So, that was YOU who got abducted! Have they had any luck finding them?'

Lizzie had seen the programme but had been dosed up with painkillers and missed both the name and photo.

'No. Like they disappeared off the face of the earth. And you?'

'Getting there. Going home in a couple of weeks. What can I do for you?'

'I've been thinking. If you want to use me in that interview, no hiding my face or any of that stuff, then go ahead. It might shake out just where Ruby Latimer is. She took us all in.'

'Marion, she tried to kill us, both of us. We can thank our lucky stars.'

Lizzie was still having mouth problems and some saliva dribbled down her chin. Marion took out a handkerchief and ever so gently wiped Lizzie's drooling mouth. Lizzie went an embarrassing pink but Marion just smiled and planted a kiss on Lizzie's forehead. Sisters in survival.

The last thing Bob Grisham now had to think about was kidnap. He would just have to make do with what he had. He knew that Lizzie was at Whittington Hospital but so what. He had other problems to take care of, like living a bit longer. Bob and Tony had been picked up by Marilyn and driven to Petts Wood where the unfortunate Franny had been "asked" for information by the Grigor team. He had cooperated. Nobody ever denied Grigor who had then been able to select Kirsty as the one he needed to talk to; with a little persuasion, she had told Grigor everything his heart desired.

Having found out what beans Franny had spilled Bob and Tony went to another of their buy-to-let empty properties four miles away. Franny, still nursing his hand and now, thanks to his brother, two black eyes, was left to his own devices, ostracised by the family. It would make him a sitting duck. Not for nothing had Grigor left him at liberty. He knew he would tell brother Bob of the clear and present danger to their whole enterprise and lives. If Kirsty had been intercepted by that man and she had told her story, no doubt Grigor would be back for the rest of the Grishams'. Franny would have a better chance with the police who had fingerprints on a couple of the body bags and bodies that matched those found in the wrecked Jag. At least in prison, Franny might be safe. What he didn't know was that he might have a short "stay of execution", quite literally as Grigor was busy with others. In a short period of time, Grigor would return to dealing with the family. It wasn't that Brad had been a friend. More importantly, Brad had been a member of his team. Touch one of his team and you touch them all. It was not just pride, but business, criminal business.

Thursday and Lizzie's wire had been removed. It took her an hour of mouth and chin exercises to start to feel more like her old self. The hospital psychologist visited her. They spoke for an hour about Post Traumatic Stress Disorder and how it could affect her, if not immediately, in the future and when she was least expecting or prepared for it. Lizzie agreed; yes, it could be a problem. Only thing was – she was Lizzie Spector – she would not succumb to anything, never had and never would! Oh, young people. Was it just bravado or was she that special?

That afternoon, DI Michael Madison came to see Lizzie. He was there officially to collect all the information she had accrued. He had cut her a great deal of slack because of her assault but now he was back and not exactly pleased. Her cavalier approach in Edinburgh could have alerted Ruby Latimer to her being in the frame. The attack on the train made her a prime suspect but now she'd vanished and no one had a clue where to find her. Collecting the documents, including the professor's manuscript, he gave her a receipt and some friendly advice—don't shadow police activity, it could be counter-productive. No need to point out that it could also be dangerous. He sat on her bed.

'Miss Spector, Lizzie. I know what you did and why, but we have a job to do as well. The suspect, not only in attacking you but with information on at least four murders and one abduction, has now apparently gone to ground. We were going to get her the day of your return for questioning, but you must have spooked her. Keep us in the loop in future. If it happens again, we might need to consider obstruction charges against you. Just advice, friendly advice.'

Lizzie nodded. He was right. She had put her profile and desire to get a scoop before law enforcement and nearly paid the ultimate price for it. She might not be so lucky next time, if indeed there was a next time. She felt a bit depressed and annoyed at her impetuosity. For a microsecond she thought about toning herself down. That microsecond flew by, out the window. It never had a chance of altering her.

Craig, Ambreen and a couple of others from her office came to see her that evening. They were upbeat and she told them that, all things being equal, she should be discharged on Saturday morning. She told Ambreen the good news about Marion having changed her mind about wanting to hide her identity. Ambreen sighed.

'Unless Ruby Latimer is found, there won't be a programme. It'll be a non-story, at least for some time. She hasn't been seen since the attack on you. Police traced her back to her house in Hounslow, then nothing. Seemingly, she hadn't even unpacked her case. It was as if she knew; She had just walked away from it all.'

'Switzerland. She's in Switzerland,' Lizzie said with conviction.

'Switzerland! Why Switzerland?'

'That's where the ghost-writer card came from. Bet you she's there.'

'I'll let the police know what you think.'

If indeed Ruby Latimer had escaped to the Alps, it must have been by unconventional means. The others left. Craig remained. Her face was almost normal again, just with some slight redness on her chin, which would vanish in a few weeks.

'Don't bother collecting me, Craig. Dad's coming to take me back up for a couple of days' rest. I need a wee bit of space.'

Craig had a concerned "hope she's not trying to tell me something" expression. He needn't have worried. She saw his hangdog expression and her eyes lit up; she smiled a still painful smile and took his hand.

'Look. I am marrying you. I need time to talk to my mum. If you want to come up on Sunday to collect me, please come. If I go straight back to your flat, the phone and all that will be going constantly. Just a couple of days, darling. To be with Mum and Dad. You understand.'

It was her last night in Whittington. "Crimewatch UK" had been planning a programme for weeks but had delayed it, pending the next-of-kin being told. No such people were available for Brad. It was agreed to screen the item.

Now, a shocking discovery. In Kent, a report was received that has led to a grisly find. In a well near the village of Cobham, police have recovered six bodies. Two of the bodies had been there for almost two years whilst the others, only two or three weeks. The bodies have been identified as a Baronet Albany Lansdowne and a Rodney Sutcliffe, both from West London, reported missing in late 2016. Lansdowne was the son of the now recently deceased hereditary peer. Sutcliffe was suspected to have connections to the London underworld but had no criminal record. The other bodies were identified as sisters, Gretchen and Lucinda Turner from Bishop's Stortford in Herts, Walter Sims from London and Bradley Atkins, address unknown. the well determined that all but one had been alive at the time of being put into the well. Body bags contained four of the six, and funeral directors have been asked if there are any of their body bags unaccounted for. Police have suspects that they are seeking.

Lizzie watched, agog, what would almost certainly be her last TV programme on her last night at Whittington. It was as if everything has come full circle. Mention of Gretchen and Lucinda again…and Walter. She felt pangs of guilt at not feeling the same anguish for Walter as for the girls. She knew the girls better. She thought back to the massage day they had all shared. Now she was the only survivor, all murdered at the behest of Ruby Latimer. *Oh, please catch that bitch. Give her the sentence she deserves*, she thought.

The next morning, Saturday, she was given the all-clear and her dad came to collect her and drive her up to Hertfordshire. Lizzie was on the mend and almost back to her usual self. She had things to discuss with her mum that only a mother and daughter could do. They stopped off for a coffee in the village, then went up to the house. It was still only midday. Lizzie now appeared to be quite chirpy, although her mum knew her daughter's ability to put on a brave face. She knew that this incident had seriously messed with her emotions, if only for a while. For one of the few times in her young life, Lizzie felt a little vulnerable and unsure. Her indefatigable nature had almost been her downfall. Should she try to curb her natural instincts or just be herself? Being herself had almost gotten her killed, and not just once. She comforted herself in the knowledge that time was on her side. It was, but she was still damaged. Mum would come to the rescue.

Mum had come to the rescue. A mum for whom the notion of a conservative-minded, slightly old-fashioned prude had been blown out the water a couple of years before by a "facts of life" exchange that had opened Lizzie's eyes to what a wonderful, open, sexually liberated woman Mrs Spector was. Lizzie had discovered that her own genetic code was from good stock. They reached home. Her dad, Jeremy, QC Jeremy, left the women and scurried off with his golfing buddies. It was now mid-Octobar but life—and golf—went on. It meant that the two would have time for a good old chinwag.

'So, looking forward to the wedding then, dear?'

Lizzie thought about the question that in itself was somewhat of a statement. For two hours, they had talked about Mr Spector, holidays planned or past, the state of the nation, the state of the garden, Rose and Todd, Craig's parents, their part in the nuptials, seemingly anything but Craig himself. Lizzie's mum had liked Brian but hadn't seen the dark side of him.

'I am indeed. Craig's a great man. I'm very lucky to have him in my life.'

'But do you love him?'

'Mum, what a question! Well, 'course I do.'

'It was just that you hesitated. If you're not sure—'

'I AM sure. It's just that I've been through a tough few weeks. He's been great, keeping my spirits up, keeping me up to date with developments, making me laugh.' She giggled. 'Oh, that was sore!' Lizzie held her mouth and gave a wince, followed by a smile.

'We like Craig but we're not the ones planning to spend the rest of our lives with him, are we? Do you both have passion for each other?'

'Passion, mother? Whatever do you mean?'

Lizzie gave a playful smile, knowing that her mother would take the bait.

'Sexual passion, bonking passion, exchange of—'

'OK Mum, yes, now we do. Took a while but I have him well trained in the art. Seems his first wife wasn't too bothered about that side of it. Me, I love sex! I scream with…'

This time, it was Mrs Spector's turn to blush, as her daughter had a couple of years previously in another explicit conversation.

'Just getting you back for the last time!'

'Touché, dear.'

'Seriously Mum, defining love is so hard. You and Dad have something I hope I can find in Craig. I'm looking for it. It's fun, the search.'

'Elizabeth, if you are looking for that perfect specimen of a man, you'll die an old maid. They don't exist. Life is one long compromise. I know how utterly uncompromising you are and look where it got you. Sex and those feelings never leave, but the embers go a bit colder with time. You need a friend and a lover. Dame Esther Rantzen. Now there's my kind of woman. Spent her whole life campaigning and doing good. Lost her husband, Desmond Wilcox, decades ago. She said that she's kept busy by everyone but has now no one to go home to and do nothing with. So sad, so true. Marry a friend as well as a lover.'

Lizzie was starting to get her chin up. It still felt a bit sore, but she had some painkillers. Her mum's advice seemed sound.

'Babies, dear. When will I be a nana?'

Lizzie had known that this question would inevitably be on the order of business. She had possibly been trying to find the right moment to bring it up, probably since they left Whittington.

'Thought you'd never ask.' Lizzie had been prepared for that one. 'Well, first thing, I'm not getting pregnant without having a wedding ring first. Then we have our careers and a few years of recreational sex first.'

Lizzie looked at her mum to see if that had shocked her, but she seemed unmoved.

'But darling, the old biological clock. Tick-tock, tick-tock.'

'...And we have discussed this. I'm going to suggest to Craig that I freeze my eggs to be re-implanted when I'm about thirty. Happens a lot these days.'

'Yes. I've read about it. Did you know you can donate some to childless couples as well? What a good thing that would be.'

Lizzie looked utterly gobsmacked. Her mum had come up with the "paying it forward" idea to top them all. She could do it for herself, for Craig AND for other women.

'Mum,' Lizzie kissed her on the forehead. 'Thanks.'

'What for, dear?'

'Just for being you.'

Mother and daughter spent a lovely few hours chatting, Mum having a gin, daughter unable to as she was taking painkillers. At 5:30, Jeremy, her father arrived in golf attire and with golf bag. They would have a lovely, relaxed evening as a family, one of the last as her wedding was set for the following spring.

Lizzie, exhausted, retired to bed just after ten and started thinking journalist thoughts again. Craig was driving up the next day to have lunch, collect her and return them both to his place. They might need to ask the police if the risk level on her had receded. If not, she might require a police presence outside for a while longer. The fact was that two of those who had tried to abduct her were still at large, one was injured and at risk himself, one was in pain and captive, one was dead, and the paymaster? Well, who knew?

'Lizzie, dear.'

'Yes love?'

'You have been very naughty.'

Lizzie was full up after another super lunch and was resting her head on his shoulder as he drove.

'Your impetuosity almost got you killed. I wasn't aware just how much evidence you'd accrued until Madison told me. We need more trust between us.'

Lizzie put on her puppy dog eyes. 'I can be naughty if you want,' meaning an entirely different kind of "naughty".

'No darling, you can't. I don't want to end up a widower before we're even married.'

Lizzie sat up and looked at him. A slight glimmer of doubt crossed her mind. Should she compromise for the sake of marrying Craig?

'Anyway,' he continued, 'we need to get this straight. I see my future with only one woman, the one in the seat next to me. Journalism has dangers but as long as we keep in contact, things should be fine.' Again, she thought about this. 'What stopped her killing you, I just don't know.'

Lizzie knew. His concern for her, the personal alarm – she'd activated it just in the nick of time – had probably saved her life. She thought again and realised that in a way, she owed him her life. She put her head down on his shoulder again and said, 'I've been so naughty.' She pushed her still a bit sore head further into his shoulder. 'But I can be very VERY naughty next week, once I'm better.' Craig knew exactly what this meant and gave an unseen self-satisfied smirk.

Chapter 47

A Ghost-writer, There Definitely was

Just because Lizzie was well on the road to recovery didn't mean she didn't suffer the occasional disconcerting flashback. These could happen normally when she was least expecting one. They were most unwelcome but extremely vivid. Craig was aware of them. He had a clinical hypnotherapist friend who, if she had wanted, would make an appointment with her. Lizzie thought it couldn't do any harm, why not. Lizzie went to the offices, not a surgery as thus, and spent some time talking about her attack. In reality, she had no conscious memory of it, apart from these flashbacks that she hoped would fade but were still happening. The session began. Lizzie, on a seat in front of Dr Helena McCormick, was not a difficult subject. Within two minutes, the doctor had her in a hypnotic state. After a few routine questions and answers about herself, her family and friends, they began.

'Lizzie.'

'Yes.' Both spoke in quiet, measured tones.

'You're on a train. Where are you going?'

'Home.'

'Where is home?'

'Craig's. Holloway.'

Where did you board the train?'

'In Edinburgh.'

That established, the doctor took Lizzie's subconscious further.

'You get up to go to the toilet.'

'Yes. I'm phoning Craig, but he doesn't answer. I leave a message.'

'What do you see?'

'I...I feel a push from behind me.'

'Yes.'

'I'm in the toilet. I've hurt my head. I'm turning around. It's her. Ruby Latimer. She's towering over me. She's really, really pissed.'

'And what does she say?'

'She says, shouts in my face, "Why aren't you fucking dead?" She's shaking me, hitting my head against the wall and shouting, "You fucking bastard." Then she punches me in the eye and the mouth.'

'What happened then?'

'I slid down the wall. I think her knee came up under my chin. It was so sore. I was searching for Craig's alarm. I remember her hands on my throat and a loud noise…that was all.'

What Lizzie had remembered was entirely consistent with what her mobile phone had picked up. Craig had listened to it on his answer service and had immediately given it to the police. A case was building against the elusive Miss Latimer.

Dr McCormick brought Lizzie back to the present. It was now apparent what was the cause of the flashbacks. The doctor seemed confident that a solution would be found. She also had another revelation to give Lizzie.

'You talked about doubts you had, doubts about you and Craig. You seem to have resolved them. This is nothing to do with hypnotherapy, recall or anything like that. I've known Craig a long time. He's a good man. He's not perfect, none of us are, but I know how much he loves you. You just need to talk a bit more but, and now I've got my wife and mother hat on, he won't let you down. You two will be fine.'

And with that, the session was over, and a short course of follow-up sessions agreed upon.

Lizzie still had uncovering work to do. She was feeling a lot more like her old self. She was back at work, part-time for a month, which meant doing only a fifty-hour week. The irrepressible Lizzie Spector. She was working from home on other items but still with a weather eye on the Latimer case. She had taken to heart what Dr McCormick had said…well, as much as she could, about Craig and keeping him informed even though it went against her nature. One of the issues outstanding was additional information that Professor Llewelyn had. She gave her a call.

'Heard about your accident, dear. Hope you're getting a bit better.'

'Not exactly an accident but yes, thanks, much better now.'

'I was as intrigued as yourself about these books. We took fifteen of her previous books and did a similar exercise to *Heavenly Hell*, slightly recalibrated to look at different aspects. The cloud came up with some interesting conclusions. I then rechecked *Heavenly Hell* and it showed not just two but three different styles.'

'What does that mean, Professor? Who's this "we"?'

'My dear, "we" is staff in the University of Bristol. It means that the author, the ghost-writer and the editor were identified. There's more.'

Lizzie couldn't wait. The professor was tantalising her as only a top-flight literary academic could.

'As I said, we ran the contents of another fifteen novels through the system. Not surprisingly, all of them showed two people, the author and the editor.'

'Not sure where this is leading, Professor. I would expect them all to have been edited, wouldn't you?'

'Now here's the rub. Her books, *Emotional Blackmail* and *Heavenly Hell*, had the same person's input.'

'Marion French. Yes?'

'No. She might have edited *Heavenly Hell*, but another person who edited *Emotional Blackmail* was the ghost-writer on *Heavenly Hell*.

The penny dropped. A ton of pennies. *One of the editors was probably the ghost-writer*. Lizzie was furiously typing on her laptop as the professor was talking. So, the identity of the ghost-writer could be revealed. All that was required was to find out who had edited *Emotional Blackmail*. Walter could have found out but unfortunately... She could ask the other editors but if it was one of them, they'd just say nothing, professional etiquette and all that. Marion French. It wasn't her. It was either Abigail, Becky or Mary. Of course, it may have been someone entirely different but there was an excellent chance it would be one of them. Ruby's agent's office and possibly publisher would have invoice records, but they would never reveal who it was. Lizzie had to talk to Ambreen about the dilemma. She had indicated that the absence of Ruby Latimer meant that the programme had been temporarily shelved but if Lizzie, in her own time, wanted to work up something, who could tell. It may still happen if Ruby Latimer came out of hiding.

The Grisham's were in disarray, to put it mildly. Both Bob and Tony were in hiding, Marilyn was now aware of the impending danger. She got herself a small calibre handgun. Franny was still in pain. Franny wasn't too bright but was

Stephen Hawking compared to three of the other men. His nails would grow back in time, if he had time. He was staying with Becky Letts, on her couch, for a few days as a favour. Becky wondered where Kirsty had gotten to. She thought Franny might know. Fat chance.

Kirsty was still in a bit more pain than Franny. Grigor was busy making preparations for her removal and final exit. The enormous pleasure, sadistic pleasure, that he gained from not just inflicting pain but in getting his victim to realise the fate that was soon to be theirs gave this man a hard-on. He salivated at what Kirsty, through her present torment and the thought of knowing she was doomed, must have felt like. Oh, the pain, oh, the pleasure.

Linda had been interviewed by police as part of their ongoing investigation, trying to deduce where the body bags had come from. She knew nothing. All of theirs were burned along with the corpses. Not totally true, was it, Linda? She'd have tackled Bob if she'd have known where he was. Mike was still butchering, totally unaware that some of his siblings had been as well. Ray, Alf and Pete were oblivious to everything—Ray because he was…well, Ray; Alf because he was either rat-arsed or stoned and Pete because he was on the run…again. Police had been visiting to see if he was there. He wasn't. Their parents were unaware of recent doings. They were permanently and deliberately unaware of doings. As ever, they turned a blind eye to the careers of their children as long as there was beer and fags dosh to keep old man Ted happy and bingo and lottery money for Ma Grisham. Grigor was busy anyway with other fish to fry. They were safe for a short while.

Ruby Latimer kept thinking about her assault. Her only regret was not finishing off the young cunt. She might have swung for her, but it would have been worth it. She remembered the almighty shove she had given her. She remembered the violent shaking, the thwack to her face and chin, the ferocious knee that she was sure must have broken her jaw as she had put so much of herself into it. She remembered a red mist throughout the seemingly "speed of light" attack. Her only regret—instead of choking her, a second kneeing to the throat rather to the chin would have finished that bastard off. Bloody personal alarms. Ruby thought of that evening. She had time to do it. It gave her a rosy glow. She needed one.

Lizzie Spector was being driven mad trying to work out which of the three editors it could be. *Emotional Blackmail* had been published five years ago. She needed to consider a strategy here. If she approached one and it proved not to be her, sure as Tuesday followed Monday, the very second she left that person would be on the phone to the other two warning them. Maybe she could work it out another way.

Given what had happened, she wondered if another meeting of the editors for coffee was in the offing. She phoned Marion, who she knew fine well wasn't the one, to see if she had heard anything. She had! A meeting the following Monday, usual place and time. She'd be there, invited or not. Lizzie now needed to see how she could identify who it was. Where was Detective Columbo when he was needed! Lizzie had five days to prepare. She might need a mind mapping genius to assist her. She sat down and tried to make a start. She got a blank piece of foolscap and wrote in the middle "Ghost-writer" and drew a circle around it. Now what?

Chapter 48

Tying Up Loose Ends

Despite their efforts in differentially retrieving DNA from the bodies of the two young women and the young man, for a variety of environmental reasons, the samples weren't brilliant. However, through painstaking efforts, results were eventually forthcoming. These were checked against the police DNA database. No matches were found, though there could have been one where some of the numbers were close but not exact. It was disappointing. The results might well turn up trumps if the person was DNA tested in future.

Funerals took place for all the bodies except one. No one had owned up to having been a relative of Bradley Atkins. He stayed in the mortuary. Madison had itemised the evidence taken off Lizzie but as most of it related to the ghost-writer story, it wasn't considered of use to the police. Lizzie, still not fully back to work, was preparing for her coffee morning. She had mind-mapped, surrounding the ghost-writer in the centre with the four editors, putting a cross through Marion but considering the other three. What did she really know about any of them? Not a whole lot. Abigail seemed to be the best off of the three remaining ones. This didn't make her unlikely, just a bit more unlikely. Lizzie had no idea about what that motivation might be; money, no doubt as there wasn't any apparent glory in finishing something off and getting no credit for doing so.

Marion was aware that after she had been released from the body bag and spent some time in hospital—she still had a couple of reconstructive operations on her vulva and vagina to come, so bad had been the assault to get her into the bag—the police had taken away her clothes for forensic testing. They hadn't told her that the testing had shown semen on her cardigan. It was in prime condition compared to that found in the bodies in the well. It came from the same person. Franny Grisham.

Franny had been left in charge of Marion when she had been their prisoner in Petts Wood. After they'd left, he'd wondered how long they would be, thinking that here was another chance for a free fuck. He felt her up. She was wet and she smelt. It was urine. He already had his member out so thought he'd be as well to relieve himself, and so he did, a different kind of relief from what his victim had not quite experienced. Stupid man. It could be his downfall, but he had the Grisham arrogance, and in any case, no one would find her, would they? The police had DNA sequencing that showed a ballpark match for a Grisham but not the one or ones they suspected. As it was, Pete Grisham had been doing six months for assault, so it couldn't have been him. Bob and Tony had scarpered and were in another of the Grisham abodes. Franny was there himself.

Police were looking for the criminal side of the family so where best to start? The "honest" ones. Linda had too much to lose. She was in a Grisham-owned house with her fiancé and was somewhat preoccupied with the exceptionally pleasurable pastime of attempted procreation. She couldn't help them much. Mike steered them in the direction of Marilyn. She was Franny's last remaining link with the outside world. He was afraid to go out, seek medical assistance or indeed, anything. She would bring him food and medical stuff for his hand. The flat was almost totally bare of furniture, with only a mattress, lamp and small portable television. The police put a tail on her, and she led them to the flat in Petts Wood where Franny was holed up. They quickly applied for a search warrant and it being granted, Marilyn having left, they forced entry and arrested the scruffy, unshaven, hapless reprobate.

'Francis John Grisham,' read DI Madison from the charge sheet, 'I am charging you with, on or about 10 July, you and others conspired to commit and committed the following murders: Miss Gretchen Turner, Miss Lucinda Turner, Mr Walter Sims, Mr Bradley Atkins. You are further charged with conspiracy to abduct with the intention to murder Miss Marion French and did cause her actual bodily harm. You do not have to say anything, but it may harm your defence if you do not mention when questioned something that you can later rely on in court. Anything you do say may be given in evidence. Do you understand?'

Franny said nothing except to acknowledge his name. DI Madison was joined by a detective sergeant. Franny had a solicitor. Marilyn had taken care of that. The interview began and given the circumstances, was likely to be very lengthy.

'We have evidence that you were present and participated in these murders.'

'Evidence?' queried the solicitor.

'Forensic evidence, evidence that puts your client in the frame for the murders and the kidnapping. His semen was found inside three of the bodies and on the clothing of Miss French.'

'So why aren't you adding the charge of necrophilia? That's surely what you're meaning as well. Am I wrong?'

Franny suddenly realised where this was heading. The solicitor had a quiet word with him. It was nearly but not quite audible.

'Would you like a few minutes to consult with your client?' suggested the DS. They stopped the recording and the DI and DS left them for a break.

'You two like a coffee?' the DS asked, and a nod indicated they would. Out the policemen went, and one returned with two flat whites. The adjournment was over by the solicitor knocking on the door.

'My client wishes to make a short statement. I have counselled him about caution, but he insists.'

'First of all, I'm not a pervert. I prefer women. I like mine alive, not dead. I didn't do anything to that Marion wotshername…'

'French, Marion French.'

'Whatever. The others were a job lot. If I got offered a deal, I might be more cooperative.'

DI Madison spoke, 'Francis, we will most certainly be adding necrophilia to the charge sheet. You are going to be remanded in custody at Brixton. Inmates don't like perverts. It would be a pity if any found out about that charge.'

His brief tutted. 'Naughty, DI Madison, could be interpreted as threatening my client.'

Michael Madison retorted, 'I think your client knows quite well what prison is like. He may not have been there before, but his young brother, Peter, is there right now. I just hope word doesn't get into Brixton; that could affect him.'

'Dear dear, DI Madison, you certainly are walking a very dangerous tightrope here. I—' At which point, Franny interrupted, 'They weren't bloody dead, I told yas. I was just having some fun with em.'

Both policemen caught a quick sideways glance at each other, that kind of "gotcha" glance.

'Can I suggest you might want to suspend the interview and advise your client that he may wish to make a written statement.' The brief acknowledged that this last outburst had let the cat out of the bag. As forensic evidence was still being evaluated and was embargoed, neither Franny nor his brief knew that the evidence already showed that the three murder victims had all still been breathing when despatched to their almost certain watery deaths. Michael Madison and his sergeant left the other two for a chat. When they returned, the solicitor said his client would begin a written statement in his cell and it would be ready for the next day.

Franny had a remand cell to mull over his predicament. He'd been in trouble before but never like this! It was like all his previous indiscretions had caught up with him. He'd always had the family around him to advise him. Franny was a follower, not a leader but when he was told what he needed to do, that was it. He'd enormous family loyalty, but he was facing a thirty stretch and if the rumour about fucking corpses got out, he could end up as one, and definitely he would be fucked in more ways than one. There were only three things worse to be accused of in the pokey than a necrophiliac—a paedophile, a nancy boy and a grass. Franny needed to find a way to offload the blame on…whoever. He reckoned he was definitely banged to rights regarding the murders. If he could only remember the name of the bird—Christie? Betsy? Ah…Kirsty. So, he would give her up in return for no more talk of him being a stiff's arse bandit. That should do it. Keep the others out of it. *What a fucking mess*, he thought to himself. *I should have kept my trousers zipped and my cock in my pants*. Tosser. He couldn't argue with that personal description in any possible way.

Lizzie was nearly back to her best. Ambreen had another story for her to get her teeth into. It was about rich people salting away untaxed wealth but still getting gongs, despite HMRC knowing about them. Juicy or what! However, she still had a bit between her teeth, that of the ghost-writer's identity. She thought she knew who it was. Her mind map had pointed to the intellectual treasure. It could only be…but could it? She went along with Marion French for that coffee. The women hadn't met for some time, or at least it felt like that.

Marion and Lizzie arrived a few minutes before the others and ordered a cappuccino and croissant. They were both well on the road to full physical recovery, but for both of them, full mental recovery was still to be achieved. Marion, in particular, after her ordeal; her beating; the body bag. It was all still too fresh for this lady. She wasn't used to circulating amongst such ferocious cretins, only editing books describing them. However, with the right therapy she would improve. Friends, and new friend Lizzie Spector, would save her sanity.

Lizzie, thanks to a few sessions with the hypnotist, was nearly there as well. As they sat drinking, eating and chatting, in came Mary. She had now lost her baby weight and looked good. She smiled at them both but wondered why Lizzie was there. Marion said she would explain when the others arrived. Just then, in came Becky and Abigail. They went up and got a coffee each. When they came and sat down, also a bit surprised and perplexed, it was Marion and not Lizzie who first spoke, 'Girls, I invited Lizzie Spector because there is some really shocking news and you all may be part of this.'

Marion told them about her abduction, the murders and Lizzie's attack. They all looked on agog, in total shock and horror. Only Becky seemed not to be surprised. She had a problem of her own.

Lizzie then started. The other three looked at each other but again, Becky was the one strangely least surprised. They didn't know what was going on with her.

'My sister, Kirsty. Met these two guys in a pub a few weeks ago. Ever since then, she's changed. I think she's got in with a really bad crowd. I haven't seen her for quite a while. She's stopped answering her phone. I'm getting quite concerned.'

The others flashed sympathetic looks in her direction. There was seemingly not a lot they could do for her.

'Have you been to the police?'

'Called them. They seemed to know. I have no idea how.'

'Know? What do they know?'

'Dunno. Just the way they were talking.'

'Sure, she's a big girl and can take care of herself,' said Mary quite unconvincingly. After several minutes of trying to reassure Becky, somewhat unsuccessfully, Lizzie sought to change the subject.

'When I was told about the murders and those who had met Walter, possibly even got a massage from him, Kirsty, Marion, I tried to work out who might have been behind them,' at which point, Lizzie took out the first of her mind maps.

'All these knew or suspected a secret, now some of them are dead, some are lucky not to be and some just plain lucky I suspect.'

The women examined the piece of paper with its crosses through three of the names. Abigail put her hand to her mouth, stood up, said, 'Sorry,' and rushed to the toilet. The others were just shocked.

'I know what this is all about,' said Mary. 'This is about Ruby Latimer, isn't it? She's disappeared. It's been in the papers.'

Abigail returned, ashen faced. 'Sorry people, it was just such a shock.'

Marilyn and Bob were sitting in the Grisham family living room in Orpington. Bob was uncharacteristically sweating, Marilyn impassive as ever. They had visitors, a man called Grigor and one called Boris, plus a couple of other young guys in really cheap-looking suits and gold-effect chains. It wasn't what you would have described as a social call. They had an offer to make them. Boris was in charge.

'Lady and gentleman. Robert, Marilyn. I know what you did. Very naughty. I decided to take some action about it.'

He had a tablet switched on and called up a short video. These two hardened petty but well-heeled criminals, Bob and his sister, jumped up from their seats at what Boris had shown them. It was totally beyond the pale. If the meeting was supposed to be some form of negotiation, it was a very not-so-funny opening gamut. Faint music was heard. It sounded uncannily like the old 60s song, *Up, Up and Away.*

'Hope they will be very happy together. Anyway, down to business. I could have done the same to you but I'm a businessman first and foremost. I have an offer to make you. Congratulations. You now have a good business operating here. I want you to continue doing it. Only difference is you will be doing it for my man here,' slapping Grigor on the shoulder. 'For that, we will reward you with thirty percent of the collections.'

Bob started to get up out of his seat, about to tell Boris to stick it up his hole, but before he could, Marilyn put her hand over his mouth and said, 'Fifty percent and not a penny less.'

Boris smiled. 'I knew you were good, lady, but I didn't think you were stupid. Forty percent.'

Marilyn took her hand off Bob's mouth and gave him a piercing look. He went to speak, thought twice about it, shrugged his shoulders and as one, they said, 'We'll take it. Deal.'

'Very sensible. I wouldn't like to have to send you on a little journey. Very bad for your health.'

Marilyn understood a lot of things and one was where the balance of forces lay. As long as Franny shut his cake hole and took the drop for them, all things considered might still not be too bad. Franny's solicitor could argue diminished responsibility and maybe get a reduced sentence. Let's face it, Franny and diminished responsibility were like yin and yan. The family would look after him when he was banged up. In any case, they had a substantial property portfolio so they wouldn't exactly starve and would be able to continue doing what they did best—extortion. Only a slight problem—the Grisham's had gone from owning the bakery to collecting crumbs off the table. What a fucking bummer.

Abigail hadn't missed much. They had all thought it best to wait for her to return. She looked quite pale. Lizzie was about to put one mind map away and take out another one when Abigail, now having another penny drop in a loud clatter, asked, 'How long have you thought that we all might be in danger?'

'Not very long. It was only when I found out about the murders. I thought it might—'

'Might what? Be a good idea to tell us we might be in bloody danger for our lives? Charming.'

'It came as a shock to me. You know what happened to me. It just confirmed what I, we...' She looked at them all, impassive including Marion. '...suspected. Ruby Latimer had a ghost-writer. Our professor in Bristol has narrowed it down to...one of three people here.'

Lizzie looked at the body language, sure that her Miss Marple style might get one of them to betray themselves. No such luck. No takers. Oh well. Mary said, 'But since she's not to be found and is suspected of murder, surely her book won't sell now.'

'Won't sell? It will sell in the millions, even more than before. It could be a publishers' ploy, of course,' said Abigail.

Maybe it wasn't one of them after all. It had to be. After another round of coffees and subtle interrogation by super-sleuth Spector, she decided she wasn't getting anywhere. The friends finished up and went their separate ways. Lizzie went back to the office, quite disgruntled at her failure to get the last piece of the ultimate mosaic.

Not so much giving it up as parking it for a while. Lizzie, thwarted by the lack of a revealed candidate, decided to forget the hunt for the ghost-writer. Seemingly flogging a dead zebra, she would concentrate her not inconsiderable talents on the HMRC programme, start to plan for her wedding and something important that she and Craig needed to discuss before it was too late.

That night, they, Lizzie and Craig were in bed. She wondered when they might be going to start having sex again, whilst he wondered the same thing. He was reticent about it, fearing she might not be up to all that smooching and for the time being, her giving head was out. He read, she lay, crossed arms propped up, deep in thought.

'Darling, you want children, don't you?'

Craig, startled by the total unexpectedness of the question, stopped reading and hesitatingly answered, 'Lizzie, only if you do. What brought that on? Was it the attack?'

Life landmarks made people stop and take stock. The attack on herself plus the loss of so many people she had known had made her reassess herself, her relationships, her future. Her *joie de vivre* had taken a bit of a dent. Lizzie was a fun-loving young woman with a very serious side to her and the now more restrained ability to put her size five in things. Craig had been a stabilising influence, but he knew she wouldn't just have asked such a question frivolously. Lizzie Spector was the least frivolous person in that bed!

'I do, of course, I do, just not right away. Not for a few years. I'd like to concentrate on my career for a bit.'

Craig stopped reading and turned onto his left side and looked at her.

'So, tell me what brought this on?'

'My mother was asking—'

'Oh, now I see, the "when will you make me a grannie" discussion. I want them when you do,' he finished, determined to complete his chapter.

'She said something I was wondering about. You know people can freeze their eggs and have them implanted later. I think it's a good idea. It could also mean helping out women who are infertile. Create a life for some other family.'

'Can I think about it please, Lizzie? A lot to consider. Why don't you look into it? Might be a runner. The thought of a lot of Lizzies running about out there. Not sure if Planet Earth is ready for it yet. Anyway, good night, darling.' He switched off his light, all thought of finishing off another page dashed. 'Any luck with your ghost-writer?'

'No,' she said somewhat curtly. She felt an arm around her shoulder. She felt a warm body at her back. No time like the present, eh? Two participants. Spooning was such fun.

Abigail drove up to Eynsham, smiling in a strange sort of way. She was thinking about what had happened and made a mental note to tell her husband. Becky had no one at all to talk to and took the train back to Orpington, not having realised that things near her had just changed ownership. Marion got a lift off

Lizzie who had driven there, a rare one-off as she would normally have travelled by tube to Charing Cross. They had become increasingly close. Marion had no idea either who the ghost-writer was. Mary got in at Windsor Station and jumped into a cab to get home. It had been raining on and off all day but now it was bucketing. She got out of the cab and ran into the house where husband George and baby George—she called them George the First and George the Second—were waiting. She kissed them both and picked up the baby for a cuddle.

'This arrived for you by messenger,' Mary opened the package and it contained some editing work for her.

'I see our bank balance is healthy. A nice cheque you put in a couple of days ago. What's that for then?'

'Oh, nothing much. Just extra work I've taken on to tide us over until you get some overtime at your work.'

'Editing must be pretty well-paid then. I should have thought about it maybe.'

'George, you're lovely. It's what I do. By the way, the doctor told me that miracles can happen more than once.'

George had a twinkle in his eye and so did Mary as well as a small bottle of pills for George. They took young George upstairs with them. She laid the parcel on the coffee table, replacing a business card that had fallen out of it that George had picked up and glanced at.

'What's "GW" when it's at home then?'

'Err…it's…er…Gordon White. That's the man I'm doing this for.'

The three of them continued upstairs. Two of them were hoping that when they came back downstairs, the start of a fourth might have just begun. Fun trying.

After her two days at the Edinburgh International Book Festival and having been totally pissed off and agitated, Ruby Latimer returned home via an Edinburgh to King's Cross train. She quickly returned to Hounslow by taxi, where she didn't thank or tip her driver. She maybe should have. He even carried her bags up for her. She was still fizzing when the driver left her and her left hand and one of her knees hurt. He called in, not to his office but somewhere else.

'Vinnie here, she's home.'

Twenty minutes of phoning her lawyer giving him utter hell, she was puffing on a fag and drinking rum and coke. Her flat doorbell rang.

'Who the fuck is it at this time of the morning?'

Her ego clicked in and she opened the door. That was it.

Ruby Latimer started to stir. She felt a cool breeze over her legs and a strange sensation that she was lying on something soft and sandy. She looked down. All she could see were her own naked breasts. She tried to speak but couldn't. Her lips were stuck together. And she was apparently glued back-to-back with another person, from shoulders to butt, calves and arms. Her palms and fingertips seemed to be stuck to those of whoever the rest of her was firmly attached to. They lay on a deserted beach, on dry-cool sand. It was approaching first light. If she only knew how very, very chilly she would soon be. She could hear some distant plane sounds. She thought she saw movement out the corner of one eye. She tried to speak but it was useless. Whoever it was that was glued to her, as both lay on their sides, was also trying to say something. That person was moaning as if in severe pain. She was aware of someone big standing in front of her. He was big and fully clothed, unlike herself.

He knelt down and squeezed her cheeks together and said, 'Listen.' They both stopped moving.

'Dying is what we all need to do sometimes, and I know you like travelling so you can do both. One could say two for the price of one, just like I have down here.'

He then got up and walked around to the other body attached to the back of Ruby. 'Kirsty. Naughty girl, killing my man when he wasn't looking. Took me ages to find you but one of the Grisham men "helped" me out. He lent me a hand and I took three of his fingernails. When you start losing fingernails, it's time to talk and he did.' The man stood up and continued his pontification. 'I am holding you both responsible for killing my man Bradley and the sentence is death.' At which point, both started to pull away from each other and make horrible muffled shrieking sounds. They remained hermetically attached.

'I was wondering just how to do it and then I read your book. An amazing story, I must say. Thanks for the idea.'

Kirsty hadn't read the book. Ruby started to attempt more screaming. She knew what he intended to do. He went over and switched on an old cassette. A scratchy song hissed out of the one speaker. It was jolly and the words were *Wouldn't you like to fly in my...* Now Kirsty understood as well. Both had by now pissed themselves, actually on each other. It dripped down onto the dry sand. He took a length of rope and went to their other end, tying it to the author's red toe-nailed, beautifully moisturised and manicured feet and Kirsty's un-manicured feet, her black-purple soles, covered in burns, which, just for good pleasure, he squeezed again and again; she tried to but was unable to scream.

Ever so slowly, they could see an object expanding and as it did, they felt their ankles being pulled until the couple were slowly becoming more and more vertical, from partly on their sides until their heads were suspended upside down in mid-air and starting ever so steadily to rise. At several feet off the ground, all they could hear was, 'Have a good trip and don't forget to write.' As an afterthought, he shouted, 'I could have left your mouths open. As you say in your book, "No one will hear you scream". Have a nice flight.'

The Glasgow to Southend early morning flight was preparing to land. A young couple bound for the capital were all lovey-dovey. The girl looked out the window and did a double take. She thought she'd been subject to a trick of the light. She thought, maybe half a mile away out the cabin window, she saw a balloon with what very much looked like an upside-down body floating and tied to the bottom of it. She went to say something to her boyfriend, but he just kissed her again.

'But—' *Oh, never mind. No one would ever believe me.* She thought, *Trick of the light.*

'I got you this book, Elaine. You said you liked that Ruby Latimer...'

THE END

283